THE DOOR AT THE REAR OF THE LECTURE ROOM BANGED OPEN. . . .

The sound reverberated through the windowless room and vibrated in Marcer's cranial resonating organ, the echo-locating chamber, like waves on the surface of a previously still pool. Two police officers strode into the room. "You're coming with us," commanded the first, a sergeant.

Marcer grasped the sides of his desk as though holding a life preserver. "The Academy of Darien has exclusive jurisdiction here, and over me."

"Police have final jurisdiction over aliens." The sergeant rushed up the platform, yanked his stick gun from its holster, and rapped Marcer hard on his right ear with its blunt tip.

Marcer's ears rang. Worse, vibrations from the blow created phantom echo-signals; for a moment the walls seemed to move closer, then recede, like looped waves in a broken window screen.

Marcer began to panic. "What is this about? I haven't done anything."

"It's the war,

"War?" Marc   What had he to do w   between the Polite Har   of Worlds and the superstitious masses of the United Emirates . . . ?

IMPOSTOR

Valerie J. Freireich

A ROC BOOK

ROC
Published by the Penguin Group
Penguin Putnam Inc., 375 Hudson Street,
New York, New York 10014, U.S.A.
Penguin Books Ltd, 27 Wrights Lane,
London W8 5TZ, England
Penguin Books Australia Ltd, Ringwood,
Victoria, Australia
Penguin Books Canada Ltd, 10 Alcorn Avenue,
Toronto, Ontario, Canada M4V 3B2
Penguin Books (N.Z.) Ltd, 182–190 Wairau Road,
Auckland 10, New Zealand

Penguin Books Ltd, Registered Offices:
Harmondsworth, Middlesex, England

First published by Roc, an imprint of Dutton Signet,
a member of Penguin Putnam Inc.

First Printing, November, 1997
10 9 8 7 6 5 4 3 2 1

 REGISTERED TRADEMARK—MARCA REGISTRADA

Printed in the United States of America

BOOKS ARE AVAILABLE AT QUANTITY DISCOUNTS WHEN USED TO PROMOTE
PRODUCTS OR SERVICES. FOR INFORMATION PLEASE WRITE TO PREMIUM
MARKETING DIVISION, PENGUIN PUTNAM INC., 375 HUDSON STREET, NEW YORK,
NEW YORK 10014.

To my men:
With love

Chapter 1

She entered the Academy precincts as a Supplicant, asking her way in an accented voice that caused the Jonists she questioned to hesitate before they answered. She straightened her back against their curiosity and tried to follow their directions, but she couldn't read the signs and wouldn't admit it to the leering men or their tall, barefaced women. Even the Harmony's famous window-screens dismayed her; when the vistas changed in time with her movements, they made her dizzy. She turned into a corridor, opened a door, and unexpectedly found herself entering a classroom. The white-gowned lecturer looked up from her—*her!*—desk display and glared at the cause of the interruption. The students twisted in their chairs, surreptitiously stretching bored muscles. One smiled; the rest looked blank, awaiting an explanation.

"I'm sorry," the Supplicant whispered, and started to back out of the room, but the corridors were empty, and she had no idea where she had gone wrong. She raised her voice. "I'm looking for Revered Researcher Gangler. Please?"

The lecturer frowned. "What do you want here? Revered Gangler is a busy man."

The Supplicant intended to present her information only to Revered Gangler, the director of the Institute of Nonterrestrial Studies of the Jonist Academy of Darien, but first she needed to enlist this woman lecturer's aid in finding him. "It is a matter of life and death. The future of humanity is at stake." Unaware she had spoken a cliché from a grade B cyclone drama, unnerved by the students' giggles, the Supplicant hesitated.

The woman Academic grimaced. "Is this a joke?"

"Please," the Supplicant begged the room at large. "I have information from Marcer Brice."

The giggles stopped. The woman lecturer fretfully scanned her silent class, then she sighed and studied the Supplicant. "Is Marc all right?" she asked.

The Supplicant shrugged. She didn't know.

The woman lecturer idly tapped her desk display, then closed the desk. "That's all for today. Refer to your syllabus for tomorrow's reading," she told her class, and to the Supplicant she said, "I'll take you to see Revered Gangler."

I. A True Jonist.

"In the beginning, life seems simple. Cyanobacteria break the double bonds binding oxygen to carbon in carbon dioxide and produce molecular oxygen as waste, meanwhile replicating themselves in a lipid envelope. Later, blue-green algae thrive. Then, in a spurt, this apparent simplicity vanishes into a diversity of multicellular forms. Much of that initial diversity is lost, but the life which does continue is in *no* sense higher, more complex, or better than the life which does not. Just as important to remember: the fragile tip of a lineage which has no sibling branches is not more successful—it could be convincingly argued it is less so— than those species existing on full bushes containing many closely related, vigorous relatives."

Marcer Joseph Brice paused so his students could absorb that crucial point, and to allow their TA utilities to transcribe the lecture into his preset syllabus annotation. He looked out from the master's speaking platform at the eighteen students, his to teach for the duration of the course: Introduction to Biological Theory. He ignored one student, a pretty girl who smiled flirtatiously and tried to meet his eyes. The attention she wanted was inappropriate. Perhaps she even hoped to discredit him by creating a scandal.

He was the first accredited Researcher of a world Academy who publicly admitted to being an Altered human. As such, he walked a fine line and used his Altered sense sparingly. Mechanical sensors would spot it—he often imagined a tally kept by Revered Gangler—but he allowed himself to send one crisp, brief EL, a pulse of ultrasonic sound, through the lecture room. The echo bounce-back registered his students' solid presence, every one of them a standard human and therefore a citizen of the Polite Harmony of

Worlds. Like all Altereds, he was only a noncitizen resident.

"A true Jonist," Marcer continued, "looks for Order, not higher meaning. Wishful thinking leads to distorted research; be careful not to fall into the trap so prevalent among the ancients: the fallacy of evolutionary *progress*."

It was Marcer's second year teaching this course at the Academy of Darien. The initial lecture was going well. He spoke with confidence, sedately but firmly, in the style he'd learned from his own professors back at the Academy of New Dawn. "There is no inevitable rise from simple to complex in multicellular life. There is no advancement toward any particular thing; there is no direction."

The Academy buildings had been scrubbed during the two-week term recess, and a harsh ammonia residue made Marcer's eyes sting and left a sour taste in the back of his mouth. He suppressed the nuisance sensations. "Remember," he said, "whatever meaning our lives have comes from the Jonist search for Order, but there is no meaning inherent in our ability to search. Human beings are not at the top of any ladder, we are simply what is here. For now."

One student was staring unhappily at the floor. Despite the best efforts of Academics, some superstitions remained in the Harmony's general population, most commonly a belief that human beings were the pinnacle of biological achievement. To defuse that fallacy, the last time he'd given this lecture Marcer had mentioned the alien Bril as an example of another intelligent species capable of searching for Order, but then he'd become entrapped in a lengthy and unproductive discussion of their extermination during the Last War. This time he avoided the reference.

A thin, earnest student stood. Marcer nodded permission to speak. "Researcher Brice, doesn't Jon Hsu's *General Principles* say that the standard human form is the ideal for examining the universe and finding Order? Doesn't that imply that it's the best?"

A year earlier, his students hadn't asked such pointed questions. They had said *human* without modifying it with the word *standard*. Opinion had become more conservative since the revelation that Jeroen Lee, one of the six Electors of Order of the Academy General, was an Altered. Marcer glanced at his desk display and found the student's name, looked up, and, in the time it took to exhale, EL-ed a rare, second time, orienting on the young man. "Acolyte Torin," he said gently, because the EL had shown no malice in Torin's aura, "that is not the exact wording of the *General Principles,* and it is not the most recent Electors' interpretation of them. My presence here speaks for itself. As for nonterrestrial intelligences, the scope of their search will depend upon their intellect and senses. That the only alien intelligence we've found so far is the vicious Bril, who were uninterested in Order, does not make humans—standard or Altered—better. That would be a moral judgment. The Jonist universe is not moral."

The wooden door at the rear of the lecture room banged open, hitting hard against the wall. The sound reverberated through the windowless room and vibrated in Marcer's cranial resonating organ, the EL-chamber, like waves on the surface of a previously still pool. Marcer braced himself for something bad.

Two constables strode into the lecture room. Both were armed with military-style stick guns, unheard of inside Academy grounds. Their crimson-and-black dress uniforms were vivid contrasts to the staid, gray granite walls, the pale blue student jackets, and Marcer's own white Academic gown. Guns held loosely in their hands, they faced Marcer across the backs of his startled students. Unwilling to dignify the intrusion with his attention, Marcer resumed his lecture. His voice was steady. "Beware of the chop logic of unwarranted overclassification . . ."

"You're Dr. Brice?" The constable sounded strained by the effort of insulting him, but the interruption was loud.

Several students gasped. Marcer's lecture faltered to a stop. It was harassment, pure and simple, to use the non-Jonist title doctor rather than Researcher, but armed police looking specifically for him was cause for a deeper concern than their failure to observe the proprieties. Marcer nodded, rather than bowing. His face felt warm. He knew his fair complexion must show a flush, but he assumed an arrogant tone. "I'm Researcher Brice. Wait outside. My lecture is nearly over."

The constable, a sergeant, sauntered down the aisle, hand intimidatingly near his holstered stick gun. The other man stayed at the door. "It's over now," the constable sergeant said. "You're coming with us, squeaker."

Worse and worse. Squeaker: Purist slang for New Dawn Altereds who, like Marcer, echo-located. Marcer hadn't heard it since leaving New Dawn, but the bite was just as he remembered it from home. "You're clearing a path for the rest of us," Marcer's sister, Miriam, had claimed. Path-breaking was difficult.

Marcer glanced at his students. Acolyte Torin had sunk into his chair and was pretending to study his hands. Marcer needed to maintain their fragile respect and, therefore, had to dismiss the class. "Think about diversity and alternatives to the idea of evolutionary progress," he said in an unhurried voice. "Do tonight's reading. We'll continue tomorrow. You may go." He closed the desk just as the constable reached the master's platform. Apparently composed, though the white gown of a Researcher was his only shield, Marcer stood with crossed arms held against his chest and watched the constable sergeant from the platform's trifling height. He didn't EL, despite the pressure to do so building in his head.

The sergeant stopped at the foot of the platform and looked behind himself, at the class. With troubled glances at the constables, the students had begun to file out of Marcer's lecture room. Acolyte Torin dawdled. "Good afternoon, Researcher Brice," he shyly said, then bowed. Others immediately repeated the courtesy.

Heartened, Marcer returned the bow. "Good afternoon, Acolytes," he answered and smiled confidently while they left. Encouraged by the constable's inaction, Marcer tried desperately to make sense of the situation. Academics had not been subject to local police jurisdiction since before the Bril Wars; that should have been true even of an Academic who was Altered.

"I let you keep your dignity," the sergeant said when the door closed on the last student. "Now, you're coming with us." The residual odor of hard cider on the sergeant's breath reached Marcer. The sergeant had stopped at a tavern before coming to make the arrest. Drunkenness made a man unpredictable even to a New Dawn Altered, and he had an uplands accent. Altereds were less common and less accepted in Darien's rural districts, or so Marcer had heard.

Marcer gripped the smooth, curved sides of his desk as though it was a life preserver, but he spoke as he would have to an unruly Acolyte. "Sergeant, I have never hidden the fact that I'm Altered. I registered when I arrived on Darien. Researcher Fields is my citizen-sponsor. But the Academy of Darien has exclusive jurisdiction here, and over me. If there is a problem, you'll have to take it up with Revered Gangler. He's the director of the Institute of Nonterrestrial Studies at this Academy."

The sergeant, a squat, powerfully built man, took the two stairs up the platform in one stride, reached across the desk, and grabbed Marcer's arm. "Police have final jurisdiction over aliens."

"I'm a sanctioned Altered; my father's a citizen." Marcer pulled himself free. An Academic appointment should have kept this from happening.

"Resisting?" The sergeant yanked his stick gun from its holster; grinning, he rapped the right side of Marcer's head hard with the weapon's blunt tip.

"Hey," the other constable said reprovingly, but he stayed at the back of the classroom.

Marcer's ears rang. Worse, vibrations from the blow created a phantom echo-signal; the walls seemed to move closer, then recede, like looped waves in a broken window-screen. Marcer closed his eyes momentarily to end the confusion between what he saw and the false EL. "I wasn't resisting," he said as he opened them, the phantom EL signal fully suppressed.

The constable sergeant aimed the stick gun at him. "You sure, squeaker?"

A stick gun could melt a hole through his heart. Protesting this gross violation of Academy jurisdiction wouldn't do him any good if he died. "I'm sure."

"Better." The sergeant took a step back and studied him. The visible elements of Marcer's New Dawn Alteration— a wide face, a slightly more prominent nose (to make room for the liquid-filled cranial resonating organ) as well as large ears—were not unsightly to standard human prejudices; they made him look younger than his thirty-two standard years. Fair skin and scattered freckles completed Marcer's fresh-faced, innocent appearance.

"You didn't have to hit him," the second constable grumbled.

Marcer couldn't tear his attention away from the gun. He gave in to the urge to use *all* his senses and sent a brief pulse. The bounce-back detected nothing he couldn't see.

"He EL-ed," the second constable grudgingly reported.

The sergeant smiled. "Do that again, squeaker, and I'll hood you."

Standard humans, like the two constables, were rarely able to hear the high-pitched pulse, and Marcer's lips had barely parted. There was no mistaking their target. They had arrived with sensing equipment, prepared to arrest *him*. Marcer reached for the General Utility, the internal communication and sorting system maintained by the Academy of Darien, intending to contact Revered Gangler himself, but the connect in his head found nothing. His access was blocked, as though he were a criminal or mentally incapable of using a utility. He was truly alone. He wet his lips, then asked, "What is this about? I haven't done anything."

"It's the war," the second constable answered.

"War?" Marcer repeated, dumbfounded. What had he to do with the emerging conflict between the Polite Harmony of Worlds and the superstitious alan masses of the United Emirates? Except for their genetic eunuchs, the unmen, pious alans disapproved of Alteration of the human genome—particularly the Altered population of the independent world of Neuland. The Harmony was currently considering a request to defend their fellow Jonists in the Republic of Neuland from a *jihad* by the Emirates alans, although the divisiveness created by Elector Lee's recently revealed Alteration and by his protégé Martin Penn's, doctrinal revisionism had complicated negotiations. Still, there wasn't a war, only diplomatic tension. The last Marcer had heard, his family's shipping company was still hauling cargo back and forth across the border. "I don't have the pain-free Neulander Alteration," Marcer said carefully. "War with the Emirates over Neuland has nothing to do with me." He shrugged. "I don't understand. Sir."

The sergeant grinned at Marcer's reluctant courtesy. "All foreigners are being deported back to the Emirates."

"Foreigners?" Marcer swallowed hard, which had the involuntary effect of temporarily increasing pressure in his EL-chamber, making him aware that he must not use it and simultaneously creating an urge to do so.

"Yeah. You're not just an Altered, you're an alien. You're being deported with the religionists." The sergeant was gleeful.

Religionists? Could it be that his family connections had

caused this trouble? Impossible that his arrest had nothing to do with his being the first Altered Academic. "This is because I was born on Safi, in the Emirates?" His voice rose in disbelief. "Sergeant, that's nothing. My parents were there on business; my family owns a shipping company. Brice-Issacs Transport. I'm Jonist, not a superstitious alan. Of course, or how could I have become an Academic? I'm a legal Harmony resident, the same as any other Altered." Marcer hoped one of his dismissed students had alerted Academy Security. The mechanical monitors and sensors scattered throughout the Academy weren't real-time monitored.

"Let's get him to the depot. You know they're probably watching." The second constable glanced around the room as though the monitors were visible to the naked eye.

The sergeant nodded and motioned with his gun for Marcer to move toward the door.

Marcer spoke humbly and for the record. "My citizen-sponsor should be informed."

"No," the sergeant said. "It's all set. Get going." He shoved Marcer.

Marcer stumbled, righted himself, then went down the two steps carefully, lifting the hem of the floor-length, white gown, his hard-earned Researcher's uniform. The emblem of the Institute of Nonterrestrial Studies on his sleeve gleamed gold and green, like tarnished copper. Faith in that Academic refuge was equally tarnished. The sergeant had claimed that it was "all set," implying collusion between the police and the Academy.

The constable sergeant returned his gun to its holster as he followed Marcer.

Marcer glanced around the lecture room. It was smaller than those at the Academy of New Dawn. He hadn't been the first Altered Acolyte educated by an Academy, or even the first to admit to his Alteration; the design of the Academy of New Dawn took into account the claustrophobia felt by local EL-Altered students when confined in small spaces. Marcer had adjusted to the closed-in feeling of Darien's Academy. He had thought he'd been accepted as a colleague there. His work was excellent; it had to be. As a student at the Academy of New Dawn, Marcer Joseph Brice had performed better than the best standard humans in order to be more than an Altered who'd bought a place in the student body with money and family connections. In the liberal climate of the times, the Academic staff had encouraged him to continue into advanced instruction, into research; they had proposed him for membership in the Academy General and forwarded his credentials to the open posting at the Academy of Darien. The Ahman of New Dawn had recommended him. "About time," Miriam had said. Had that time vanished?

Marcer stopped in the center aisle, nearly at the door, turned, and studied the sergeant. EL bounce-back signals provided subtle insights into character and truthfulness as well as location—speculation was that this emotional aura was a learned interpretation of minute physical signals—but Marcer couldn't EL. He smelled the alcohol again and took the chance that the sergeant's aggressiveness was bluster. "You know this is specious," Marcer said quietly. "I'm not a foreigner or a religionist."

The man shrugged. "It's not my problem. I do as I'm told."

"Not much of a Jonist."

Both constables looked askance at Marcer. The junior constable brought out his stick gun; the sergeant sullenly removed a length of worked leather from his side pouch. Straps hung from it. The thing was sewn, not molded, giving it a medieval appearance, and it had, in fact, been modeled after the hoods which covered the heads of hunters' falcons, preventing use of their eyes.

"I didn't EL," Marcer said, backing away until he bumped into the row of student chairs. Hoods not only blocked the Altered ability to echo-locate, they also blinded the wearer. The disorientation of enclosure was terrible. Home on New Dawn he'd seen news reports of hooded prisoners—Altered bandits, agitators, or plain criminals, all dehumanized by the hood, and made ridiculous. They shuffled and floundered and whined as they were led away like panicked animals.

"Wear the hood or take off your gown," the sergeant said. "Your choice. Either way, you're being deported. Right now."

Take off your gown. The Academy *had* sanctioned his arrest. That was why the sergeant, uncomfortable as he seemed, was confident. Marcer had become a liability and an embarrassment to his colleagues when Elector Jeroen

Lee was exposed as Altered. No Academic would arrive to question the arrest. The cowards of the Academy were using subterfuge to be rid of their Altered Researcher.

The gown had a front closure. Beneath it Marcer wore an ordinary, pale blue shirt and comfortably shabby pants, nothing which would inspire the respect or self-confidence provided by an Academic gown. "Your word, officers, that if I take off the gown, you won't use the hood, too?"

The sergeant hesitated long enough that Marcer knew he'd guessed correctly. They had intended to hood him anyway.

"You have *my* word that I won't cause any trouble," Marcer said. The fact that his Alteration was not visually disturbing gave him an edge in dealing with standard humans: he could pass as standard, and they felt awkward not treating him as one. So Marcer watched the sergeant with polite but expectant attention. The two constables exchanged a look, perhaps communicating through their police utility. "Whatever else I am," Marcer added, for them and the monitors, "I am a member of the Academy. My word is good."

"All right." The sergeant shrugged at the other constable. "Neither of us will use the hood unless we have to."

Marcer bowed, gravely but only to the depth an Academic would normally use. "Thank you." He hoped they would keep their word to an Altered man.

He felt the gown's thin, worked rice-paper fabric between his fingers. It was the cheapest kind. He had several double-silk gowns, gifts from his uncles and father, and one of rose-petal silkik hand-woven by Miriam, but he rarely wore them. It seemed impolitic to remind others that his family was wealthy, so he had lived entirely within his Researcher's salary. The stiff rice paper slipped through his hand. He had an awful thought: if he took it off, he might never wear an Academic gown again. In the tension over the hood, he'd overlooked the main point: they intended to ship him to the United Emirates, where he'd be a stranger, an infidel, a scorned Altered, and possibly an enemy.

To voluntarily take off the gown would symbolically renounce his rights as an Academic. Jeroen Lee had been revealed as a secret Altered, yet he had not been removed from his position as an Elector. At least not yet. It was possible that the Harmony would become more tolerant, rather than less; it was too early to tell. Marcer needed to preserve his Academic rank. The two constables were waiting.

"No," he said. "I've changed my mind. I'll come with you wearing the Academic gown to which I'm entitled, and without a hood, or we can struggle, and you can shoot me and explain to everyone how and why you did." Except during exercise drills, he hadn't been in a physical confrontation since childhood, but Marcer tensed, fully intending to do whatever he could against two armed and trained policemen.

The junior constable gripped his gun; the sergeant held the hood. Neither moved. Marcer waited, sweating. "There will be a record of this," Marcer reminded them. "You won't be able to claim I resisted." He spread his arms. "I'm not."

They said nothing, but the junior constable holstered his stick gun and the sergeant returned the hood to his pocket. Marcer took a deep breath and released it slowly.

The sergeant opened the door. Students lined the corridor, standing in silence. Curiosity or respect? Marcer didn't know, but was relieved he'd preserved his honor. Several bowed. He nodded at them. None of his colleagues was there, not even Ted Fields.

"Let's get him into the coach, fast," the sergeant muttered. The other constable pushed Marcer through the hushed crowd.

A rice-paper gown wouldn't prevent him from being exiled.

II. Girl child.

The creature's nails clicked a warning against the cool, tile floor. Nisa looked up from her painting just as Qadira, her stepmother, the houri bitch who had stolen Nisa's happiness and ended her mother's life, followed her strange pet through the door. Nisa gritted her teeth and clenched her brush more tightly. Her hand trembled. She set the brush into its tray at the bottom of the easel and pretended to study her current project, a painting of a man on horseback, a copy of an ancient Persian miniature from a book her parents had given her before her father had been Blessed with a holy wife. The bright colors were gaudy but cheerful, and Nisa's father enjoyed riding horseback. She hoped her gift of the painting would sweeten his attitude toward Nisa, his only daughter.

Qadira came so close that had Nisa extended her hand, it would have brushed Qadira's arm, so close that Nisa smelled the cloying musk that enveloped her like heavy fog. The houri moved with catlike speed and stealth, but her face was wolfish. The backward slant of her cheeks didn't lessen her beauty, yet a caricature would have shown the similarity between her appearance and that of her ugly pet. Both came from Paradise, but only the houris were called holy. Nisa would have liked to paint Qadira's portrait, but wouldn't give her the satisfaction of refusing.

"Not morning prayers. Father miss Nisa." Qadira hissed the last words, drawing them out, making the sound of Nisa's name offensive. Though Qadira's sentences were awkward, her clever way of filling sound with emotion kept her meaning clear. Nisa's father called Qadira's labored grammar holy speech, but Qadira's tone, when she spoke to Nisa, was anything but divine.

"Of course he missed me, once you pointed it out." Nisa turned her chair to face Qadira directly. Totsi, Nisa's own pet, humped his head from the center of his back, the better to see and hear. "Hush," Nisa whispered and stroked her pet. Totsi was a talish, an animal native to Bralava's southern continent. At rest, he looked like a fat, fuzzy snake.

"Wrong," Qadira said. "Father discusses marriage of you after prayers."

Her marriage. Nisa glanced down, patting Totsi to keep him still. Gilt paint glittered on Nisa's index and middle fingers. It had left a faint brand on Totsi's soft, gray-blue hide; Nisa tried to wipe the paint away with her thumb, but only spread it. In her lap, Totsi coiled around Nisa's hand protectively; his lumpy head hunched into his back again. Nisa bent low and kissed him.

Qadira's pet watched Nisa and Totsi. When Nisa met its saucer eyes, it stiffened and grumbled deep in its throat. At the moment, its hairless skin was emerald green, the color of Paradise. It raised itself onto two legs and stood easily, at least as comfortable upright as a human toddler.

Erect, the creature was taller than Nisa was while seated. When she stood, the creature came as high as the bottom of Nisa's chin. Qadira gestured, and the creature returned to all fours.

"My father will be angry if you don't get pregnant soon," Nisa taunted her stepmother. She had overheard servants' gossip.

Qadira sighed, but Nisa had no sympathy for the houri's worries. "What vulgar thing that?" Qadira pointed at the picture.

"A present for my father." She smiled at her own, neat work. The original had been painted on old Earth in the first millennium of the Prophet, God's blessings and peace be upon him. Nisa hoped the finished painting would remind her father of happier times.

In one deft motion, Qadira reached across Nisa, picked up the vial of gilt paint, and dashed the paint across the nearly finished work. It ran through the sky like a golden cloud, covered the rider's face and the bulk of his horse, then pooled in the calligraphy border which dedicated the picture to Nisa's father. Paint dripped over the easel's ledge and onto Nisa's lap.

Nisa jerked Totsi out of the way and grabbed a damp cloth to blot the paint. The rider's face had become a shadow. All but the two rear legs of the horse was gone. The picture was ruined. Nisa bit her lip. Totsi quivered with Nisa's reflected fury, but Nisa had learned not to argue with Qadira. Despite the houri's peculiar, pidgin grammar, Qadira always won because Nisa's father was the final arbiter of any quarrel.

"Sharif no like useless vulgar." Qadira's musical voice danced across Nisa's defeat.

Qadira's creature came closer, putting itself between Nisa and its mistress as if suspecting danger. The thing had a vinegar scent at the best of times, but the stench worsened with its mood. Its foul odor encouraged Nisa, though it stung her eyes. She chuckled. "Sharif?" Nisa's voice was breathless and harsh. No one else called Nisa's father, Sheik Radi Khalil Sharif, by that title. It was bragging, to make so much of the fact one was *shorfa,* a descendant of the Prophet, God's blessings and peace be upon him. Before he had been Blessed by his pilgrimage to Paradise and a marriage to a houri wife, Nisa's father had disdained such references. Once he had told Nisa that there were many kinds of *shorfa*. Sheik Radi had explained that a thousand years earlier, back on old Earth, if one had money or power, it had been possible to obtain a decree that made one a sharif. After that, all descendants were *shorfa*, too. Who knows what kind of sharif our family is? he had asked. Nisa doubted he would want to be reminded of that conversation anymore. "Paradise changed the *Sharif*," Nisa told Qadira, "but be careful he doesn't change again and see you for what you are. Just another woman, and maybe even a barren one."

Qadira laughed, beautifully. Her creature huffed in its throat as an accompaniment. "Marry quick," Qadira said, "else die."

Aleko Bei, Emir of all seven worlds of the United Emirates, had invited Sheik Radi to undertake the pilgrimage to Paradise. It was an honor impossible to refuse without appearing disloyal, and disloyal men did not keep their heads for long. Sheik Radi had left with his wife's blessings and returned with Qadira, a houri second wife.

Sheik Radi refused to believe that lovely Qadira had caused his first wife's death. Heavily pregnant with yet another son for Sheik Radi, Nisa's mother had tumbled over the rail of the high marble staircase from the woman's floor, the fourth and highest level in the Sheik's city mansion. Enthralled by his new, holy houri wife, Nisa's father had seemed barely to notice Riva's death. Only Nisa apparently remembered the lazy family afternoons in the country when they would ride to a hidden place chosen by her mother and some secretly arranged treat would be waiting: gifts, games, a special meal. Once it had been Sheik Radi's brother, Nisa's Uncle Tuwma, just arrived home from the capital world, Qandahar. That time, Sheik Radi had whispered to his wife that he loved her. Nisa had been the only child close enough to overhear. Her mother had been modestly but not entirely covered outdoors on the grounds of their own estate. Nisa remembered the sun on her mother's face, her mother's smile as she gazed at Sheik Radi, the smell of hot oil and roasting lamb as the unman cook began preparation of an outdoor meal.

Nisa had known Qadira was poison from the first. When Sheik Radi had returned with her from his pilgrimage, Riva had supervised the preparation of a feast honoring his return and the arrival of his new, second wife. Qadira had refused to eat, saying nothing was to her taste, and she had loudly suggested that Sheik Radi put his "old woman" aside, claiming it was improper for a holy houri to be second to any merely human wife.

Nisa looked one last time at the spoiled painting, then unsnapped it from the stand and crumpled the damp paper. It made a tight ball that fit between her palms, but it was only paper, not a weapon; she tossed it to the floor. "The Prophet, God's blessing and peace be upon him, said there should be no compulsion in marriage," Nisa said. "I don't want to marry any man, but I'd sooner marry an infidel Jonist than one of your Sons."

The women from Paradise were demons, not holy. When Qadira's houri friends visited, their faces were lovely, but stiff; their expressions showed joyful serenity all the time. Qadira looked on Nisa with that same tranquil delight and stepped away from the easel. Her hips swayed the silk of her long caftan in careless eroticism. "Stay, then. Wither. Age. Father hates to fat old daughter. Wait. Qadira end you." She snapped her fingers. "Poof." The hard noise punctuated a wicked laugh.

Totsi raised his lumpy midriff again, forming a head, and rolled slightly so as to look down at Qadira's creature; he curled and slapped himself, as though echoing Qadira's snapping sound. Totsi was homely, but a chauvinistic childhood impulse had caused Nisa to insist on an indigenous creature as a pet. Back then, her father had humored her, as though she had been *his* pet. In Bralava's Native Life Reservations, talish hunted in packs, using their deceptively torpid bodies as bait. Totsi's snap was the prelude to a leap. Nisa put her arm around Totsi, hugging him close to keep him safe from the houri's creature. Many houris had these ugly companions. They roamed the city freely. It was a crime to harm them; Ziller said the beasts were called jinn by the ignorant. Nisa thought they had it right.

Qadira's creature huffed and whined, then Qadira whirled around to face the doorway in a graceful swirl of silk. Nisa's father strode into Nisa's studio.

"Beloved." He looked only at Qadira, as though they were alone, although this suite of rooms had belonged exclusively to Nisa all her life. The Sheik crossed the room in three long strides and took Qadira's extended hand gently in his own, subtly supporting her trifling weight despite the fact that the houri stood alone quite as well as anyone.

Nisa no longer attempted to vie with her stepmother for her father's attention. She smoothed the wrinkles from her paint-spattered smock, one sufficiently worn that the golden spot Qadira had caused was lost in other stains. Nisa set Totsi on the floor at a distance from Qadira's creature and rose to greet her father when his attention could be occupied by someone other than the houri wife who Blessed him by their marriage. Nisa didn't understand what about the venomous Qadira entranced her father, but though he might grumble about Qadira's lack of a pregnancy, he also seemed to worship the wife who, when she eventually bore him a son, would bear him a Son of the Prophet, God's blessings and peace be upon him.

Qadira directed her husband's attention toward Nisa. "Messy child." She shook her head gently.

Sheik Radi frowned at Nisa. Nisa lowered her eyes. He had not spoken to her, so, following Qadira's recently imposed protocol, Nisa said nothing. When her mother had been alive, Nisa had spoken freely.

"Nisa, you should know better," Sheik Radi said. "You're seventeen. You should act . . . womanly. Stop playing with paint and prepare yourself for marriage." He gestured dismissively at her easel and the various sketches and paintings hanging from a line around her studio walls. "Representation of life is a suspect activity, even for men."

Totsi squirmed against the side of Nisa's foot. She gently pushed him out of sight and didn't answer her father.

"Bad thing." Qadira indicated Totsi while trembling as though the diminutive talish was a tiger. "Bites me."

"Totsi did no such thing! Where did he bite you? Show me!" Outraged and terrified, Nisa realized she could be fighting for Totsi's life. The pet was her last friend in the house. Qadira had replaced their entire staff with groveling unmen of her own choosing, and Nisa's six brothers were usually away. Besides, to please their father, they generally took Qadira's side.

Uncharacteristically, Qadira backed down. "No. No. All right."

Sheik Radi looked sternly at Qadira for a moment, then his gaze softened as she wiggled closer. "Fat girl." Qadira look sadly at Nisa.

Nisa never knew where Qadira's attacks would go, only that they would be embarrassing, demeaning, or, if they were alone, threatening. This time, however, Qadira made a rare mistake. Qadira was slender, with tiny hands and feet and huge, dark eyes, but Nisa's mother had been voluptuous. Sheik Radi had liked it. "I look like my mother," Nisa whispered.

It seemed that his infatuation with the houri hadn't entirely displaced Sheik Radi's memory of his first wife. He cleared his throat and glanced through the window, which overlooked the women's courtyard. Nisa would have preferred a brighter studio, but it was out of the question for a woman to be exposed to strangers. The dark rooms of what had been Riva's suite were directly across the courtyard. Sheik Radi looked from them to Nisa. "Yes, you do."

Qadira's creature emitted a low cry and was ignored.

"Nisa. You didn't pray with us this morning," Sheik Radi said, but his tone was mild.

It would have been useless to point out that a mere two years earlier Sheik Radi had performed the ablutions and prayed only irregularly, except for Friday afternoons. Nisa bowed her head. During that earlier time such submissiveness would have made her father chuckle. "I prayed here." It was untrue. "Karim has friends in the house; I thought it would be best."

Sheik Radi nodded; Nisa suspected he did not enjoy their estrangement, either. "That was modest behavior, Nisa; I hope to see more of it from you. They'll leave for school tomorrow, then you can join us."

"Pictures, Sharif?" Only Nisa heard falsity in Qadira's humble reminder. The houri gestured around the room, indicating Nisa's many paintings. Nisa's favorite was her own design, not copy-art: a still life of a red vase with flowers on a table. It looked real, unlike her landscapes. She couldn't get permission to remain outdoors long enough to complete one. The clumsy veil and cover also slowed her work. Her father had absolutely refused her request for art lessons, even while her mother had been alive.

"No holiness . . ." Qadira shrugged eloquently, without speaking aloud the supposed injunction of the Prophet, God's blessing and peace be upon him, against representational art. Nisa reached for the picture book, ready for an

argument. It was true she went beyond religious subjects
and calligraphy, but there had always been pictures as well
as patterns in Muslim art. Why not now?

Nisa let her hand drop and her words remain unsaid. She
wouldn't win the argument, and once entangled in it, she
could lose her last pleasure. Her father was frowning at an
incomplete portrait of Nisa's cousin, Uncle Tuwma's daughter, Hulweh. Nisa spoke in resigned desperation, before her
father could forbid her to draw. "When will my marriage
take place?"

"Then you agree?" His stern tone was a reminder of the
horrid scene when he had informed Nisa of her engagement
to a man more than twice her seventeen common-count
years, a stranger named Idryis Khan a'Husain. He wasn't
even from Bralava, but from Qandahar, and besides being
a houri's Son and a cousin of Aleko Bei, he was a military
fleet commander, unlikely to be someone she could love.

"What choice do I really have?" Nisa asked bitterly,
which she'd vowed to herself she would not say. To watch
her words as though she were a servant in her own home
was another humiliation. Tears in her eyes made her turn
away.

"Peace." Qadira rested the palm of her hand against
Sheik Radi's chest. "Nisa agree."

"My beloved is wise." He took Qadira's hand and
kissed it.

The way Qadira manipulated her father gave Nisa hope
that she might twist a husband as easily, even without the
houri's holy advantage. Nisa could be a virgin only once.
"I apologize, Father," Nisa said. "I accept your choice."

"Good. Your wedding will take place when a'Husain re-
turns from his trip to the Polite Harmony of Worlds." Her
father smiled at her.

Qadira hissed, delicately. "Infidels. All die them
Neulanders."

Her father's lips tightened. Nisa suppressed a smile. In-
tolerance was Qadira's major failing. It made her incautious
around Sheik Radi. She yearned for war against the Republic of Neuland and, if necessary, against the huge and powerful Harmony of Worlds. Her aim wasn't conquest; she
wanted to kill all Neulanders.

"I've always hoped to see the Harmony," Nisa said.
"Perhaps, if he travels there often, my new husband will

take me." Once there, she could ask for asylum. Then she would study Harmony-style window-screens and have a new, independent life.

"Not with war imminent." For the first time since the matter of her marriage had been broached, her father showed paternal concern. "It isn't safe."

"Jihad," Qadira whispered.

Nisa didn't follow civic matters—her opinions didn't matter, anyway, since women had no voice in public life—but for once she was in complete agreement with the houri. Perhaps her husband-to-be, trapped inside the Harmony, would die before their wedding.

III. The outcasts of the Harmony.

The constables turned Marcer over to a blue-clad Harmony soldier as soon as they arrived at the transient depot. Marcer's new guard, an older man than the constables, looked curiously at Marcer's white Researcher's gown and his wide, minimally Altered face. "Seems strange to deport an Academic," he said.

Encouraged, Marcer eagerly agreed. "My name is Marcer Joseph Brice. I'm a Researcher in Nonterrestrial Studies at the Academy of Darien. I don't belong in the Emirates. I'm from New Dawn."

"It's Academy politics," the constable sergeant warned the soldier. "Don't get involved." He clapped his junior constable on the shoulder. "Come on. It's done. Let's get out of here."

Neither constable had spoken to Marcer during the long ride to the depot; they didn't speak as they left. Denial of his humanity made the illegal procedure more palatable.

Marcer needed time and access to a General Utility to argue his case. He turned to the soldier. "This isn't right," he said. "Please, will you let me contact the Academy? Right now, I'm cut off from all operating utilities." He had tried unsuccessfully, over and over, to gain access to any of Darien's public systems. "I'm sure I can straighten this out."

The soldier stood still, eyes fixed on the horizon, obviously and rather clumsily consulting the military access utility or some communication docket. Marcer opened and closed his fists against the cold and looked around so he wouldn't seem to stare at the soldier. The lowering sun made the ice crystals embedded in the frozen soil glisten like fresh blood. A hoist ship rested on a vast plain of frozen black soil outside the temporary compound; its freighter or commercial liner would be waiting in orbit to rid Darien of the outcasts of the Harmony.

Marcer didn't know Darien well. His Academic appointment had begun during the northern continent's winter, when the city of Next was icebound and its flat countryside a frigid waste. The work of settling into his new position had occupied his time; sight-seeing would have come later, and in a more hospitable season. It was winter once again and Marcer still had no good idea of the location of this gated compound, except that it was on a boundless, empty plain well outside the city. The soldier was unarmed, but even if Marcer ran, it was much too far to consider escaping on foot to plead his case before the Academy.

Revered Gangler had always been correct in his dealings with Marcer, but vaguely disapproving. Still, there were others in the Academy who would actively support Marcer's right to a fair hearing. Ted Fields, for one, and much of the younger faculty. Most probably they didn't know what was going on, and surely Revered Gangler hadn't decided this on his own.

Inside the compound, several dozen wailing women huddled at the flimsy, minimally functioning gravity fence. They stretched the wire and begged the preoccupied soldier to let them leave. A few called to Marcer for help, seeing only his white gown and misinterpreting his escort. Because travel was his family's business, Marcer understood and spoke Ufazi, the Emirates' major language, but the foreign voices were too many for him to make out individual requests. The high-pitched, frantic pleading of the alan women made him uneasy. He looked away.

The soldier came out from the utility. "They say you're Altered," he told Marcer and looked pointedly at the Academic gown, implying Marcer was an impostor.

"Yes, I am." He cleared his throat and bit down on his urge to EL while trying to sound reasonable and calm. "More than 40 percent of New Dawn's population is Altered; it's an Extreme World, barely suitable for humans, but, like Darien, we're near the border and there's trade."

Enough travelogue. "I was admitted as a Researcher at the Academy of Darien anyway, and proposed by the Academy of New Dawn for General Membership. I'm the first." He glanced modestly down, then looked back directly at the soldier. The man's accent came from one of the inner worlds, Flute or Rockland, where Altereds were rare. "But they aren't deporting me because I'm Altered. The real problem seems to be a mix-up because I was born on Safi, in the Emirates. My parents were there on a business trip." Stop babbling, Marcer told himself. "Give me a chance to petition the Academy. Officer, the Harmony is my home."

"Politics," the soldier said slowly. "And you an Altered Academic born outside the Harmony." He shifted his feet and didn't meet Marcer's eyes. "I'm sorry, but you have to go inside the compound."

Marcer glanced at the black lifting body of the hoist ship and shivered in the cold. Mud sucked at his thin, indoor shoes; the ground hadn't been sealed, and the heat generated by the deportees who had passed this way had made the path ooze. Its fetid odor reminded Marcer of the stench of dead, improperly preserved organisms during student fieldwork. The hem of his white gown was becoming brown. Marcer lifted it slightly, though the cheap cloth would be ruined by dampness, so the stain was irrelevant.

An eerie voice from the compound's interior rose over the fence. Rhythmic, high-pitched, and insistent, it echoed in Marcer's EL-chamber. He recognized it from mandatory classes on non-Jonist superstitions: a muezzin's call to prayer. "What is that?" he asked anyway.

The soldier shrugged. "God-talking. It's too much trouble to stop them. Come on." He gestured at Marcer to continue toward the compound.

Marcer didn't move. "Alans." He put disgust into his tone. "Officer, don't put me in with them. They're barely human." The unofficial, but common, belief was that religionists were Flawed. Because his extended family included a few religionists, Marcer considered that notion excessive, but the wailing women and chanting men made him wonder. Belief in gods wasn't just exotic, it was alien.

The soldier looked from Marcer to the alans, then back again. Marcer held his breath against the urge to EL, to know what the other man felt. "They also said you're a religionist."

"Not true! I'm an Academic! Of course I'm Jonist."

The man shrugged, his mind nearly made up against Marcer.

Few Harmony officials were susceptible to bribes, but Marcer had overheard his father and uncles discuss getting Special Import Licenses under the table. He wished now that he had listened more closely, and that he hadn't been so self-righteously concerned with his own Academic status if Brice-Issacs Transport was involved in a scandal. Some of his Issacs cousins would have known what to do; they'd listened, but they were standard humans, citizens, more comfortable straying from the narrow path of Jonist Order. A bribe would have to be offered delicately, and only if his situation was truly desperate. "Let me stay in the head-quarters instead." Marcer lowered his head and kept it bowed like a favor-seeking Supplicant.

"Sorry, no." The soldier moved his hand so that he almost touched Marcer, urging him forward.

Desperate enough. Marcer took a single step, then stopped again. "If you got a message to my father, both he and I would be grateful. Brice-Issacs Transport is fairly a substantial business on New Dawn." He couldn't look at the man.

"A message? ND is a six-day trip from Darien." The man merely seemed surprised.

"I'd pay, of course," Marcer added.

"How? All deportees' funds are frozen." The soldier walked slowly toward the gate, forcing Marcer to follow him in order to continue the conversation.

The muezzin's call started again. Marcer's gut tightened. They were only a few meters from the gate. The women cried out their wretchedness, begging Marcer and his escort to save them from demons: jinns. Women extended their arms beseechingly; one lifted a small child over her head and implored Marcer to take her and raise her in the Harmony. Raise her free, the woman said.

"I'm charging it!" the soldier shouted. The women were obviously familiar with the gravity fence; they scrambled away from it as the soldier counted to ten, slowly. He delayed longer than his count, until a woman who had tripped on her long scarf managed to put some distance between herself and the wire marking the compound's limit. She was soaked in mud and panicky, but safe when the click of expanding boosters ignited. The air along the fence became iridescent, as though a thin sheen of oil coated it, but that was the only visible manifestation of the local increase in gravity. The soldier turned to Marcer. The open gate was the only break in the gravity fence. Once across that barrier, Marcer would be lumped with pious alans. He would have no status and no rights. He would be penniless, dependent on charity from men true Jonists despised.

"Time to go inside, Researcher." The soldier gestured again. His expression was sympathetic. "Even if I could send a message, it'd take too long to get there to be of any help to you. You're going out tonight." He inclined his head toward the hoist ship.

"There'd be a reward," Marcer said quickly, in a low voice. "If you got a message to my father, I mean. I could wait here. Brice Issacs has a local agent on Darien. I don't know him, but I'm sure he'd pay."

"Reward? Are you offering me a bribe?" The soldier shook his head. "They knew what they were doing when they decided to deport you. Get in." He reached for Marcer, but Marcer had stepped forward rather than let the soldier force him.

Marcer breathed deeply to quiet his gut. The wet-soil taste in his mouth had the bitter flavor of foliage alien to New Dawn. The muezzin's call had become a group chant. Marcer didn't understand a word of it. He tried one last time. "Officer, I've done nothing wrong. There's been no trial. I'm an honest man trying to stay in the Harmony because it's my home. Please. Call Ted Fields at the Academy. Researcher Fields. I'm sure he'll straighten this out. But if you won't, then please—let my father know where I'm being sent." With as much dignity as he could manage in the mud and chill, Marcer went through the gate. His life as a Harmony Academic was over.

Chapter 2

The Supplicant listened to the Harmony Jonists argue among themselves, unimpressed. The woman lecturer had led her to Revered Gangler, who had then brought in Researcher Theodore Fields, a man who introduced himself as a friend of Marcer Brice and earnestly told her to call him Ted.

Revered Gangler's office smelled faintly of almonds. Not a scrap of paper was in sight anywhere, and there was no decoration on the white walls. A real window instead of one of the marvelous window-screens opened onto an unexciting view of a cloister garden. The Supplicant watched a man and a woman seated outdoors on a garden bench with their backs to her. The man put his arm around the woman's shoulders. She leaned close and kissed him. The Supplicant looked away.

Revered Gangler was one of the rare Harmony people with wrinkles and age-spotted skin. However old he was—probably very old indeed, since Harmony Jonists looked thirty for at least a century before beginning to age—Revered Gangler sat ensconced in his tall, straight-backed wooden chair and frowned whenever his attention passed over the Supplicant. He barely acknowledged her. She was unimportant, the messenger and not the message. Only that insignificance had allowed her to remain in his office during their discussion. "How can we be sure this isn't an Emirates' trick?" Revered Gangler peevishly demanded of his fellow Jonists.

"The sensors and monitors say she's telling the truth." After four hours, Ted Fields's deference for Revered Gangler was wearing thin.

"The truth as she knows it." Revered Gangler sighed and shook his head. "Brice's background might support his working with the alans against us; it's said that he's a religionist."

"That's got to be false. I know Marc." Ted Fields stood, so that they all had to look up at him. "He was treated very badly, but I can't believe he'd turn on Jonism or the Harmony. The data he collected look reliable. I trust him as a field researcher, a Jonist, and a man. Besides, if it's even possibly true, then it should be forwarded to Center. Let the Electors decide."

The woman lecturer stirred. "What about Ahman Klee? She'll be furious if she's sidestepped."

"I know where the order to deport Marc came from!" Ted Fields strode away from the other two, toward the Supplicant, then seemed actually to see her. He hesitated, bowed, then quietly said, "Thank you for bringing us this information. Thank you for being Marc's friend." His smile widened as he appraised her as a woman. She blushed, but kept herself from looking aside.

Revered Gangler watched Fields through hooded eyes, an old, cold man wary of excitement roused in the young. "*Do* you?" he asked. "You think it was only Klee?"

The Supplicant sat perfectly still. Had Marcer Brice been *sent*? Was someone in the Harmony already suspicious of Paradise? If so, rousing the Harmony to action might not be as difficult as she'd feared.

I. A game that someone has to win.

"What's that smell?" Hulweh asked Nisa.

Paintbrush in hand, Nisa sniffed, then looked up from the uncompleted watercolor portrait of her friend, Hulweh. Behind Hulweh, Qadira's creature watched them from the studio doorway, its stink more foul than a wild dog's. It was alone. "What do you want?" Nisa called out, as if the thing could answer.

The creature swaggered into the room. Nisa flicked her brush at it. A dot of pale blue paint landed on the rounded crown of its head, just above its eyes, nearly a match for its currently turquoise hide. The creature blinked but didn't retreat. It sat on its rump and swiped at the paint with one of its front paws. Except for the heavy claws, those paws looked like crudely articulated, cartoon hands. The short

thumb was opposable. Nisa had seen the creature walk upright carrying odd scraps of booty to Qadira's rooms, looking as if it were her dwarf henchman or a demon jinn.

Released from her pose by Nisa's distraction, Hulweh
had relaxed on the divan. She took a honey-dipped pis-
tachio roll from the low side table and licked the sweet,
sticky glaze. She squinted at Qadira's creature. "It *is* ugly.
Does it bite?"

"Not where anyone can see it. It's sneaky, just like its
mistress." Nisa gazed into the creature's gray saucer eyes,
repulsed and fascinated by the greed in them. The thing
wanted.

"You shouldn't insult the houris." Hulweh lifted her teacup and slurped noisily as she drank, but the polite sound
failed to erase the indiscretion of mentioning houris aloud.

"I'm not afraid of Qadira. I hate her."

"Hush. You're not a child anymore, to say such things."
A cousin as well as a friend, Hulweh's father was Sheik
Radi's younger brother. Nisa could confide in her. Classi-
cally beautiful, with Persian eyes and ruby lips, Hulweh was
twenty-eight to Nisa's seventeen, an old maid, but Hulweh
didn't care. Their disinterest in marriage was a bond between them.

Nisa wouldn't be restrained. "She's why I agreed to
marry Idryis Khan a'Husain. I have to get away from her.
And that." She pointed dramatically at Qadira's pet. Now
sprawled on the floor, watching them, it had taken on the
ivory color of the tile.

Hulweh peered at it. She had weak eyes, left uncorrected
by her father; they gave her the unfocused look of a
dreamer. When reading, she held the pager so close she
seemed to be smelling the screen, yet she read constantly.
There was a pager on the floor next to the divan, a smuggled Harmony romance she'd brought to share with Nisa.
Hulweh was addicted to Harmony stories of women in love,
and women adventurers overcoming danger. Without good
vision, without the ability to paint, Nisa would have found
it difficult to think, yet Hulweh was clever. She went outside her home more often than Nisa had permission to
leave hers, and Hulweh always knew what was going on in
the world—although some information probably came from
her excellent unman housekeeper, Ziller. "Have you met

a'Husain, now that you've agreed to marry him?" Hulweh asked.

"No, but I saw his picture." Idryis Khan a'Husain seemed a massive, brooding man, a dark, heavy spot against the outdoor background of the picture. Somber, not someone who laughed.

Hulweh didn't ask about his appearance. "He's military, like most of them."

"Most . . . ?"

Hulweh set her cup on the table. "Sons of the Prophet, God bless and keep him. Children of the houris. There aren't many on Bralava, compared to our other worlds. I looked up this Khan. He's important, Nisa. Aleko Bei is his cousin. With such a close relation to power he has to be careful not to offend the Bei; otherwise, the Bei might decide he's a rival and have him killed. Especially since he's a Son. Some people say only a Son should rule the Emirates. They say that's why Paradise was found."

"Men." Nisa shrugged, dismissing the subject. She wet the brush in her mouth, tasting the familiar iris blue chemical dye, and returned to work on Hulweh's portrait.

"Nisette, know the ground you're walking on." Hulweh leaned forward, the better to see. "This isn't a game. The Sons are dangerous. Idryis Khan a'Husain is . . ."

". . . in the Harmony," Nisa interrupted. "Maybe he won't return. After all, we're supposed to be at war with them."

Hulweh made a rude sound. "That's all talk. There's no war now, and there won't be one. The Harmony won't fight for Neuland."

The creature rose onto all four feet like a dancer rising on her toes. It seemed to inspect Nisa's painting.

"Shoo." She moved the brush to flick more paint on it, then decided to ignore it as she caught a dark gleam in its large eyes. She turned her back on it to face Hulweh. "What do you know about all that?"

"The truth. Our men turn every incident into a move in a game that someone has to win." Hulweh peered nearsightedly at Nisa, frowning like an exasperated mother. "You should take your mind off color and line once in a while and visit your real life, Nisa." She sighed. "Our quarrel with the Harmony of Worlds is over Neuland, but Neuland is independent, not part of the Polite Harmony.

There's no dishonor if the Harmony refuses to defend Neu-land. Neulanders are Jonists, but even so the Neulanders are a different Jonist sect. Neuland actually attacked the Harmony twenty-some years ago. Besides, Neulanders are genetic conversions—pain-free Altered humans—and the Harmony despises them, same as we do. The Harmony won't help Neuland once it's clear our men are serious about taking Neuland."

Annoyed at being lectured and to prove her own knowl-edge, Nisa said, "The Harmony already *has* defended Neu-land. Their warship destroyed one of ours." Because of it, Nisa's youngest brother had begged their father to buy him a military commission. He wanted to fight infidels. Qadira had approved, so he was training on Skodor and Nisa was confined at home with only Qadira and her father.

"Oh, that." Hulweh licked her fingers, then picked up the honey roll again. "Their ship fired on ours because some Harmony people were in danger on Neuland. The thing you have to remember about the Harmony, and all Jonists, is that they're afraid to die. They're godless. They believe this is their one and only life. It makes them cowards."

Disappointed by predictions of the unlikelihood of war, Nisa pushed her easel away. It rolled farther across the tile floor than she had intended. She went to Hulweh. "But if they do fight," she insisted, "then they have almost forty worlds, and we have seven. Eight if you count Paradise. They're the ones with the big fleet and the planet killers. We'll lose."

Hulweh sipped more tea. "You sound as if you hope we do."

"Husbands can die in wars."

Hulweh coughed. Her face turned red. It was a minute before she could speak. "Not fleet commanders. They stay in their command ships, far from the battle. And there won't be a war, anyway. Is the war why you agreed to marry him?"

Nisa shrugged. "Qadira says it's a jihad; she wants to destroy Neuland. Qadira gets what she wants." As Nisa said its mistress's name, the creature nosed closer. Its breath warmed her right arm. Its foulness overpowered the smell of the paint. She didn't look at it, but her body tensed. Qadira's pet was an animal, she told herself. It didn't understand human speech, yet there was at least a monkey intelligence behind its big, malevolent eyes. "There are plenty of worlds outward. I don't even know why we want this Neuland place."

"Neither do I," Hulweh admitted. "Except the houris are behind it."

"If there was a war, would the kitchen express shut down?"

Hulweh jumped off the divan, knocking her cup of tea to the floor. Sharp-edged ceramic fragments flew everywhere. Tea pooled like muddy water in the grout. "You have no sense at all!"

"What did I say?" Nisa asked, nervously pretending innocence.

Hulweh glanced at the open door. Nisa's studio was the public room in her small suite, her substitute for a sitting room. It opened onto the main hall of the women's floor, but Nisa and Qadira were the only women living on the fourth floor. With Qadira out of the house, Nisa and Hulweh were alone except for the creature and unmen servants. "Don't even think that name," Hulweh said. "Your father would lock you in a room until your wedding if he heard you say it. Forget them. The kitch . . . they'd be useless to you, anyway. They only get women into the Harmony because they bribe border guards to wink at smuggling them; no guard would let you through, or me either. The Khalil family is too important."

Nisa wanted to break the serious mood. "Why don't you take my fiancé?" she teased. "I'll get another." She bit into a honey roll, relishing the composition of nutty crunch and honeyed gluten. She enjoyed sweets, and luxury, but she wished for freedom more.

"Maybe not. What man will pay a decent bride-price when, for the cost of a trip to Paradise, he can have a holy houri bride?" She spoke with forced gaiety. "The way things are, you're lucky to get married."

"I wish I wasn't marrying this Khan. He's almost forty!" Nisa lowered her voice. "Hulweh, he has another wife. I'll be second."

"Well, that's not so bad. A man happy with his first wife doesn't take a second." At Nisa's dark look, Hulweh put her hand across her mouth. "Oh, Nisa. You know I didn't mean your mother. She had a good marriage, a happy life.

Your father was forced to marry again. The Bei practically ordered it. And you'll be happy, too. No one ordered Idryis Khan to marry again. It won't be so bad. A husband will protect you from the worries of the world. Look at us. I read. You paint. Our lives are easy because we're sheltered by our fathers and our husbands."

Nisa shook her head. "My father keeps me from doing everything I want to do. I can't study art. I can't go outside and paint a landscape if I want."

"But you'll always have me to pose for you." Hulweh stood, arms extended. When Nisa didn't go to her, she went to Nisa and hugged her. "Nisette, your mother died too young. I can't be her replacement."

"I don't want a replacement!" Nisa stamped her right foot on the floor. "I don't want a husband, either!"

Qadira's creature grunted. Nisa glanced sideways at it. The thing was staring at Nisa's pet, Totsi, who had entered the studio from Nisa's dressing room, where Totsi had been dozing on a cushion beneath the domed skylight. Alarmed, Totsi was humped high, his midsection eyes oriented on Qadira's much larger pet. Qadira's creature was scrutinizing Totsi like a man trying to sense a woman's shape beneath her chador. The thought of a man watching her like that made Nisa shudder. "I'll run away from him," she said.

Hulweh seized Nisa's arms. "Don't cross a'Husain. All men are dangerous, but these Sons are worse." She held Nisa at arm's length, bit her lip, then released Nisa.

"What is it?" Nisa asked.

Hulweh hesitated, then said, "You're his third wife, not his second. I checked. There was another, but she had an *accident*. Her family received compensation and didn't make a fuss."

A man could do anything to a daughter or a wife.

"He has a reputation among men as honorable and competent, so maybe it was an accident," Hulweh added, speaking so quickly that Nisa knew she didn't believe it. "He avoids his other wife, but he's generous with money. The Sons all have a problem with their tempers. I suppose they hate that they can't have children." All Sons were sterile, but Nisa didn't care that she would be childless.

Qadira's creature made a *huff-huff-gulp* noise. Totsi squirmed into a ball as tight as Nisa had ever seen a talish form. Totsi was terrified. "Go away." Nisa waved her hands in the creature's face. Most animals would have moved, but this one glared at her, then lazily batted at her vacated chair. It tumbled sideways to the floor. The creature moved languidly toward the table, with its tray of pastries. Hulweh snatched them up, and it turned, walking instead toward the uncompleted watercolor. Nisa couldn't avoid admiring its musculature. If dance was poetry, then the creature's walk was polished prose, the strongest possible argument against static portraits. Unfortunately, Harmony-style window-screens were banned by the imams as improper reproductions of reality, a usurping of the prerogatives of Allah.

The creature stared at the unfinished painting. Without warning, it licked the picture. Its long brown tongue lingered on the paper as though savoring a treat. Nisa stood frozen as lines smudged and colors muddied. The creature's jaws snapped shut. It turned toward Hulweh.

"That thing is smart." Hulweh returned the pastry tray to the table, chose another roll, raised it to her lips, then thought better of it and replaced it on the tray.

The creature looked from the ruined portrait, to Hulweh, then back to the portrait.

"What's it doing?" Hulweh asked.

"It's discovered art," Nisa said.

Hulweh tried to smile, though the attempt was feeble. "It's not *that* smart. Well, I'd better leave." She glanced at the door.

"I thought you were staying the whole day," Nisa protested.

"Ziller is waiting for me downstairs."

Totsi uncurled himself slightly. His head humped cautiously up, like a child peering around a corner. Qadira's creature grunted, turned, eyed Totsi, then looked at Hulweh. It took a step in her direction.

"Is it going to lick *me*?" Hulweh retreated, moving toward the door. "Ugh."

The creature watched her.

Nisa didn't know what Qadira's ugly thing intended, but Hulweh was her guest. Nisa placed herself between the creature and Hulweh. "No!" she shouted, waving her arms menacingly. "No! Go away!"

The creature gazed at Nisa, apparently unimpressed. Its alien eyes were like a dark night sky: unreachable; beyond understanding; yet laden with meaning. Nisa didn't know whether its stare was a threat or a friendly gesture; women couldn't make the new pilgrimage. Paradise was for men.

The thing turned away first. It looked beyond Nisa, at Hulweh.

Nisa stamped her feet hard against the tile floor. "Go away!"

The creature turned. It opened its mouth. It made no sound, so that the effect was similar to a yawn, but the rows of teeth were conspicuous, sharp and frightening. There was no mistaking the creature's meaning. It expelled a foul, noisy breath at Nisa. The biting scent—a cross between harsh onion and lemon—made her eyes tear.

"You're right; you'd better leave," she told Hulweh without loosening her attention on the creature. The thing clicked its mouth closed, but Nisa's eyes didn't immediately stop tearing.

Hulweh rushed to the door, grabbing her chador from the hook where she'd flung it.

The creature surged forward on only its hind legs. Nisa threw herself at it. It sidestepped her with frustrating ease and raced Hulweh to the door. It won.

Hulweh stopped. The creature blocked the doorway. It stared as if daring her to try to walk past it.

"Can you call someone to come?" Hulweh's voice quavered. "Nisette, are *you* all right?"

"Fine." Nisa's hand was damp with spilled tea. She had broken her fall by bracing herself and had landed near the shattered teacup. She picked up a sharp piece and got back to her feet. The call panel was near the door. "Push the caller if you want, but no one will come. All the unmen are afraid of it. And of Qadira. They won't help."

The creature seemed to be waiting. Nisa approached it cautiously, holding the jagged ceramic fragment behind her back like a hidden knife. "How can anyone believe she's holy? Or that this jinn comes from Allah's Paradise?"

Hulweh shivered. "It's listening. Will it let me out?"

The creature's saucer eyes were on Nisa. She once again moved to a position between the creature and Hulweh. The creature was motionless. "Yes. Just walk steadily. Don't run. I'm sorry, Hulweh."

Hulweh's grin was sickly. "Next time, you come to my house." Hulweh scooted through the doorway. Nisa fol-

lowed her. The creature didn't. Once in the main hall of
the women's floor, an echoing, excessively large place, Nisa
dropped the broken ceramic piece. She and Hulweh hurried
down the massive, central staircase, passing the private
rooms of Nisa's father, the closed access to the second
floor, and ending on the ground floor very near the kitchen.
Nisa glanced up. The dizzying expanse of stairs and railing
were empty, except at the very top. Qadira's jinn had come
to the edge of the staircase. It stood on two legs and was
staring down at them.

II. God-dance.

Marcer went a few meters inside the gated compound,
then stopped, repelled by the stench of the alans and the
outlandish sight of them at prayer. He turned back to the
gate. The gravity fence whined as it powered down once
the gate was closed; the soldier walked off to his stillpost.
That post may as well have been on another world. The
soldier was free. Marcer wasn't. His gut twisted. *Do something!* his body goaded him. *Run! Fight!*

He swallowed hard and forced himself to think. That was
the way to escape this trap. He had to suppress emotion
and pretend he was in the field. The first rule of fieldwork
was to gather data.

Marcer faced into the compound again. The women near
the fence eyed him. No one came close.

The compound was clearly meant to be temporary. A
shelter had been installed, along with three rows of incon-
gruously pastel fiberfoam lavatories. Most of the odor came
from those. The shelter was a sloped roof, a lean-to, which
gave minimal protection from the brisk west wind. The
fence around the compound perimeter was outlined with a
triple height of red wire. The ground inside the fence hadn't
been sealed either, and the heat generated by the throng
of milling deportees had produced a field of oozing mud.

Women, a few with children, huddled in the sheltered
area; so did a very few men. The women at the fence were
more numerous than those in the shelter. The latter wore
voluminous fabric coverings, which hid their bodies except
for their eyes and their hands; those women near the fence
were also covered, but with oddments of clothing. One

nearby woman had a pale yellow dress draped over her head, its sleeves tied under her chin. Her eyes were red and swollen. She watched him, a Jonist Academic locked inside the gate, with a mixture of fear and hope. Marcer turned to study the compound's men.

The muezzin's call had been replaced by a group chant. The men had arranged themselves in long rows perpendicular to the fence. One man led them, though he didn't face his congregation. The textbook illustration of this alan group prayer had been labeled "visible signs of superstition." Like crops in farmland, the alan religion grew rows of men.

Sight was passive. Echo-location was tactile, active. Heedless of sensors, Marcer turned in a slow arc and EL-ed the compound.

His first impression, after months in the close confines of a city, was of unrestricted space. The fence was an insignificant interruption. The mist in the air gave a shimmering quality to the bounce-back, akin to the shiny reflection of sunlight off metal, but gentle and more diffuse, as though the deportees stood in clouds, not mud.

An EL pulse didn't resonate color, but there were perceptible textures that gave a similar effect. The soil had the malleable quality of all mud, but a softer consistency than the common clay of New Dawn. The shelter roof and the lavatories were solid but echoed their makeshift nature by a lack of consistent density. The bounce-back from men and women had a supple feel, as though the pulse was absorbed slightly into their bodies before the bounce-back, giving an indistinct impression of a skeleton bounded by soft structures. The bounce-back signals were discrete, so that if he strained and thought about it, the effect was jerky, like vision by strobe light, but to EL natural; his mind bridged the gaps so that the information flow felt as continuous as any other sense.

He EL-ed the women at the fence, flinched, and ended the EL.

Those women were terrified. When human beings were the target of an EL pulse, there was a halo effect. New Dawn Altereds called it an aura. To EL a person also scanned body language. Body language was emotion.

The general public was largely unaware of the full scope of a New Dawn Altered's ability, but the information was available. Marcer thought the best Academic report on the topic was one written decades earlier by Jeroen Lee, long before his elevation as an Elector, entitled "Practical Empathy: New Dawn as an example of unintended consequences." While most discussion focused on the EL-derived insight as though it was intellectual—"You're a walking lie detector," Ted Fields had once joked—early in his career Jeroen Lee had grasped the intimacy associated with the knowledge. Particularly when emotion was strong, an EL bounce-back was visceral. Marcer felt the women's terror in his heart as well as his head. For a moment, it became his emotion, too.

In search of calm, Marcer EL-ed the praying men. They knelt in mud like irresponsible children bent on dirtying their clothes, then bowed, stood, and repeated the sequence, prostrating themselves again. Absorbed in their motion, most were oblivious of him, serene. Up and down they went. A liturgy. Jonism had its formal aspects, but nothing to compare with this physical manifestation of prayer, this god-dance. Marcer's mind tried to give it meaning, as though the bodies were writing the letters of a word across space, but if so, he couldn't read. Prostration in the mud reeked of a self-abasement antithetical to human dignity. A harbinger of things to come in the Emirates? Not if he could help it.

In near unison, the men rose to their feet. Camouflaged by their upright posture, curious but wary, Marcer went forward, picking his way as carefully as he did in a field survey of wild creatures.

"Don't go closer, sir," a woman warned in a carrying whisper. She spoke common language, not Emirates Ufazi.

Marcer hesitated.

Gingerly, with frequent worried glances at the praying men, the woman came to him. She wore a black scarf-like thing over her head and a black coat that grazed the muddy ground, rather than the impromptu getup of the rest.

"Why shouldn't I?" he asked.

"They'll kill you for intruding." In normal clothing she might have been pretty, but, accentuated by the dismal clothing, her dark-shadowed eyes and her grim expression, were what Marcer mostly noticed. He didn't EL.

The men were rising to their feet. Confined, unarmed,

absorbed in their chant and motions, they looked harmless, but there were many of them. He was alone.

"If you need to question them, wait until their prayers are over." The woman came closer still and lowered her voice. "There's a Son among them. You shouldn't have come inside alone." Her foreign accent was thick, but didn't garble the words.

His white Academic gown had fooled her into thinking he was in the compound on Harmony business. Rather than rectify her mistake, he asked, "Which one is he? The son of the important man?" Marcer scanned the lines of men, but they were an aggregate.

"An angel's son," she said, "one of those they call Sons of the Prophet; I don't know whose child he is except they say he's important." She indicated the man leading the prayers. "Stay away from him, sir. Sons are dangerous."

The rows of men moved in nearly military precision. The leader's movements were graceful but tightly controlled. He performed them while seeming unaware of leading the congregation.

"Thank you." Marcer gave the woman a curt bow and moved forward to disassociate himself from her. Those women near the fence were obviously pariahs to the other alans.

"Sir, listen," she said, following. "Please. We want to stay in the Harmony. We *need* to stay. All of us. If you send us back, you're sending us to our deaths. Show mercy, please." She placed her hand lightly on his arm and looked suggestively into his eyes. "I'll do anything you ask. Anything. I don't want to die. If I go back, my husband will let me rot in the Woman Eater—in prison."

He didn't believe her, despite her desperation. Woman Eater. Her fear was real, but her melodrama was ridiculous. "I can't help you. I'm being deported, too." He shook off her hand and strode away, annoyed because she'd smudged his gown.

The alan prayer was over. The rows had dissolved into clumps of men. Worried that he would lose track of the leader—an angel's son!—Marcer edged toward the several hundred men. He hoped to enlist the leader's help in arguing that his birth on Safi was meaningless.

"Jonist!" One man bellowed it, then the catcall was

taken up by others, enough so that the voices became threatening.

Marcer glanced outside the fence. None of the soldiers was in sight. He wondered now at his wisdom in continuing to wear the Academic gown. It hadn't done him any good with his own people and could make for trouble with the superstitious alans. He stared impassively at the jeering men. There was nowhere to run.

The throng of men parted. The angel's son walked directly to Marcer. The nearby women scurried toward the gate. The alan men fell silent. The entire compound was watching. Were the soldiers?

As he approached, Marcer studied the alan leader. Taller than average in the compound, though shorter than Marcer, he carried himself with overt authority. Not a subtle man. He was muscular. His conservative, businessman's suit wasn't muddy; he'd prostrated himself on a rug or mat which he no longer carried. His hands and feet were smaller than expected for his body size. He held his hands open at his sides. Had Marcer known how to read it, his face might have provided clues to his age and achievements, but Marcer was too inexperienced to determine much. In the Harmony people chose the age at which they wished to stabilize their appearance. Besides, this angel's son was bearded, a rarity in the Harmony. His hair was jet-black. It had been cut very short. His dark face was gaunt, but not with the look of privation; it was the stark expression of a warrior on a mission. The mission was Marcer.

Though it felt like cheating, Marcer EL-ed, the better to know this alan leader. The bounce-back was no different than if he had EL-ed a stone. The man was present and moving, but there was no halo effect. Nothing. Shocked and disbelieving, Marcer EL-ed again. He listened deeply. The alan leader hesitated momentarily—the muddy ground. His right hand tapped against his leg. Nevertheless, the subtleties of the alan's body language did not form a consistent message that Marcer was able to interpret. It was like the jumbled bounce-back from certain animals, but this was a man, and Marcer had had no trouble with the bounce-back from other alan men.

The so-called angel's son flushed. He scowled at Marcer as he walked and did not stop again until he was only an arm's length away, too close for comfort in the Harmony.

The crowd strained to hear, as though Marcer and this alan had been thrust onstage into a play. If so, Marcer didn't know his lines.

Harmony protocol called for the alan to bow first since he'd approached Marcer. The alan didn't bow. Neither did Marcer. They looked at each other, each vaguely belligerent, but not stupidly so. Like the woman, the alan probably assumed Marcer was a Harmony administrator.

The alan set his feet apart as if readying for a fight. It reminded Marcer of male chimpanzee social skirmishing, a standard lesson in the introductory class he had so recently been teaching. The man's insistent attention was aggressive. Marcer guessed the alan could stand all day in that pose, and that he would, if only to preserve his supposed dignity and avoid moving first. The game of social chicken was childish. His inability to sense an aura and know the other man's emotions made Marcer uneasy, but also curious. "My name is Marcer Joseph Brice," he said. "I am a Researcher at the Academy of Darien. I *was,* rather, until this morning." To be polite, he spoke Ufazi.

"Are you here to spy on us, Researcher Brice?" the alan leader asked immediately. His voice was a surprise, low, courteous, and unthreatening.

Marcer's knowledge of Ufazi had apparently aroused suspicion. "No." He smiled—carefully. "I'm being deported, too, unless I can stop it. I was born in the Emirates. On Safi."

"A Jonist Academic deported to one of our worlds? That isn't credible." His tone was reasonable, and yet the alan hadn't deigned to introduce himself. He circled Marcer in an exaggeratedly hostile manner, as if inspecting merchandise with which he was dissatisfied. Fieldwork, Marcer reminded himself, and struggled not to show offense.

The alan stopped in front of Marcer again, but even closer. "This is a naive method of inserting a spy into the Emirates, Researcher Marcer Joseph Brice. Typical of your insular Harmony. Return to your usual posting; your career as a spy is over."

Marcer parted his lips slightly, as if taking a breath, and sent a compressed EL pulse. As Marcer listened to the bounce-back, the other man's muscles tensed, then loosened, and he made a small, low, perhaps involuntary sound. He stepped back, then forward, as though an impetus to violence was being alternately released and suppressed. Marcer, however, felt no emotion in the bounce-back. Nothing. This man was strange.

Impulsively, Marcer bowed. "I *was* born on Safi. There must be records. I'm being deported against my will. I am not a spy. I have no desire whatsoever to go anywhere in the Emirates."

The alan leader grinned, showing teeth. It was a peculiar expression, chilling, predatory, and yet false. "I am Idryis Khan a'Husain, favored Son of the Prophet, God's blessings and peace be upon him. You are nothing. An infidel. Less. Jonists are pagans."

Finally there was a reaction from outside the fence. The soldier left his stillpost and watched. Farther away, a group of soldiers came down the hoist ship gangway. If this Idryis Khan a'Husain attacked, they would be forced to remove Marcer from the compound. He'd have a chance to argue his way to freedom. Besides, he would never survive being deported if he cowered before this man. Marcer gazed disdainfully at the alan religionist. "I've told the truth," he said. "If you don't believe it, you're a fool."

Idryis Khan looked at the soldiers. Marcer followed his look outside the compound and didn't see the low blow coming. The alan's fist hit Marcer's groin. Bent over, involuntarily groaning, he heard laughter and congratulations. Marcer slowly straightened, glad he had not fallen into the mud. He backed away from Idryis Khan. Many of the watching alans faded into the background, but those remaining shouted their leader's name like a banner: Idryis Khan.

The soldier returned to his stillpost. Those on the ramp watched alertly, but did not advance.

Idryis Khan a'Husain had noticed. "They're not rescuing you. Come close again, Researcher Brice. I'm sure I can do better."

Before Marcer could react to the threat, Idryis Khan a'Husain lunged and struck him, this time in the face. The blow vibrated inside his head, making a false bounce-back, like an optical illusion. His Altered sense interpreted it as a stream of arrows shot into the sky, arrows his eyes could not see. Marcer swayed, but kept on his feet.

The right side of his face ached, but not badly. Marcer suspected the alan had pulled his punch. He breathed deeply. The world steadied; the phantom signals were sufficiently slight that they could be ignored.

Idryis Khan watched Marcer.

Marcer touched his cheek and felt blood. He straightened. "I've told you the truth," he said. "I'm no better off than you are. Worse—I'm not returning home." He EL-ed—it gave him an earlier opportunity to dodge—and waited for another blow, but this time he intended to be ready to respond in kind.

None came. Idryis Khan was like a spring with the pressure gone, relaxed but with the potential for more violence if pressed. "What else?" a'Husain asked. His mild tone reminded Marcer of a bad recording. It sounded artificial, a step removed from real life. "That alone—being born on Safi—isn't enough, if you really are an Academic."

He was right, of course. Even as he felt the pressure to EL, Marcer didn't want to admit his difference. Altereds weren't accepted in the Emirates. Bad enough he was a Jonist. Marcer shrugged. "I am a junior Researcher in Nonterrestrial Biology at the Academy of Darien. The rest is politics."

"Nonterrestrial Biology." A'Husain repeated it under his breath. Marcer, had he been a standard human, would not have heard it, but his Alteration also enhanced his hearing. Much louder, a'Husain said, "You are a spy."

"I'm not." The alan men were crowding closer.

"Brice," a'Husain mused aloud. He made another circuit around Marcer, examining him like a buyer at an ancient slave market. Marcer didn't protest. A'Husain stopped at his starting point, facing Marcer. "You're a Jew," he said.

"No."

"Your name is Brice. Born on Safi. Brice-Issacs Transport is a shipping company, running goods between the Harmony and us. Yes, you're a Jew. *That's* why they're deporting you."

Marcer clenched his fists. Inside the Harmony, to be a religionist was worse than being an Altered; it was a matter of character. Truthfully, his ancestry might have been a factor against him. His father, Lavi Brice, and other relatives, used obsolete tribal affiliations to advance business in the Emirates, where religion was important. Harmony authorities probably knew it. Marcer and his sister, Miriam, had been forced to study what Lavi Brice called "the classics," including the myths and superstitions of the Bible; a few members of the extended family had peculiar customs into which Marcer had never inquired. Marcer had disassociated himself as much as possible from the Marrano elements in his background, but they did exist. "My paternal grandparents were Jews," he admitted, "though not my mother's. I'm not; I'm entirely Jonist."

"A Jew born on Safi." A'Husain nodded, his suspicion confirmed, though there was no reaction in his face. "A Jew sent away by his brother Jonists. So, Joseph, how does it feel to be in the pit and on your way to Egypt? What dreams will you interpret once you're there?"

The soldiers would have monitors in the compound. Marcer understood the mocking reference, but didn't want to show it. "My name is Marcer," he said. "Joseph is a family name, my father's grandfather. Is Egypt one of your cities?"

Idryis Khan smiled. It made his face look like a mask. "A Jew who denies it. Then if you aren't a spy, you're stateless. Which is it?" In one smooth, quick movement, he grabbed the collar of Marcer's gown and ripped it. The gown's closure opened, exposing the clothes underneath.

Marcer recoiled. A'Husain still had the collar, so the thin rice-paper fabric tore. The right side of the gown dragged in the mud, ruined.

The men behind a'Husain called encouragement, but he only said, "So we know who you really are."

III. Jinn.

"Have you ever seen one of those creatures up close, Ziller?" Hulweh asked breathlessly. She and Nisa had run into the huge ground-floor kitchen of Sheik Radi's house. "The houris' pets?"

The half dozen servants looked up from their work of chopping vegetables and washing laundry. The wide exterior doors were open to the domestic dock, where a fruit delivery was in progress, and the sweet bouquet of stickpeaches battled the canal stench wafting inside. Ziller was seated with Joho, Sheik Radi's chief cook, at one of the long worktables, a plate of dainties in front of him along with a half-empty, perspiring glass of pale yellow, foam-topped liquid.

Nisa glanced back at the corridor, listening, but she didn't hear the click of the creature's nails on the stairs. It hadn't followed them.

Ziller stood and made twin, brisk bows to Nisa and Hulweh. "I've only seen jinn from a distance," he told Hulweh. "It's best to avoid them when they're loose on the streets; they bite." Old Ziller was thin, unlike most senior unmen, whose greatest pleasure was food. Ziller had presence, a dignity that unmen usually lacked.

"Young Mistress, can I offer you and your guest some refreshment before you inspect the kitchen?" Joho asked Nisa. As he did, he stepped in front of the table, blocking their view of Ziller's drink. Nisa recognized it as ale—alcohol—which unmen sometimes drank. That they had offered ale to Ziller meant they were absolutely certain Qadira was not at home.

The women's staircase ended near the kitchen because when the house had been built women had run households. No more. Unman servants did it; women were protected from working, nearly protected out of any useful existence except as baby factories. Still, a woman's household inspection rights were given lip service.

"Nothing for me, thank you," Hulweh answered quickly. She bowed, though it was unnecessary to bow to an unman. Hulweh claimed that unmen were women with a penis; she liked them.

"No, nothing then, Joho," Nisa said, coming closer.

Hulweh deliberately turned her back on Ziller and Joho and drew Nisa with her by hooking her arm through Nisa's. "The jinn would have attacked me, but Nisa stopped it." Nisa smiled uncomfortably at the gaping underservants Hulweh had addressed, then realized Hulweh's purpose and looked outside, onto the dock. The sweating deliverymen—men, not unmen, for such heavy work—had unloaded their cargo. The household staff would bring it indoors.

"You were very brave, Nisette," Ziller said. "Did it try to bite?"

Nisa and Hulweh swung around to face Ziller and Joho again. The alcohol had vanished from the table, secreted away by one of the servants.

"Not really," Nisa said. "The creature was acting strange.

Usually it stays with Qadira or in her rooms. Maybe it was just disoriented."

"It licked Nisa's portrait of me!" Hulweh exclaimed with a theatrical shiver. "That thing is ugly!"

For all her shrewd political analysis, Hulweh often acted silly around men and unmen. Nisa frowned. "I don't think it wanted to hurt us; it seemed curious."

"You!" Joho shouted at his kitchen staff. "Get back to work." Hairless, like all genetically engineered unmen, Joho was the only servant who predated Qadira's arrival as Sheik Radi's wife. Every household servant was one of the docile, sexless human unmen. They lacked a libido, were impotent and sterile, so the kitchen was a place where women could routinely still go uncovered and unannounced. Nisa visited the kitchen only rarely. Unlike Hulweh, she distrusted unmen.

"If Gidie knew you had ale," Nisa said in a low voice to Joho, "he'd fire you, and not even your cooking skill would save you." She wanted the unman to know she was aware of his indiscretion. Let him be indebted to her.

"But you won't tell him, will you, Nisette?" Ziller asked with a wide conspiratorial smile. Ziller was Housekeeper General of Hulweh's father's city home, but he had been born on the vast Khalil estates in the north. Nisa had known him all her life. Ziller had protected Nisa from Hulweh's teasing brothers, and her own; he had slipped sweets to her when, during Ramadan, the fast became too much for a child; he had admired her paintings. He was the one who had comforted her when her mother died. Unmen were competitors to women, but if there was one unman Nisa trusted, it was Ziller. "Of course not," Nisa said. Embarrassed, she turned to Joho. "Didn't Gidie tell you to keep that door closed?"

Gidie, the new Housekeeper General at Sheik Radi's home, was an unctuous creature of Qadira's choosing, but he did not get along well with the staff. Joho grimaced. "As soon as we're done, Young Mistress."

They never obeyed Nisa.

"If it isn't too bold," Ziller said, "I would like to offer my congratulations."

For a moment, Nisa didn't remember what he meant. "Oh, that," she finally said. "Yes, thank you." Mention of her impending marriage made her anxious to talk of something else. "You should come upstairs, Zil, and see my latest work. I've been playing with how light illuminates different surfaces, trying to copy what the ancients did, but make it my own."

"I hope Idryis Khan is as grateful as he should be to have such a talented and beautiful wife," Ziller said. The pedestrian compliment had been warmly spoken.

Nisa blushed as she thanked him, and turned immediately to Hulweh. "Will you come tomorrow so I can repaint your portrait?"

Hulweh twisted slightly from side to side, then said, "You visit me instead. My brother Mernisi is home from Skodor."

Qadira's creature had frightened Hulweh. Was that its plan? "I'll try." It was no secret that, even escorted, Nisa was rarely allowed to leave the house, but sometimes she used it as an excuse. When working hard on a painting, Nisa often viewed any interruption as unwelcome, even visits with a friend.

Hulweh draped her chador loosely in place. She had only to go through the house to her covered car. "We should leave," she told Ziller.

Leave-taking could be a lengthy process, but by wearing the chador, Hulweh showed she was serious. Nisa walked with Hulweh through the servants' hallways rather than through the courtyards, until they reached the public—male—portions of the house. Ziller had gone ahead.

"Why are you so hard on Joho and the others?" Hulweh whispered. "Unmen are the natural friends of women."

That was the common opinion. Nisa shrugged and didn't answer. They didn't speak until reaching the main streetside entrance to the house. It was majestic and empty. Before Bralava had become one of the worlds of the United Emirates, the Khalil family had been hereditary leaders of the northern plain. The grandeur seemed wasted now that this was merely a private home.

"I'm sorry," Nisa said.

Hulweh hugged her. "For what? Little sister," she said, using the diminutive, "you know you can never offend or anger me."

Hulweh smelled of honey and the vanilla scent of her

favorite shampoo. When they parted, Nisa said, "I wish I were a man."

Hulweh shook her head. "What would you do? Life isn't easy for them, either."

Ziller opened the door. Bright sunshine lit the hall, itself an answer. "If I was a man, I'd marry you," Nisa whispered, "then we could live happily ever after."

"Silly girl." Hulweh kissed her, then pulled her chador close and hurried through the open door.

When they were gone, Nisa passed through the kitchen— she wasn't really welcome there—and climbed the staircase to the women's floor. Qadira had removed all decoration from the walls, claiming that Nisa's mother's choices were too lively. She hadn't replaced them; the holes, hooks, and uneven fading where rich carpets had hung made the emptiness desolate. *Paradise must be dreary,* Nisa thought. Men never discussed it. Even its location was secret, to protect it from infidels.

Nisa stopped in her studio doorway. Despite the stench, at first she didn't understand. The easel was tumbled on its side. The watercolors seemed to have been swirled and spattered throughout the room as if by a spinning wheel. The easel's legs were broken. The pad of watercolor paper had been chewed and spat in clumps on the walls. A greenish yellow fluid, lumpy with bits of disintegrating paper, dripped from the walls and stained the divan and tables. Globules spotted the hanging pictures and the pale, thin drapery at the windows. The odor of bile and bitter venom signed the work.

Nisa gagged. Her eyes ached. Her impulse was to run, but her artist's eye picked out details in the confusion. Horrible ones.

Totsi's body was partially covered by the broken easel. Pinkish blood pooled on the floor among the bits of paint. It would stain the grout. Nisa held her breath and entered the fouled room slowly, careful to avoid stepping on regurgitated matter. She circled around to approach Totsi's inert body from the other side. In the area between the easel and the window Nisa found Totsi's head. Chunks of flesh were missing, and the rest had been chewed. It lay in the center of a puddle of yellow urine. Qadira's creature was gone, but it had left its message.

IV. Martyrs.

The gravity fence whined as it was suddenly fed full power. The sunlight dimmed as the compound was cut off from the world beyond. Four armed soldiers rushed through as the gate opened. Their boots made wet, spurting sounds as they hit the mud; two others stayed on guard at the open gate.

What they wouldn't do to defend Marcer, they were doing for his white Academic gown.

"Stand away from him!" the lead soldier shouted at Marcer. Marcer was happy to oblige. He moved toward the squad.

Idryis Khan a'Husain watched them come. His face lacked expression; his posture seemed relaxed. His alan followers also watched and waited, but excitedly. Because of them, the atmosphere in the compound held the kind of tension that was the prelude to a riot. But why? An alan rebellion against deportation to their own worlds made no sense, beyond a kind of vicious pride.

Weapons at ready, three of the soldiers formed an arc facing the alan crowd. The majority of those interned in the compound, mostly businessmen, had moved off toward the shelter, but there were at least 150 younger, agitated men ranged behind Idryis Khan a'Husain.

The platoon leader addressed a'Husain in clumsy Ufazi. "You. Come with us."

A'Husain was as inert as a grenade before the pin is pulled. From among the alan men behind him came unimaginative insults: Jonist pigs. Godless sons of whores. He was silent.

Marcer took a step toward the gate. No one else had moved. Eyes seemed to turn to him. He stopped. "Officer," he said to the platoon leader, embellishing the soldier's rank, "get me out of the compound and there won't be any more trouble."

"Are you hurt?" The platoon leader didn't look away from a'Husain. From the quick movement of muscles around his eyes, he was troubled by the alan invective.

"No." Marcer EL-ed and felt hatred and resentment rising from the alan men like waves of heat coming off a fire. Most were silent, but those men hated just as much as the others, however unreasonable it was. "No, but you can't take him out of here and leave me, because if you do, I'm dead, and you'll have killed an Academic. It's simplest just to transfer me."

The platoon leader was unprepared for this situation. Marcer could sense his confusion even without EL-ing.

A'Husain had looked away from the soldiers and was studying Marcer. He held a portion of Marcer's gown in his hand, like a drooping banner.

"Let's go," Marcer urged the soldiers.

"All right," the platoon leader said. "Both of you." He gestured toward the gate with his weapon.

Finally. Marcer's relief made him smile.

"No." A'Husain crossed his arms over his chest while continuing to study Marcer. Behind him, men cheered as though the refusal was a victory.

Marcer remembered something his father had said: *Alans all want to be martyrs.* Idryis Khan seemed to want to create an incident, even start a bloodbath that would decimate his own people and possibly increase the likelihood of war. Marcer had a duty, as a Jonist and a man, to prevent such chaos if he could. He stepped between Idryis Khan and the platoon leader, though not in the line of sight of the soldier's firearm. "What has he done?" Marcer asked in the common language.

The soldier glanced at Marcer. "He attacked an Academic."

The alan Khan had done that earlier, without repercussions. Marcer shook his head. "He tore a cheap gown."

A'Husain scrutinized the soldiers, who seemed to ignore Marcer's statement. The platoon leader gestured again with the tip of his stick gun. "Come along, you," he ordered a'Husain.

The alans behind a'Husain were businessmen, not warriors, but their growl was feral. Marcer EL-ed, feeling the mob's tentative, unconscious, and, so far, slight motion forward as well as their bitterness.

The soldiers had guns. They would survive a melee. Marcer probably wouldn't, and neither would the alan Khan or most of his mob. *Alans all want to be martyrs.* They were willing.

Marcer removed what was left of the ruined gown. Without it, in his casual, comfortable shirt and pants, Marcer projected no particular authority. He looked at each of the four soldiers, and said, "You came inside to rescue me. I'm fine. Now let's get out of this compound."

Jonist soldiers were rational and well trained, but they remained human animals. The angry crowd had triggered a streak of stubbornness in the soldier. "You're coming, too," he ordered a'Husain. He must have given a command through the Military Utility because the other three men moved in unison to cover him as he went forward to grab a'Husain.

The crowd hissed, but stayed back. The three soldiers had trained their weapons on them, so although the alans shouted, the alans didn't move. A'Husain appeared passive, but when the platoon leader was off-balance, reaching for him, a'Husain suddenly screamed something bloodthirsty and leapt onto the other man.

The soldiers could have killed a'Husain, but whether by design or not, a'Husain always kept a position that would force them to hit their comrade, too. They didn't shoot.

A'Husain used his hands like claws. He scratched. He ripped the soldier's clothes and then his flesh. It was the raw attack of a madman who was brilliantly skilled. The soldier struggled, but a'Husain absorbed his efforts as though the soldier's blows were meaningless.

The soldier wouldn't win.

"Get the gun!" an alan shouted, apparently unaware that Harmony military-issue stick guns were personally keyed and wouldn't fire for others. A'Husain ignored the gun, but used the muddy fragment of Marcer's Academic gown to try to throttle the soldier. The soldier twisted and nearly got loose.

Another troop of soldiers, their image distorted by a scatter-field, rushed through the gate.

A'Husain flung the soldier into the mud, dived after him, and bit the man's shoulder. Blood spurted. The Harmony soldier screamed, a high-pitched, sickening sound.

Two of the three soldiers already on the scene entered the fight. They tried to pry a'Husain from their leader, but the alan held on with his teeth. A'Husain had become a beast.

Involuntarily, Marcer EL-ed. Just then, a'Husain looked up. His beard was bloody. His face was impassive. There was nothing in his eyes.

"Stop," Marcer yelled. "You can't win."

The two soldiers used the momentary respite to topple a'Husain. Though it took two of them, they pinned him on the ground. "Shoot!" one screamed at the third man.

Fight or flight was biology. The alan crowd was ready for a fight. To kill their leader, their angel's son, would start one.

The soldier took aim.

"No!" Marcer flung himself between the soldiers and a'Husain.

The shot didn't come. The second squad had arrived. They overwhelmed Idryis Khan a'Husain by force of numbers, but whatever slim chance Marcer had had to avoid deportation had vanished. He saw in their eyes that by saving an alan, Marcer had committed treason.

Chapter 3

Darien to Center-Sucre was a seven-day trip. The Supplicant traveled in the company of Researcher Fields and Revered Gangler, so she traveled as an Academic. As Fields explained it, that meant the cabins were smaller, but their workmanship was better than in the deluxe accommodations purchased by businessmen and government officials.

Her cabin was magnificent. She had left Bralava as a refugee, in the poorest accommodation possible, a transport web. Twelve days spent naked, hanging suspended in semi-adhesive confinement netting (except for brief rotating meals, group showers, and forced exercise) had given her too much time to brood, but against all odds she had managed the first and hardest step. She would complete her mission.

In contrast, her cabin now was a three-meter square, entirely paneled in window-screens. According to Ted Fields, they were probably the Master's certifying project of a licensed artisan. Around all four sides of the room illusionistic fluted pilasters supported a frieze of false and fanciful animals (or possibly bizarre but genuine ones she didn't know) and flanking cabinets with latticed doors. Sometimes the doors seemed to be ajar. Various objects appeared to be inside the cabinets. They changed daily, though they were generally antique: sometimes a caged songbird and candlesticks, sometimes hard-copy books so natural they seemed ready to read; once there had been keys and several times reproductions of ancient sculptures. For days, the Supplicant found herself reaching for an interesting item only to touch bare, flat walls.

The deception was flawless. The inventiveness was tempered with a bitter humor best shown by the imitation mirror which, in early morning, reflected her as a child, and aged her as the day wore on, until finally, very late, it would show no one at all as she stood gazing into it.

Ted Fields blamed himself for his failure to prevent Marcer's deportation and had removed all decoration from his cabin. His had been less interesting, anyway—two window-screens which showed identical views, except one was in daylight and the other in the dark—but the Supplicant thought it a stupid, useless penance. She said nothing. If such a simple effort could expiate his guilt, she envied him. Her own guilt ran deeper. Meanwhile, she was traveling toward a place where she knew no one, where she was an ignorant foreigner carrying a disputable message from an unreliable source. Consequently, she smiled at Ted Fields and learned to flirt; she would need allies.

I. Uninjured peace.

Marcer Brice arrived on Bralava to a hero's welcome. Every man deported to the Emirates and set loose by the Harmony freighter's dump-and-run was treated to a series of welcoming speeches. Most were in Ufazi, and Marcer could understand them, although the mayor of the city of Shores spoke in Fars, a local language. The speech made by Josip Gordan, the governor of Bralava, an appointee of Aleko Bei, was the last, the longest, and the most fiery. It referred to war with Neuland, and if necessary, the Polite Harmony of Worlds, as an inevitable jihad and ended with an alan communal prayer.

"Just sit respectfully, with your head slightly bowed," Matthew McCue whispered to Marcer as he demonstrated the proper posture. They were on the floor already—the heroes had been given everything except chairs—arranged in tidy rows in an immense and very beautiful open-air courtyard.

Marcer copied McCue's pose. Those few deported traders who were not alans did the same. All women had mysteriously vanished. Marcer worried about those who had been refugees in the Harmony. Throughout the trip to the Emirates they had begged the crewmen to let them maintain their asylum in the Harmony. Several had given their bodies to the freighter's crew as an enticement for a return trip back to Darien, but every one of them had been dumped on Bralava with the men. What had been done with them? Marcer looked sideways at McCue, his mentor in understanding the ways of the United Emirates. "Lower," McCue whispered.

Marcer bent his head farther, though his entire body remained bruised from the thorough beating the soldiers had given him at the compound, and he was sore from spending the trip to Bralava wrapped in semiadhesive transport netting. He hadn't had money to bribe the crew to let him rotate down from the overcrowded stacks more than their illegally brief minimum of twenty minutes once a day. The crew had done well pursuing their racket among the wealthy businessmen the Harmony had expelled. McCue—a trader who'd been tied in next to Marcer—had offered a loan. Marcer had refused; he could endure the trip. He'd arrived in the United Emirates a penniless foreigner, owning only the clothing on his back, which the welcoming committee had given him, but better that than to arrive already in debt.

Seated, McCue seemed a taller person than he did standing. He had the upper body of a larger man; only stubby legs caused his lack of height. His massive arms were strong, yet his waist was thick with fat. Moles on his forehead and beside his right nostril made him ugly. He had yellow teeth and dandruff. He smelled of seasoned sweat, though he'd paid to rotate down and stay out of the webbing for hours each day, and those trips had included use of washrooms. He rarely met Marcer's eyes, and, when he did, his glance was furtive. A crossman of the Protestant sect, not an alan or a Jonist, he'd taken Marcer under his wing on the ship. Marcer didn't trust him.

The Harmony crew of the freighter had not originally permitted the alans to pray. During their release from the transport webs the alans had prayed anyway, and those who could afford it prayed five times each ship day. At first there had been a confusion of threats and skirmishing, then the crew—which knew that ungrateful cargo who spoke against them strongly enough might convince the Emirates to rescind the freighter's safe-conduct—relented. Marcer had grown accustomed to the *Adhan,* calling them to prayer, to the ritual wash and murmur of the *Shahadah* prayer, and then the alternating postures of *rak'ah;* he couldn't understand what was said, since he knew no Arabic, but the peaceful ritual had soothed him, too. It was a good time to think.

Like his namesake Joseph in the Bible, he'd been sent into exile without reason or justice. He could hope it was temporary, but first he had to survive. Everything he'd been, every honor he'd achieved, was meaningless and lost; he had to begin again. Until he could find a way home, it was expedient to view this new world, Bralava, as an unexpected stint of fieldwork.

The reception had been preceded, for Marcer and a few other suspicious characters, by a terse interrogation. He'd been labeled an indigent, classified as a Jonist and an alien, but issued a plastic card that was his temporary Permit to Live. "No unlicensed begging," the official had said. "One week to find a stable, registered job, or you go to the Citadel." McCue had warned him to expect as much. "But once you're let in, they'll never bother to chase you down," McCue also explained. "Just don't request a permit extension, and they'll forget you exist. And get an unregistered job, or the owner will report you for subversive activities when your first paycheck is due, to avoid paying. Businesses using unregistered labor have their own worries." He grinned as if to say he had done as much himself.

It was nothing like the scrupulous Harmony, and Marcer's status could hardly have been worse, though when he showed the card to McCue, McCue claimed that wasn't so. "You're legal, despite being a Jonist Academician," he said. "The rest is details. I'll bet the Khan put in a good word."

Idryis Khan a'Husain was on the dais with the Emirates officials. McCue said a'Husain was an important nobleman, a cousin of Aleko Bei, but had only laughed when Marcer asked about his being an angel's son and told Marcer to ask the Khan himself. Throughout the speeches a'Husain had sat—the officials had chairs—looking stern. As usual. His expression rarely changed. Time spent in webbing ten meters away had taught Marcer that a'Husain was arrogant and stubborn. Obviously rich, a'Husain had refused to pay off the crew, so he and his most determined followers had spent as much time in the transport webs as Marcer and the other indigents. A'Husain had spent a fair amount of that time staring at Marcer from across the naked bodies of the men between them. Marcer didn't want anything from that peculiar man and doubted very much that a'Husain had done anything for him, a Jonist.

No one knew Marcer was Altered. His Academy status probably made them assume he wasn't, and he hadn't volunteered the information. There were already too many strikes against him. Emirates officials were unlikely to detect his echo-location since the ability was an obscure Harmony Alteration essentially confined to a single, underpopulated Extreme World. Though his Alteration was a secret, he was free to EL and did so frequently, which made him feel like a child again, spending summers at his maternal grandparent's grange on New Dawn.

The men prayed. Marcer watched their long, evening shadows dance shapes across the intricately patterned walls. His echo bounce-back confirmed the visual harmony of the arched walls. An abstract tracery linked them and repeated their design on a smaller scale in carved stonework inset with blue-and-gold mosaic. The deep blue sky above was filling with stars he could not identify; perhaps one of them was home.

The courtyard was part of Government House, an enormous complex containing offices as well as the governor's residence. According to McCue, it stretched over six city blocks. Governor Gordan *was* the government, since Bralava, uniquely in the Emirates, had never had a single emir, only a group of chieftain sheiks. The attributes of executive and legislature were combined in Governor Gordan; his power was personally exercised. The only check on it came from Aleko Bei himself, or from competing lesser powers: local noblemen, religious leaders, and the military. Idryis Khan a'Husain was a military fleet commander, a Son of the Prophet and thus a holy man, as well as Aleko Bei's cousin. On the dais, the governor deferred to him.

When the prayers ended, the reception broke up. The Emirates style was to dissolve into smaller and smaller groups, whereas in the Harmony a meeting ended more formally, usually with passage to another place and a slow, individual drifting away of the uninvited. McCue grunted and motioned for Marcer to help him up. Marcer extended his arm. McCue grasped it and raised himself hand over hand, as though Marcer's arm was a rope to climb. Bralava's gravity was heavier than standard, but the difference from Darien was minor. More oppressive was the humidity.

The evening temperature was moderate, but the effect was of a cooling steam bath, clammy. Marcer couldn't remember much about Bralava's native life except a brief encyclopedia reference to "continental shrouds of mangrove-form forests" and that it was the source of an exotic, expensive imported fish, the wema, which had once been served at an Academy banquet.

When he was standing, McCue nodded at Marcer. "Goodbye, Researcher. My assistant, Velkic, heard that the Harmony deported even independent traders; he is waiting outside for me. I enjoyed our chats. Good luck." He rubbed his forehead with his hand and began to shuffle away.

Startled, Marcer called his name. "McCue!"

McCue turned back. He hadn't said anything, but the interest he'd taken in Marcer had been an implicit promise. Marcer planned to be self-sufficient, but he needed a crutch for a day or two. He had twenty-six ceramic Harmony counts, everything that had been in his pocket when the constables arrested him: pocket change for the Academy providers, enough for a snack between classes. "You'll give me a job?"

McCue chuckled and wiped his face again. "You're an Academic, not a salesman or an accountant. You have nothing to recommend you but a family relationship with a shipping company I rarely use, B-I Transport." He pronounced the name "buy," rather than with the usual initials. "My freight is more delicate than B-I is equipped to handle. Then again, they're as honest as anyone in the Harmony, which means not honest at all unless you have something they want. Do they want you, Academician? Is giving you a job a good investment?"

Lavi Brice would certainly repay McCue, but was it wise to put his father in McCue's debt? "Yes," Marcer said. Survival first.

McCue laughed outright. "Then ask them for help. B-I runs both sides of the line. Even with the border closed, they have an office on Safi; that's a four-day trip. They may have a local agent on Bralava. Go to him for funds."

Marcer stared helplessly; he'd be out on the street for at least that night. If a local agent existed, he would be a stringer, not family, and difficult to convince without documentation. Marcer wet his lips, tasting the strangeness of a new world in his own sweat. "Put me up for the night,

McCue. Give me a letter of introduction. I'll pay you back. Whatever you want that I have."

McCue shifted his weight. "A promise like that from a man who wore a white robe once, and may wear one again, is worth something." He studied Marcer. "If he can be relied on to remember and repay."

"One night, McCue . . . It isn't so much. I need to learn the city." Two weeks ago Marcer had been as high as any avowedly Altered man had ever gone in the Academy. Now he was nothing, and so ignorant that he didn't even know what was outside the door of Government House. It was humiliating to have fallen so far, so fast.

"I'm Christian, Researcher. We're tolerated here in the Emirates, more so than in the Harmony, but I walk a thin line. Helping you will do nothing important for me. And you're being watched." He gestured.

Marcer turned to where McCue had indicated. Idryis Khan a'Husain was observing them. Still on the dais, ostensibly engaged in conversation with the governor, his attention was over the governor's stooped shoulder; his eyes met Marcer's. A'Husain nodded infinitesimally, a slight motion that could have meant, come here.

"Go to him," McCue said. "He's too proud to show it, but you interest the Khan. He would be a valuable connection. Use him. Good luck, Researcher." He turned his back on Marcer and walked away. This time Marcer didn't try to stop him.

If McCue wouldn't help, then Idryis Khan a'Husain might be Marcer's best alternative to the streets of a foreign city, but reliance on a'Husain made Marcer uneasy. Beneath his superficial composure, beneath the pious alan style, a'Husain was unique, the only person Marcer had ever EL-ed from whom he sensed no substantial halo. That lack made Marcer want to avoid the Khan for the reasons standard humans avoided darkness, because they couldn't know what was there.

There was no choice. Marcer picked his way through clusters of men, some still cross-legged on the floor, on a zigzag path toward the dais. As he arrived, a'Husain glanced down and, although seemingly indifferent to Marcer's arrival, said a farewell to the governor, bowed in the indolent alan manner—though a'Husain never accompanied a bow with the ordinary alan kiss or hug—and left the dais. He came directly to Marcer, then stared with an unwavering, unnerving attention while standing uncomfortably close.

Marcer cleared his throat. "You wanted to speak with me?"

"McCue is a Harmony spy. Best you don't leave with him."

The ugly crossman seemed an unlikely agent of the Harmony. Despite his standing as a Supplicant, Marcer chuckled. "On Darien, you called me a spy. Have you changed your mind?"

"I was wrong about you—probably. I'm not wrong about McCue." He persisted in watching Marcer.

It was difficult not to react to the threat implicit in his prolonged unwavering attention. A'Husain's stare seemed aggressive but, hanging in the shipboard webbing, Marcer had realized that a'Husain didn't necessarily intend offense or aggression; he was merely indifferent to whether or not he gave that impression. Marcer looked away to break their connection. "They say that men who . . ." He stopped. A'Husain was not someone with whom it was ever safe to banter.

A'Husain was still watching. "What do they say?"

Marcer took a chance. "That men who see conspiracies everywhere are conspirators themselves."

"Very true." A'Husain's tone was amused. It seemed a good time to ask for a loan or other assistance, yet Marcer hesitated. He trusted this alan noblemen-soldier much less than he did McCue.

"A goal of prayer," a'Husain said, apropos of nothing, "is to reach a state of *salaam,* uninjured peace."

"Ah." Marcer didn't know how to respond. "Did you?"

"I felt you behind me, watching."

Alarmed, Marcer took a step away. "I assure you, I wasn't watching you, Khan."

"Perhaps not with your eyes. I've felt you other times."

Marcer flushed. He had EL-ed during the prayer. "I was looking at the courtyard. This place is very beautiful. Different from anything in the Harmony."

A'Husain nodded as though accepting a personal compliment and moved close again. He smelled of scented soap. "You must be an excellent biologist to have risen so high, despite your ancestry. The Jonist Academy is all intrigue and politics."

Praise from a'Husain made Marcer uncomfortable. "I haven't risen so very far."

A'Husain briefly touched the edge of Marcer's sleeve, a touch so insubstantial that it was visible but not felt. "It is unrealistic for you to imagine that the Harmony of Worlds will take you back willingly. It would mean admitting a mistake, which they rarely do. Consider this a new life."

Kindness from a'Husain was more alarming than his stare. Marcer wanted to get away from him, even if it did mean the street. The climate was easy; he spoke the language; his presence was legal. In the morning he would locate B-I's agent. He could survive without help. "Perhaps you're right, Khan," he said in his most diplomatic manner, and began a bow which would have been a farewell. He was moving backwards when a'Husain seized his arm in a hold as hard as his previous touch had been gentle. Marcer remembered the edge of violence just below this man's surface and didn't try to pull away.

"You not only need the Harmony's permission to enter their border, you need Emirates permission to leave. *My* permission." Their eyes met. A'Husain's grasp on Marcer tightened. "Those Jonist fools would eventually have managed to kill me," a'Husain continued, "though it was obvious even to you that I couldn't abandon my people. I owe you my life. It's not a debt I want, but it is also not one I take lightly. Despite that, I will not allow you to leave for the Harmony if doing so will injure the Emirates or me. I will keep you under my observation. There are other things than a spy that the Harmony might send here."

"You don't owe me anything, Khan." Marcer bowed as gracefully as his stiff body could manage, relinquishing the debt.

A'Husain released him but remained near enough that Marcer heard a low rumble from the back of a'Husain's throat, like a satisfied cat's purr. "I doubt you are an assassin," a'Husain said, "still, it is suspicious that you—a biologist in the Jonist Academy—were deported. Too convenient."

Exasperated with a'Husain, and having decided not to ask for favors anyway, Marcer used Ufazi's rude, familiar form of address. "I have nothing to hide. Perhaps you do, Khan, but nothing that matters to me. I'll be on my way."

"No. You will come with me for tonight."

This was his world. Marcer bowed, acquiescing to the inevitable, which in any event put a roof over his head. "I would be grateful."

II. Innocent.

Governor Gordan gave no indication Marcer was anything other than an honored guest. An old man at only seventy-three—early middle age in the Harmony—Gordan was scrawny, his hands were spotted with blemishes like freckles, his hair was thin, and he exuded an odor of cloves and grease, as though he applied a pungent cream to his body to remind himself he was alive. He extended his hand to Marcer and joked that his bones were too old for a proper Harmony-style bow, altogether jovial with a Jonist infidel despite his earlier fierce speech excoriating exactly such men.

Idryis Khan a'Husain and three local noblemen were also present. All shared the generous meal of exotic fruits and fancifully erected sculptures of grains and meat, using ladles or their hands to partake. A vegetarian by choice, Marcer had more than a sufficient selection. Meals on the transport ship had lessened his delicacy over communal dining.

The dining room was small, part of the private quarters of Government House. Its focus was an open overlook to a sunken, fragrant flower garden. They sat on the floor, using silk cushions to make themselves comfortable. The talk was irrelevant to any political or personal concern, and their polite attempts to include Marcer only clarified that he had no knowledge of the poetry of Jabira, the water garden recently installed in a park in the Emirates capital city of Deka on Qandahar, the Sufist music revival, or any other thing particular to the culture of the United Emirates. Despite this deficit, every man continued to treat Marcer with gentle respect. They ignored his past, his accent, and his awful charity-issue clothing. Marcer was embarrassed, not by them but by the knowledge that no Harmony gathering of similarly exalted notables would have been so courteous to a deported Emirates subject.

"Several ships from my command will arrive in this system over the next several weeks," Idryis Khan said, seemingly idly. "The men will want planetary leave. I'll grant my permission, but they'll also need yours, Josip."

The governor gestured at a servant to clear the table. The other guests had fallen silent. "I apologize, Khan, but that is impossible. Our facilities aren't adequate."

"They'll rotate down, if need be."

The governor shook his head. "A few of your officers, perhaps. No more than five or six, and an honor guard of ten. That's all I can allow on Bralava at one time."

The servants were frozen in place, no longer working.

"This is an insult," a'Husain said quietly. "We are on the same side, you and I. We both serve Aleko Bei. I will report your discourtesy to my cousin."

Governor Gordan pulled his fingers through his gray beard. "Of course, Khan," he said, "but those are my orders. From the Bei."

"This suspicion of the Sons is unjustified." A'Husain pounded his fist on the table, shaking the dishes. The gesture seemed inconsistent with the serene expression on his face.

"*All* Sons are not suspect," one nobleman said. Governor Gordan glared, and the other guests shushed him. A'Husain appeared not to notice.

"And how will my officers attend my wedding?" a'Husain asked. "In shifts?"

Governor Gordan didn't answer. He gave a curt order to the servants, and they began to remove the meal's remains.

At the mention of Idryis Khan's wedding, Marcer realized he had seen no women at all so far on Bralava, not even among the Government House servants, who, to Marcer's increasingly bleary eyes, looked like bald, wizened boys. Perhaps the women deported by the Harmony were safe in some private, women's portion of this world, but Marcer didn't believe it. McCue had confirmed the existence of a woman's prison within the Citadel, locally called the Woman Eater. Marcer listened to the governor and a'Husain. This was not the moment to ask about the women.

A guest, Sheik Radi Khalil Sharif, broke the silence. "You have taken a house, Khan?"

A'Husain delayed, then slowly turned his attention from the governor to Sheik Radi. He nodded. "Yes, Sharif. Outside of the city, but not too far. The countryside is quieter.

My life is generally too public." The tension had passed
without an outburst from Idryis Khan. The others quickly
resumed their conversations.

Sheik Radi glanced at Marcer, who had happened to sit
between them. "Your friends are, of course, welcome,
though I planned a private and modest wedding celebration, since it is not your first and you have no family here."
He used archaic, extremely formal language.

Idryis Khan glanced at the governor. "That would be
best, Sharif. And I prefer that the marriage be concluded
soon."

Sheik Radi nodded, but his attention drifted to Marcer.
He seemed troubled and about to speak, then apparently
he reconsidered. The talk returned to the superficial, but
unlike male conversations in the Harmony, the subject of
women or wives was never approached, even tangentially,
by anyone.

Ship time had not been well synchronized with the local
day at the city of Shores. Marcer struggled to suppress his
yawns. A'Husain touched the back of Marcer's hand. Marcer
looked up, startled. "The journey here was unpleasant,"
a'Husain told the other men, "and I'm afraid that I must
ask to be excused, even from such pleasant company. I
expect Researcher Brice, though reluctant to say so, must
feel the same."

The men apologized as though their presence had become rude, and Idryis Khan a'Husain was gracious in accepting their apologies while denying the need for them.
No one moved, though it was late already even in Shores.
More, and stronger, coffee was brought by the bald servants, whom Marcer finally identified as unmen, the Emirates Altered genetic eunuchs. They passed pastries. Marcer
wasn't hungry, but he took one anyway and tried to eat it
so as not to be discourteous. He would gain nothing by
offending these men.

Nearly an hour after a'Husain had spoken, pleading urgent but unspecified business, the three other guests finally
took their leave. Only Idryis Khan, Governor Gordan, and
Marcer remained. Idryis Khan had told Marcer he would
stay overnight in Government House. After a silence during which Marcer ached to ask the way to his room, Governor Gordan gestured for more coffee for the three of them.
"An Academy Researcher?" the governor said to a'Husain.

"He seems a tractable enough fellow." Both men studied Marcer.

"A nonterrestrial biologist," a'Husain said finally. "It's unsafe to trust the Harmony. Why did they deport him?"

Governor Gordan smiled, exposing his stained teeth. "Given your impending marriage, I had assumed you had managed to bring him here yourself to help produce an heir. Or for other reasons."

"No." A'Husain clenched his fists, then opened them.

Gordan shrugged. "A questionable background at such a time as this . . . Don't underestimate the provincialism or the sectarian insularity of the Polite Harmony of Worlds, Khan. I imagine your new friend is innocent of intrigues, and that your encounter was chance. Perhaps he can eventually be convinced of the truth of the teachings of the Prophet, God's blessings and peace be on him. My own distant ancestors were Christian." His old eyes were hooded, but the governor smiled at Marcer. A servant poured steaming coffee into the governor's cup. He drank it in two gulps.

"An easier hurdle than Jonism," Idryis Khan said, "although you may be right; his family are Jews."

They were discussing Marcer as if his presence was irrelevant; their dialogue was mysterious. How could a nonterrestrial biologist produce an heir for Idryis Khan? Marcer EL-ed. Idryis Khan had no aura, but Governor Gordan's deep distrust of Idryis Khan, mixed as it was with respect and even affection, surprised him. Emirates political and personal intrigues were beyond him. "I should leave," Marcer said.

A'Husain clamped his hand around Marcer's wrist. "You will do as I tell you." He released his grip. Marcer abruptly realized that a'Husain must dislike extended physical contact. He seemed, in fact, to touch Marcer more than he did anyone else.

"Governor," Marcer said. "I have a permit that says I'm a free man on this world. Am I free to go?"

"You are my guest's guest. You must ask him." Using both arms, the old governor lifted himself up from the low table, tottered a moment, waved a helpful servant away, then stood looking down on a'Husain. "You lead a lonely life, Khan," Gordan said. "I have worried about you since your last visit to Bralava. I mean you well, for your own sake and for that of our people. Despite the Holy Book, Jonists have one thing right: take what pleasures you can without doing harm." He glanced at Marcer, then back to the Khan. "He attempted to be agreeable tonight. There were no Jonist outbursts or disrespect shown to anyone. No arrogance. There's hope for him. You may find some equanimity yourself with someone you can respect." He smiled like an indulgent uncle. "I think you should let him live."

Marcer jumped to his feet. No one moved to stop him. The room had just one door, plus the open garden access to an enclosed courtyard. Government House was a palace in the midst of a city Marcer had not yet even seen. Where could he go?

Governor Gordan chuckled. "You frighten him, Khan. You frighten too many people, perhaps even the Bei. Well, it is up to you." He nodded, then walked stiffly, on arthritic legs, to the door, turned, gestured to the servants to follow and bid both of his guests good night, leaving Marcer alone in the closed room with Idryis Khan a'Husain.

Marcer's heart was racing. His palms were damp. He couldn't resist the impulse to EL, though it told him nothing. He had been stupid. He hadn't noticed subtle signs because in the Harmony, such things were obvious, not hidden. He, a trained field biologist, hadn't recognized a'Husain's interest in him for what it was. In the Emirates, a perversion.

"Sit down, Marcer."

Marcer walked away from the table. He swallowed hard and felt the pressure build inside his head. Did a'Husain feel pressures, too? An urge to violence?

A'Husain sighed and got up, walking to Marcer with his hands open and arms at his sides. "Are you afraid of me?" a'Husain asked. "There is no reason to be."

"I'm defenseless, Khan, a stranger here. You claim I might be a spy. The governor of this world suggests you let me live, then shrugs and leaves us alone. Of course I'm concerned." He suppressed an urge to EL. The Khan seemed able to hear it, even if he didn't know what it was.

"I give you my word," a'Husain said quietly. "You won't need to be afraid of me if I can trust you." He came slowly to Marcer, his face fixed in a smile that was as artificial as a forest-scented breeze from a window-screen.

"Do you believe me?" a'Husain asked. He stood too close.

Marcer blushed and knew it showed on his fair skin. Like any proper Jonist, he had experimented sexually. The physical act was not impossible or abhorrent to him, although he found male bodies unappealing, but if power was an aphrodisiac, it wasn't working for Idryis Khan a'Husain. More than anything, Marcer wanted to escape. "Yes," he lied, because anything else would insult a'Husain.

As swiftly as a striking snake, a'Husain touched the back of Marcer's neck. His fingers were cold. The contact was ambiguous: firm enough to be a threat, with his thumb on Marcer's throat, but his fingers moved in Marcer's hair in a tentative caress. Marcer was several centimeters taller than a'Husain, but there was no doubt who had control.

"From the first time I saw you in that camp on Darien," Idryis Khan said, "when I called you a spy and you called me a fool, I knew I had to have you. Why? What makes you different?" A'Husain's hand moved from Marcer's neck to his jaw; he stroked Marcer's cheek. His beard brushed Marcer's shirt. They were so close that the fragrance of a'Husain's scented soap was as strong as perfume, though it did little to cover his male pungency.

Marcer stepped back. "I understood you were getting married."

A'Husain sighed, but didn't physically pursue Marcer. "That's for politics and advantage. You can understand such things. I have watched you, Marcer. In the camp, on the ship, and now here. You act honorably. By their nature, women cannot. They are never worthy companions for a man. They have one purpose."

Marcer couldn't block the need anymore. He EL-ed. At so intimate a distance, the bounce-back showed a'Husain's raised pulse, the changing rush of his blood: his physical need and nothing else. With the other man's warm body so close, the emotional silence of the bounce-back was eerie. Marcer had always shared his partner's passion, an empathic enhancement of their connection, but this felt as if Idryis Khan was a puppet or an animal.

The Khan reached for him, but Marcer evaded his touch. "I know how things are in the Harmony," a'Husain said.

"I've been there. Men take whatever pleasures suit them. That's what I want for tonight. Pleasure. In matters such as this, Gordan can be trusted to be discreet."

The Harmony was considered a continuous orgy of eroticism by the people of the Emirates merely because Jonists did not conceal the existence of, or the human need for, pleasure. A true Jonist didn't believe any form of pleasure was degenerate, perverse, or illicit. The Electors had never promulgated a sexual moral code; such things had nothing to do with ethics. There was one rule: consent. Idryis Khan seemed oblivious of the need for it.

"I'm flattered, Khan," Marcer said, "but you misunderstand the Harmony and me. Jon Hsu's *General Principles* says that pleasures which harm no one are good; Jonists don't need to be discreet. That doesn't mean that all of us enjoy things which require discretion here."

Idryis Khan stared at Marcer. Marcer found himself evaluating whether or not he could defend himself if the Khan attacked him. A'Husain looked like a child holding back a tantrum. His hands had fallen into fists. His eyes glittered. He did not blink. It was the look he'd had before attacking the soldier. When he spoke, the timbre of Idryis Khan's voice was shrill. "And do you enjoy such things?"

Certainly not with you. But Marcer couldn't say that. "No," he said, and bowed, backing farther away. "I mean no disrespect." He wondered if refusal was a mistake and whether he'd made an enemy. On the other hand, he hadn't sunk so far since being deported that he had to prostitute himself.

"Trickster," a'Husain said. With the exceptionally quick movements of which he was capable, Idryis Khan a'Husain grabbed Marcer, pulled him close, and kissed him. The Khan's beard was soft against Marcer's face; his lips were hard. The arms around him were like steel bars holding him in place. Just as Marcer began to struggle, the Khan pushed him away.

Marcer fell backwards onto the floor, breaking the fall with his hands. He stared up at the Khan.

"Is your answer still no?" the Khan asked through clenched teeth.

"Khan?" Marcer said. He meant to ask whether he had a real choice, then saw in the Khan's taut body how great his tension truly was. No word games, then. Should Marcer do something he would despise in order to placate this man? Marcer rose to his feet, the better to face Idryis Khan. "I'm sorry, no."

"I owe you a life." The Khan turned away in a hard, jerky motion very much unlike his usual grace. "Run. Get out of Government House before I hurt you. Run. Then we're even." A'Husain picked up a coffee cup from the table and threw it in one rapid motion. It shattered against the wall near the door. "Run," a'Husain said. "Or else I'll kill you."

Marcer ran for the door.

III. Home.

Lost in the immense Government House, Marcer stopped a servant and asked the way to the nearest exit. The unman pointed down a stairway, then continued on his way. At the bottom of the stairs two swarthy men with weapons but no uniforms guarded double doors leading outside. Another, opposite set of double doors appeared to be the entrance to a private area, perhaps the governor's apartment. Marcer felt the guards' attention, but they did nothing to prevent him from leaving.

Once outdoors, Marcer found himself on a wide veranda which doubled as a dock. Water lapped against stairs leading down to a canal. A row of unpretentious buildings lined the opposite bank; most of them were dark. The air stank of cut foliage and salt. Night didn't bother him, except the darkness made him homesick for New Dawn. An EL showed the ruffled pattern of the waves and the way the buildings on the far shore nestled against each other like children leaning on their mother, but no one was about. It also showed the dock had no access to the streets of Shores.

Carefully, because the steps were slick, Marcer went to the water's edge. A small boat was tied to a marble post; a much larger, ornate craft was moored in its own slot. There was nothing to prevent him from taking either boat. The guards protecting this private entrance couldn't see the dock. Marcer sat on the second to the last step and considered his next move.

Fear of the man and not the sexual act had sent Marcer out into the night, but refusal had been the right thing to do. A relationship with an alan nobleman would shrink his chance of petitioning successfully for reentry to the Harmony to zero. It was over, and he was alone on the steets of an alan city.

If he could reach a street. If there were streets in Shores. There must be. Government House must connect with pavement on some frontage. He needed to locate shelter he could use until sunrise. He didn't even know the length of Bralava's night, but the world was classified as a Familiar, so it couldn't be far different from standard. Nothing to worry about.

He returned to the doorway he had just used. The guards barred the way. "But I just came out," he protested.

They didn't answer, which was a hard argument to dispute.

Marcer tried to push past them. Impersonally efficient, they sent him sprawling onto the veranda.

"How am I supposed to leave?"

Apparently they didn't care, but he wasn't to return inside.

Marcer went back to the canal's edge. He could swim to the other side. It wasn't far. He dipped his hand into the water. It came out slimy and smelling of oily putrefaction. The stories of the Emirates inadequate hygiene were true. He'd never thought of himself as unreasonalby fastidious, but he wouldn't swim in a sewer.

Marcer inspected the smaller of the two boats, imaging it inside his mind via EL bounce-back signals. There was no motor, nor any engine panel, just a plastic carapace with three molded hard-plastic seats. No oars. There was no way to propel the thing. To take the larger boat, however, would certainly bring about a pursuit and his arrest.

"Get away from my boat!" a woman called.

Marcer swung around, then nearly slid into the water as he briefly lost his balance. By the time he was stable, she had come down the steps. He couldn't see her through the bright, handheld light she shined in his face, but a cursory EL showed a slender, feminine figure, taller than most alan women from the compound. She was wrapped in a full, loose cloak like those of the other women—black, since it blended into the night. It covered her so well that he couldn't discern much more than her outline. Even so, Marcer felt what he hadn't with a'Husain, the muddle of intelligible human emotions, mostly satisfaction and curiosity. She held the lantern in one hand and an ungainly double-sided oar in the other. The oar was poised to whack him.

"Sorry," he quickly said. He bowed. "I was a guest in Government House, then I got lost, leaving. I'm trying to find the street."

"A guest?" She didn't believe him. She'd seen his clothes, perhaps.

"A guest of a guest. I left abruptly. Now they won't let me back inside. I need to find my way into the city."

"You're the Khan's new playmate." Her voice was throaty, amused. "I heard him throwing things when I was dilly-dallying inside, so I left quick. What happened? Was he too rough for you?"

Her accent, with its Fars sonority, differed from the sharp, cultured tones of the men he'd met at dinner. Theirs was the Ufazi he'd learned from his father. She slurred her words; her consonants were hard. Though she was a woman, he had first supposed she was a servant, but her lascivious observations and the transient nature of her boat's mooring made him consider another option, so he was careful not to insult her. "He wanted something I was unwilling to do."

"Ah, so you're particular." She lowered the oar. "Well, I'll give you a ride, since the old man told me I wasn't needed after all—though he'd sent for me specially. He paid, so all's well. Where are you going?" Her build seemed too slight to row the boat effectively, yet she handled the oar with wiry strength. As she spoke she went past him toward the water, trailing harsh perfume like a vulgar banner. She set her handheld light on the ground. He had a fleeting glimpse of her eyes, which were lovely, but the lighting was poor and she was wearing a veil. She spoke with the relaxed confidence of a beautiful woman.

"I don't know where to go," he admitted. "I just arrived on Bralava today." He held out his arms in a wide shrug and winced at his soreness, a consequence of the webbing.

She dropped the oar across the boat with a thunk, then sent it sliding backward toward the boat's midsection, where it rattled into place in cutout slots. "I guessed you weren't from Shores, by your accent. So, where *are* you from?"

"New Dawn."

She straightened her back from the work of installing the oar and turned to him. There was a long pause, then she asked, "Isn't that in the Harmony?"

"Yes." He was tired and didn't think it necessary to tell his story to a whore. "Can I have a ride? Anywhere."

"Climb in." She tugged on the rope, bringing the boat closer. He accepted the invitation and, edging past her, put his right leg over the boat's side. As soon as he placed weight on the boat, it rocked and started to float away, taking half his body with it. He was nearly pitched into the canal, but she pushed his buttocks and he fell instead into the boat. His knee struck one of the seats, and he yelped. She jumped in after him. The boat tipped and rocked crazily. Marcer managed to right himself and get onto the rear preformed seat. By then, the boat had steadied, the woman was in the middle seat and rowing toward mid-canal. She put out the lantern and rowed harder as she found the current.

"So you're from the Harmony," she said eventually.

"Yes." It was an invitation to talk, and she was doing him a favor, but the rocking of the boat was making him sleepy.

"A Jonist?"

"Yes." He roused himself enough to add, "I hope you're not offended."

"Not me," she said. The oar slapped the water, hitting something that clinked. "I wasn't brought up strict. I wasn't really brought up at all. I just survived."

She didn't continue, and Marcer didn't pursue the comment or the thread of bitterness in her tone. He watched the buildings they slowly passed. They entered a larger canal which had other traffic. She grunted with effort. The rhythm of her strokes on the water was regular and soothing. Marcer kept still; she knew what she was doing. He leaned back while holding the edge of his seat and stared up into the sky. Low on the horizon was a moon, distinguishable from a star or planet by its bright crescent shape. It was larger than either of New Dawn's native satellites and looked like a lopsided wink. He yawned and pulled his arms close to his chest against the dank night's chill. The water-slap of her oar hitting the water was monotonous and pleasing.

He didn't realize he'd fallen asleep until he awakened, puzzled and disoriented. She was shaking him. "Come on," she said. "You're too big. You have to get yourself out of the boat, unless you want to sleep in it all night."

He rubbed his eyes and yawned. The gentle lapping of the water against the boat's side was tranquilizing. "I may as well; I don't have anywhere to go."

"That was a joke. The bats would roust you and arrest you for idleness, encroaching, and curfew-breaking. You'll have to hotel it."

He blinked and wiped his eyes as she switched on the light. An EL revealed the wharf around them, a series of slots along a pier; they were in one slot, tied fast with rope. She was home. She'd done as much—more, even—than it was reasonable for him to expect from a stranger and a woman in this biased place, but he had no resource except her mercy. Her actions and the trace EL bounce-back, her aura, made him decide she was trustworthy and kind. "I have twenty-six Harmony counts," he said, "and nothing else worth money. I was deported from the Harmony; I don't know anyone in Shores. Where should I go?"

She stood looking down at him, hands on her hips. "In that case, you should have stayed with the Khan." She sighed, and reached down to help him. "Well, you didn't. Come on."

He took her hand, then almost released it, startled by its rough, seamed texture, as though there were ridges across her palm. She helped him onto the dock, which was built of hard plastic boards. Her perfume irritated his nose. "You can carry the oar," she said. "If I leave it, it'll be gone in the morning. You're *really* tall."

He nodded, realized she might not have seen it, then merely bent down and took the oar, too tired to respond. It was heavier than he'd expected, solid. She brought the light, but turned it off; the streets were lit intermittently, where the streetlights weren't broken.

They walked side by side. "Where are we going?"

"Home," she said. "I'll put you up one night, since you had the good taste to refuse the Khan."

"Thanks." He rested the oar on his shoulder. "I think you saved my life by being there tonight," he added, reconsidering his poor show of gratitude. She was a woman of the Emirates offering hospitality to a foreign man. It spoke of her confidence and her charity, or else her recklessness. "You don't like Idryis Khan a'Husain?"

She didn't respond immediately, and he realized it might not be a prudent question to answer. Finally, she said, "The houris' Sons are all crazy."

Houris. He'd been told about angels in the Harmony common language, but in Ufazi they were houris, the virginal women of Paradise mentioned in the alan Qur'an. He absorbed the information uncritically, too tired to examine it. The street was paved with uneven bricks, over which a sheeting had been spread. It had broken, pitting the street into bumps and gullies. There was no sidewalk, but there was very little traffic, and none of it vehicular. The buildings were one- or two-story with blank, windowless walls facing onto the street. She turned into one, entering by a low, narrow doorway. He lowered the oar from his shoulder in order to enter, then banged his head anyway. The cramped passage smelled of bleach. They entered a paved brick courtyard with one tree in its center, crossed the yard, and went partly through another, shorter passage lined with doors. She opened the second door, then stepped aside to let him in.

"Home," she said. "You can sleep on the floor."

"You're very generous," he said sincerely, and turned to her just as she switched on crude lights, bulbs rather than sun-stones. They illuminated the room. He stood fixed in place. She had removed her veil. He saw her face. She was hideous, the ugliest person he had ever seen.

Chapter 4

The Supplicant had adopted the Harmony style of dress immediately upon reaching Darien, but on the ship to Center-Sucre she began using their clothes to her advantage. Still uncomfortable with the immodesty of the clinging, flesh-baring apparel, she discovered it was easier to wear if she thought of herself as an actress in costume. She impersonated the bold, arrogant, mysterious Supplicant without quite believing she was that woman, but then had no difficulty displaying her body to men. She knew no women who fit the part she now performed, so she modeled her persona on heroines of Harmony novels. To be a woman of the Harmony, she had to pretend.

The irony of being an impostor woman was not lost on her, nor was the fact that no one recognized it; that was precisely what she'd entered the Harmony to fight. She discovered how easy such an imposture was. Men didn't see women, they saw an image they wanted.

Ted Fields stayed as close as a bee guarding honey. Another man, a Jonist officer on his way to a post at Center, asked to escort her to a shipboard entertainment. She refused; the officer could do nothing to further her mission. "You're beautiful," Ted Fields murmured, pleased by her rejection and probably assuming it had to do with him. "Pure. Sweet."

All men want a virgin.

I. A good living.

She had full lips, tinted crimson, a much darker shade than the pinkish scar tissue zigzagging along her cheeks and forehead. As Marcer continued to stare, those gorgeous lips frowned and her warm, brown eyes narrowed. Her eyes

were large and lined with thick lashes, but they lacked eyebrows. Her jaw was puckered by furrows of scars. He
couldn't read expression in her distorted face. Grisly disfigurement was unknown inside the Harmony. Any competent medic could have fitted her face into a healing skinsack
and restored her to a human physiognomy.

"It gives me a good living," she said.

"I'm sorry," he mumbled, and dropped his gaze. He
bowed, then winced as he straightened and confronted her
ghastly face again. Yet it was interesting. He couldn't look
away. A shiny line of scar showed where her eyebrows had
been; they seemed to have burned off. Other scars looked
like cuts. Their eyes met. This was a woman, not an exotic
mask. "My name is Marcer Joseph Brice. Thank you.
Thank you very much for letting me stay the night." Made
uneasy by his fascination with her disfigurement, he forced
himself to study the room instead of her face.

Tiny and anachronistic, like something from the antique
past, the room was stupid; each device required its own,
manual switch. A half-open door led to a simple kitchen;
he guessed the other, closed door was a washroom and that
the tall corner closet probably contained her clothes. A
ladder leaned against a wall; there was a covered opening
in the ceiling, presumably to an attic or open-air roof. The
walls were dusky beige, which darkened the room, and one
wall was hung with a rug of abstract design. A low sofa
below the rug doubled as a bed. Covers were folded back,
exposing the linens—though they were obviously not linen,
but the shiny, cheap, synthetic fabric, flast. There were two
mismatched chairs of a material that looked like wicker but
had a rougher grain. She had loosely covered their seats
with cloth. Open shelves held a variety of jars and knick-
knacks. Against the far wall, a table had the only mechanical device, other than the electric lamps: a viewing screen.
The crowded room was no larger than the entrance to his
Darien apartment, which was only stock Academic housing.
Though he hadn't EL-ed, he was a bit unsettled by its small
size. Snug was not a compliment on New Dawn; still, this
was just large enough to avoid discomfort, and it was neat,
clean, and efficient.

"Does it bother you?" she asked belligerently.

"What?" He immediately felt foolish and turned back to
her, telling himself to look at her in exactly the way he

would have looked at any other person, except that confronted by her unsightliness he couldn't quite remember
how that would be. "I'm sorry," he said. "Yes, it does
bother me. I'll leave if you want."

"No. At least you don't *like* it." She lowered her head,
incompletely hiding it, and came farther into the room.
With her back to him, she swung off her heavy cloak, drap-
ing it across a chair. Below the modest covering, she wore
a pair of loose translucent blue pants shot with gold thread,
and a matching, knee-length tunic. Not silkik, but expensive
for the surroundings. Businesswear for a whore. A whore
who looked like this?

Yet viewed from behind, she was exquisite. Her long
dark hair was loose and fell to the small of her slender
back. It gleamed with red highlights in the electric light.
The silk tunic exposed the shadow of her shapely figure.
He wondered if there were scars elsewhere on her body.
Curious, he EL-ed. There were scars but not as many as
covered her face. The bounce-back should have been the
ugly auditory equivalent of her visible mutilation. It wasn't.

The unevenness of her skin, while repellent visually, in
EL bounce-back provided texture. It was the difference between velvet and silk. In the aural vision created by his
Alteration, a smooth complexion was not necessarily superior. Her velvet texture was, if anything, more interesting.
Her unsightliness was so immaterial to his altered sense of
beauty that, although he had EL-ed her on the Government
House dock when they first met, he hadn't noticed her mutilation until he'd seen her. Perhaps her beauty when he
EL-ed came from her aura. It shone. There was goodness
and generosity; there was sadness. She was tarnished silver.

She turned around.

"How did it happen?" he asked.

"They pay. It doesn't hurt me. Just go to sleep."

He watched as she moved quietly about, putting her
cloak away, then her shoes, generally keeping her back to
him. She pulled hard at them, and several folded blankets
fell off a shelf. She picked them up and extended them to
Marcer. "Here. The floor all right?"

"Of course." He took the blankets and noticed her
hands. His impression of them as ridged and rugged had
been correct. There were burns and cuts all over them. The
fingernails of her left index and middle fingers were miss-

ing. In spite of the injuries, none of the damage prevented her from freely using them. Very careful butchery.

Marcer finally understood. She allowed men to torture her for fun or sexual excitement. There were men who *liked* doing it. They paid to abuse her. That was how she earned her living. He couldn't find a proper expletive and fell back on one his father sometimes used. "Holy God." He sank down into a chair, his long legs spread awkwardly in front of him.

She chuckled, starting to relax with him again. "I thought you were a Jonist from the Harmony."

He stared, momentarily seeing her as nothing more than a fieldwork problem. She'd said it didn't hurt. It must not; no one would endure that much suffering only for money. If it didn't hurt . . . "You're a Neulander!" It was as much a question as a statement.

The Republic of Neuland was populated almost exclusively by Altereds of a particular type, supposedly the result of a genetic accident during the first generation of settlement, but more likely an Alteration purposely incorporated into their local human genome by Neuland's pioneers. Neulanders were pain-free. Someone with the Neulander Alteration would feel nothing but a mild pressure when cut, or painless heat when burned. Combined with their freedom from pain, Neulanders had a special healing capacity to regenerate tissue quickly after injury: RHF, for Rapid Healing Factor. It was so fast that Neulanders used skinsacks only with difficulty. The entire Alteration complex also occurred in a category of native animals, the best-known of which were the hummers. If she was a Neulander, it would explain both her scars and her ability to get them. "Who are you? *Are* you a Neulander?"

She shook her head. "My name is Linnet Wali. I'm from here. Shores. I never knew my parents; maybe one was from Neuland, though I've never heard of a Neulander visiting Bralava. Anyway, it's late. You can use the bathroom after me."

He bowed. "Of course."

She nodded curtly and entered the washroom. He spread the blankets; the floor would be a vast improvement over shipboard webbing. He stretched out as best he could between her furniture, repositioning nothing, lying on his side with his legs pulled up around a chair. From behind the closed bathroom door came quiet sounds which only his preternaturally acute hearing let him recognize as muffled sobs. He wanted to comfort her, and yet he was a stranger, perhaps even the cause of her sadness. Uncertain what to do, he listened and did nothing.

She returned; he didn't look up as she turned off the light. The rustle of stiff, flast bedsheets said she'd gone to bed.

How could anyone disfigure another person for pleasure? Why did she let them? Even if it didn't hurt, what must be the humiliation of enduring it?

He'd met her outside a private entrance, probably to Governor Gordan's quarters. Marcer became too angry to sleep. That withered man was her customer. That hypocrite who had recommended the Khan not kill him, but hadn't bothered to try to prevent it, had scarred this woman. The food Marcer had eaten at Government House was a weight in his gut. He got up. He went to the washroom, but was taken unawares by its primitive design. The toilet was a hole over a cesspool. He gagged at the stench in the claustrophobic room, then all of the late dinner came uncontrollably up. As he retched, he worried that she would believe he'd been sick because of her appearance. She didn't deserve that.

She was awake, eyes open and staring blindly into the dark, when he returned. He wasn't sure what to say to reassure her. He stood awkwardly, trying to think past his fatigue.

"You can leave if you want," she said.

He shook his head, forgetting she wouldn't see. "I sat next to a'Husain. It was a long meal. The conversation was pleasant. But you were in the same building at the same time, waiting to be hurt. And he wouldn't have let me leave except he owed me a favor. None of this seems real. A month ago I had a good future doing work I loved and now I'm an indigent sleeping on a stranger's floor. I don't know if I can come through this the same man I was."

"Worry about tomorrow, not ten years from now. And you don't need to sleep on the floor." She held open the covers. "You can sleep in a stranger's bed. Nothing is ugly in the dark."

He EL-ed, feeling her shape, and smiled because to him she wasn't ugly. He hurt all over. His head spun with fatigue and repellent information. Could Linnet Wali of the shining aura have so little pride that she let men violate her for money? He felt like Gulliver, the only normal man in a topsy-turvy country. "I can't," he said. "Thank you. I'm sorry, but I'll be asleep the minute I put my head down."

She laughed. "Sleep is all I offered. So come to bed."

II. A good omen.

Idryis Khan sent Nisa a gift. Her father brought it to her the day after the Khan's arrival on Bralava. She was in bed, staring at the wall in the doltish stupor she had perfected, her mind seemingly glazed by the medicines her father's doctor had prescribed without having seen her, when told she was in a female frenzy.

Sheik Radi opened the white silk gift box. "Beautiful!" he exclaimed with the rigid enthusiasm with which he had dealt with her since Totsi's murder. He held up a heavy gold necklace encrusted with pink tourmalines and small clear diamonds. "Try it on, Nisa." He extended it to her. The gold segments struck each other and jangled, disturbing the silence. Light from the window made a glittery rainbow through the diamonds.

"Look. Matching earrings." Sheik Radi tried to pass her the box, but Nisa didn't move her hand to take it. He set it beside her on the bed, then sat in the comfortable chair in front of the courtyard window. "Nisa?" He was becoming impatient. "Ingratitude is unbecoming to a woman."

Another of his platitudes. She wondered where he got them. "I'm sorry," she mumbled.

"It's all right." Her father sounded tender. From nowhere she remembered his tears after her mother's death. He had cared for his first wife, but he had believed in the innocence, the holiness, of his second.

Nisa sighed. Her pet was dead. All her favorite paintings had been destroyed by Qadira's creature. They couldn't be repainted; they would be unalterably different if she tried. They had been a record of her life, a visual diary. It was gone. "Give the necklace to Qadira," Nisa said. "She already has my mother's jewelry."

Sheik Radi slapped her, but lightly. She was an invalid.

"These are yours, a gift from your betrothed. You'll show your respect for him by wearing them when he visits. And I will punish you if you dishonor me by having another tantrum."

Tantrum. That was how he described her fury upon discovering Totsi dead, her studio in shambles, her work destroyed, and the untouchable Qadira to blame. A man might rage, but a woman had a tantrum. Nisa gazed at him. Tears welled in her eyes as she remembered Totsi, who had never harmed anyone; he'd loved her, and he'd been destroyed by Qadira's hideous beast. Eaten. She sniffed, remembering the awful smell. She let the tears overflow. They tasted salty when she licked a corner of her mouth. "I won't, Father," she promised, and produced a wan smile. "It's good the Khan is here. Do you like him?"

Her father's lips tightened in an unnatural smile. "He has *taqwa*; he knows what is right. But you must not be jealous of his time. The Sons are different from other men, with different needs."

Curious, Nisa wished she could ask more, but too great a curiosity would make him aware she wasn't as torpid as she seemed. It didn't matter. She planned to run away before the wedding. A little guilt might speed her escape. "I know he has another wife; I'll be second. Will I live in her house?"

Sheik Radi roused himself from other thoughts. "No. No, she stays on Qandahar. You'll be here. He purchased a house. The marriage papers are being prepared."

Nisa had nothing to do with her wedding preparations. Her father—actually the housekeeper, Gidie—had planned the modest celebration and ordered her a new wardrobe. Had she seemed interested, then Nisa might have arranged the clothing for herself, but only the appearance of being drugged would fully explain her new, retiring demeanor to her father. Meanwhile, she was supervised less closely, Qadira rarely visited, and her horrid pet was banned.

"Will the celebration be soon?" she asked. No one had mentioned a date.

"Soon." He stood, patted her, then took the necklace from the box and placed it in her hand. "When you see him, Nisa, tell me what you think. I will sign nothing until you do. It's an advantageous alliance for us. Old Josip may distrust him, but Idryis Khan is a Son, a cousin of Aleko

Bei, and a rich, powerful man, but if you don't like him . . . Tell me."

She was touched. A woman truly could get more with honey than with vinegar, but a woman shouldn't have to either. "I will miss you when I'm married, Father."

Sheik Radi kissed her forehead. "You remind me of your mother. Those were good times; we were young together. A strong woman is not always a bad thing." He sighed, then looked down again at Nisa. "If war does come, and the Khan is called away, then you can stay here."

"Will there be a war?" Since war hadn't managed to come soon enough to kill off Idryis Khan, she no longer wanted it. She needed an open border to the Harmony.

"I hope not. I frankly see no reason to awaken a sleeping giant. On this, I agree with Idryis Khan. The Harmony of Worlds has never bothered us. Why fight them over Neuland? And the Harmony doesn't want war either. They're sending a delegation here to negotiate."

"Here to Bralava? Why?" Qandahar was the capital; Bralava was a boring backwater.

Sheik Radi patted her head and looked out the door. Nisa bit her lip. If he wanted to leave, she couldn't stop him without seeming too interested. However, smiling good-naturedly, clearly humoring her, the Sheik did answer. "History. We're the closest world to them, but the real reason is that Bralava was where our people and the Harmony cooperated against the Bril during the Last War. They probably think that's a good omen; Jonists are superstitious. Even though the negotiation is secret, they claim it's important that the popular attitude toward the Harmony is better here."

Nisa nodded, and didn't do anything more to prevent her bored father from leaving. Once he was gone, she lay back on the bed, eyes closed, letting her body relax from the effort of indolence. To do nothing was difficult work. She waited until she was sure that her father wouldn't return with a final question or send Gidie to fit her for the new clothes again.

Finally, Nisa sat up. She examined the jewelry she'd pretended to disdain. There was a bracelet as well as the necklace and earrings. As a set, it was probably worth more than any other single piece of her jewelry, but if she pried the stones loose, the individual stones were not large. She tallied her important jewelry: amber beads from old Earth; a sikt stone ring; a long string of red pearls from Amudjar; and the white-on-black cameo that had been her mother's. Would it be enough to bribe her way aboard a ship to the Harmony? The kitchen express would be safer, but she had no way to contact them. Hulweh had been her only hope, but Hulweh hadn't known anything.

Nisa tiptoed from the bedroom to her studio. The bare walls and the ammonia odor of cleaning solution strengthened her resolve. She sat cross-legged on the floor, looking at her remaining art supplies.

Paints: oils, tempra, and watercolors. Stirring sticks, rags, and containers. Paper, canvas, vellum. Clay—she'd tried pottery sculpture. Knives, for cutting the hard clay. Lots of knives, but all innocuous in context. Sharp steel. She closed her eyes and imagined sketching the largest, one suitable for butchering. How to draw the sharpness of that edge, or reproduce the expectancy she felt when viewing it? How to render the glint of sunlight reflecting off the metal surface without resorting to clichés? Much as she ached to, she couldn't paint or sketch; it would interfere with her disguise.

Her father intended to marry her to the son of a creature like Qadira. A Son of the Prophet, God bless and keep him. From his picture, he looked like any other man, but how was that good?

Nisa unscrewed the cap of a black-glass container. Despite the residual odor of the oils, she had rinsed it carefully. Inside were fourteen tabs, her cache of medicine. She added another, the morning tab she hadn't taken. She had tossed the first few away, then she'd realized they would be useful. It could be important to have a secret weapon.

A husband might forbid her from drawing. A husband might beat her. She would have no control over her own life. If she was married before she could run away, then these might be useful to slow her husband's pursuit of her. And if she ran before she had a husband, then she would use them to kill Qadira's creature.

III. An exile, waiting.

The Bralava agent for Brice-Issacs Transport was terse. "Not a chance," he said.

Marcer squinted into the tiny screen. Like any New Dawn Altered, even when he didn't EL, the illusion of reality given by a screen—especially a rudimentary two-dimensional one like Linnet's—was inadequate and uncomfortable. It was worsened by distortion around the screen edges and by thin, black lines which moved randomly across the stringer's image. "Brice-Issacs will repay you," Marcer said. "I just need a small advanc . . ."

The agent, a man named Viho, interrupted. "I can't confirm anything, since the Harmony closed the border. Could be you're who you claim to be. I won't take that chance. If there is a war, then I'm sitting with a deficit account for B-I, and the owners are on the other side."

Marcer raised his voice. "Some are on Safi. They'll confirm what I've said."

Viho leaned impolitely forward, so that the screen failed to encompass all of his face. "The big money is on the Harmony side, not here, and anyway, I don't care. B-I isn't my only account, Mr. Brice." He omitted even the Emirates equivalent of Marcer's Academy title. "All trade across the border is shut down. That self-righteous Harmony of yours has left me holding a collection of empty accounts. The Jews and the Jonists knew what was coming and didn't warn me! I'm not digging myself any deeper for an incidental B-I relative left stranded in my zone." He cut the connection. The screen subsided into flickering lines. Marcer turned it off manually.

With the screen's illumination gone, the room dimmed. Linnet hadn't opened the shutters. Marcer stood for a moment, hands clasped in front of him, then he turned and bowed to her. She'd been listening. It was unavoidable in her tiny apartment. "Thank you," he said. "I'm sorry that I can't repay you for the call, but I will as soon as I have funds."

"Do you expect those funds soon?" Linnet mugged a broad smile to show she was joking, a habit probably developed because her scarred face gave nothing away.

He didn't answer.

"Never mind, Marcer," she said. "One call is not a heavy expense." She pulled her loose robe around her body and went into the kitchen.

He listened as she opened cabinets. Strong, afternoon sunlight came through cracks in the shutters. They both had slept through the morning. His clothes were badly wrinkled; he had spent most of the night in them. She had been naked, but he hadn't noticed until she awakened him. Propped on her elbow watching him, her rapt attention had roused him. She had smiled when, upon opening his eyes, he blanched and shrank back from her. She had covered his mouth with her hand, stifling the beginning of his apology. "Never mind," she had whispered. "You can always close your eyes." She had slid her hand over his lips and touched his right cheek, then her hand had toyed with his earlobe, slipped down his neck to his chest. She had caressed him, gently, through his clothes, but when he began to touch her, she had pushed his arm away. "No. Consider this rent." Her hands went farther down his body. "You seem willing to pay."

She had opened the banded collar of his charity-issue shirt, then slipped her hand along the closure, parting the fabric all the way down. The trousers had an elastic waistband. She pushed it below his hips. She bit her lip as she worked, and though he purposely watched her, eyes wide, she didn't look into his face again, except once. "Are you fixed, or do I need something?" she asked.

"I'm safe." He'd taken the regular six-month tab only a month earlier.

Marcer had EL-ed and felt her shape in his mind. Visually she was quite horrible, but the bounce-back was like summertime after a long winter, not only warm but pleasingly diverse after the cloak of cold, sleek snow. Her rough texture was fascinating; her aura was lovely. He forgot she was a whore, forgot she wanted him to be passive and afterward was embarrassed when she casually told him that he was "really quite good," as though they were both professionals, sharing pointers.

She returned from the kitchen carrying a round, red spongy something, a knife, and half a loaf of bread. "Hungry?"

He wasn't, really. "No."

"Eat anyway. It's the first law of poverty: never refuse

food. Here." She set her load on the table and pulled out the second of her two chairs. "Sit down."

She was so cheerful that it hurt his ears to hear it, as if gaiety was emotionally too loud. The unfamiliar surroundings made him only too aware he was an exile, hoping for a chance to go home. He imagined the span of emptiness between Bralava and the Harmony as an echo that would never return in his lifetime. "At Government House," he said, "we sat on pillows on the floor."

"I'm not authentic." She enunciated carefully, using a word from the Harmony's common language rather than Ufazi. Something learned from a client? He hoped no one from the Harmony had ever hurt her. "I don't want to be. Some day I'll go to the Harmony. Sit."

He hadn't meant his comment as a criticism. He smiled, trying to be a good guest, and sat at the table. To overcome his awkwardness, he took her hand. "I'm lucky to have met you."

She shrugged, and drew her hand away. He wondered if it were possible for her to blush through the facial cicatrix. "Do you know how long it's been since a man spent the entire night with me? And cared about *my* pleasure?" she asked. "I've been repaid." She arranged the table so that they each had a cloth in front of them, then she cut the bread into equal hunks and passed one to Marcer. She sat in the other chair and placed the red something between them. It smelled sour.

A shaft of sunlight lit her cratered face. She caught him looking, but didn't turn away. Neither did he. He was thinking of the difficulty a woman alone must have in a society as backward as the Emirates. "There were women on the ship, deported when I was. Do you know what happened to them?"

She knew. He could tell from the way her eyes dropped and didn't need to hear her answer to know that it was bad. "They're in the Citadel," she said. "The Woman Eater. There's supposed to be a trial, but whether it happens or not, those women are dead."

"Holy God." He said it softly, with feeling. The women hadn't exaggerated their danger. "I should have believed them. I might have been able to help." He couldn't imagine how, when he hadn't been able to help himself, but he would have tried.

"Why?" she asked. "They're nothing to you. You should be thinking about how you're going to support yourself," she said. "What do you know how to do?"

It was a good question. Nonterrestrial biology was not something practical, like being a medic, which could translate into a job. "I'm a nonterrestrial biologist, specializing in synecology, the study of ecological interrelationships among communities of organisms. In the Academy, everyone is also a teacher. Could I get a position in one of the local schools?"

Her eyes showed her disbelief in such a plan.

"Tutoring, then? I need a job where I can earn enough to get to Safi as soon as possible. I can stay with relatives there until the political situation improves."

She shook her head. "No one would hire a Jonist infidel as a teacher."

He cleared his throat. Cast adrift in a place where a civilized education wasn't useful, he had no experience at unskilled labor. "I'm healthy," he said. "I'm fairly strong. What do you think I should do?"

She observed him with her head tilted to one side. "So smooth," she said, rubbing her blemished thumb across his palm. "A handsome face and a good body. Your ears are big. Clean-shaven men always seem younger than they are. The way you keep your lips just slightly parted makes you look harmless. And blue eyes are so innocent." She picked up his hand and examined it, then pushed at his forearm muscles. "Detail work. Mind work. Nothing heavy. Am I right?"

"Yes." He pulled his arm away and pushed his chair slightly back from the table. The friendly atmosphere had changed. He was on trial, or at auction.

She winked. "Go to the Khan, Marcer. He likes you or he wouldn't have let you leave. Go back. He'll give you a show job, something dignified. When the border is open, you can go home and forget you were ever here."

His face reddened. Ask a whore and get advice on whoring. Her aura was a lie. Though it was legal in the Harmony, prostitution wasn't respectable; an Academic would never partner with a whore. "I won't go to a'Husain. Anything else?"

She ripped a chunk of crust off her bread, dipped it into the red substance, then ate it. She watched him, waiting.

He understood. Was he willing to live like a poor man? He picked up the bread and tore a section off, but hesitated before putting it into the sour-smelling spread. "What is it?"

She shrugged.

"I don't eat meat," he said. "Dairy and fish, but nothing that moves on land."

She gaped as if he was a lunatic, then shrugged. "It's not meat."

"All right." It was probably not rancid, just unfamiliar. He dipped his bread and ate, trying hard not to inhale. The texture was gritty.

"It's whifle," she said. "Made from a sea plant. It almost never goes bad, and it's cheap. Healthy." She took more. So did he. "There are always job openings at the fisheries. They'll take a Jonist. No one stays long."

He didn't ask why. "Does it pay well?"

She smiled widely, stretching the scar tissue of her face. "It won't get you to the Harmony too fast, but it's enough to live on."

"I'll try it." He wondered what limits Linnet put on her customers to prevent them from doing more damage than her Neulander RHF Alteration could heal. If they amputated a limb or even a finger, she couldn't regenerate it. He EL-ed and felt the shining halo of her individuality again, her core, but its beauty didn't entirely dissolve his resentment.

"I'm a work of art," she said.

He had been staring. Marcer looked away. "Isn't there anything else you could do? What about the fishery for you?"

"No one can do what I can."

"Any Neulander could," he snapped, "but I've never heard of one doing anything so degrading."

She got up suddenly from the chair. It tipped over backwards and clattered on the floor. "Spoken like a man!"

She had taken him in. "I apologize."

She righted the chair. Her robe had come open. She covered herself, retying it quickly as though concerned he might see what he had already touched. "If I had gone to the Harmony," she said, "I'd be back and in the Woman Eater. How is that better?"

He had no reply to that. Linnet went to the kitchen and

returned with two cups of tea. She set one in front of Marcer, then sat down and continued eating as if nothing had happened. When she glared at him, he began eating again, too. Whifle wasn't as awful as it smelled. Like an exotic form of cheese, it was a taste he could acquire if he had to.

Linnet sipped her tea. "The fishery is hard work, and it's nasty, but nothing pays as well that'll hire a Jonist foreigner. It's a registered job, legal."

He was reminded of McCue's advice. "I'd heard unregistered is better."

"Sometimes it is, but the fishery won't cheat you. They can't afford to lose a good worker."

The work must be very bad. Marcer nodded to let her know he understood and that he could do it.

"Down the street is a flop that's cheap but clean," she continued, her tone that of a protective mother. "They're honest enough that you won't be murdered or robbed while you're asleep. You'll have to share a room with two other men. There's a communal kitchen; if you contribute, you can share the meals." She glanced around the table and mumbled something to herself about needing sugar. She set her cup on the table, sighed, and, without looking directly at him, said, "Or you could stay here with me. I don't bring clients home, but I've had them follow me. It would be handy to have a man to discourage them—and to keep away the pimps."

She made it sound as if he would be the one doing the favor. "Why are you helping me?" She did nasty, sordid work that strained his tolerance for consensual *pleasure*. Such a person should have been embittered and vicious, not kind.

"Because I can," she said. "Because it's something I can do."

Chapter 5

The Supplicant was surprised when Revered Gangler knocked at her cabin door two hours before they were scheduled to descend to the surface of Sucre. Their small delegation would stay in the surface city, Sucre-semp, while petitioning for permission to visit Center, the enclosed Harmony capital city which rode the sky above Sucre's jungle. Center was where the main Jonist Academy was located, alongside the Harmony's central government.

"The situation is tricky," Revered Gangler said. He barely glanced at her, like a pious Muslim afraid to see a woman's face. "The old days of unanimity and uniformity are gone."

He clearly regretted the change. The Supplicant nodded to encourage him, and gestured toward the room's sole chair.

He didn't sit. "Lee is the only biologist of the six Electors, the one most likely to understand, but if we associate this with him . . ." Revered Gangler sighed. "Do you see?"

She did. "Lee is the one who is Altered and who hid that fact for years? He has the Neulander pain-free Alteration?"

"Exactly. He's in disgrace, but he's not out of office. He won't resign, and most younger Ahmen . . ." —he paused as if to check her comprehension, as though she didn't understand Jonist ranks, or know that the four or five hundred Ahmen, though appointed by the Electors, also elected the six Electors when a vacancy occurred—"The Ahmen support him, even though we've learned he isn't a citizen. They won't allow a vote to impeach. Now his close associate has begun preaching a new interpretation of Jon Hsu's *General Principles.* So, Center is in turmoil. It's a bad time for a new crisis. If we went to Lee, his endorsement could make your information into another source of factional debate. Particularly since Marcer Brice is Altered."

The Supplicant gaped at Revered Gangler. "He is?"

"You didn't know?"

She sat carefully down on the edge of the bed. "He never told me."

"Well, he is," Revered Gangler said grimly. "A rare type, but when the vote to hire him came up, I did some research. He echo-locates, an old mammalian trick. That's supposed to be all there is, but you can't change only one component of the human brain without affecting others. The mind settles into new shapes. Empathy doesn't sound like a bad thing, does it? Except it's not a human ability. Jon Hsu defined humanity by how we perceive the world, by our sense and our senses—as it should be." He looked directly at her. "I voted against hiring him."

"Then why are you here?" she asked, almost the first question she had dared address to him.

"Because he's right." Revered Gangler paced to the door, turned, then came the two short steps back to the Supplicant. "Being Altered doesn't make a man stupid. He's not. He did good work at the Academy. And because it's us against them, humanity in its broadest sense, even including Altered humans, against these creatures."

"You believe his information?"

"The more I look at it, the more I do. We won the Last War against the Bril, but now we've found a new enemy, a worse one because they slip onto human worlds as impostors, not in ships."

The Supplicant stood. Revered Gangler backed up a step. "We can go to Sanda Brauna," he said. "She's a botanist by training. Or Kurioso. He'd like to steal some thunder from Lee by discovering this. The trouble is, either of them might refuse. It isn't clear-cut. And this is important!"

Vehemence in an old man made the Supplicant smile. She understood what he wanted: an excuse not to go to Elector Jeroen Lee and someone to blame for that choice if it backfired. "We will go first to Elector Brauna," she said. "This is something a woman will understand."

I. Circumlocutions.

Nisa had never imagined that she might like her future husband. If Idryis Khan a'Husain had a houri mother, Nisa saw no sign of it. There was nothing like Qadira about him, nothing sneaky. He was one of those men to whom no likeness did justice; regardless, she wished for a sketch pad. Noble, regal, he had the uncommon knack of sitting still without seeming bored or boring. Taller than either her father or any of her brothers, he held himself like a caliph. She burned with fury at the Jonists who had mistreated him—almost killed him, he admitted. His proud face was tanned; his hands were wide and strong; she found herself wishing for him to touch her.

They weren't alone. Her father and brother, Adem, were there. She did not talk directly to her Khan, nor did he address her, yet they managed to converse via circumlocutions. Of course, as befitted her station in life, she was modestly covered. Only her eyes showed, and the Khan hadn't had female relatives visit to inspect her. She wondered what reports of her appearance he did have and wished he could see her.

"My new house is north, along the seashore," Idryis Khan said in a refined accent, facing her father. "There is a concealed terrace, safe for a modest woman's use, which overlooks the ocean; the day I saw it sunlight struck the water quite beautifully. The air was golden. I thought an artist would enjoy it."

An artist! Her father had never taken her drawing seriously, not even her mother had, yet her Khan had heard of it and had chosen a house because she would like it.

"It's far outside the city," her father said doubtfully. "A difficult distance for a woman to visit her family."

"A woman rarely travels," Nisa said eagerly, to give the Khan's choice her approval. She couldn't sip tea or eat without setting aside her veil, so she sat quietly while the men did both. Idryis Khan ate in small bites, not greedily like Adem. He smiled slightly as he sipped his tea, as though aware she was studying him, and if the Khan's smile seemed a bit strained, it was undoubtedly the fault of their chaperones. She remembered her mother's answer when, as a child, Nisa had asked about her parents' marriage. In those days, young men and women on Bralava had mixed more easily, at closed, private parties under the supervision of their parents. "I looked at your father's smile," Riva had said. "I looked at his parents and both seemed contented in the presence of the other. Some men spent all their time talking with friends; your father spoke with his female cousins, too, and watched over his sister, your aunt Cala."

"Is there game on the grounds of your new estate?" Adem asked, interrupting Nisa's reverie. Idryis Khan made Adem look like a boy. Dressed for an afternoon polo match in which he would play, Adem wore a bright red team shirt that made his face florid. She couldn't imagine her Khan wearing such a thing. He had too much dignity.

"Adem is an excellent hunter," Sheik Radi explained with evident pride.

"It isn't virtuous to obtain one's pleasure from the injury or death of a living thing," Idryis Khan said, startling both father and son into silence.

Nisa shifted in her chair. She hadn't imagined she might feel such a thing about any man, but perhaps she could marry the Khan and be happy. Nisa's mother had said that a woman should look for true respect and for kindness in a prospective husband's eyes. The Khan's eyes were dark, but his actions—choosing a house for her and acknowledging her art—were a better indication of kindness and respect than any physical feature. Though his physical features were excellent. Nisa was glad of the veil. Her face had warmed as she imagined marriage to the Khan. She never considered her mother's additional advice: Beware of infatuations.

"Are you giving testimony in the trial of the wild women?" her father asked. Nisa knew he was simply making conversation, but she liked the way Idryis Khan answered, taking the question at face value.

"I was present throughout the whole indecent business on Darien and on the ship." Idryis Khan motioned with his hand as though to say that the matter had been beyond his power. "They ran from their fathers and husbands to live among infidels, which is dishonorable, immodest, and forbidden. Did not the Prophet, God's blessings and peace be upon him, say that no believer should be permitted to bring disrepute onto the community of Islam?"

Sheik Radi murmured perfunctory agreement, but Adem

startled them all by quietly asking, "Is that what the women have done by running to the Harmony? Or have we men disgraced Islam by failing to protect women as the Qur'an requires?"

Sheik Radi shifted his teacup in his hand and didn't reply to what may have been disguised criticism of the circumstances of his first wife's death. The Khan inclined his head at Adem. "Nothing is simple," he said gently, forestalling argument.

Despite the fact that Nisa had intended to do precisely what the wild women had done, meeting the Khan had convinced her that she should not run away—at least not until after their marriage, if she then changed her mind about him. Then the disgrace would be his, and not her father's. Adem's comment she dismissed. It came from his resentment of the Khan's disdain for hunting. Besides, more protection was precisely what women did *not* need.

Sheik Radi cleared his throat. "And was it on Darien that you met your friend? The Jonist Academician? How is he?" The question was gossipy, arch, and unlike Nisa's father.

Her Khan motioned with his hand as though waving a fly away. "I haven't seen him since that dinner. He left shortly after you."

"Ah." Her father sipped tea and watched her Khan. "I'd had the impression you intended to employ him."

"A Jonist? No. But since he belonged to their Academy, I deemed it politically useful to treat him kindly, in case he is ever reinstated. Governor Gordan thought well of him. After you left he mentioned that the Jonist might be led to submit to Islam. He did seem tractable, but I was wrong. He disappeared among the lower elements of the city."

Adem yawned, but Sheik Radi eased back in his chair, nodding. "I'm glad you don't favor a war against Neuland and the Harmony." He glanced at the closed door and the servant beside it, then lowered his voice. "Frankly, the attitude from the capital has disturbed me."

The Khan sighed. "You're not alone. The Bei shouldn't listen so closely to"—he also dropped his voice—"certain advisors. However holy, they are women, requiring *our* protection."

The men discussed the newly begun negotiations with the

Harmony, but Nisa paid no attention. Once, she lifted her hand, pretending to pat her veil in place; her sleeve fell back just enough to expose the bracelet, part of the set the Khan had given her. He noticed. Well-bred, he said nothing, but the message had been sent and received.

Later, when her Khan had gone, Nisa's father seemed pleased. "Do you like him?"

"Very much."

Her eagerness made him smile. "You'll make a good wife." It was the highest compliment he had ever paid her. "I'll set a date with him for the celebration."

II. Triage.

Wema were in season. Marcer cursed them in Fars gutter talk acquired from his coworkers, and meant every syllable he said. More than a meter long, with four bulbous eyes that seemed to move and focus after death, the wema's dead eyes watched Marcer. Gutting fish probably wasn't the worst work in Shores. Sanitation jobs were more repellent—he'd been surprised there were such jobs, after seeing the canals—but sanitation paid better. It took family connections to get that work.

The Lashkari Kumbar Fish Processing Plant was well lit and frigid, a morgue for fish, but apparently some step in their transportation from ocean to warehouse was not quite cold enough because the flat wema bodies were slimy, a sure indication of bacterial growth. The surfaces showed brownish discolorations; the intestines, when he made his cut and spilled them onto the moving entrails tray, stank of putrefaction.

"What the matter with him?" a man down the line shouted periodically. Actually he cried it, and tears dripped from his half-closed eyes; Marcer didn't know the reason for his grief and didn't care; the man had done the same thing for days, and the pathetic had become merely annoying. The workers wore rubberized long coats and thin gloves made of a similar impermeable material, but the air in the cavernous place was filled with a fine mist of pinkish blood and bits of viscera; it settled onto them all like a glaze. Sometimes the crier, a small, hunched fellow, wiped his tears on his own encrusted shoulder, making Marcer shudder.

"Shut up!" the next man—an unman, actually—on the line often yelled. Once or twice a shift he turned and waved his filleting knife at the crier, who would hang his head in shame and be silent for a while.

Marcer tried to ignore them. He cut fish—not fish in the classic, terrestrial sense, but the word had been extended to any water-breathing water-dweller for centuries. Despite the clothing, the fish-gut dampness reached him. So did the cold. He paced himself. Originally he had been assigned to the canning line, where the worst wema carcasses were sent by inspectors Marcer likened to triage nurses: this one to the cans; this one to be filleted and sold to the rich. Working the canning line required no thought, and there were few opportunities to make mistakes. After three days he had been moved to the filleting tables. To fillet properly required a decision for each individual wema precisely where to make the cuts. It put choice, albeit of a much reduced and trivial kind, into the job. It also meant an extra fifteen rials a day. The inspectors always nodded approvingly when they passed Marcer. He was good at this horrible work—doubtless the result of his excellent Academy education. During the first week he had occupied his mind unraveling the wema life cycle, guessing their habits and habitat. Now, wema were just dead fish. He hated them.

He was too tall. He had to bend to work at the filleting boards and stoop to rinse the gutted fish. Each morning when his shift ended, just before sunrise, his back ached. The day shifts received four long breaks for alan prayers and personal necessities, but the night shift, though it paid twenty rials more, had only one long break, for midnight lunch, and two very short ones. He would stand at the railing overlooking the canal from which the fish arrived, watch the dawn and slowly straighten himself erect, working his shoulders and rolling his head. Sometimes he observed or EL-ed the shoreline, studying the scavenger species living there, pretending to still be a biologist.

He made 120 rials a day. Food was forty to eighty rials a day, depending upon what and how much he ate, and if he bought extra for Linnet. She discouraged it, which increased his eagerness to contribute. Each visit to the public bath was six rials, more for extra services like soap or to use the laundry. A bed would have cost thirty-five in a dormitory with five unmen—rent was cheaper if a man was willing to live with eunuchs—but Marcer had only paid it for one night. He lived with Linnet.

She called his a good job. He always had something left, if he didn't need clothes, shoes, transportation, or entertainment. Marcer finally understood why there were so many alans. Life in poverty required the pooling of resources. In fact, that was the unmen's purpose in the human ecology— to support parents and brothers.

Marcer's knife slashed a fish's belly. Wema were native to Bralava, alien to him, though not exceptionally exotic. His work was nonterrestrial biology of a close and immediate kind: He identified the organs spilling from his cuts, the heart, the brain, the liver. He stood for hours in a mounting pile of fish entrails, the debris that wasn't sent along on the moving tray for processing into fish meal, fish oil or some other product he had long since vowed never to use again. He remembered how tasty he'd thought wema were at that long-ago Academy banquet. Not once had he guessed what the fish would someday mean to him. His deviation from complete vegetarianism had been avenged; he would never eat fish again.

Inattention was dangerous. He nicked his right index finger through the glove on the sharp edge of the knife, then glanced furtively around. No one had seen. If he followed company rules, he would have excused himself, washed and bandaged his hand, then bought new gloves from the company store. He didn't. The company charged each worker one hundred rials for a second pair; the first was free, making Lashkari Kumbar a benevolent employer. Under the pretext of rinsing a fillet, Marcer flushed his cut. There wasn't much blood; diluted by water, the pink color matched the wema's.

The chemical preservatives in the water stung his cut. He ignored it, just as he ignored his back. His conscience was a more difficult matter. His blood might cause biological contamination. He could afford to buy a new glove. He had 420 rials saved. He rationalized that the damage was already done. Frustrated, anxious, he continued gutting fish.

When the night shift ended, Marcer joined the long line to turn in his gear and collect his daily pay from the superintendent. The workers called him boss. Marcer didn't know his name. He didn't know most of their names either because they used nicknames. His was "Giant."

"Tonight?" the boss asked as he handed over Marcer's money in a folded bit of green paper with squiggles of Arabic writing on it, unintelligible to Marcer except for the numbers.

The next night shift was that of the alan holy day, when many of the alan regulars didn't show up. "Time and a half pay?" Marcer had been ready. Linnet said Lashkari Kumbar was supposed to pay time and a half for Friday work to everyone, not only alans, but for several weeks running he'd received only his regular wage.

"You Jews," the boss said, shaking his balding head in disgust. He sighed. "All right. Time and a half."

One hundred eighty rials. Marcer nodded. "Then I'll be here tonight." He walked away. The third-class fare to Darien in transport webbing, back when there had been regular service, had been 10,289 rials. By the time he earned that much, the cold conflict between the Harmony and the Emirates would probably be over, unless it got hot.

The problem wasn't really money, it was whether the Harmony would let him return once the emergency ended. He could send a message to his father then, asking for money. His scrimping now was probably irrelevant, but he did it anyway to pretend he had some power over events. It kept him from feeling like a leaf in a tornado. That and Linnet.

The indoor factory lighting seemed bright, but when he went outdoors into natural sunlight, he squinted. He was registered as a Jonist. Why had the boss called him a Jew? It reminded him of Idryis Khan. Marcer looked back, intending to ask, but the boss was gone.

Marcer stood at the railing. A ship was off-loading a fresh load of wema, raising its iced pits and dumping the cargo into a factory sorting bin. Wema were demersal fish, bottom feeders, and they were caught with nets. Useless, rough debris picked up with the fish spilled into the bin: souring vegetation left over from the mangrove-form forests mentioned by the encyclopedia; waste fish like the cruly, the baet, and something obviously terrestrial, introduced by accident onto Bralava. An ugly thing. Catfish?

With the stink of fish and offal still on him, Marcer had no desire to eat either breakfast or dinner, but he craved conversation enough that he considered stopping at the café where some of the night shift spent their days. He remembered long dinners back on Darien with Ted Fields, Gwen Asher, and Hana Skarit, drinking cheap blush wine from Flute and tossing around ideas about everything from the cardiovascular systems of *M. Amacuro B. gesii* to the reproductive habits of the now exterminated Bril. This was another life. Alans forbade alcohol to everyone, and black-market rotgut would have been a major expense, but Marcer wished for its temporary oblivion.

The public bath was a luxury, yet he went every day. Human contact was not a luxury. He needed Linnet, but was tired of spending his days in the apartment. There was no good public place in Shores to go with a woman, though every now and then they strolled in the local suq, shopping for groceries and gossip, Linnet so covered with cloth that it was a wonder she didn't suffocate. Idryis Khan a'Husain was in the news; more ships under his command had arrived. He was popular in Shores because he was a Son— still rare on Bralava—and because he was allied with Sheik Radi Khalil, a generous benefactor to the city's poor. The Khan had made no obvious move to trace or contact Marcer. But what about the boss calling him a Jew? Who else would, but the Khan?

"Hey, Giant!" yelled a fishery worker called One Eye, for obvious reasons, from the open-air café, "I need a partner for a game of issi."

They had taught him the game and then been astonished when he won the second game he played, and then the next three. To him it was simple, a matter of spatial organization and frame patterns. They played for money, however, and though he could have won quite a bit, to do so offended his sense of fair play. Besides, they would have been angry, and an infidel who was the center of trouble might be fired from the factory. He shook his head no, and One Eye groaned. In the distance a faint vibration, inaudible to standard humans, made Marcer look up into the pink sky. A hoist ship had just lifted a load toward an interstellar vessel. Meanwhile, he was stranded on Bralava. The *Adhan* began calling men to *Fajr,* morning prayer. Always the outsider, Marcer hurried away.

III. Jinn.

Marcer walked the nineteen blocks from the fishery to Linnet's neighborhood, stopping once at the public bath and once in a small, local suq where he made careful purchases of day-old rolls, cheese, and two apples from merchants who had come to know him. He used a shortcut through the courtyard of a vacant building. In the alley behind it he saw another jinn.

Beautifully camouflaged, he might have missed the jinn except for echo-location, which he no longer was reluctant to use. Freedom from sensors set to detect it was the one privilege he had in this alan city.

Jinn were demons in alan mythology; that the locals called these animals jinn indicated their dislike of them. By law, jinn couldn't be harmed. They seemed to know, and it was a canny merchant who could prevent them from stealing.

"Hello, girl," Marcer whispered. Jinn were so graceful and quick that female nomenclature came naturally. He got down on one knee and extended his hand. He wasn't certain the jinn was female; he hadn't noticed sexual distinctions, or any genitalia among those he'd encountered, but a female gender was essential to a species. Even in creatures which reproduced asexually, each individual was female. Marcer thought of them as roving explorers surveying neighborhoods and events with intelligent curiosity.

Like the others that he'd encountered, this jinn seemed fascinated by him. She approached slowly, her birdlike head tilted to one side; she exuded a sweet, mint smell. Doglike, she licked his hand. *Don't terrestrialize,* he reminded himself, but he wasn't, really. Categorizing body types and movements was only shorthand. He had been raised on a world classified as Extreme; he knew that licking his hand wasn't necessarily affection. Clearly, however, the jinn were interested in him, though they generally passed people without a glance. The difference between him and other humans was his ability to EL.

The jinn weren't native to Bralava and were unlike anything there. Linnet said they were from Paradise, brought back by Blessed men as pets for their houri wives.

Interesting pets. Very adaptable, and flexible in their behavior. Jinn could walk on either two legs or four, though they were quicker and had greater endurance on four. Their skeletons and musculature were compromises; they weren't built for distance travel, but for disguise. Only their eyes didn't change color. Those eyes frightened many people. At night or when the animals were fully camouflaged, those huge eyes were all that was visible as the jinn moved throughout the city.

It was early, the time of day Marcer sometimes spent walking, learning the city. There was no hurry. Linnet was often slow getting home. With gradual movements, although the jinn were rarely spooked by human actions, he reached into the net bag and withdrew a rice-flour roll, his cheapest purchase. Jinn teeth indicated an omnivorous diet. "Take it." He offered the roll. Animals, which didn't share food, generally accepted it from strangers. Some nonterrestrial animals could be tamed.

The jinn peered at the browned bread and briefly licked it, but Marcer guessed she was only being hospitable. "You're too well fed." He smiled. As if it was a real conversation, he gestured at the jinn's enlarged belly. "Or are you pregnant?"

He wondered how they reproduced. It was rare for animals of such apparently high intelligence—jinn curiosity reminded him of apes, or the carls native to Rockland—to be asexual. If they were. He wished for access to a lab.

The jinn huffed, which Marcer had learned meant boredom, and glanced over her shoulder. He couldn't speak and EL simultaneously, and he lost his appeal to the jinn if he went too long without EL-ing. He EL-ed. The jinn lunged suddenly and snapped at his wrist.

Marcer drew back in time. "Nasty," he scolded. He tore the bit of bread the animal had licked off the roll and replaced the roll in the bag. "I get the message." He dropped the crust he had torn from the roll. The jinn stepped on it as she approached Marcer again. Her mouth was closed.

Marcer EL-ed and took a step away, then waited for the jinn. She followed. He'd done this several times with other jinn. They would follow him while he EL-ed as though he were a latter-day Pied Piper. Once he led one for seven blocks. He took this one to the end of the alley, then stopped EL-ing. The jinn sat down and stared at him, seemingly puzzled, then watched as he walked away.

Marcer checked at the dock. Linnet's boat was in its slot. He dropped another bit of bread at the canal's edge and watched the mad scramble between a pale, wriggling native crawler and an immigrant Urfa fen-hen. The native won.

Jonist Academics rarely had an opportunity to investigate nonterrestrial life beyond the admittedly large borders of the Polite Harmony of Worlds. The thought that he might one day be envied made Marcer smile. A week before being deported, he'd received a paper back from the Academy, his second as primary author: "Comparative Susceptibility to *Leishmania major* infection in native vertebrates of three genetically isolated worlds." *The Journal of Synecological Studies* had rejected it despite favorable peer review. It should have warned him, but he had assumed the rejection was impersonal, his work too mundane, and never considered the possibility of personal danger.

He sighed, wiped his hands on his laundered pants, and stole a flower from the Park of the Holy Martyrs on the way to Linnet's apartment.

A neighbor was standing idly in the courtyard. Seeing Marcer, he nodded a greeting, and called, "Good morning, Giant. She has someone with her."

Though Marcer detested her work, he considered Linnet blameless. He had learned how few choices a lone woman had in Shores. Her customers, however, he judged to be monsters. She hadn't brought any home since he had stayed with her.

The neighbor nodded, seeing through him. Altered empathy wasn't the only kind. "Listen, Giant. It's better for someone who doesn't get hurt to do it and be paid." The neighbor, like many in the building, was an unman. He wore the livery of an elegant store in Gracious, the richest shopping district of Shores, and he was going to be late for work.

Marcer EL-ed him and was reminded that not only women had hard lives. Unmen were sexually inert, but not sexually unusable. The neighbor had waited to safeguard Linnet.

"You're right," Marcer said, and touched the unman's arm. "I'm here now; go on to work or you'll lose your job. And thank you."

The unman glanced once more at the passage to Linnet's door, then he nodded and left. Marcer crumpled the flower in his hand, rolling it so tightly that its scent embedded itself inside his palm. He tossed the crushed flower to the ground and sat, waiting, beneath the lonely courtyard tree.

Linnet's door opened. Marcer stood, impatient to see the brute who, perhaps on his way to work, had decided that the best start to his day would be to hurt a woman. Out of Linnet's apartment strode Matthew McCue.

McCue's well-cut suit made him seem massive rather than fat, but he was clearly the same man who'd been deported with Marcer. He patted his sweating face with a cloth handkerchief and looked uneasily about, out of place in this working-class district. He saw Marcer, who gaped at him. Startled but not surprised, McCue stopped. "Good morning, Researcher Brice," he said in the Harmony's common language, not Ufazi. He bowed.

Marcer rushed at him. "McCue? You know Linnet?" Ufazi came more naturally to Marcer in this situation. The image of this wretched, ugly man cutting her, burning her, and then, most likely fucking her in the same room where Marcer spent some of the only good moments of his exile was too much. If he'd had a filleting knife, Marcer would have gutted McCue where he stood. "Bastard!" The Ufazi insult had no meaning in the Harmony, but Marcer wasn't thinking like a Jonist. "Come here again, and I'll kill you."

McCue extended his pudgy hand as though warding Marcer off. "You're being unreasonable, Brice. The woman is a whore."

Marcer grabbed McCue's jacket and shook the man. Though her appearance hadn't worsened over the weeks, it hadn't been easy to ignore what was done to Linnet. To know who did it made overlooking it impossible.

Linnet stepped outdoors wearing her yellow caftan, her usual attire while at home. Her hard-soled clogs clicked staccato taps against the concrete passageway. She looked at both of them. "Marcer. Are you planning to drive away my customers one by one?"

"I know him."

"So do I," she answered. "I've been paid. Let him go."

Reluctantly, Marcer released McCue.

McCue wiped his face and didn't leave. "No. We'll talk.

Inside." Marcer recognized the mercantile avarice in McCue's stout, ugly face. The trader saw an opportunity.

"All right," Linnet whispered. Another neighbor had overheard them and eased open his door. Uncovered, though modesty was unnecessary around unmen, Linnet scurried back to her apartment.

McCue studied Marcer with more assurance, taking in his wet hair—drying anything in Shores's humidity was slow—and the net bag of bargain food clutched in his right hand. The apples shone very red in the light, but they smelled overripe. "This will be interesting on your Academy résumé, Researcher."

"Shut up, McCue." Both Marcer's hands were clenched.

McCue skirted Marcer warily and returned to Linnet's room. Marcer followed.

To Marcer's impoverished senses Linnet's familiar home no longer seemed quaint or claustrophobic, but comfortable. Marcer stayed by the door but looked for blood or other signs of McCue's attentions. He EL-ed. Nothing. She must already have cleaned the traces away.

McCue sprawled against the pillows on her neatly made bed as though he owned her place. He exuded cunning like the sweat he kept mopping off his forehead. "Tell him," McCue ordered Linnet.

Linnet stood at the entrance to her kitchenette, arms crossed over her chest. "He is a customer, a valued customer," she said forcefully.

Marcer imagined McCue's gruesome pleasures and felt sick.

"Nonsense," McCue said. "I was here to collect on a debt." McCue pursed his lips, controlling a self-satisfied smile. "Little Linnet owes me a considerable amount of money. There is nothing personal between us."

Truth. Marcer EL-ed and felt it in the bounce-back. McCue was sly and shrewd; his aura flickered evasively—but not just then. Marcer set his bag of food on Linnet's table and nearly smiled. McCue wanted him to ask about the debt. "Is he staying?" was all Marcer said.

Linnet stared down at her floor.

"You could help repay her debt, Brice, since you enjoy protecting her."

McCue apparently didn't realize Marcer's disposable income was usually fifteen rials a day.

McCue's tone sharpened. "You could help her become beautiful again. But beauty costs."

Whereas at first her face had been a hideous mask, Marcer had come to see that she was lovely beneath what had been done to her. With his echo-location and his eyes, he saw the tiny areas of unmarked, perfect skin and the curve of her elegant jaw. He imagined her nose before it had ever been broken. "She's beautiful already to me."

Linnet stared at him.

McCue guffawed. "Periodically, in order to satisfy men not so discerning as a Jonist Academician, she has to be repaired," McCue said. "A man gets no satisfaction from gutting a wrecked building. Cutting an ugly woman is less . . . stimulating than cutting a beauty." McCue sighed theatrically. "She owes me quite a lot, and, if it's not paid, there will be consequences." He levered himself to his feet using his arms. "Since she won't feel pain, I'll have to be creative."

Marcer wished his ability to EL really was the secret weapon that cheap Harmony melodramas claimed for Altered capabilities. He swallowed hard, glanced at Linnet, then EL-ed. McCue was serious. "How much does she owe you?"

"Leave him out of this, Matthew." Linnet walked between them as though protecting Marcer.

McCue detoured around her. "She owes me 118,000 rials. Plus change."

Marcer waited for Linnet to deny the outrageous sum. She stayed silent and wouldn't meet his eyes. "Health care is more expensive here than I thought," Marcer said.

"There's more involved than just my face." Linnet returned to the kitchen doorway, then in a stronger voice, she added, "None of it concerns you. Go away, Marc. Forget this."

"Go back to the Khan," McCue said, "and I'll cancel ten thousand of her debt."

Marcer understood. "Idryis Khan a'Husain. You want me to see him." He used Linnet's euphemism. "The Khan said you were a spy."

"Did he?" McCue chuckled. "I am."

"He didn't mention you were also a pimp."

McCue wasn't upset by the insult. "I'm a trader. My merchandise includes information." He glanced, barely, at

Linnet. "Also travel papers, tickets, and permissions. Money lending, when necessary to make a transaction work. Pimping, if it gets me what I want."

Twice when Marcer had complained about the fishery Linnet had suggested asking the Khan for a job. He had assumed she was mocking his former, easy life. Had she actually been working for McCue to resolve some of her debt? "What makes you think he'd care if I showed up?" Marcer asked.

"Because he asked me to bring you to him. I've kept track of you, Brice. He knew I would. I came here to tell her to throw you out, to increase the pressure on you."

"I don't believe you."

"Yes, you do."

Marcer sat down at the table. Linnet joined him there, busying herself by removing the food he'd brought from the net bag. "Thank you," she said, as though they were alone in the room, but Marcer saw his offering for what it was: old cheese, bruised fruit, and stale bread. He covered her nearest hand. "If I did what he wants, would you stop letting them hurt you?"

"No," she said with quick certainty. "But thank you for believing that I can be hurt." She gently removed her hand from beneath his.

Marcer studied McCue. He was a fixer, a man who got things done, and such men always had their own profit in mind. Marcer stood, to be physically higher than the contemptible McCue. "Am I bait? Do you plan to blackmail him?"

"Idryis Khan? I wouldn't dare. I wouldn't survive the first demand for money. But he fascinates me. The Khan, his Blessed father and his houri mother. She vanished recently, and not to return to Paradise. Odd. Idryis Khan and the other Sons should interest you, too. They usually avoid outsiders, but Idryis Khan likes you. I saw it back on Darien. He attacked the soldiers, but you were the original provocation. He finds you appealing, Academician, and if nothing else, I'd like to know why. Another ten thousand if you can tell me."

"You really are a spy."

"The celebration of his wedding is this afternoon. You'll attend it with me. What do you have to lose? A job at Lashkari Kumbar Fish Processing? I'll have them fire you.

A certain style of virginity?" He grinned. "I'm generous. Come to the wedding, and I'll reduce her debt by twenty thousand."

"His *wedding*?" It seemed grossly vulgar, but it would be a public setting and probably safe.

"Why not?"

Why not? Linnet was wringing her hands. Her grip was unknowingly too strong and powerful enough to break bones. Marcer forced one of her hands away from the other; he held it until she looked up. He only saw her eyes. "Do you want me to do this?" he asked.

To EL was unnecessary. She needed his help, but wouldn't ask. "It's my problem," she said.

"All right." Marcer turned to McCue and caught him glancing surreptitiously at a status he wore on his wrist. A businessman, with other appointments. "I'll go to the wedding with you, but that's all. When the party's over, I leave. And you'll reduce Linnet's debt by half."

McCue was a happy man. He didn't try to bargain. "Fine. I'll never see that money anyway. My fault for lending to women." He dropped two gold sovereigns—one thousand rials each—on the table. "Buy yourself a decent suit, Brice, and get some rest this morning. You're hunching your shoulders like a laborer. Your hands look chapped. Be at my office at noon. If you're not on time, then I'll tell the Khan where you live. Believe me, you're better off going to a man like that voluntarily than waiting for him pick you up. He'd take Linnet, too, most likely."

Marcer picked up the heavy coins. "This doesn't add to her debt or start one for me."

"Of course not." McCue was as genial as he had been on the ship. "It will be reimbursed by the Khan. He paid me handsomely to find you." McCue nodded a cocky farewell, opened the door, and let himself out.

IV. Blue.

The room closed in upon the two of them once McCue was gone. Neither spoke. In distress, Marcer EL-ed. The walls had become too confining and the ceiling too low for comfort. He smelled of dead fish, despite the bath. His charity shirt was threadbare from too vigorous washing.

Linnet went into her kitchen and returned with cheap ceramic plates, the kind that chipped rather than deformed temporarily when dropped. She peeled her apple with a knife. Marcer picked up a roll, then set it down again. "Why do you owe so much?" he asked. "Skinsacks are rudimentary medicine. It couldn't be so expensive, even here."

She set the half-peeled apple on her plate but kept the knife in her hand. Seemingly oblivious to what she did, she ran the cutting edge back and forth across the ball of her thumb. "There's more to it, but I can't involve you."

He tried to imagine what secrets Linnet could possibly share with a man like Matthew McCue, a trader operating on both sides of the Harmony/Emirates border. A crossman spy for the Harmony? He shook his head. "I am involved, Linnet, I'm Jonist. I believe that knowledge is powerful, and that searching the universe for Order is right. If you don't tell me what's between you and McCue, then you're asking me to do this blind."

She smiled, facing her plate. "You're not a proper Jonist, anyway. I know you. You believe the universe is moral. You try to do what's right, not what's most advantageous."

She seemed to believe Jonism was a merchandise market with each person a trader seeking profit. Frustrated, he shook his head. "What about McCue?"

"He's not so bad. He has reasons to cooperate with Idryis Khan, but he didn't just drag you off; he let you present yourself with dignity."

Just like the constables on Darien had allowed him his dignity while taking him to exile. Marcer pushed his plate aside. It clattered against Linnet's. "Have you been watching me for McCue? Is that why you've pretended to be my friend?"

The knife's edge pierced Linnet's thumb. Blood welled up from the cut, but Linnet didn't notice; she didn't feel it. Red drops fell onto her plate and were absorbed into the roll, staining it. "I never pretended anything with you," she said. "Matthew already knew you were here. He even went to Lashkari Kumbar. But yes, I told him, too."

Marcer was fascinated by her cut. She continued to run the knife up and down her thumb, unaware that the blade had entered her flesh and that each stroke sent it deeper.

She noticed his attention and glanced down, then tossed

the knife onto her plate and put her thumb in her mouth,
sucking it like an infant. It disturbed him though he knew
she felt no pain. Did she *enjoy* abuse? Did it stimulate
some peculiar Neulander eroticism? The Republic of Neuland was infamous for its torture parties.

Marcer picked up the two gold coins and rattled them in
his hand. They represented a good start on a trip to Safi,
or more than enough to send a message there, a call for
help. The Emirates branch of the family were openly religionists—they were Jews—but it would be safer to stay with
them than to remain here on Bralava. It showed no weakness to ask for help. After all, he had managed for more
than a month on his own. Yet he hadn't been alone. He'd
had Linnet. His departure for Safi wouldn't help her at all.
He set the coins back on the table. "All right. But I wish
you would tell me the truth."

"Knowing wouldn't help you." She smiled in the way he
imagined her smiling for a client just before she was hurt.
Falsely, to placate him. "You should wear blue to compliment your eyes. You need new shoes. And get a small present
for the Khan."

"On his own money."

She examined her thumb. It was no longer bleeding. A
thin pink line, nearly lost among her other scars, was all
that showed. Marcer glanced at his own hands. The spot
where he had cut himself at work was lightly scabbed. If
he pressed his finger hard against the table, the scab would
break and the wound would bleed again.

"I'll shop with you if you want. I would enjoy it."

He needed air. He got up and went around her to the
kitchen. Its window overlooked the canal. Bralava's moons
made tides, and the tide was low, exposing the bare, reaching roots of a mangrove-form plant trying to establish itself
in the tidal zone. If it wasn't ripped out, a grove would
slowly form, clogging the channel. A four-legged crawler,
larger than the one he'd fed, scampered at the water's edge.

Linnet joined him at the window. The top of her head
came only to his chest, so that while he stooped to see out,
she was on tiptoe. Rather than look at her, he studied the
canal margins. Across the canal, men were cleaning a barge.
A young child played in the mud. Children drowned in
Shores's canals every week. No statistics were kept, and
accurate news was hard to come by in the Emirates. People

relied on rumors, not newscasts. Gossips agreed those deaths were a form of birth control. Daughters.

Marcer put his hands lightly on her shoulders. It was a trick, a way of sensing vibration, a poor substitute for EL that he had learned in New Dawn's Academy, where students were forbidden to use Altered abilities. "The only thing that costs so much," he said, "since you avoid drugs and gambling, is interstellar travel. But here you are, still on Bralava."

"Here I am."

He felt her tension, a hint that he was getting closer to the truth. "There are women who enter the Harmony for asylum," he said slowly. "Some are poor."

He knew he was on the right track because she said nothing.

"McCue's business takes him back and forth across the border all the time." Marcer meant it as a question.

"It did." She faced him, causing him to drop his hands to his sides. "I heard gossip last night that Idryis Khan might not testify against those women. That would help them, but even if it didn't help *them,* without the Khan's . . . interest there won't be a meticulous investigation of how, exactly, they left the Emirates, or who helped them leave."

That was their connection. Linnet arranged with McCue to smuggle women into the Harmony. That was the reason for her debt, and part of the reason for McCue's anxiousness to please Idryis Khan.

McCue didn't seem to be a humanitarian, a man who would risk himself to smuggle women, but then, McCue was deceptive. A spy, but for whom? The highest bidder? McCue had mixed motives, at best, for the help he gave alan women, but Linnet acted from principle. He would be helping *her* as well as McCue.

Marcer took Linnet into his arms. She leaned against him. She hadn't perfumed herself with the jarring fragrance he'd finally realized she used to cover the smell of blood. Her face was certainly *different,* but not all differences were ugly. The Neulander Alteration was a clever reworking of some basic themes of biology. The results should be no more disturbing than his own wide face and large ears.

They'd slept together, but, afraid of losing his only friend, Marcer had always waited for her invitations to do more than sleep. He stroked her face with the palm of his hand.

Touch had become as pleasing as his ELs of her. She was a rare, exotic creature. He couldn't imagine purposely injuring Linnet. He didn't believe she wanted to be cut or burned. He kissed her. The contrasting normalcy of her lips was arousing.

"Marcer," she said, interrupting, "don't go. Idryis Khan is unpredictable. He might have you locked up."

Marcer remembered the cold, impervious shell that was a bounce-back from the Khan. He was a man of stone. "I'll be fine," Marcer said. "It's his wedding. Besides, the Khan let me go once. He will again."

Chapter 6

The Supplicant had been flown to Center in a guarded coach, then lectured for two hours on the protocol for meeting an Elector. She must bow first and to the proper depth; she must speak respectfully but without fawning, which could be interpreted as un-Jonist. "But I'm not a Jonist," she protested, startling them.

"You're a religionist?" Ted Fields was shocked.

Religious belief had ceased to matter to the Supplicant; she believed in the threat of alien invasion. That was enough.

"It doesn't matter," Revered Gangler said. "She has important information. The Electors will listen."

Ted Fields turned away like a child embarrassed by his elders, and wouldn't look at the Supplicant. Perhaps he thought he was in love, but if all went well, soon she would have little use for him. Still, when eventually he glanced at her, she said, "I'm not Muslim, anymore. I don't understand Jonism. I'm just a woman."

He smiled. "How do you like Center?"

He had never been there before either, yet he sounded like a tour guide. Center, the city of which the Jonists were so proud, was said to float above Sucre-semp, but what it really did was hover. The air on Sucre had been heavy and sickly sweet, but Center's cleansed air smelled artificial, as though it were the product of a chemistry lab rather than a world. Light from the sun-stones seemed real enough, but it wasn't the light of Bralava's sun. The ornamentation, even the window-screens, was garish. She realized she was homesick. "It's wonderful," she said.

I. An esthetic problem.

Nisa studied her face as an esthetic problem. Her eyes were dark. Should she make them even darker, perhaps mysterious, or lighten them to look lively? Her lips were a bit thin, but she could widen them with color. Her skin, at least, was flawless. Brush poised, she stared into the mirror as if it were a canvas awaiting her decision where to paint. Idryis Khan would see her after the ulama chosen to officiate publicly proclaimed their marriage. A special reverence room, where her Khan could look at her for the first time, had been filled with white roses, peonies, and lilacs.

"Beautiful." Hulweh walked into Nisa's dressing room, a windowless recess between Nisa's bedroom and her studio. Ziller, dressed as a guest, followed. He closed the door neatly behind them. Nisa had prevailed in a minor battle to actually invite him, not merely to allow him to attend as Hulweh's servant.

"Thank you." Nisa turned to Ziller. "My eyes," she asked. "Darker or lighter?"

"Darker. Let me do your eyelashes."

Hulweh laughed. "I meant the Khan. He was standing with your father when we arrived. He *is* handsome."

"Looks are a poor basis on which to judge a man." Ziller took the brush from Nisa. "Look up."

"You're a prune, Zil." Nisa was motionless, letting Ziller use the brush to extend her eyelashes.

"Is that real?" Hulweh lightly touched Nisa's new gold necklace. It was two fingers wide; a rare, opalescent soft diamond dangled from it, flashing ruby red as it picked up color from her dress.

"Yes." Nisa glimpsed herself in the mirror as Ziller stepped back, still holding the brush. Perfect. "And it wasn't required by the marriage contract. He sent it this morning." She raised her arm to exhibit the matching bracelet. Her coiffure nearly hid the tiny, soft diamond earrings.

"Generous." Hulweh ululated cheerfully but softly. Nisa blushed and had to suppress a silly grin.

"Never judge a man by his courtship," Ziller said.

Hulweh put her hands on her waist and shook her head. "How *should* we judge them, then? And why are we having this discussion before a friend's marriage? Don't you think Nisa is nervous enough?"

"No." Ziller smiled, however. "She isn't nervous at all. She's radiant and mysterious. Look at her."

They both did. Nisa smiled at herself in the mirror. She pursed her lips. She arched an eyebrow.

"She's not mysterious, she's vain," Hulweh joked.

Nisa laughed and stuck out her tongue at her reflection. She leaned back in the dressing-table chair, satisfied. Such things being subjective, there was no ideal woman's face, but she knew that she was, indeed, quite beautiful.

"Will you let us know what the men are talking about?" Hulweh teased her unman servant. By virtue of his ambiguous gender, Ziller could attend both the men and women's parties. "The women's conversation will all be about Nisa's dresses." She gestured. By tradition, Nisa would change into seven different dresses during the party. They hung in the dressing room like a splendiferous silk and silkik rainbow awaiting sunlight. Gidie had done her proud.

Ziller shrugged. "Men are bores. I thought I'd stay at the women's party with you."

"Ziller!" both Nisa and Hulweh burst out.

Something scratched at the closed door. Hulweh grabbed Ziller's arm; she turned to Nisa. "I thought that thing was locked up."

"It is. I haven't seen it since you were here. Weeks ago." Nisa stood. She was concerned that, from spite, Qadira might have released her creature. Ziller matter-of-factly went to the door and threw it open as if to surprise whatever was on the other side. It was only Gidie, officious in his white-and-gold livery. He bowed, while frowning slightly at Ziller.

"They're ready for you downstairs, Mistress Nisa," Gidie said, far more formal with her than usual.

Nisa nodded regally, as befitted a woman married to a Khan. "I'll be there shortly." To her friends, she said, "A bride should enter alone. I'll see you downstairs."

Ziller shook his head. "Nisette, be careful." Hulweh slapped his arm. "Everything will be fine," Ziller continued more positively. "But be proper. Demure. This Khan is like all Sons, traditional. Save your high spirits for your friends."

"Of course." Nisa wasn't listening. She had returned to

her self-examination in the mirror. A bit of silvered rouge, she thought, just beneath the eyebrows. It would match the glitter of her silver-and-green silkik dress, the next she planned to wear. "I'll see you downstairs."

Ziller placed his wrinkled hand gently on Nisa's shoulder. "Not too long, Nisa. Remember, a modest woman doesn't make a grand entrance." Then they left Nisa alone to complete her toilette.

When they were gone, Nisa opened a drawer and removed the black jar in which she'd hid the tranquilizing tabs. She shook it like a rattle, listening to the clatter. She put it down, then immediately picked it up and left her small suite headed for Qadira's, where she hadn't dared intrude before.

Qadira's door was closed, but none of the women's rooms would lock. She listened, with her hand on the knob, and heard nothing but her own breathing. She didn't know what she would do if Qadira was inside rather than downstairs, but she turned the knob and pushed the door hard, letting herself in.

The suite was the largest on the women's floor; it had belonged to Sheik Radi's mother, Nisa's grandmother, and it smelled as stuffy as Nisa remembered from her childhood. The first room, a sitting room rather than a studio, was furnished with heavy, old-fashioned furniture, upholstered in dark colors. Pale light from skylights didn't lift the gloom; the lamps were off. The only change from her grandmother's day was that nothing hung on the walls, neither carpets, pictures, nor contraband Harmony windowscreens. The place had the ordered look of a room that's seldom used. Qadira had houri visitors, but they apparently didn't sit here; as for Sheik Radi, she went to him. The door to the private rooms of the suite was closed. Nisa had been committed from the moment she entered the first room, so she went on.

The door opened onto a hallway. Unlike Nisa's, it didn't overlook a courtyard. Again, the only natural light came from skylights. Nisa wondered how her grandmother had borne the sense of enclosure. As for Qadira, she didn't care.

Nisa turned right and opened all three doors. Each room was fully and uninterestingly furnished in the style her grandmother might have chosen for young children. Qadira hadn't changed anything in the nursery. At the hallway's end, Nisa turned and went back the other way.

"Qadira!" she called. No one answered. The silence and general air of neglect buttressed her resolve. She passed the public room. She opened more doors, searching. This portion of the suite had windows overlooking the outdoor garden. These rooms showed use. In one, clothes had been strewn over a divan, and the chair at a dressing table was pushed aside. There were no books, no art on the walls, nothing to show how Qadira spent her time. Nisa supposed she merely sat, plotting.

At the last room, she found the creature's lair. Once she opened the door, she was overwhelmed by the rancid stench of sweetness gone bad. The room was a treasure trove of trash. Its pungency made Nisa's eyes tear. Worried about her makeup, she hesitated a moment before going inside.

A nest made of a collection of shiny fragments embedded in an accumulation of colored cloth was at the wall opposite the door. It held bits of table linen, a gnawed box, and what might have been a canvas stolen from her room; altogether it was a cache of worthless, dirty junk heaped up into a cozy bed for a demented scavenger. Seated within, its alert, alien eyes fixed on Nisa, was Qadira's creature.

Nisa gritted her teeth, then smiled. "You ugly thing," she crooned. "You beast. You killer." She unscrewed the cap of her black container. The creature glanced at the door, which Nisa had left ajar. It stood, moving slowly.

The creature was much heavier than it had been a few weeks earlier. The weight was centered around its midsection, announcing the cause: Qadira's creature was pregnant. Ugh. What kind of ugly pup would it have?

"A treat," Nisa sang. "I have something for you, you monster."

The creature glared, but pregnancy slowed it, and the pet shambled only a step forward. Nisa tossed the tabs at it. Several hit it in the face, others fell into the folds of the nest, but most dropped at the creature's feet.

The thing bent down. It sniffed. They were citrus-flavored, though Nisa smelled nothing but the foulness of the room.

"A treat!" she said brightly. "Eat them! Umm, so good!"

The creature looked at her suspiciously, but then it lapped up several tabs at once. It liked their taste and ate more, rooting among the debris to find them. Nisa watched and grinned. Only after the thing had eaten ten or twelve did she realize how long she'd spent on her revenge. It was still eating as she hurried downstairs. Tardy was a poor way to enter into marriage.

II. An acre.

The foreign elegance of the reception was lost on Marcer, but not so much that he was unaware it must exist. The room was stately: high ceilings, walls of white marble inset with black-and-gold arabesque patterns. A fountain burbled in its center. Huge windows overlooked a formal garden.

Men milled about, abundantly attended by unman servants. There were no women. McCue said they had a separate party in an adjacent room. There was no music. Two unmen performers chanted in nasal singsong. There was no alcohol. Waiters dressed in snow-white tunics and pantaloons circulated with tea, coffee, and fruit juice, as though dispensing drinks at a superior children's party. Conversation was stilted and did not include Marcer.

His new, blue cotton suit looked like a tradesman's uniform. He'd decided to keep as much of McCue's money as possible, and had only spent four hundred rials, but he felt as though he'd worn a sign that read, "I don't belong."

McCue must have lied about the Khan's interest in him. Sheik Radi, the host and father of the bride, had been gracious to Marcer but was obviously bemused. Idryis Khan avoided Marcer. He looked magnificent in the maroon uniform of Marshal of the elite Descent Assault Force, one of the units he commanded. Several of his officers were also present, though they stayed aloof from the other guests. Uniformed men—not unmen—guarded the house.

Marcer sipped juice and hugged the wall, trying to disassociate himself from McCue and remain inoffensive. After the ceremony, he intended to slip away. He wouldn't be missed.

Governor Gordan, Linnet's most regular customer, was

across the room, engrossed by his conversation with two younger men. The governor stroked his beard and nodded sagely, with hypocritical kindness. Damn him. He didn't look like a monster. Marcer started deliberately toward him, uncertain of his intentions. Josip Gordan couldn't be accused of hurting anyone, raping anyone, or causing distress to anyone except Marcer.

McCue intercepted Marcer. "The bride is late," McCue complained. "The Khan cannot be pleased. Go to him."

"The Khan has no interest in me." Marcer's zanth crystal glass was half-full of an unidentified, sweet yellow juice he didn't like. He handed the glass to a passing servant.

"You've made yourself so conspicuous, what else can he do but stay away?" McCue seemed to find the situation amusing. "Well, he'll know I didn't dress you. On the other hand, he won't believe I gave you your advance; I'll have to absorb the two thousand rials." He sighed with patently false grief. "Approach him."

"No." Marcer smiled at McCue, daring him to complain. A recorded call to prayer began. Alan men moved to perform ablutions at the fountain. Marcer and McCue remained silent. They were nearly the only exclusions from the alan fellowship. The men formed rows facing the niche indicating Makkah—an abstraction on worlds other than old Earth. Marcer sat with McCue on the room's margins. Unman servants prayed alongside guests, an alan practice condemned by Jonism, which viewed hierarchy as natural, but which Marcer privately admired. The religionist mind was different from his own, but he respected men whose principles were reflected in their actions.

A prolonged lag occurred before the women filed in through a side door. They formed rows behind the men. Veiled, cloaked in voluminous chadors, they looked like shapeless bags of laundry. Marcer wondered idly how the Khan chose a particular woman to marry. Their low position in Emirates society made women fungible. Mate choice, the drive to bind one's genes with those of someone likely to produce thriving offspring, was less important than political choice and social or religious superstition. No wonder the Harmony's population was healthier.

The *rak'ah* were finally about to begin when a lone woman, clad like the others in a plain black chador, rushed into the room. Marcer had assumed the bride was one of the women already present, but this, he supposed, was the actual bride making a separate entrance. All eyes turned toward her. The alan prayer leader paused, delaying prayer again while she entered the women's ranks. She walked demurely, head down, but she slowed her pace as though enjoying the attention. The folds of her chador swung about her body, giving shapely hints. Marcer EL-ed. Most men disapproved.

A man cleared his throat, and then, as one, the prayers and alternating postures that accompanied them began, but a subtle attention to the women's rows lingered among the men, an awareness which hadn't been present before.

After prayers, instead of a Friday afternoon sermon, the holy man read the marriage contract aloud. Marcer was curious, having attended few weddings even in the Harmony, since marriage was rare among Academics, but the contract was in Arabic. He understood nothing. Idryis Khan a'Husain and the woman then stood in front of the congregation and made statements, fortunately in Ufazi.

Idryis Khan went first. "In the Name of Allah, most gracious, most merciful, with His help and guidance, with all my trust put in Him, with my sound conscience and awareness of responsibility, with my free choice and goodwill, I, Idryis Khan a'Husain, marry Nisa Khalil Sharif, and take her as my wife according to Sharia, according to Allah and the teachings of the Holy Qur'an, in conformity with the inspired tradition of Mohammed, the Messenger of Allah."

Nisa. She looked tiny beside the Khan and mysterious in the chador. There was something undeniably erotic about concealment. It gave sexual imagination free rein. To do so seemed improper, but Marcer EL-ed and felt the outline of the woman's voluptuous body inside his mind. She trembled, radiating an aura of pleasure and excitement. The Khan wouldn't be needing him.

Nisa stated her acceptance in a small voice. The Khan's stern expression didn't change. Marcer had forgotten how a'Husain felt in EL. Without an aura, he was a black spot on the horizon. Idryis Khan didn't radiate emotion, he cast it back like a mirror.

When Nisa finished, women shouted and ululated. Men gathered around Idryis Khan and the girl's father, congratulating them.

The women left, although the room had accommodated them easily. The unman servants resumed their duties. Trays of sweet drinks and cookies circulated. McCue whispered that these were traditional accompaniments, but that there would be a banquet.

"Go wish him many sons. It's their tradition." McCue grinned as though the felicitation was a trick.

"Later." An offer of congratulations seemed polite, but Marcer was reluctant to approach the Khan. So were others. The alans admired yet seemed to fear hin. They were a community; a'Husain was separate, different, and, the alans assumed, better.

"It's rude to wait. I'm going." McCue demonstrated his sincerity by walking toward Idryis Khan and Sheik Radi.

Best to get it out of the way. Marcer joined the well-wishers, but remained at their edge. Taller than all of them, he looked over their heads. So far, the wedding was boring. He scanned the room.

Governor Gordan was leaving. The door to the large entrance hall, from which double doors opened onto the street, was guarded by the Khan's men, who opened it for him. The governor glanced back as though he wished to remain, then sighed and left.

Marcer abandoned his efforts to reach Idryis Khan. He hurried after Gordan but the guards stopped him at the door. "I must speak to the governor," Marcer protested.

"You're not allowed to leave," a guard told him.

"He just did." Marcer gestured stupidly at the door.

"*You're* not," the guard said. "The Khan wants to speak with you." The man was almost rude.

McCue had been right, after all. Protest was useless. Marcer turned back toward the party. Conversation was more restrained. Idryis Khan was watching him; so was Sheik Radi and a scattering of others, including McCue. Marcer's face reddened. He returned without looking at anyone.

Idryis Khan came part of the way to meet him, dragging his new wife; she was the only woman still in the room.

Marcer bowed, Harmony-style, as if to a superior. "Congratulations on your marriage," he said, only to the Khan. After several weeks in Shores he knew not to address the wife. "I hope you'll have many sons."

Idryis Khan stopped in the middle of a reply bow and

glanced at his black-clad bride. "A woman is an acre, Marcer, a field on which to grow men. This acre will be barren. I won't have any sons with her."

The woman made the beginning of a protest.

"Go back among the women, wife." Idryis Khan had been holding her hand fast, but he dropped it. He seemed to look through rather than at her draped figure. "And never make me wait for you again."

The bride hesitated only a moment, then she turned and ran for the door to the women's party. The ringing of her heels on marble was like an echo bounce-back. It told Marcer that she was hurt, humiliated, and very, very angry.

III. A brave girl.

Nisa knew her marriage was a terrible mistake the moment after their covenants, when Idryis Khan, newly her husband, seized her hand. His grip was that of a man holding a bridle, not a bride.

It got worse. He did not lead her aside to the private reverence room. He did not smile and send her back with the women, either. He did not even pretend happiness. "That was immodest," he said tightly. "It's wicked to disturb prayers."

She had no answer, but he didn't wait for one. He kept her by his side throughout the congratulations, displaying her like an ornament, forcing her family and his friends to acknowledge her presence, punishing her for her late entry. His friends had to compliment her, knowing she was listening. Her father, brothers, uncles, and cousins were forced to hail him as family while his wife stayed wantonly among the men. Many hung back; the governor didn't offer congratulations before he left. Her hand ached from his pressure on it.

The worst came when the Khan towed her across the room to greet a very tall man in a cheap suit who seemed as mortified as Nisa. The man, however, kept glancing at her as if trying to pierce her veil with his eyes. He was odd-looking: clean-shaven, with wide, high-boned cheeks, wide eyes, and big ears, as if his face hadn't been assembled quite right, though the result was engaging. His hair might once have been short and neat, but now was overgrown. He spoke too quickly and with an accent, but his voice was kind.

The Khan's wasn't. Neither were his words. Some men claimed that women and unmen had no souls. The Khan was even more cruel. An acre! Her last hopes for her marriage came crashing down with the word. She had deluded herself, convinced by a handsome face and deceiving manners. She had no importance to him. All fields are alike in the dark.

When he finally released her she ran, thankful for the veil because it hid her tears. The women's party was through a door, across a short corridor, and in another, smaller room. Nisa ran for it, needing Hulweh and her other cousins. Poised to yank open the door, she realized everyone would have noticed her delay. They would have assumed the Khan had taken her to the reverence room. Her face would show all of them the truth.

As she tried to compose herself, Ziller left the women's party. "Nisette?"

Alone of everyone, except her mother, he could not only recognize Nisa beneath a chador, but know when something was wrong. She nodded, afraid to speak for fear of crying.

"I've been waiting. We all have. Did your husband keep you so long?" He was teasing, trying to jolly her out of disappointment.

"With all the men," she blurted.

Ziller frowned and glanced at the door to the men's party.

"Zil, it's all gone wrong. My husband says I'm an acre!" Her voice broke. She had traded masters, her father for a stranger. "He doesn't care about me."

"He doesn't know you," Ziller said stoutly. "You'll show him who you are. Come inside with your friends, Nisette. Women understand."

"Nooo," she wailed. Qadira was there, with the other houri wives. They would laugh and make sly comments in their broken dialect. Nisa was sure that somehow this was Qadira's fault. After all, Idryis Khan had a houri mother. Nisa tried to back away.

Ziller caught and held her hand with nearly a man's

strength. "Don't give up, Nisa," he said. "Take time to sort this out. You have to be a woman now, not a child."

She'd heard the rumors of bride suicides. She was frightening her friend. Nisa took a breath, held it, then spoke with only a tremor in her voice. "I'm fine, Zil. I would never do *that*. I'm going upstairs to fix my makeup. Tell them I'll be there soon."

Ziller nodded. "Not too long, Nisette. You're a brave girl."

She nodded. He kissed her forehead through the cloth of the thin, indoor chador, winked, then opened the door to the men's party.

Nisa walked the corridor, entered the women's courtyard, and took the path across it without noticing the lilies and sweet-smelling rithas. The corridor continued on the far side of the courtyard and led to the women's staircase. She smelled roasting mutton and heard the clatter of dishes from the nearby kitchen, but it was around the corner; no one saw her. Her legs felt heavy as she climbed the staircase; rarely had it seemed steeper. The women's floor was silent.

In her haste, she must have left the door to her suite ajar. She hesitated on the threshold, then went inside. The studio was empty, her belongings having been packed and shipped to her husband's house. "An artist," she whispered aloud. He must have laughed as he wooed her with lies. She should have refused to marry him; her father would have allowed it.

Heedless of her hair, she pulled off her chador and tossed it on the floor. Immediately, a telltale scent made her eyes sting. She crept slowly forward to her dressing room. That door was also open. She wished she had the chador to muffle the stench; it was fierce. She went in.

The room was deserted. Her dressing table was untouched. Each of the seven new dresses hung ready for her to wear, one by one, during the party. She never would. They were torn where Qadira's creature's claws had snagged them; they reeked, polluted by the creature's urine.

IV. These misogynist men.

As he watched the Khan's bride hurry away, Marcer considered the reproductive advantages of female reticence.

The social and economic handicaps of women also leveled the reproductive playing field. Women needn't compete with other women in order to marry and reproduce because men never knew them.

Yet—to be an acre! The Khan's power over his wife was despicable. Had men forced the chador on women to conceal their sexuality, the official position, or to conceal that they were human?

"I'm pleased you came." Idryis Khan's quiet voice was intimate. He turned one of his artificial smiles on Marcer. Some guests were watching.

As was becoming increasingly habitual to him, Marcer EL-ed. He registered the guests' curiosity and incipient scorn as reflexively as he registered their presence. It was background information, like the chanting unmen across the room. "Now that you've seen me, will you tell your men that I can leave?" Marcer nodded coldly at the guarded door.

A very few standard humans could hear an EL; the Khan seemed to be one of them. He tilted his head as though to hear better. "No," the Khan said. "You'll wait for me in the courtyard, the one beyond the last door on the right. After dinner. I need to talk to you." He walked away.

Marcer shuddered as he watched. The Khan was alive, but to Marcer's sixth sense he felt as dead as a carved headstone.

Marcer rejoined the party. He had no other choice. He avoided McCue but Sheik Radi's approach surprised him. "What did the Khan tell you?" The Sheik's tone was decidedly unfriendly.

Marcer was tired of trying to fit into the Emirates. He bowed in the blunt Harmony style. "He said to meet him after dinner." Let Idryis Khan bear the brunt of his new father-in-law's anger.

Sheik Radi looked up into Marcer's eyes. He was a thin, dour man, not handsome but regal, the kind who, whatever his actual competence, looked the part of a superior. "For what purpose?"

After several weeks in the city of Shorcs, Marcer knew that questioning a guest was contrary to alan tenets of hospitality. He answered anyway. "I have no idea. I haven't seen him since the dinner with you at Government House."

Sheik Radi relaxed, but only slightly. "Was it on your account that the Khan refused to testify against those women?"

Marcer glimpsed Matthew McCue taking a sight on Marcer like a surveyor plotting his lines. What hurt McCue also hurt Linnet. "The women?" he asked, hoping his face didn't give his false insouciance away. "The ones deported from the Harmony? I know nothing about it, Sheik Radi. Nothing at all. As I just told you, I've had no contact with him."

"You came with the infidel, McCue. The Khan's guest."

The comment didn't require a response. Marcer nodded in agreement, let it become a bow, and started to turn away.

"I'm surprised you haven't petitioned the Harmony delegation for permission to join them and return to the Harmony," Sheik Radi said in just the tone to capture Marcer's attention.

"What?" Marcer spoke too loudly. Others looked, including Idryis Khan.

Sheik Radi smiled. "The delegation. It's an open secret that they arrived from the Harmony to negotiate an end to the state of emergency. Governor Gordan mentioned earlier today that they're being quite reasonable. He left because he had another session with them."

Sheik Radi knew precisely what he was doing in giving this information to Marcer. He even glanced at his new son-in-law.

Marcer cleared his throat. "Where are the Harmony officials?"

Servants were arranging pillows around a series of low tables they'd carried in; they had begun gently ushering guests to suitable positions. Sheik Radi watched, smiling, apparently satisfied that his duties as host were being adequately performed. "They're at Government House," he said. "You'd better hurry. They leave Bralava in two days." He walked away.

Marcer was led to a table far from anyone important. He barely noticed. These misogynist men, with their foreign social graces and insular superstitions, were controlling his life. McCue hadn't told him that Harmony officials were

on Bralava, although he'd certainly known. Idryis Khan
wanted him to stay for reasons Marcer couldn't fathom.
Sheik Radi didn't. Had it not been for Sheik Radi's pique
over the Khan's treatment of his daughter, Marcer would
never have known a way of returning home existed.

Home. Jonists defined home as the place, people, and
philosophy a person is willing to defend. There was nothing
here for him, nothing at all in the Emirates, except for
Linnet. He could take her with him, but first he had to
return home. That meant getting out of this house and in
to see the Harmony delegation before Idryis Khan
stopped him.

An elderly little Altered unman, who introduced himself
as Ziller ba'Lezin, was seated at the table beside Marcer.
The guest on Marcer's other side was a relative of Sheik
Radi from a rural province, apparently dependent on him,
and across was Zafar Maqsood, an aide to the governor,
and recent arrival from Qandahar. McCue was at another
table, minimally closer to their host.

Food was presented communally, not in individual portions. It would once have seemed unsanitary, but Marcer's
mouth watered with anticipation. It was the best, most plentiful meal he'd had since leaving the Harmony, good
enough to disregard temporarily the existence of a Harmony delegation. He set aside his scruples and even ate a
grain-based casserole which had been flavored with lamb.
He couldn't eat without thinking of Linnet and wishing he
could take something back to her. Fruit was served at
meal's end, most of it cooked. He bit into an uncooked
white oval fruit, very sweet but with a disagreeable mushy
texture, as if the fruit were rotten. The next one Marcer
tried was the same size, but rounder, red and delicious. It
would travel well. Maqsood watched. "You have expensive
tastes," he said. "Fortunately your Khan is a rich man;
mine is only a bureaucrat. He must be agreeable to everyone, and entirely halal."

The Sheik's relative blushed; the unman examined his
hands.

Marcer didn't particularly care if alans thought he was
Idryis Khan's lover. Apparently, however, this Maqsood
was partnered with Governor Gordan, Linnet's client.
"Does Gordan like to hurt you?" Marcer asked.

Maqsood frowned. "Those ugly rumors aren't true." He

hunched his shoulders and turned slightly, so he faced the Sheik's relative instead.

Marcer knew better, but now, with an official delegation from the Harmony so close, the governor's peccadilloes were less important. They might even be a basis by which he could bring Linnet to the Harmony as a refugee.

Tea was served. The unman sighed and excused himself. Marcer noted that he left through the door to the women's party.

He sensed attention on him and looked up. Idryis Khan, seated beside Sheik Radi, was watching. He inclined his head toward the door he had mentioned, where he wanted to meet Marcer. Dinner was breaking up; men were moving around to converse with other men. Servants were removing the low tables.

Marcer didn't acknowledge the Khan. This was Sheik Radi's house, and Sheik Radi didn't want Marcer there. All that was necessary to get past the guards was to make Sheik Radi aware he wanted to leave. Marcer put several red fruits for Linnet in a pocket. It bulged a bit, but he was an ignorant Jonist, he might as well act the part. He excused himself and left the table, moving directly to the guarded door, prepared to make a scene.

McCue immediately joined him, as though their walk had been planned. He put his arm around Marcer's waist like an old friend, and even leaned into him, using his considerable weight to make Marcer's path veer. "He'll kill me if you leave," McCue said. "Talk to him first. That's all I ask. Please, Academician."

Marcer glanced back. The Khan was watching intently. He met Marcer's eyes, then raised a glass of tea as though in salute. He let it go. It shattered on the floor. Marcer ELed as it fell. In the bounce-back, glass splinters formed a temporary pattern, like a snowflake, as they rebounded off the floor. The surface tension of the tea droplets gave them the misleading texture of protoplasm, as though Idryis Khan had smashed a thousand helpless creatures.

There was consternation at the main table. The Khan studied Marcer, and only when Marcer nodded did the Khan turn away to make polite apologies to Sheik Radi.

Marcer owed McCue nothing. He had lived up to his agreement to attend the wedding. Regardless, he couldn't let McCue die. He allowed McCue to steer him away from the door. "All right," he said while watching the Khan make superficial conversation. "I'll talk to him, but then you'd damn well better get me out of this trap."

V. The multiplicity of uniqueness.

The courtyard, apparently one of several in Sheik Radi's house, consisted of a formal garden cut by a winding, man-made stream. Foliage was positioned in rows that were perfectly straight except where pierced by the channel for the stream. Marcer took a path paved with colorful mosaic tiles; it went in a straight line through the garden, crossed the stream twice, and ended at the waterfall fountain where the stream originated. A bench and flowers of a type unknown to Marcer were placed near the waterfall. He sat on the bench, unmoved by the unnatural display. Gardens were the domesticates of the plant kingdom. He had never liked them.

He didn't have long to wait. Idryis Khan followed Marcer's route to the fountain. They watched each other as he approached, and when the Khan stopped just in front of Marcer, he stood too close. "Why did you try to leave?" Idryis Khan asked without preamble, in the tone of an offended host.

Marcer's anger was slow to build, but it had been gathering all day. "Why are you holding me prisoner?"

Idryis Khan's next comment was spoken more gently. "I needed to talk to you."

"I have nothing to say. I'm only here because McCue bribed me."

Idryis Khan sat down so close beside Marcer that Marcer felt the warmth of the Khan's body. Conversation would be awkward because Marcer could neither see nor EL without turning toward the Khan. On the narrow bench, that seemed too personal. "How much did he pay?" the Khan asked.

"Two thousand rials." Marcer would not mention Linnet to Idryis Khan.

"You're cheap."

Marcer smiled without friendliness. "You've never filleted fish for ten hours a day." He flexed his shoulders, reminded of their ache. He had worked the entire previous night, then walked the city much of the morning.

"I asked you here to offer you a different job."

"My inclinations haven't changed." Marcer left the bench.

The Khan cleared his throat, though the sound seemed deeper. His hands were fists. "You don't know how to behave respectfully, but you should learn. Quickly."

Marcer's instincts told him to back down, but a Harmony delegation was just kilometers away. "I intend to return home to the Harmony." He EL-ed automatically, having momentarily forgotten Idryis Khan had no aura, none of the fuzzy emotional fringe that the minute movements of a human body created.

The Khan's fists opened. "This is your home, unless I help you leave," he said in a more conciliatory manner. He rose from the bench to stand with Marcer. "I will, if you help me."

Marcer remembered how, on the ship, Idryis Khan had never twitched or squirmed. He didn't use glancing, sideways looks like other men; he rarely scratched or turned in an aimless manner. His hands kept still unless they were performing a definite task. His ability to do nothing over a protracted period of time was impressive and unusual.

"Marc," the Khan said, "I told McCue to bring you here because I need the services of a biologist. I prefer an infidel. I'm offering the job to you."

Marcer laughed, but briefly. It was an excuse. "An alan nobleman has no need for a nonterrestrial field biologist."

"What do you know of my needs?" Idryis Khan's anger was in his voice. He seemed, despite his impassive face, to want to say more, but instead he stalked to the side of the stream. The waterfall splashed into a basin, then a trough led from the basin to several rows of plants as regularly spaced as alan men at prayer. From the shape and color of the plants, they had little in common with Bralava's native life, though it was possible they came from another, ecologically isolated area or continent. The variety of life had drawn Marcer to nonterrestrial biology. Nothing was as capable of surprise; nothing displayed the multiplicity of uniqueness better.

Marcer shrugged, though the Khan was facing the stream.

"I don't want a make-work job from you. I want to get back to where I belong."

"And where is that?" the Khan whispered.

Marcer flushed and didn't answer.

The Khan continued gazing into the water. Marcer looked but saw only a rippled surface, then a thin, orange shape rose up, gulped air, and submerged again. It was too brief a sighting to identify the creature.

"Shouldn't you return to your guests?" Marcer prompted. He wanted to leave and attempt a visit to Government House.

The Khan finally looked at him. "It isn't make-work. To the Harmony, you're an embarrassment. If you leave the Emirates now, it will only be for some independent world on the human frontier, one that will make your work in the fish-processing plant seem comfortable, and your adjustment to life here to have been easy. The Harmony doesn't want you. Even the Independent worlds are tending to limit immigrants to . . . Never mind." He clasped his hands behind his back, returned to the bench, sat, and placed them on his lap. He looked up. "My offer is sincere. I have a use for a professional biologist, *only* a biologist. No . . . affection for me is required. Take the job, Marcer Joseph Brice." He looked steadily at Marcer's face. "The position could well lead you back to the Harmony."

If Idryis Khan had shown emotion, then Marcer might have been convinced. The Khan's tone seemed sincere, even vulnerable, but it had to be a lie. Marcer's deportation had been political. An appeal could succeed. If nothing else, his father would find someone to bribe. He didn't need to trust this violent stranger.

The Khan must have read his face. "You still refuse."

Years of dealing with teachers and superiors who believed he shouldn't be in the Academy had ingrained in Marcer a formal but obstinate style of deference. He bowed to a punctilious depth. "I won't accept any position that would appear to be an adaptation to the Emirates."

"I wish you would have accepted willingly, but you'll take the position." The Khan stared in his disconcertingly assertive way. To return the look was like gazing into animal eyes; Marcer wasn't certain what was behind them.

"Your relatives on Safi haven't met you," the Khan said,

"but they knew about their cousin, the one who made his father so proud by becoming a member of the Jonist Academy despite a certain handicap." Marcer knew what was coming. "Now I understand why you were deported."

"Yes, I'm Altered," Marcer interrupted, to have it over. However much he fought the feeling, to admit that he was Altered made him ashamed. This was particularly difficult because he had hidden the truth. Worse—he'd enjoyed the freedom from being Altered.

The Khan still studied him, perhaps seeing him not as a man, but as an example of an Alteration. "You could be imprisoned for failure to provide the information," he said.

Marcer straightened, only then realizing he had slumped. From what he had seen on Bralava, he could have been imprisoned any time Idryis Khan, a Son of the Prophet, a Marshal in an elite military force, a fleet commander, and a cousin of Aleko Bei, asked. This was a test more than a threat. If he gave in, the Khan would own him. "Then tell the governor," he said. "There is nothing I can do about it."

The Khan blinked. "Explain your Alteration."

Marcer spoke quickly. "I have an extra sense, a limited ability to echo-locate, to EL. It's not as well developed in humans as it is in the terrestrial mammals which acquired it naturally, but it's effective. New Dawn, my homeworld, is dim, and also has a long seasonal darkness in the hemisphere with the only continent. When it was settled, Alterations were popular in the Harmony, even advised for immigrants to worlds rated Extreme. New Dawn Altereds were genetically engineered on the Academy recommendation."

"Echo-location would be a useful skill for a spy."

"What use would it be to EL?" Marcer asked, alarmed. "It's easy to detect and doesn't give information a spy wants. You know I'm not a spy."

"Who really knows another man? You didn't volunteer the truth." The Khan finally looked away.

Marcer breathed easier. Idryis Khan had treated Marcer with a certain courtesy, but there was violence always lurking just beneath his calm. "The truth is that I'm tired of being Altered. And it was hard enough being a Jonist in that compound, without being Altered, too. Then it was too late to mention it without making it a confession."

"A man should know what he is and reconcile himself to it."

Idryis Khan was right, in theory. This was real life. Marcer glanced around the courtyard. A woman in a black chador had entered it from the direction of the party. He must have heard her footsteps, perhaps subliminally. She stopped and seemed to search for them. Marcer assumed this was the bride, but he EL-ed anyway. Even through the covering, it showed him this was a different woman. Like the Khan, she had no aura. Like the Khan? Houris' children were always male. Could this be a houri?

Idryis Khan seemed not to notice her. "I haven't told anyone you're an impostor," the Khan continued. "I won't. In exchange, you will take the position on my staff."

"No."

Impatiently, the Khan said, "You don't have a choice. I didn't get the help I wanted on my trip to the Harmony, but now you're here. Whatever else the Jonist Academies produce, they don't graduate incompetents. You will work for me. You'll start immediately."

He sounded grimly serious. Marcer had to get away from Idryis Khan and this house; the Harmony delegation would be in Shores for only two more days. "My answer is no. You'll have to find someone else for your mysterious project." He bowed.

Before he could rise from the bow, Idryis Khan had him pinned. Marcer's head was on the ground. Idryis Khan's left arm was around Marcer's throat, his fingers pressing against the jugular; his right held Marcer's arms down. Marcer struggled, but the Khan pressed harder, choking him. "You won't leave the house except with me." The Khan's voice had the soft tone of a man speaking to his lover. "You have a job to do. If you don't do it, I'll kill the whore. McCue told me about her. A monstrosity." He released Marcer.

Marcer stumbled, hit his right knee on the ground, but then managed to get upright without falling. He rubbed his throat, watched the Khan, and didn't answer.

The Khan tore a showy lavender-and-yellow flower from its stalk, twirled it between his right index finger and thumb, then shredded it. He tossed the remains into the basin. The fragments circled once, then were captured by the main current and drawn into the stream. They disappeared from view.

"What is it you want a biologist to do?" Marcer asked.

"Investigate Paradise." Idryis Khan noticed the woman. She had come closer. He bowed and held the position. "Mother," he said, "my friend was just returning to the party."

Chapter 7

Elector Sanda Brauna received the Supplicant in a hothouse the Elector maintained within her apartment on Center. Its curved windows looked down on Sucre's surface, although it was difficult to see more than tiny patches of sky through the riotous jungle growth. As the Supplicant waited to be acknowledged she stood as she had been instructed, in a position that was a civilian counterpart of military attention; all the while Brauna reclined on a lounger sipping a frothy pink liquid. The Supplicant knew of the rigid hierarchy among Jonists, but it seemed odd to have a woman as a superior. White-blond, slender, and beautiful, Brauna looked no more than a few years older than the Supplicant, although in the Harmony physiognomy was deceiving. Ted Fields claimed she was more than a hundred years old.

Whether by age, guile, or indecision, Elector Brauna gave no hint as to her opinions. "I've reviewed Researcher Brice's data and listened to Revered Gangler's annotation," Brauna said. Her voice was youthful, too. "Come closer, girl. Tell me about yourself."

The Supplicant began her rehearsed speech. "I've come because of a danger that will eventually affect even the Harmony."

"Stop," Brauna interrupted, holding up her hand, palm flat. "I want to know who you are and why you are here."

They had not told the Supplicant to expect this question. They had not prepared her for the reality of a woman with power, who met her with arrogance but no ceremony and watched her with the direct attention of someone truly interested. It was up to the Supplicant to shift interest to belief, then belief to action.

Revered Gangler cleared his throat, but otherwise the hothouse jungle was silent. Elector Brauna had a stocky, well-muscled guard nearby, but only after the Elector glanced once at him did the Supplicant notice the extremely tall man in a black uniform, his back to the shadowed overhanging foliage, who seemed to take in everything, as though his eyes were cameras. What should she say to explain herself? "I'm a woman. And that's why I'm here."

Sanda Brauna glanced at Revered Gangler. Before Brauna spoke, the Supplicant was sure that she was disappointed. "I would describe myself as more than merely a woman," Brauna said.

The Supplicant smiled nervously. She tried to think of a response that would be true, convincing, and which she could state in the foreign Harmony language. In discussing why he opposed war against Neuland, she had overheard her father say that war should be fought only for honor or advantage.

"You *are* more," the Supplicant said, "and so I come to you because only you, the one Elector who is a woman, can defend the honor of women who are not more. Women in the Emirates have one function—to bear children—and are being usurped even from that. All women, including those here in the Harmony, will respect your guidance and support of their sisters.

"And who am I? I am one of them." The Supplicant bowed, as much to compose herself for the rest of her appeal as to show deference. "With your support, we can show the blindness of men and how they need to . . ."

"I have no complaint against men," Brauna interrupted. She smiled slightly. "At least none from the Emirates."

So much for honor. The Supplicant bowed. "Elector, outside the Harmony, men rule women, a weakness these aliens exploit. Marcer Brice's data is true; the aliens are real. I've seen them. The Harmony government may not care just now what happens in the Emirates, but the Electors of Jonism should. To save the Emirates not only increases Order, it spreads Jonism by showing its superiority: clear thinking compared with alien lies made possible by religious superstitions. An Elector responsible for establishing Jonist Order in the Emirates would have great prestige, greater than that of any other Elector; it's possible that such a person would become chief of the Electors. And political advantages often lead to material ones."

Revered Gangler gasped. She'd been impertinent in suggesting that any of the six Electors would or could become the leader of the others, but the Supplicant had remembered another of her father's dictums: Every member of a council of equals dreams of becoming dictator of the rest.

Sanda Brauna smiled disarmingly. "Tell me more, my dear."

I. Spoil.

Nisa never knew how long she stared at her ruined dresses. She sat on the edge of the dressing-table chair and watched her hands clench and clutch each other. Strong, muscular hands, accustomed to painstaking work, they'd masked the fact that she was ultimately helpless. She hadn't even managed to kill the creature.

But she would.

Roused from her stupor by images of violent death, Nisa shivered. Her hands were cold. She glimpsed herself in the mirror. A strange, pasty smile was fixed on her face; her eyes were blackened by smeared mascara. She saw the ravaged dresses behind her and rifled through the dressing-table drawer. She needed something, anything, with which to finally execute Qadira's creature. All she found was useless feminine frippery.

She remembered her art supplies, stacked in boxes in her bedroom. She hurried there, only to find their contents spilled across the floor. The creature seemed to know what she valued. Broken jars of paint had rolled, spreading color randomly, so that her floor looked like an abstract painting by a madman.

Nisa's shoes clung to the sticky floor. She had walked into a puddle. Black paint was dyeing the margins of her dress; her shoes were ruined. It didn't matter. She knelt in the paint as she searched through her tools: spatulas, paintbrushes, palette knives. Nisa picked up a fairly sharp knife, coated with a yellow glaze which smelled of oil paint, but perhaps wasn't. Unconcerned, she hefted the knife in her hand and retraced her steps, calling for the creature. Nothing came.

Nisa listened, then heard the click of its nails on tile; she hurried toward the sound and found it near the women's stairs. The creature blinked its huge eyes as it saw her, and rumbled like approaching thunder. It sat down on its rump.

Nisa held the knife like a paintbrush. "You had to ruin everything." She spoke as if the thing understood, and it did seem to listen. "I was leaving," Nisa said reasonably. "I would have been gone tonight. All you had to do was stay out of my way." She felt the knife's sharp edge with her thumb but winced as she almost cut herself.

It licked its right front foot absently, keeping its attention on Nisa, but then the creature moaned like a sick child. It lurched onto its hind legs. Standing, albeit awkwardly, it was a head shorter than Nisa, but pregnancy left it poorly balanced. Its belly protruded; every movement seemed difficult.

It had moved well enough to ruin her dresses. She extended the knife like a sword.

The creature vomited, spewing vile, lumpy liquid at Nisa. The stench was a nightmare. Nisa jumped back. It didn't reach her.

The thing glared from dark saucer eyes. It seemed to have difficulty with camouflage. Most of its skin was gray, but its belly was a livid red. The belly undulated. Qadira's creature wailed at a pitch so high that it set Nisa's teeth on edge, so high that for a moment Nisa couldn't hear it.

Alien distress was still obviously distress. Nisa recognized the cause. The thing was in labor.

Nisa looked at the knife in her hand, then down the staircase. Guests were celebrating her marriage. She had a husband who called her an acre. Her father wouldn't take her back, and if he did, she wouldn't want to live her life as Qadira's foil. To run, though, meant to leave everything she knew. And everyone. Was freedom worth loneliness and fear?

Yes. She wanted to be a person, not a woman.

Besides, all of her dresses were destroyed. If she went down, her cousins would whisper, her aunt would fuss, and Qadira would taunt her. Hulweh would stand by her side, but Hulweh was an old maid, an oddball with less status than Nisa.

All she had to do was leave. If she waited, her new home was far outside Shores, and she didn't know what precautions Idryis Khan would take. The time to act was now.

Qadira's creature didn't matter. All it had done was strengthen her resolve. Nisa started toward the stairs.

The creature lurched at her. Nisa jumped away. Though slow and awkward, the thing had vicious teeth and an unsatisfied will to harm her. Did it understand that the pills she had given it had made it sick? Was its cunning intelligence enough that it knew she had caused its confinement?

Nisa extended the knife. "Get out of my way, ugly thing. I'll kill you if you don't. You deserve it." She moved sideways to go around it to the stairs. The thing followed her with its eyes. When she was close, it lunged, jaws open, ready to bite.

Nisa thrust the knife clumsily forward. The creature fell back onto four legs, lowered its head to protect itself, and snarled a sound like grease sizzling.

It crouched; it fixed her with a chilling stare. Nisa took another step. It attacked again, fearlessly. It didn't seem to realize that the extra weight of pregnancy had slowed it. Nisa used that advantage. She kicked it as it came at her. It stopped momentarily. Her knife connected and dug into its flesh. It repeated a high-pitched noise and hopped clumsily sideways.

Nisa still held the knife. Her grip tightened as the creature moved. The knife ripped along its belly until the screaming creature went too far and Nisa pulled it out.

The foul smell exuded from the cut reminded Nisa of her slashed dresses. She held the knife ready to thrust again and studied her adversary.

The wound was healing.

She couldn't take her eyes away. Like a zipper closing, the line of ripped flesh mended itself as she watched.

Except for its panting, Qadira's pet looked untouched within minutes, and while it healed, it snapped viciously at her each time she attempted to reach the stairs.

"I have to leave," Nisa whispered to herself.

As though it understood, the creature twisted, plunged heavily at her, and tried to bite. Nisa screamed and escaped.

It raised itself onto two legs. Its belly rippled, but it shook its head, then leapt suddenly at Nisa. This time it reached her. Its teeth grazed her arm. She barely felt it.

It didn't attack again. It staggered away, its belly heaving. Nisa examined the bite, which was shallow but oozing.

There was no pain even when she touched the wound, as though her arm was anesthetized.

She still held the gory knife in her hand. Nisa raised it and charged the creature, screaming her own name like a battle cry.

It didn't try to run. She struck, sliding the knife into the thing's gut and pulling it down through the creature's flesh as easily as cutting through butter. It was a much deeper wound than the first. Intestines slithered out the rent in its skin, though the wound edges were healing. Nisa struck again. And again. It made no attempt to dodge.

Red blood splashed from the wound. Blood covered Nisa's arm to her elbow and spattered her clothes. Alien organs gushed through the opening. Another thing emerged, too: a boneless, limblike appendage. She stopped slashing at Qadira's creature and stared, trying to make sense of it. It looked like a newborn talish.

Totsi was being reborn from the body of her killer. Nisa dropped the knife and scooted back.

The talish wriggled half in and half out of the closing wound. Its mother—Qadira's creature—looked at its own gaping middle and licked the visible portion of the talish. The gesture seemed curious, not maternal.

Talish were native to Bralava, not Paradise. Talish were born from talish, not from creatures like this thing.

The gash was much bigger than the healed first cut Nisa had made. The edges tried to mend themselves, but the protruding talish and the creature's own slimy, stinking intestines were in the way, blocking any closure of the wound. The talish struggled forward; as it made headway there was a nauseating sound of flimsy tissue tearing. Eventually, the talish humped, forming a head just as Totsi had been accustomed to do.

As the newborn struggled to reach the light, Nisa saw another talish behind it, possibly a full litter.

"Stupid."

Nisa looked up. Qadira was at the top of the stairway, her chador open, her hijab veil pushed down.

Her creature whined and struggled to reach the houri. Qadira rushed to it. She dropped to her knees beside her pet and put her arms around the thing, cradling it, careless of its wound or the talish struggling to be born from Nisa's crude cesarean. "Stupid," she crooned.

Blood loss and the rents in its belly would already have killed any other being. Nisa watched Qadira caress her creature with the tenderness of a mother comforting her child. Her pet was dying. Qadira knew it. Dry-eyed, she watched Nisa and, horribly, her expression was the same eternally pleasant one she always had.

Nisa picked up her knife again. "I killed it to protect myself. It came at me!" She waved the knife.

Always slow of speech, Qadira didn't answer but as she embraced her pet, her eyes never left Nisa's face.

The talish fell out of its unnatural mother with a wet plop.

"Spoil." Qadira shoved the squirming innocent away, and when her pet tried to retrieve it, she tightened her hold on it to prevent movement. Fragile cilia, the threadlike filaments on the bottom of the newborn talish, waved randomly, searching for purchase on the ground.

"Spoil?" Nisa repeated. There were baby machines, but they were a bad substitute for a mother's womb; she'd never heard of a surrogate creature. Nisa edged around the creatures from Paradise, one beautiful, one ugly, trying to reach the stairs.

The creature shuddered and pushed itself hard against Qadira. She turned on Nisa. "Go die you bad, you rot, you bad match wife!"

The creature's blood was being absorbed into Qadira's dark chador and the pastel gown underneath. Her clothes were as ruined as Nisa's. Her clothes. That was an idea. It would be only fitting to take dresses from Qadira. Nisa smiled at the thought of Qadira's rage. "That creature attacked me. It ruined my clothes. If I've killed it, I was justified."

The creature whined. The high-pitched noise made Nisa's head ache.

"I talk of Khan. He kills you, I say." Qadira reached over her pet, extending her empty, bloody hand to Nisa. "You see, you die today, you bad. Go."

Talish were usually speechless, but the newborn let out a thin scream, looking for comfort from its mother while lost in a pool of the creature's blood and poison vomit.

"The Khan?" Nisa hesitated. "You think he'll kill me on your whim?" She tossed her head, though she remembered only too well that she was merely an acre to him. Nisa sidled around her on the way to the stairs.

Qadira looked impassively at the mewling talish cub, then swiftly picked it up and banged it hard against the floor, smashing it with apparent moral and physical ease. Blood trickled from the wound. "Spoil," she said. "Nisa spoil. Sons do for mothers." She made a loud, calling sound that sent a shiver of fear through Nisa.

Nisa threw the knife at Qadira. She'd never thrown a knife before and hadn't aimed. It tumbled like a broken airframe falling from the sky and skittered across the floor. Qadira didn't flinch, but she stopped her clamor. "Sons do for mothers," she repeated.

Her creature moaned, and she cradled it. "Stupid," she murmured, and hummed bits of an ancient lullaby.

Nisa walked determinedly around her and her dying creature. Qadira didn't try to intervene, but as Nisa started down the steps, Qadira's hostile voice stopped her one last time. "Go die. Run."

Nisa ran.

II. Flagrante delicto.

Marcer went directly to Sheik Radi. "Your son-in-law is holding me captive at this party," he told the Sheik. "I want to leave. This is your house. Please let me."

"No." Sheik Radi turned his back on Marcer and resumed his conversation with a white-robed ulama, an alan cleric. The cleric frowned at Marcer, then spurned him, too.

Marcer clutched Sheik Radi's arm. "Why not? You know why he wants me." He slipped sexual innuendo into his voice.

Sheik Radi turned and smiled tightly. "Indeed I do, and I approve. He explained at dinner." The Sheik nodded at the ulama.

The ulama, an older man with a dark, weathered face, frowned again. "A worthy endeavor," he said solemnly. "Shame on you for your unwillingness to help."

"What?" Marcer glanced around the room, then EL-ed. Idryis Khan had not returned. "What did he tell you he wants?"

Sheik Radi sighed. "To have sons." He turned again to

the ulama. "It was my one qualm about this marriage, that the holiness of a Son would prevent my daughter from bearing children." He looked back at Marcer. "You are an Academy-trained biologist. You Jonists are clever. It is your duty as a man to help. That you've refused requires us to compel you."

"The Khan is lying to you," Marcer said. "He will humiliate your daughter."

Sheik Radi's face reddened. He started to raise his arm as if to strike Marcer, but the ulama came between them. "Not a guest," he said.

"That an infidel would accuse a Son of the Prophet, God bless and keep him, of lying!" Sheik Radi said. "And at the Khan's own wedding party! If you weren't my guest, I would teach you respect. If you don't mind your manners, you will be locked in a room until the Khan is ready to fetch you." With that, Sheik Radi and the ulama turned their backs on Marcer and marched self-righteously away.

Marcer had become socially invisible, though he caught guests casting covert looks at him. He stayed near the edge of the party, trying to think of a way out of the trap into which McCue had led him. He needed a diversion, but there was no one who would help him. Perhaps he could get himself thrown out of the house if he were sufficiently obnoxious. He wished he could pretend drunkenness; that would offend alans.

McCue was keeping a low profile. He was still at his table, blowing into a glass of hot tea while making polite conversation with another trader. Marcer strolled over, then crouched on his heels just behind McCue. "Get me out of here, you bastard," he whispered in a low voice he hoped was menacing. "He's not the only one who can threaten."

McCue's companion pretended not to hear, despite his pained, polite expression. McCue smiled into his glass. "But I believe *him*."

Marcer hadn't planned it, but he reached around McCue's fat belly and jerked the tea glass from McCue's hands. He dumped the hot tea into McCue's lap.

McCue screeched as his groin burned. He jumped up and away from the table, holding his pants as far from his skin as he could. "You . . . you . . . you . . ." he said between squawks of pain. He hopped from leg to leg, squealing like a pig on a grill.

Marcer gazed dispassionately at his handiwork, unashamed. Guests and servants rushed to help McCue. Marcer stood aside, hoping his uncivilized conduct would get him thrown out, but the Sheik was smiling, not apoplectic. Marcer had hurt a man no one liked.

How to get out and to Government House? Marcer paced, careless of observers. He noted the doors: one for servants, one for the front entrance hall, one to the women's party. The old unman with whom he'd been seated alternated between the two parties; Marcer watched him leave yet again.

With support from two servants, McCue left the party through the servants' exit. Marcer wished he had kept closer to McCue.

Idryis Khan returned and went directly to Sheik Radi. The Sheik smiled, but he seemed disturbed; Marcer was too far to eavesdrop and he didn't want to move closer to Idryis Khan. There was no denying his animal magnetism, but the man was a volcano waiting to erupt. If Marcer escaped, he would be furious. Marcer's only safety lay with the Harmony commission.

Marcer had been staring, and Idryis Khan looked his way. The Khan nodded at Marcer as though they were in league. Marcer walked away without acknowledging the Khan, pacing the room, listening to the exclusively male voices and feeling deprived; half the human race was missing. Unmen couldn't fill the vacancy; they were too like oversize children.

Women! The alans were unreasonable on the subject of protecting them. Marcer took a glass of tea from a passing servant. An obvious attempt to inspect the feminine pulchritude of the women's party would be obnoxious. It could incite the alans to expel Marcer from the house.

Using artful indirection, Marcer made his way closer to the door to the women's party. He had to be outrageous, so that even the Khan couldn't control the alan crowd's reaction. He was almost at the door when a servant waylaid him. "Can I help you, sir?"

"Where's the toilet?" Marcer was purposely loud. The prim guests looked away, embarrassed by bodily needs. Alans! Their very politeness worked to his advantage.

The servant indicated the door the servants used. Marcer nodded, but stayed where he was. After a brief hesitation, the servant went on his way.

To rush at the forbidden door would alert the men. Marcer EL-ed. The pattern of men in the room reminded him of alan prayers. He sensed a message hidden in their movements. He EL-ed again. Three guests wearing the uniform of the Khan's Descent Assault Force glanced his way; so did the Khan. Odd. He wondered if the three were also Sons.

The women would be frightened. Even Linnet, a prostitute and bolder than most alan women, feared being seen. Marcer walked several steps away from the door as he considered the unavoidable harm to innocents. He was procrastinating.

Enough time had passed since he EL-ed that the Khan and his men no longer seemed focused on him. He took the last few meters to the door at a hurried walk, yanked open the door and went through.

Behind him, someone tittered nervously. Someone cursed. Men came running. Marcer broke into a run, too. They wouldn't be able to stop him in time. He was in a vestibule or hall. Another door was opposite.

He opened the door and heard high-pitched feminine voices. Except for Linnet, he hadn't spoken to a woman since being dumped on Bralava, and he suddenly felt shy. This room was a smaller version of the men's, but more ornate and therefore less stately. Two all-female couples danced to recorded music. Many women were elderly, which to Harmony perceptions seemed a matter of medical neglect.

The door from the men's party opened. Marcer entered the women's party, closing and locking the door behind him. He EL-ed, to get his bearings.

A woman noticed him. She screamed. Other women looked. More screamed; some shouted at him. Women seized napkins to hide their faces. Two raised the hems of their dresses over their heads. One withered matron slumped to the floor in a faint. Two very beautiful ones, who had been alone at a table, stood, looked curiously at him, and came forward.

There was no need to go farther inside, but Marcer couldn't leave until the men found him in flagrante delicto.

He kept his eyes down so as not to panic the women any more than he already had. He would be evicted from the house or he would not.

An unman servant rushed Marcer, yelling for him to leave. He tried to push Marcer out the door, but was too much smaller than Marcer to be more than an annoyance. The unman realized when he couldn't open the door that it was locked. He released the catch.

Men burst into the room. The women's screams worsened. They turned their backs to the men and surged into the farthest corners of the room. They tripped over each other as well as over the tables, scrambling to escape. A few lost their wraps, exposing themselves in their effort to avoid their saviors. The two women who had come forward ran away with the others.

Three men pounced on Marcer and held him while another punched him in the face and the groin. The men wouldn't let Marcer hunch over or fall. "Get him out of here!" a clear-headed woman shouted.

Good, Marcer thought. He gave no resistance as they dragged him into the vestibule and pressed him against the wall. Surrounded, Marcer stared into the wild eyes of men who minutes earlier had been tranquil, and was frightened by their quick descent to violence. "I'll leave," he said. "I'm sorry." He'd gone too far. They would kill him.

The shouting stopped. Like a champion entering the ring, Idryis Khan walked through the parting men, directly to Marcer. His expression was as impassive as ever, but his fixed eyes were those of a maniac. Marcer fought to get away, but he was securely held. More and more men poured into the vestibule, but everyone hung back. Idryis Khan was the principal victim; his bride had been despoiled by Marcer's eyes; his wedding party had been defiled. They waited for him.

Marcer turned his head away from the Khan as though to shield himself from a blow. It didn't come. Marcer dared a glance at the Khan. His face had a fixed grimace. His lips moved, but he didn't speak. He seemed as likely to howl. As if from afar, Marcer heard a high-pitched scream. The Khan shuddered.

"Let me leave," Marcer begged. "Let me go."

Marcer's plea snapped the Khan's restraint. His right hand became a fist. Marcer struggled to get free and failed.

With the deliberation of a paid executioner, Idryis Khan punched Marcer's jaw. Next, he kicked Marcer in the gut, then another hammer punch that cracked Marcer's head against the wall. Marcer's vision darkened. His ears rang. His head filled with jagged, random, senseless noise. False bounce-backs made him sense a huge hole, just in front of him. With careful aim, Idryis Khan kicked Marcer squarely in the groin.

The Khan stepped back. Other men took their turns, punching and kicking. If they had held any clubs or weapon, Marcer would have died.

Marcer couldn't see; he couldn't EL. He hadn't the strength to spit out his blood and it dribbled from the broken corner of his mouth. Eventually, much later than he wished for it, he was pounded into unconsciousness and knew nothing more.

III. Leaving home.

Filthy, reeking of the creature's nasty odor, Nisa stopped on the bottom stair. She needed clothing, men's clothing. To reach the servants' quarters, where their clothes would be, she had to cross the kitchen. The kitchen was also the quickest way out, but today it would be bustling with cooks. Designed to protect women from strangers' eyes, the house was not easy for a woman to leave.

"Nisa!" Ziller came around the corner from the kitchen, clearly having intended to check on her upstairs. She murmured a brief prayer of thanksgiving.

Ziller clapped his hands together. "You're not covered. Where have you been? Your guests are . . ." He stopped, stared, sniffed, then took a step back. His nose wrinkled, and he eyed her dress incredulously. "What happened?"

"There isn't time to explain." She had to be gone before they missed her; Ziller already had. "Ziller, if you truly are my friend, get me men's clothes. Something from the servants. Please." Her hands touched her necklace and she remembered the need for money; her hoard of jewelry was packed and on its way to the Khan's house. His last gift would have to be enough to buy her free of womanhood and him.

Ziller gaped. "What happened?" he asked again.

Surprised by her own impatience, she shook her head. "I have to leave or the Khan will kill me. That's what the houri said. I believe her, but even if it isn't true, I want to get away."

"Did you kill her?" Ziller moved back from Nisa, looking down the kitchen corridor. For help?

Her dress was foul and bloody. Her right arm ached; she had stabbed with vehemence. Her left arm was still bleeding. She had no regrets. "No. I killed her pet. Help me, Zil?"

Ziller bit his lip, dithering.

"Please? I need you. Who's in the kitchen?"

"Stay here." Ziller left without declaring himself. Either he would return with her husband and father, who would compel her obedience, or he wouldn't. Nisa sighed and collapsed onto the bottom step. Her dress, wet with the creature's blood, was clammy against her legs. She leaned against the rail and looked up. Qadira would come down once her creature was dead. Nisa wouldn't escape if Qadira raised an alarm. "Hurry," she whispered.

The Qur'an forbade what she was about to do. The moment she impersonated a man or unman, she would be subject to arrest. There should be no coercion in marriage, the Prophet, God's blessings and peace be upon him, had said. She had been coerced. She hung her head, aware she was rationalizing. She hadn't been coerced, she'd simply been born female.

Ziller returned carrying a small bundle of clothes. He didn't hand the bundle to her. Nisa pulled herself upright by holding the rail. "Nisette, are you certain?" Ziller asked. "Do you know what you're doing? It's not too late. Go back to the Khan. Submit."

It would be easy to submit and let events take their course, but however much submission was extolled as faith, for her it would be defeat. "No." Nisa's only models for boldness were male. She pretended she was a man and tried to play the part of her father, even deepening her voice. "I've planned for this. I know what I'm doing. Just help me get out of the house. Who's in the kitchen? Is Gidie?" She couldn't trust any of the house servants.

"Where will you go?"

Nisa's knowledge of the city was limited to what she had seen from covered carriages and canal boats. She'd never walked anywhere. City maps were wildly inaccurate. Well, she would learn as she went. "First to the suq to sell this." She touched the necklace.

Ziller studied her face. Nisa wanted to shake him and tell him to hand over the clothes, but Ziller was a friend and knowledgeable. "Is there no other way, Nisa?" he asked. "Life in the city is dangerous. There is no assurance of any happy end once you step through the door."

She took his hand, only then noticing that hers was sticky with blood. He didn't draw back. "If I leave with my new husband, then he'll kill me. I believe that. Houris get what they want. But even if he didn't, Ziller, so long as my life continues as it has—with my father or a husband—I can't be who I am."

"You're talking nonsense." Ziller sighed, but handed her the clothes. "From the laundry," he said. "Lightly soiled, but much faster to find and unlikely to be missed for days. Hurry. Some commotion started just after I left the party. Everyone in the kitchen has gone to watch. You won't be seen if you're quick."

Nisa started to hug him, then remembered the condition of her clothes. "You're wonderful."

"And you need a bath. You won't get one on the streets. Avoid public baths, of course." Ziller leaned forward, careful to avoid contact with her filthy clothes, and gave her a peck on the cheek, then he withdrew a small purse from his pocket. It jingled as he handed it to her. She didn't protest—it would have been foolish—but there were tears in her eyes. His, too. "Nisa, be careful," he said.

"One last thing, Zil." She took a deep breath. "Do you know how to contact the kitchen express?"

He didn't answer. "If you've nowhere to go, then get a message to me. I'll try to help. But not immediately, dear girl. I'm sure they'll watch Hulweh once you're gone, and me." He glanced back toward the kitchen. "Now, be quick! Change clothes! Go! I have to return, or they'll know I helped." He left without a backward look.

Nisa, holding the clothes at arm's length to keep them clean, ran the short distance to the servants' washroom, just outside the kitchen. She was lucky. It was empty.

The door had no lock, but she pulled it tightly closed. Windowless, the only light was above the tarnished mirror. The deep sink had hot water, though the lavatory was an old-fashioned hole in the floor. It opened over a cesspool, which could be flushed into the canals. The room smelled as though a flushing of the bunghole was overdue, but it smelled better than she did.

Nisa stripped off her filthy dress with difficulty; drying blood made it adhere to her. She kicked it into a corner and only then did she look at what Ziller had brought: a pair of loose fitting pants and a long-sleeved tunic overshirt, both in thick, white cotton which would hide some of her curves. The shirt was smudged; the rest was wrinkled but fairly clean.

The pants had a side pocket, but it wasn't deep. Worried that the jewelry, which she couldn't wear, would fall out, she stuffed it instead into her underpants and giggled weakly, wondering if the bulge was manly. She pulled the pants on, then looked down. Her shoes would give her away. Ziller hadn't provided others, so she kicked them off. Better to be barefoot. Fortunately, she hadn't painted her toenails.

She glimpsed herself in the mirror. Her profile revealed a womanly figure. She tore through her discarded clothes and found an unstained portion of her white slip. She ripped it along its seams until she had a usable rectangle. That she wrapped around her breasts, binding them flat. With the extra material tucked in, she looked chubby. She pulled the tunic over her head. Done.

She was a boy—until she looked into the mirror. Makeup and long, elaborately styled hair showed a girl in servant's clothing.

Nisa wet the hand towel and scoured her face with hot water. There was no time to be gentle. Her eyes smarted as diluted color dribbled into her eyes. She squeezed them tight and rubbed them, her lips, and her cheeks. Overlooked, her earrings caught on the rag and she nearly pulled the left one out. She bit her lip and took both earrings off, thrusting them into her pocket.

How much time had passed?

She needed scissors. The kitchen. She stood motionless, listening, and heard only her heart. She cracked the door open and held the doorknob in her hand, ready to pull the door closed if voices were near. Still nothing.

She looked one last time into the mirror. Her face was red from scrubbing and dark beneath her eyes, but she didn't look like a woman on her wedding day. Her left earlobe had bled. She wiped it with the edge of her sleeve. Her upper body looked thick, but not curvaceous. "You're fine," she whispered to encourage herself, and started to open the door.

Her ruined dress, shoes, and underskirts were in a corner. The streaked hand towel was at the sink. She closed the door again and one by one dropped every evidence of her presence into the bunghole. The dress shimmered at the bottom, but with luck it would become covered with muck or flushed out before it was found.

Three or four minutes had passed. The servants might have returned to the kitchen. There was only one way to find out. She opened the door. Silence. She tiptoed, barefoot, into the hall. No one was there. Head down, she walked into the kitchen.

Two of the catering cooks hired for the party were working at a table on the far side of the kitchen; their backs were to her. If they noticed her entrance at all, they didn't turn. She went directly to Gidie's desk, opened the drawer, and removed his scissors. Kitchen shears would have been better, but she didn't know where they were kept. She held the scissors behind her back and walked sideways, to the huge, low drain where major cleaning was performed. She leaned over it, hiding her head as much as possible, and turned on the water.

Nisa took long hanks of her hair and clipped it raggedly, in only six cuts, to about the length of the nape of her neck. Around her ears, she lopped it shorter, but still left enough to cover her pierced earlobes and her torn ear. Men usually wore their hair clipped closer to the scalp and much neater, but this would do. When she was done she used her hands to help the long, dark hair flow down the drain. She rinsed her face again and set the scissors atop a counter. Done.

Nisa straightened. The two hired cooks were hard at work decorating something. She'd been very lucky, so far. She ran her fingers through her cropped hair. Her head felt light. She shook it, as pleased as if she'd set a burden down.

The delivery door to the canal was already open. Nisa walked out of the house.

The kitchen dock was screened from the formal canalside entrance twenty meters away by a low wall and a border

of potted bushes. If not for them, the mob of angry men
would have seen her. Instead, she was out of sight when
she heard voices. One was her father's. The words were
inaudible, but she recognized his anger.

Greatly daring, Nisa crept to the low wall and, staying
down, she peered between the bushes. The focus of the
enraged men was a man lying motionless on the ground.
As she watched, Nisa's brother, Karim, kicked him. The
body, perhaps even a corpse, was driven a bit closer to
the water—Karim's intention. A fat man protested but was
shouted down.

Made curious by the violence, Nisa brushed the leaves
aside and tried to identify the victim. She couldn't. He'd
worn blue, but the suit was as ruined as her dresses. Even
crumpled on the ground, he looked to have been a tall
man; he was curled to protect his midsection. One limp
hand reached in her direction. An elderly guest kicked the
victim again. The prone man was a short distance from a
tumble into the filthy water.

Despite Qadira's threat, Nisa had supposed Idryis Khan
was better than this mob. She was wrong. He spat sharp
words at the fat man and paced the dock like a dog looking
for a way to attack through a fence. She didn't see him
strike the victim, however.

The men were losing interest in their stationary target.
Attention shifted to the fat man. Nisa wished she could
have sketched the moment he realized no one would support
him. He raised his shoulders in a slight shrug, acquiescing
to the mob. It wasn't enough. When the fat man tried
to back away from the dock, Karim grabbed him. Men
shouted encouragement. For what, she couldn't hear.

Before long the servants, now hanging about the rear of
the crowd, would return to work. If she hadn't left by then,
she would be discovered. The kitchen dock also had street
access, so streetside deliveries could be made directly to
the kitchen. It was a neighborhood of mansions; she would
be conspicuous, but there was no choice. She needed to go
around the house, then walk to the east end, a poor district.
Nisa started to back away from the bushes. There was a
splash. She had to look.

The mob's victim was in the canal and as she watched,
Idryis Khan shoved the fat man into the water, too. The
Khan's shout was loud enough that she heard it easily.

"Then save him yourself!" Men laughed. She never would understand men.

The unconscious man first sank, then bobbed to the surface. He floated on his back, moving with the slow current toward the kitchen dock. When waves from the fat man's fall caught him, for the first time he struggled to stay afloat. His inefficient movements weren't much help. The fat man, however, swam better than Nisa had expected. He reached the other's body, checked him, and dragged him with the current toward the kitchen dock. Nisa scooted backward. On the main dock, men laughed, joked, and straggled into the house. The last to leave was Idryis Khan. He watched the two men in the water until it was certain the fat man would manage to bring them both to the kitchen dock. Only then did he rejoin the guests.

Nisa had delayed too long. A caterer came from the kitchen, carrying a stack of cartons. He saw her, and said, "Stop sunning yourself, boy. There's work to do."

He thought she was a spare, a dayman hired for the party; he hadn't seen through her disguise. Nisa grinned. The caterer frowned and shoved the cartons at her. "Here. Put these on my flattop. The white one." The man indicated one of the docked boats, then went back to the kitchen.

Why not? The cartons were bulky but light, probably empty. She carried them to the barge and placed them on the deck, then looked out over the water. A boat would be faster and much less conspicuous, except for the theft itself. This one smelled of cinnamon. She hadn't eaten, and wondered if there were leftovers, then realized her stupidity. She had to go.

The barge rocked. "Hey! Boy!" Nisa looked over the side. The fat man was holding on to the barge. Only his head showed, and occasionally he glanced down and sideways, presumably to the tall man he'd saved.

Afraid her voice would give her away, Nisa didn't answer. She hunched her shoulders and started off the boat. "Come here!" the fat man screamed. "Help us up! I'll pay."

She went back, pointed at the ladder built into the pilings of the dock, and left the barge again. The epoxy-embedded wood was rough under her bare feet. Walking far would be difficult.

"Boy! Come here!" The fat man's head bobbed up and down in the wake of a passing powerboat. Too tired to climb up, he clung with one arm to a rung of the ladder; his other arm supported the barely conscious victim. That man was riding low in the water; the fat man was having trouble getting himself, let alone another man, up the ladder. The victim's eyes were open and staring dully. Nisa abruptly recognized him. He was the man with the accent, to whom the Khan had described her as an acre. Well. The Khan had seemed to like *him*. Imagine what he might have done to *her*!

The victim would drown unless she helped. Maybe both men would. Nisa bit her lip and looked up at the sky, then back to the water. She was being foolish. She should think only of herself. Nisa went to the top of the ladder, unable simply to walk away. She lay across the dock to brace herself and reached down for the fat man. So close, the water stank of fish and garbage.

"Haul him up," the fat man said. "You," he angrily ordered the victim, on whose behalf he'd been tossed into the water, "Raise your arms, Brice, or I'll just let you go."

Brice groaned. His battered face was ugly with incipient bruises; his left eye was swollen closed. His head wobbled, but he gritted his teeth—his mouth was battered and his lips were cut—and raised one arm out of the water. His wrist was limp.

"Grab the ladder!" the fat man yelled.

Brice tried. His hand slapped against the dock. Nisa stretched, reached for it, and missed. His arm fell back into the water. Slowly, he raised it again.

"Get up!" The fat man was furious. As the crest of the next wave hit, he shoved Brice up, though it meant releasing his support for Brice's head. Nisa grabbed and grasped one of Brice's arms. He was heavier than anything she'd ever lifted.

"Pull!"

Brice slipped out of Nisa's grip as the current sucked him down. He kicked feebly and stayed afloat. Their eyes met. He struggled through the water and lifted his arm to her. She leaned farther out, sure he would die if she didn't bring him in.

The fat man moved aside to give Brice better access to the ladder. Nisa didn't think Brice had the strength left to use it. His fingers closed around her wrist, and she was happily surprised when, with his other hand, he grabbed a rung. She seized his arm with her free hand, then shifted position so she held his wrist in both her hands instead of depending on his weak grip. He leaned against the ladder, resting, while the fat man swore foul curses and clung to the ladder, too.

Brice couldn't heave himself up from the water. The fat man couldn't help. "When I say 'three,' then do your best," she whispered, having read in one of Hulweh's Harmony romances that a whisper gave less information about the speaker's voice.

"One." She shifted position so that, rather than hanging over the edge, she was crouched on the deck, ready to pull him up.

"Two." Brice looked at her. His mouth was open and his one good eye blinked.

The wave arrived. "Three." With every bit of strength she could muster, Nisa tugged and dragged him up. He scraped against the edge of the dock; the fat man shoved from below, more unsteadying than helpful. Brice himself managed to grab a mooring post as he rose. Among the three of them, he was pitched onto the dock with his legs dangling, feet just above the water.

"Good," Nisa said, as though encouraging a child. She staggered back. Her shirt was damp. She hunched her shoulders and kept her gaze modestly down, only now realizing these men had seen her face.

"Well, finish the job," the fat man called irritably. Brice exhaled noisily and scuttled the rest of the way up. He lay like a landed fish, shivering and coughing.

The fat man called, "Help me up, too!"

Brice was in the way and Nisa doubted she could move a man his size outside the water. He looked up, then gave her a faint smile. He rolled his one good eye, sufficiently alert to have heard the fat man, then wiggled out of the way like a weary snake.

Nisa went to the top of the ladder again, leaned down and extended both hands. The fat man nearly pulled her into the canal before she got free of him. Better braced, she signaled. Working with her, the fat man climbed and was pulled from the water. Landed, he sank onto the dock next to Brice, then rolled onto his back and sat up. He wiped his face, glanced at his ruined clothes, and patted them as though to dry them.

"McCue?" Brice said. He lay supine on the dock. "Thanks."

The fat man, McCue, snorted. Water dripped off his nose. Both men were beardless; both seemed foreign. Nisa tried to remember the guest list. McCue was the name of one of the four infidel traders the Khan had invited. She didn't recall anyone named Brice.

Not that it mattered. They weren't her guests anymore. Elated—she'd just saved a man's life; possibly two—Nisa still hadn't escaped. Soon someone would look for the bride. She started to leave, intending to go around the house.

"Don't you want your payment?" McCue called.

She couldn't seem peculiar, but the money was irrelevant to speed. Nisa went back and held out her hand. Using his hands to hoist himself up from the deck, McCue stood, reached into a waterlogged pocket and withdrew a coin. Rather than simply give it to her, he took her hand and examined it.

Her nails! They were polished a pale pink, almost a natural color, yet obviously not. They were trim and smooth; her hands were small. Afraid she'd been discovered, Nisa said nothing. McCue placed the coin in her palm. "A girly-boy?" he asked.

She didn't answer.

"I don't give a damn." McCue shrugged. "Even dirty you're rather attractive. If you're not one, you should consider it. Meanwhile, take us down the canal into the suq district, and I'll pay you three hundred. Generous, but I don't want to walk through the house or try to hire a hack streetside."

She shook her head.

"It'll be half an hour's work, at most. Four hundred."

Nisa cleared her throat. This was an opportunity to leave, if not unobtrusively, then in a manner unlikely to be challenged. It would give her additional cash, delaying the time she would need to sell the conspicuous jewelry. "No boat," she whispered.

"Borrow one of the Sheik's," McCue said. "Just return it later today. Five hundred."

"I'll do it," she said, lowering her pitch as much as she could.

McCue helped Brice to his feet, and they tottered after Nisa. The tall man limped and grunted, but managed better than she had expected. She wondered if he'd been playing dead when he'd been so still.

She led them to the boat the unmen were allowed to use to visit family or friends; the shopping barge was too big, and its absence would be immediately spotted. McCue helped his tall friend settle into the prow, then sat down himself on the narrow plank that was the only real seat, except for the steersman's. He left that for Nisa. She boarded cautiously. The boat was smaller than any she'd ridden. It rocked underfoot from their unsteady weight. She sat in the steersman's seat. The two men waited.

Nisa didn't know how to start an engine. There was a handle-thing and two buttons, none labeled. She stared, hoping the answer would come. She had never driven anything mechanical. McCue watched her, eyes narrowed in irritation. "Cast off," he said. "I'll pilot us where I'm going, but you, boy, had damn well better get this boat *back* in one piece. I won't be responsible to Sheik Radi."

"Yes, sir," she said huskily and humbly, grinning to herself because everything had worked out so well. She untied the lines around the mooring posts and sat quietly as the fat man started the deafening engine, then pulled the boat aggressively into the canal. She was leaving home.

Chapter 8

The Supplicant watched her audience as she told them about her first meeting with Marcer Brice. Revered Gangler stared down at his hands; he'd heard the tale before. The tall, black-clad man, who had inched closer, was a sponge, showing nothing but his absorption of her information. Elector Brauna's expression revealed a distaste for Marcer Brice, the man. "Altered, isn't he?" she asked.

The Supplicant nodded. "So I've been told."

"But an *acknowledged* Altered," Revered Gangler interjected. "And not the Neulander Alteration."

The Supplicant was surprised to hear him defend Marcer Brice.

"Have you met with Jeroen Lee?" Brauna's tone sharpened. She leaned forward in her lounger.

"No, Elector." Revered Gangler wet his lips. "But I have reason to believe Researcher Brice was deported at Elector Lee's instigation."

"Oh? Did he want to dispose of other Altereds in the Academy?"

The Supplicant listened to Brauna's arch tone and heard the depth of her enmity toward Elector Lee. It had to be something personal, something the Supplicant might use to sway her. "Elector Brauna," the Supplicant said shyly, "we would never have presented this to Elector Lee. He has the Neulander Alteration. How could he be objective? The Republic of Neuland is the aliens' target."

Elector Brauna chuckled. "You're a smart girl. You're right; this is one issue he can't co-opt for his own aggrandizement. You'll have dinner with me tonight. Here, in my apartment."

I. My real life.

The boy was a woman. Marcer lay in the boat and let the deception continue, too spent to care.

"You fool," McCue bellowed over the engine noise. He drove the boat too fast, bouncing them into the air with each wave they hit. Every jolt sent a lance of pain through Marcer. He didn't answer. McCue was right. Marcer hadn't understood alans well enough. He was lucky they hadn't beaten him to death. Still, the gamble had worked. He was alive and free of Idryis Khan, but he owed his life, in significant measure, to Matthew McCue. It rankled.

"What did you think you were doing?" McCue shouted.

"Getting out of your trap." Marcer shouted, too, to make himself heard, but his jaw ached, and the buffeting wind hurt his broken teeth.

"You don't say no to one of the Blessed Sons. He could have killed you, but that bastard wouldn't quite let himself. The rest hung back, afraid of him." McCue turned a tight corner, and they entered a much wider canal. He jerked the power back; they slowed. Even so, they left an overloaded rowboat rocking crazily in their wake. McCue waited until it was possible to speak in a normal tone. "What did he want?" McCue asked.

"Me."

McCue scowled in disbelief. "You're not that handsome, Researcher," McCue said. "What did he really want?"

Amused by his own pique, Marcer wondered if McCue was right. Marcer had assumed the Khan's job offer was a sham. What if it wasn't? McCue always knew more than he said. Did he know Marcer was Altered? "Me," Marcer repeated. Why tell McCue anything?

McCue wrenched the boat hard to the right, down an even wider canal. The turn threw Marcer against the boat's side. He grunted with pain and the effort of righting himself.

The girl disguised as a boy had listened avidly. The city of Shores wallowed in gossip. She probably hoped for information she could sell. *Good luck to her,* Marcer thought. He knew firsthand the difficulty of earning a living in Shores. Her impersonation and Linnet's choice were two of a woman's very few options.

They entered an open area the size of a small lake, where a mass of stationary interconnected pontoon boats floated. McCue slowed until they left no wake. Marcer had heard of Shores' floating suq, but hadn't visited. Boats cost money. He walked the city.

The girl was studying the suq as though she had never seen it, either. From her lack of skill with a boat, likely she hadn't. Marcer took the opportunity to examine her more closely. Her face was smudged and gray around the eyes, but with the artless appeal of a gamin. She also had a ragged, dirty look, which explained why McCue hadn't questioned her status as a day worker. At the same time she seemed soft, not hardened by the streets, which with her delicate features made McCue's guess she was a girly-boy—a female impersonator working as a prostitute—plausible. He EL-ed and noted her compressed breasts and that she carried metal in her crotch and in her pocket. Coins?

She noticed Marcer's attention and quickly lowered her eyes. Her face reddened. Marcer guessed she hadn't been at her deception long.

McCue let their boat cruise slowly forward until they were beyond the pontoon island, then he turned down another canal and picked up speed. Marcer EL-ed, to get a sense of where they were, but recognized nothing. "Where are you heading?" Marcer asked. "Take me to Government House. I'll leave, and I swear I'll send back a reward and pay off Linnet's debt, too."

If McCue heard, he didn't answer. Marcer had to wait as the breeze touching his broken front tooth sent a shudder of pain through him, then he said, "I know about the Harmony delegation. Take me to them, McCue. Please." Marcer gripped the side of the boat and tried to sit straighter. "I want to go home."

McCue pulled aggressively back on the power. "Idiot. Make this your home; you have no future in the Harmony. Their delegation won't see you."

"Yes, they will. The Harmony *is* my home. I'll never be comfortable here." Yet in odd ways he had been comfortable in Shores: able to EL freely; able to trust another person, Linnet, as he had trusted no one since his mother's death, not even his father or sister, who made plans for him and had their own ways of using his success. He didn't miss the ambition which had driven him for so long, though he did hunger for work with intellectual excitement. Yet the Harmony was his home, the place where he wasn't an outsider, the place he would willingly defend with his last breath, and Jonism was how he structured his life.

McCue gestured. "Why should they take you back? Look at yourself!"

Marcer did. He looked like a drenched bum. The blue dye had run unevenly so that parts of his new suit were deep, turquoise blue and parts were grayish white. Still wet, the cloth clung to him like a Neulander's bodysuit. The pants, originally a bit too short, now ended well above his ankles. He had lost both shoes. Concerned that it was gone, he reached into his pocket for his money his entire fortune, 2223.25r—and was relieved to feel the bulky lump of coin and damp paper. In the Academy there was a saying: *Clothes make a merchant; a mind makes an Academic.* "The delegation will see me because I'm a member of the Academy. They'll know my expulsion was a mistake."

McCue laughed. His clothes were in better shape than Marcer's, though McCue still looked silly. He gentled the engine back and entered another canal, this one lined with stark, commercial buildings and nearly deserted warehouses. Signs in curvilinear Arabic script were meaningless to Marcer, who was now effectively illiterate. The disguised woman looked attentively at them; Marcer guessed she could read.

"The only way you'll ever see the Harmony again is if you have something they want," McCue said. "You don't. You muffed your only chance when you refused Idryis Khan. At the very least, you would have had some political information; he's important. Accept the truth, Researcher. You're here to stay."

Marcer refused to believe it. "You could get me inside Government House, McCue," he said. In the Emirates, there was always someone to bribe. "What have you got to lose? Help me and I'll be sure there's something in it for you."

McCue finally noticed the supposed boy's interest in their conversation. "You! What agency are you with?"

She studied her hands a moment, then looked up. "No agency." To Marcer, her artificially low voice was a giveaway, but he'd found that standard humans were inattentive to aural clues. McCue scowled, but his suspicions seemed unrelated to her gender.

"Why was a girly-boy at Sheik Radi's house?" McCue asked. "He doesn't use them."

She shrugged, keeping her shoulders hunched to hide her breasts. "Just day work."

"You're a spy. For who?"

"He's not a spy," Marcer said. "Leave him alone. He's some boy who happened to be there when we needed help. Be grateful. And if you don't take me to Government House, I'll get there anyway, and I won't owe a damn thing to you."

McCue looked steadily at Marcer. "Is that so, Researcher? Nothing at all?"

Marcer flushed, truly repentant. "I apologize. And I thank you. You saved my life."

McCue grimaced. "Did I, Researcher? I suspect the Khan would have ensured somehow that you survived. I wouldn't have acted if I thought it would make him my enemy; I thrive as his tool."

If McCue was right, the Khan would be after Marcer again. "I need to get home. This isn't my real life. Help me one last time."

As competently as any professional steersman, McCue maneuvered the boat against a temporary loading zone on a small dock adjacent to a white-painted warehouse. He cut the engine. The boat bumped against the dock. "You're too much trouble," he told Marcer. "And you're selfish, like every Jonist I've ever met. You don't understand morality or duty."

"And *you* do?" Marcer snapped. A merchant!

McCue stood to his full if undistinguished height, rocking the boat. "Tie us up," he ordered the impostor boy. "Yes, I do," McCue told Marcer. "And I don't believe in coincidence. Idryis Khan a'Husain, a fleet commander and an important Son—an extremely ambitious one—goes to the Harmony. What does he investigate while he's there? Not your military preparedness, but your relationship with Altered Neulanders. He tried to hire private tutors specializing in Neuland's biology. Then you, an Academic, an expert in nonterrestrial comparative biology, are deported to the Emirates on the same ship as the Khan.

"Are you aware, Academician, that the entire Harmony

deported only one shipload of Emirates nationals? The one you were on? Oh, they'd claim it was because of negotiations, but . . ." McCue was ready to say more, but then he noticed the boat was drifting away from the pier. "I told you to tie us up, you lazy son of a whore!"

The impostor boy had made a halting attempt to hitch the boat to the dock, but the mooring post was now beyond her reach. She was staring woefully at it, rope in hand. Marcer guessed it was inexperience rather than laziness which had made her fail, though she had been paying more attention to their conversation than her work. She wouldn't be able to maintain her deception long; her lack of skill at male occupations was too obvious.

McCue yelled imprecations at her as he returned to the steersman's seat.

"McCue," Marcer said, "are you a spy for the Harmony?"

"I am a member of the human race," McCue said grandiosely. "I have questions. Why are the Emirates so interested in Neuland? They've never owned it; it would give them no critical advantage. And Idryis Khan; is he loyal to Aleko Bei? Why did he marry Sheik Radi's daughter? The Sheik is a local power and Idryis Khan has never shown an interest in Bralava. And by God, I want to know—who the hell are these houris?"

"The houris? What do they have to do with anything?" Marcer was curious about the holy women—demons to the women in the Darien compound—but he had supposed they were merely a special category of alan women created by religionist superstition.

"I'd like to know exactly that." McCue restarted the engine, steered the boat out into the canal, then back toward the same dock. He maneuvered the boat into position and glowered at the disguised girl. "This time, tie us up!"

Marcer was faced directly into the sun; he shaded his eyes with his shaky hand. "Where are we?"

"Colchi District. My warehouse," McCue said. "And here is one last bit of free advice because you're ignorant, not hopeless: Go back to the Khan tomorrow morning—not now, while he's angry and occupied with his new wife—go back and tell him that you're sorry. Do *whatever* you need to do to return to his good graces. Get close to him, then watch and learn and listen." McCue cut the engine.

The girl had managed to rope one mooring post, but she hadn't tied the boat to it. Instead, she held them fast by clinging to the rope. The stern was already drifting with the current.

"You!" McCue yelled at the girl. "If you think you can make a profit from what you've overheard, just remember that I've been there first." McCue butted her out of his way and clambered up onto the pier like a man mounting a horse, though he groaned with effort. He grabbed the rope from around the post and cast it back at the boat. "Get off my dock! And if you don't return that boat to Sheik Radi, I'll send him after you!" He started to stomp off toward the white building.

Marcer struggled to get up and failed; the attempt made him woozy. His body had stiffened. His chest and stomach were bruised, but his dunking in the canal, though it had left an oily residue, had rinsed away the blood although he saw fresh blood seeping from his surface wounds. His broken teeth ached. He wouldn't get far alone.

"Hey!" the woman called. Her voice was suspiciously high, as though she'd forgotten her masquerade. "You didn't pay me!" She started out of the boat, but it already had drifted away from the dock, and perhaps she thought better of a physical confrontation. She had something important to hide.

McCue turned back, grinning. "First lesson a dayman should learn, if he's going into business for himself, is to get the money up front." Chuckling, McCue started away again.

"McCue!"

McCue's heavy sigh was visible, but he stopped and turned back, arms crossed against his ample chest, waiting.

The boat's drift made conversation increasingly a matter of exchanged shouts. "Just tell me what's going on," Marcer called. "There are things you know that I don't." Marcer's neck ached from looking up to the dock. *Everything* hurt.

"Ask the Khan!" McCue walked away.

II. A dangerous person to help.

Idryis Khan, her father, and the houris belonged to another life. Nisa sat where McCue had been and gingerly pushed the lever. The boat sprang forward. She pulled the lever back and studied the controls, trying to concentrate on them rather than on what she had overheard. It was good to know that others were suspicious of the houris. She had almost volunteered her own information, but it would have meant revealing herself as the Khan's newly-wed wife.

What would a real dayman do? She looked at her remaining passenger, this Jonist named Brice. His mouth hung foolishly open, but he didn't seem to be a fool. He closed his mouth again and waited, as though too exhausted to speak. She wished he wouldn't look at her so directly. He was a man; he must have some money, and cash would be useful.

It was difficult to force herself to sound confident while remembering to lower her tone. "You want a ride? I still haven't been paid. We're not going anywhere in this boat until I am."

He smiled. A front tooth was cracked diagonally; he looked like a child cutting his first teeth. Both eyes were darkening. His right cheek was swollen. He had resettled himself stiffly, obviously hurt, and even picked up his right leg to rearrange it, rather than moving it under its own muscle power. "Can you drive a boat?"

Her bluff called, Nisa pushed the lever forward to demonstrate. The engine gulped and chortled like a sneering man and when she gave it more than the minimum power, the boat lunged forward and up, beyond her control. They were headed for the opposite shore. She turned the wheel frantically. The boat lagged, then changed direction suddenly and too fast. She wanted dry land or to give it into someone else's charge. Palms sweating, she steadied the wheel and pulled the power back to idle.

"Very good," he said.

Pleased by his unexpected approval, Nisa's enjoyment was punctured when he added, "Help me to the wheel. I'll drive."

"Pay me first."

"I don't have to pay you anything. You can't drive, and it's not your boat."

It was her father's, but she couldn't tell him that. She wasn't unhappy to relinquish control; besides, his presence was good cover for a runaway wife.

She supported him when he lurched upright, shaking the boat. She managed to rest his weight on her shoulder rather than against her side. He didn't gasp in surprise and was apparently unaware her shape wasn't that of a man. McCue had called her a girly-boy. From jokes and innuendo, she suspected it was a good disguise.

Brice dropped into the seat, then leaned forward, resting his forehead against the console. He was genuinely hurt, barely able to function. "What did you do?" she asked.

He looked up, puzzled.

She gestured at him with a loose, unladylike movement of her hand. "To get beat up."

He grinned, displaying more broken teeth. "Exactly what I'm doing now. I'll drive the boat where I'm going, then you can take it wherever you want."

Nisa sat where she'd been while McCue drove. Since it was Friday there wasn't much commercial traffic, but a heavily laden barge was approaching. It looked huge in the water, as though it would fill the canal.

"Are you going to Government House?" she asked. If he met with his fellow Jonists, she could be on her way to the Harmony much faster than she'd expected if she managed to attach herself to him.

He looked as though he wouldn't answer, then reconsidered. "Not immediately. McCue's right that I won't get in alone, like this, but I have a friend who might be able to help." He sat, lost in thought as the barge came steadily toward them. Nisa touched his wrist. He looked up. She pointed at the looming barge. He pushed the power lever. The boat jumped, then they were skipping forward toward the opposite shore, then back to the canal center. The barge bore down on them.

He didn't know anything more about driving the boat than she did. "Get out of its way!" Nisa shouted. The barge blew a horn. It echoed in her head.

Brice winced. He drove the boat to the side of the canal, near the bank, and slowed to let the barge go by. Two jeering deckhands called down insults as they passed. The wake rocked them. After it passed, Brice glanced around, checking their position, then moved the boat forward, following the barge. Its burning fuel trailed a foul smell. Soot settled on them.

"I know you're a woman," Brice said. The boat was

going at a moderate clip, but it seemed less noisy than before. She heard him too well.

She shivered at the cool breeze coming over the water. "That isn't so," she said, but her denial was uncertain.

"I don't intend to tell anyone," he continued, disregarding her statement.

She didn't trust any altruism from a man, but was relieved that at least he didn't know who she actually was. There would be a reward for finding her.

Brice looked at Nisa, studying her, evaluating her, yet not as a woman. She bit her lip and looked directly back. "I'm not looking for any profit, or anything else from you," he said. "If you need to lie to earn a living, it's not my concern. But you're not doing a very good job, and it's a dangerous game to fail at. The police bats will pick you up."

She would be caught and returned to her husband for punishment; Qadira said he'd kill her. Or she might be killed on the street. Brice knew half her secret. Nisa tried to consider her options calmly. To tell him the rest was risky but felt right. This was a man who might get her into the Harmony. "You were at my wedding," she said quietly. "I'm Nisa Khalil, Sheik Radi's daughter." She hesitated, then added, "Idryis Khan a'Husain's wife."

Openmouthed, he studied her face, which would tell him nothing except that such scrutiny from a man humiliated her. She kept her head high. "The acre," he said.

She turned away, then forced herself to look back. "Yes."

Brice slowed the boat as they reached the conglomeration of pontoon platforms and moored crafts they had passed before. Near them, the area had some traffic. Marcer Brice stopped the boat; others went around them. "Holy God, they'll be looking for you. The Khan's bride. That means they'll be looking for me and McCue since you left with us."

His stare was accusing. Nisa had never considered the effect of her flight on anyone but herself. She lowered her head guiltily, and yet, what else could she have done?

"Do you want to go back?"

"Never," she said. "I want to go to the Harmony."

He chuckled, then winced as if that hurt. "That's two of us."

"I do," she insisted. "Will you help me?"

"You're a dangerous person to help." He spoke carefully, enunciating with unusual precision. "But I know someone who might help us both, someone I have to warn, too, about the Khan. This person is . . . special. I won't take you there unless I'm sure that this isn't a whim, and that you won't betray my friend even if you're caught."

His friend was a woman. Nisa was certain, however abnormal it was for a man to have a woman friend—but then, this was a Jonist from the Harmony, an infidel to whom the word normal didn't apply. "I'm running from Idryis Khan, too," she said. "If he beat you so badly and he likes you, what do you think he would do to a runaway wife? He has never seen me. He doesn't care about me. Even if it was a whim, I'm committed."

He gazed at her, openmouthed again, then pushed the lever; the boat jumped forward, its nose in the air for a moment before it settled down. He steered them around the suq. She was on her way to the Harmony of Worlds.

III. A good enough reason.

Marcer clenched his jaw to keep from groaning as he struggled upright. He was sorry that, after leaving Nisa an hour earlier, he'd taken Linnet's suggestion to rest briefly on her bed. His chest was tight; his lungs burned and his arms felt liquid, unable to support his weight, but Linnet was a Neulander Altered. She didn't feel pain, and he would not display his pain to her.

She placed her hand gently against Marcer's chest. Her scars felt glassy smooth, but hard. "Lie back. There's no reason to get up yet."

"Isn't Idryis Khan a good enough reason? Besides, the girl is waiting for me." However, he let himself be convinced by her touch.

Linnet placed a cool, damp, malodorous rag over Marcer's eyes. "I know," she said. "It smells like burnt grease, but it will keep them from blackening and bring the swelling down." Before he could object, she also arranged a poultice across his ribs. It smelled sour and vaguely alcoholic. Folk medicine, but it was the best she knew. That and the generic painkiller—provenance and efficacy unknown—

purchased over the counter at the local suq, were all he had.

The search for Nisa would be intense once the Khan discovered she was missing. If the girl was found, then at least she couldn't implicate Linnet. He had left Nisa with the boat in another neighborhood. He worried, though, about the Khan's threat against Linnet.

Speed was imperative. Marcer had to get inside Government House before the Khan caught up with him, as he surely would eventually. He had to save Linnet. The rag slipped down his face as he forced himself into a sitting posture. Marcer reached for it just as Linnet did. Their hands met. She touched his cheek comfortingly but briefly, like a nurse on the job. He wondered if she studied gentleness; it couldn't come naturally to Neulander Altereds.

Linnet smiled, a parting of her beautiful lips that pulled her scar tissue cheeks into odd shapes. He knew her face intimately. He had EL-ed her often in the last weeks, in the way a child ELs his mother, to make a soothing presence palpable inside his mind. She was the only person on Bralava whom he trusted, the only good to come from his deportation. "The guards at Government House know you, Linnet. You can get me inside, then I'll find the Harmony delegation. Will you help get me in?"

"No," she said.

Taken aback, he gaped at her. She'd done so much for him, he had given no thought to a possible refusal. He wiped his face with the smelly rag and glanced out the open window onto the courtyard. Two unmen neighbors were chatting; they'd seen him hobble to Linnet's room and would remember it if police bats arrived. "I should leave; I wouldn't have come except to warn you." His voice was husky as he spoke the lie. He had come to her for help. He knew, from her aura, that she cared for him. He cared for her. Why had she refused?

He lifted his legs, using his hands to move the right leg, and swiveled so he was on the edge of the bed. His right knee throbbed.

Linnet sat next to him. She placed her hand on his thigh. "Marcer, she's the Khan's wife, as important a woman as exists here. You left the wedding with her. Save yourself. If you help her, the Khan could do anything to you."

"I can't abandon her because it's risky to help."

"She has no claim on you."

"She's alive. She says if he finds her, the Khan will kill her. I believe it. Please, help me help her."

"I am helping *you*—to stay alive. They will never let you near the Harmony commissioners. There must be more guards around them than there are martyrs in Paradise. If you go to Government House, you'll die."

"It's my life."

"And I believe it's worth something, even in Shores and not the Harmony."

"But Nisa's isn't?" He got painfully to his feet, keeping as much weight as possible on his left leg while trying to pretend the pain was irrelevant, then gave up the attempt to impress a Neulander with his fortitude. He hissed as fire seemed to travel up the nerves from his knee and send his body into flame. The painkiller should have been working to dull it.

"Nisa." Linnet repeated the name thoughtfully. "What is she like?"

He smiled, recalling her wild attempt at driving the boat, but deliberately avoided physical description. "Spunky."

"Then this Nisa is pretty or you wouldn't call her spunky." Linnet's tone gave away nothing of what she might have felt at another woman's prettiness.

"You'd like her," he said. "She's determined, not desperate, but she doesn't know the city and doesn't realize how much she doesn't know. She's intelligent. Probably stubborn, too. She has something—jewelry, I think, or coins—hidden in her clothes. She wants to be free. She wants to go to the Harmony, but a girl with her background won't survive alone in the city for long."

"Then she won't survive. One thing I've learned is that not everyone can be helped." Linnet reached for a glass of water she had brought earlier for Marcer, then didn't take it. She brushed at her clothes as though they were dusty.

"We can try. You helped me, a shiftless Jonist. I'm honor-bound to pass on the favor."

She didn't smile.

"I was lucky to find you, Linnet. Now she's found me."

Linnet shrugged uneasily. "Coincidence isn't destiny."

Marcer felt he was making progress. He EL-ed solely for the halo effect. He had never admitted his Alteration to her. The omission felt like a falsehood, particularly since she was Altered, too.

The bounce-back was wonderful. Her cut-velvet skin seemed to glow in combination with her aura, no longer tarnished silver, but golden with love, hope, and melancholy. He put his arm around her. She astonished him by pulling gently away. It unsteadied him physically and emotionally. Was the halo effect of his EL wrong? She saw him sway and braced him by returning to his side.

"Can you suggest a place for Nisa to hide?" Marcer asked. "She looks enough like a boy that she shouldn't be spotted immediately."

"No one sees a woman. She should have stayed in a chador. Every stupid runaway wife pretends to be a boy. They'll be looking for one. Men aren't idiots, even when they're . . . vile."

Did Linnet hate men? Had she been kind to him because of a deal regarding her debt to McCue? They knew very little about each other. She had no understanding of his life in the Harmony. He didn't know what had driven her to make the choices she had. He had talked about his family, but she had never mentioned anyone. Sex had little intrinsic meaning in the Harmony, nor would it necessarily mean much to a whore. He winced at the thought. "I'll warn Nisa." He turned. He had walked three blocks after taking a water taxi from the dock where he'd left Nisa; he didn't relish the walk back. Marcer limped toward the door, glancing out the window as he passed. The two men had left. The courtyard was quiet.

Linnet caught his arm. "Marcer. You're still going to help her? Why?"

"She has no one else." True, but his chance to meet with the Harmony commission was slipping from his grasp because of the Khan's wayward wife. "If she's found, I believe Idryis Khan will kill her. I can't stand by."

"Is that Jonist Order?"

He hadn't given Order a thought. Were proper Jonists selfish, as McCue had claimed? He shrugged. It hurt.

"Did she promise you her favor?" Linnet's face was inscrutable, but her bland tone insinuated something obscene.

Disturbed, but rather than showing it, he made a deprecating gesture across his battered body. "Do you really think I'm in shape to do anything like that?"

She didn't answer. It was said that pain-free Neulanders lacked empathy because they never felt pain. He didn't believe that now, but it was possible she didn't understand the discouragement pain created. "Linnet, do you think all men are evil?"

"Not evil." She seemed embarrassed for him. "Just subject to certain desires. Don't worry, Marcer, I understand them. And she wasn't wearing a chador."

He was appalled by Linnet's acceptance of alan ideology concerning the irresistibility of uncovered women. "Linnet, in the Harmony, anywhere but in the Emirates, woman are as visible as men. Seeing a woman is routine. Normal. I'm not overwhelmed by it, and I doubt any man is. If they say otherwise, it's only an excuse. We've been together for weeks and I haven't tried to, well, rape you."

"But look at me. My skin is my cloak."

He looked; he met her eyes. Her face was uneven, individual and peculiar, but he didn't find it repulsive. "I like the way you look."

She turned away. Her beautiful thick hair, always hidden by the heavy alan cloaks when she was outdoors, caught sunlight from the open window. He EL-ed, feeling the tortured scars on those parts of her body that her clients found most interesting. Damn them to alan hell. He took a painful, awkward step closer. "Linnet."

As if unaware of him, she said, "I'll help the girl; I may as well. McCue isn't brave. When he gives my name to the bats, they'll come here anyway."

He worried for her. "I'll take charge of Nisa, but you have to get away. Even if McCue doesn't tell the police, Idryis Khan will. Would your . . . patron at Government House help you?" Marcer hated to put her in a position of asking Governor Gordan for anything, but didn't know how else to protect her.

She hugged her arms around herself. "We never speak. It's his rule. I must not make a sound. And no, he'd never help me."

It was horrible and humiliating. No wonder she was afraid whenever she went to Government House; no wonder she'd been so pleased by her dismissal on the night the two of them had met. Her thin, scarred shoulders, barely visible through her indoor clothes, trembled slightly. Uncertain whether his touch would be welcome, Marcer's caress was hesitant, a slow, warm brushing against her back which brought her close. Preoccupied by the need to comfort her, he didn't feel the irregularity of her skin beneath his hand. She turned to face him. Her eyes were dry.

They looked at each other. The blemishes across her checks, which distorted her face more than the cicatrix on her forehead and the misshapen flesh of her chin, were vile, nasty to see because Linnet's disfigurement was entirely man-made. Its existence was scandalous. It didn't hurt, she said. Holy God. He wanted to hurt the men who hadn't hurt her.

Marcer stroked her cheek with the edge of his hand. He forced himself to feel the imperfections and to enjoy them, as he did from an EL. He guessed she forced herself not to flinch or turn away. Even after a violent beating, he did not look nearly so damaged as Linnet.

She blinked. Her beautiful, dark eyes glistened.

"I like the way you look," Marcer said again, and he bent down—carefully, leaning his weight against a chair for support—and kissed Linnet, tenderly, on the lips. Her mouth yielded to his, her body relaxed against him, and though she was the one who broke the embrace, she stayed close, looking up. Her lack of facial expression was troublesome. Sight was a constant sense. Empathic information from an EL could substitute, but it was intermittent, intentional, and made him feel guilty, a legacy of Academy rules and shame that he had never explained his Alteration to Linnet. He wanted to say something loving, but every phrase he knew was trite. "I won't leave for the Harmony without you," he said instead of a more passionate declaration.

"What would your family say?" Linnet asked. "Returning with an ugly prostitute from Bralava?"

He hoped the bruises disguised it if he flushed. His father, a standard human, would never understand; his sister Miriam would call him crazy. "They'll be grateful to you for helping me. They'll come to care about you, as I do."

"Perhaps. If they're not really Jonists—like you."

Disconcerted by her comment, Marcer glanced outside. The light in the courtyard had changed. It was shimmery and reflective, like sunlight on water, but Linnet's courtyard didn't have a fountain.

"I'll go to the girl," Linnet said. "You're too conspicuous."

There wasn't a sound from the courtyard, although usually at dusk it was bustling. It looked empty, but there were no shadows. Marcer EL-ed.

"We'll meet somewhere I've never used with McCue. I have a friend who . . ."

"Quiet!" Marcer's bounce-back was giving information totally at odds with the tranquil scene his vision showed. Men were out there, armed men he sensed but couldn't see. He closed his eyes as he did when an EL signal was distorted, and he EL-ed again. "The bats are here, outside, using a scatter-field," he whispered.

Linnet froze, then inched toward the window as if afraid to see. She squinted as she peeked into the courtyard. "There's nothing."

He EL-ed. "There are eight men with rifles."

"I don't see anyone."

He wrenched himself away from the compulsive need to recheck yet again, the usual result of an incongruity in sensory information. "It's true. They're preparing for a raid. On us."

She stared.

"It's a scatter-field," he said impatiently, then glanced about and EL-ed her room for anything with which to fight them off or a means of escape. "Is there any other way out?"

"The roof . . . Are you sure about the bats?" She didn't believe him.

"Yes." He couldn't EL through the ceiling, but the flat roof was partly visible from the courtyard, and use of a roof was an ordinary extension of an apartment in Shores. They would expect it.

"The kitchen window opens directly onto the canal," she said. "My emergency door."

Of course. She was already part of an illegal conspiracy and had thought such matters through. He limped into the kitchen.

Linnet followed as though humoring a delirious patient. "But the courtyard is empty. Why do you think anyone's there?"

The kitchen window was already open. "They're there. Believe me. I can see them." The window was high over the sink. It was large enough to accommodate a small adult. He wasn't small, though he might have squeezed through before he'd been beaten. He would never manage it now. He EL-ed. The drop to the canal seemed to be four or five meters. Even if he made it, he wasn't in shape to swim. "Get out of here, Linnet. You can make it free. I don't think they're watching the canal." It was his fault that she was in danger; he was the one who had raised the Khan's wrath.

Linnet wouldn't leave quickly unless he convinced her, but this was a poor time to admit his Alteration. An explanation would take too long. "Trust me," he said, "If ever you've trusted anyone—if you've ever wanted to—then trust me now. I *know* armed men are out there. There isn't time for me to tell you how. I'll say that Nisa let me off and then continued on her own, that you had nothing to do with her. I'll tell the bats that you left Bralava with a patron." The kitchen window was in shadow. The breeze coming in was cool, raising goose bumps on his bare chest.

"You truly see police bats outside?" she asked.

"Yes!" Though he had to balance on one leg, Marcer seized her arms and pulled her to the open window. "Believe me. Go. I can't make it. You can. The canal is clear." He EL-ed again to be sure. "Hurry. I want you to be safe."

Linnet walked deliberately into the back of the kitchen and took a sealed, dark plastic bag from a drawer. She placed it inside her dress, trapped in place by her underclothes, then she kicked off her sandals and climbed onto the sink. She had planned this escape. She touched her concealed bag as though for reassurance it was there. Its bulk made her look pregnant. She scooted to the window, gazed outside searchingly, then turned to Marcer. "Where is the girl? Nisa?"

He looked into the apartment's main room. The courtyard was quiet as a grave. He would hear when the bats began their move. "Don't go to her," he said, looking back at Linnet. "She's dangerous."

Linnet touched the side of his face; her hand felt cool against his warm skin. "You're the only man I know who cares for whores and strangers. If you care, so will I. Where is she? I won't go until you tell me."

There wasn't time. He told her the dock where he'd left

Nisa. She nodded and jumped quickly through the window. He heard a splash, but resisted the urge to look.

Marcer hopped back to the main room on his left leg, then lay down on the bed. He didn't look into the courtyard. His head was pounding. His skin was hot. He would have to go to the Khan to keep Linnet safe, but that was a better reason than McCue's babble.

He covered his eyes with his forearm to shield them from the bright, late-afternoon light. He was in that position when, a few minutes later, police burst through Linnet's door.

Chapter 9

The Supplicant dined alone with Elector Brauna. They sat adjacent to each other at a high, white porcelain table in the clearing of her hothouse garden. The rather frugal meal of rice and vegetables ended with an extravagantly rich chocolate dessert. They were served by servants who, though male and female, reminded the Supplicant of unmen in their submissive passivity—though for unmen, that wasn't uniformly true. "Subs," the Elector named them with disdainful chagrin. "Better to use mechanicals. No toolman really can be trusted." She sighed, while looking very beautiful in her gossamer robe.

Elector Brauna was the first woman with whom the Supplicant had been alone since leaving the Emirates. She missed the intense friendship that existed there between women. Exposed constantly to the eyes of men, in the Harmony there was always sexual tension; she could relax with Brauna. The Supplicant tentatively placed her hand over the Elector's. "You can trust me. All women are sisters."

Sanda Brauna gazed at the Supplicant, her expression unreadable. "As the heart grows older it will come to such sights colder," she said, "and yet you will weep and know why."

Puzzled, the Supplicant nodded slightly. She didn't understand, but the rhythm was sad.

"Poetry," Elector Brauna briefly explained. She continued:

"Now no matter, child, the name:
Sorrow's springs are the same . . .
It is the blight man was born for,
It is Margaret you mourn for."

Brauna sighed. "It's a short poem by Gerard Manley Hopkins,

a long-ago religionist from old Earth. The best poetry is written by religionists. Strange. We Jonists don't have the knack."

"Ah," the Supplicant said, for want of anything better. She hadn't envisioned Elector Brauna reciting poems to her.

"Do you read poetry, girl?"

To be called "girl" by a woman who seemed nearly her own age made the Supplicant feel patronized, but then, Elector Brauna was her patron. The Supplicant shook her head. "No. I paint. Painted. I haven't done anything since I left home." She lowered her eyes. "I'd like to paint a portrait of you."

"Paint? With permanent colors? How delightfully archaic." Brauna shifted position in her chair. "I might enjoy that. And there will be time. By and by. I've arranged for you to stay in Center, here in my residence. Security advised it. Revered Gangler and the Researcher will be lodged in Center, too, inside the Academy, although their contributions are at an end. After I make the alien threat known, you'll be safer under the protection of an Elector, where the merchants and soldiers can't question you willy-nilly.

"I'm having a full survey report prepared. I'll present it at an Electors' Special Conclave. This Brice's data will be an appendix."

This Brice. Elated, the Supplicant smiled and bowed from her chair. "Thank you, Elector." With the support of an Elector, surely the Harmony would act.

Brauna nodded. "Incredible! And those alan men don't recognize the danger! Opening our borders to female refugees from your worlds was one policy for which I fought; now I see how dreadful their plight was." She gazed into the Supplicant's eyes. "Occasionally, I find I have no use for men." Brauna smiled, bent closer, then hesitated. The Supplicant returned the Elector's smile. The Supplicant's expression must have encouraged Brauna, because she gently stroked the Supplicant's cheek, more than any Jonist man had dared.

Ever since entering the Polite Harmony of Worlds, the Supplicant had been expecting a seduction of some kind.

I. Teacher.

Nisa supposed she was a ninny to wait so long, but Marcer Brice had said he would be awhile and he was her best hope of reaching the Harmony. Besides, he had an honest face beneath the bruises and no incentive to turn her in to her father or her husband. Idryis Khan a'Husain. Nisa spat, as she'd seen men do.

A covered woman was coming toward her. Twice already Nisa had redirected taxi customers; Brice had parked them at a commercial pier. The woman was close enough that Nisa could just make out her eyes though even they were covered by a black gauze veil, marking the woman as scrupulously pious; if so, it was odd for her to be on the streets unaccompanied by a man. Idlers watched the woman with a mixture of disdain and avarice, but no one bothered her. "Over there!" Nisa called irritably, and pointed to the line of taxis. "I'm not for hire!"

Nisa continued to scan the pier. With his limping gait and extreme height, it would be impossible to miss Brice. Maybe he'd been captured. How much longer should she wait?

The pious woman stopped at Nisa's slot. "My husband sent me," she said in a tremulous whisper. She moved closer, turning her back on everyone but Nisa and lowered her soft voice even more. "My husband is a teacher," she said, startling Nisa by using the archaic Arabic word, *idryis,* instead of Ufazi.

Nisa scrutinized the woman suspiciously. "What's your husband's name?"

"Hey! You're not licensed!" The nearest water-taxi owner, a heavyset man with a scar dimpling his forehead, jumped out of his boat and onto the dock with practiced grace. "You can't pick up a fare."

"It's private," Nisa essayed as an answer.

"That's a lot of . . ."—the boatman glanced at the respectable-looking woman in the chador—"hot air. You can't pick up anyone off this dock without a license."

"He's family," the woman said. "This boy is my husband's cousin, sent to take me to their cousin Nisa's wedding party." She spoke meekly but with certainty. "Forgive him. He didn't know where to wait."

There'd been enough hints. Nisa was ready to accept the woman as a messenger from the Jonist Brice. She stood and, hoping her maritime inexperience wasn't obvious, she extended a hand to help her into the boat. The woman wore gloves, so it was proper.

"I don't believe a word you're saying, either one of you," the boatman said. "I'll let it go this time, just in case this isn't a cheat, but don't come around this dock again. You hear?"

Nisa dared only nod. The boatman glowered, while Nisa pretended to settle the woman on the single passenger bench. To make good her escape, Nisa would have to start the boat and maneuver it away from the pier without alerting anyone to her ineptitude. She took the steersman's seat, said a quick *Shahadah* under her breath for luck, then started the engine on the first try. She grinned.

The boatsman was still glowering at them from the dock. He shook his head as Nisa dared increase the power from idle, then hurriedly lifted the mooring rope off its pole, tossing it into the boat. Nisa's heart skipped a beat as she realized how close she had come to pulling down the dock or capsizing the boat, hardly inconspicuous, and how would she have looked wet? She waved at the boatman, who shook his head again, now seeming more disgusted than angry. Nisa let the boat drift at the lightest throttle possible. It wasn't so difficult, as long as she went slowly.

They left the pier. The boatman returned to his taxi. Nisa concentrated on not hitting anything. When the woman, in a more authoritative tone than before, started to speak, Nisa hushed her. "I don't know what I'm doing!"

The woman laughed. "Who does?"

"I mean I don't know how to operate this boat."

"You're doing fine. This is a no-wake area. We're only going around the corner and down a bit, then we'll abandon the boat. They'll trace it too easily."

Nisa wasn't sure she trusted this woman; she seemed too ready to dispose of Nisa's property. Nisa turned to her, but there was nothing to see but the dark nullity of a chador. "Who are you?"

"If I give you my name, then you can give it to others if we're separated," she said in a sensible, serious voice. "Call me Fatima. I'll call you . . . Suliaman."

Nisa grinned at her new name. As they left the dockyard, other boats sped around them. One man shouted that she was a traffic hazard. Nisa increased the power slightly, then quickly pulled it back when the boat plunged forward. Better to be noticed for her slowness than for an accident. Speed frightened her.

The woman settled her chador around herself. In places where it touched her body, the cloth looked damp. "If you were going to run, why did you make it so public? Stupid girl. You could have waited a few days. Now they can't hush up your disappearance."

"I did what I had to do."

The woman didn't reply. "There," she said. "Go left. This inlet is busy, and the people are poor. We'll leave the boat at one of the piers and hope someone steals it. Then its position won't tell the bats where we went. Do you have any money?"

"I can sell the boat," Nisa said sullenly.

"Forget the boat. That would take too long."

As Nisa made the turn, they passed a pier so deteriorated that on one side its tilted planks were underwater. No boats were docked there, but a pack of young boys were diving from its edge into the murky water. Each time one dived, the pier shook.

The boys noticed the woman in the boat. Two of the older ones began to catcall and point at her. One pulled his penis from his pants and shouted obscenities. Nisa gaped. She had never encountered such a display; she had never traveled in such an area. When she left home, an escort always guarded her from such things.

"The Harmony border is closed," the woman probably not named Fatima said. She ignored or was oblivious of the boys. "The independent worlds that accept runaway women won't take anyone as important as you."

Nisa bowed her head. "Where is Marcer Brice? Are we going to Government House? I thought Brice was taking me to the Harmony with him."

"Why should he?"

Suspicious, Nisa put the boat on idle. "Where is he?"

"I had to leave him. I think he'll be captured—all because of you."

"Why are *you* helping me?"

"Because he asked." In a milder tone, the woman continued, "Because I've helped other women and know better than most what to do."

"Are you with the kitchen express?"

The woman chuckled. The chador muffled the sound. "No. I don't qualify. I'm independent."

Nisa gave the boat more power. With anger as an incentive, it was easier to add a bit of speed. She felt tricked. She had entrusted herself to Brice's care and expected passage to the Harmony. This woman was an interloper, a critic, and seemingly so leery of Nisa that she wouldn't give her name or show her face.

Nisa sensed the woman's eyes on her and stared back, noticing how like a child hiding under a blanket a seated woman in a chador appeared. Her own stolen, white cotton servant's clothing was elegant in its simplicity; if fat McCue thought her a girly-boy, she must still be beautiful. The contrast between the covered woman and unencumbered boy would make an excellent painting. She would call it *Black and White* or *Captivity and Freedom*. "So. Then I'll have to wait in Shores?"

"Yes. Do you have a plan? Friends who will hide you?"

"No." She thought of Ziller, but it was too much to ask of him or Hulweh. "Isn't that what you know how to do?"

Fatima sighed. "You had best stop acting like a spoiled child. You're not Sheik Radi's sheltered little daughter anymore."

Nisa realized she'd been rude. "I apologize," she said. "It isn't easy for me to beg for help, and I'm disappointed that I won't get to the Harmony anytime soon. I'm frightened every time a man looks at me. There seem to be too many choices, but none of them is safe or good."

Fatima didn't answer. The canal's stink was worse than usual. "There." Fatima finally pointed to a shabby but structurally sound pier near what seemed to be a local market. "We'll leave the boat and go up the street separately. I'll buy a chador. That isn't a suspicious thing for a woman to do. When I leave the shop, you come to me; I'll give you the package and wait for you. Find a quiet, private spot, put it on, then I'll take you to a place where you can spend tonight."

"I don't want to be a woman anymore."

"You're not. You're an impostor. Watch out! You have to dock us first without crashing."

Nisa grinned: an impostor woman.

II. Waiting to win.

Idryis Khan stood in front of an open window, outlined by the sunset. His dark form echoed the shape of the Citadel, the island prison in the bay beyond him. Marcer suspected the prison view had been planned. A sea breeze, saltier and cleaner than the canal stench, made the room seem fresh; the open window made it airy. The view of the Citadel cast a chill.

Marcer had been deposited at Government House by the police bats who'd arrested him and wrecked Linnet's home. The bats had been replaced by two soldiers under the Khan's command. They held him, one on each side, while waiting for the Khan to turn around and inspect the prisoner.

The interview room had the impersonal polish of a public place; since it was an alan room and lacked significant furniture, it seemed spacious. Marcer didn't EL at first because the Khan would recognize that he had. After several silent minutes he decided it didn't matter. The EL relieved some stress and the pressure in his head. It told him nothing about Idryis Khan's thoughts.

The Khan shifted position, then turned to Marcer. The soldiers saluted. "You may leave," the Khan ordered them, with a gesture. Marcer regretted their departure; he was forced to stand with his weight only on his left leg. His right knee had become increasingly swollen. It was painful to the touch, and he could put no weight on it, so he was continually off-balance.

Idryis Khan studied Marcer with the stony attention of a gargoyle. After the soldiers closed the door behind themselves, the Khan said, "You look poorly."

"Thank you. You did most of the damage." It was foolish bravado and possibly untrue. He had little memory of being beaten.

"I apologize." Idryis Khan bowed with the enthusiasm of a man saluting an ape. "Your error was the result of your Harmony upbringing. You didn't intend any dishonor. As for the woman, I am aware that you had nothing to do with her disappearance, although perhaps McCue did. When she's found, I will deal with her personally."

"What will you do?" Linnet was with Nisa.

The Khan waved his hand, dismissing the matter. "The Harmony delegation is nearby. My soldiers have orders—my orders—to take you to them. Plead your case, Researcher Brice. And when afterward you are still marooned in the Emirates, then the guards will return you to me."

"And if I'm not marooned?" He wouldn't be. No proper Jonist would deny him a hearing before his peers on Darien.

The Khan never answered. He walked past Marcer without glancing his way, opened the door, and left. Immediately, the soldiers returned. They seized his arms and marched him down a long corridor. At a pair of guarded doors, in unison, they yanked him off his feet. The Government House guards opened the door and the soldiers dragged Marcer forward to the Harmony commission. It was a piece of theater designed to reinforce his status as a prisoner and make him seem reluctant. He didn't care. The Harmony delegation would see through it.

They were at dinner, ten Jonist commissioners plus Governor Gordan and the aide Marcer had met, Zafar Maqsood. All twelve were seated on pillows on the floor; all except Gordan and Maqsood squirmed uncomfortably. There seemed to have been little conversation for Marcer's entrance to interrupt.

The room reeked of coriander and cumin, as though Governor Gordan had purposely insulted Harmony palates. The plates of the Harmony group were virtually untouched. The ten of them—exclusively male—wore Harmony-style suits, better tailored and sewn of fabric with a finer, tighter weave than what he'd seen on Bralava. None was bearded, and they had a straightforward look of strength and vigor, without the overripe appearance of age characteristic of important men in the Emirates, like Gordan.

When his broken teeth hurt, Marcer realized he was grinning. He fixed his expression into something more serious and tried to bow, but the Khan's soldiers jerked him sideways, toward the foot of the low, rectangular dining table. The painkiller was finally working or Marcer's euphoria was medicine for his aches. He walked forward on his own once the soldiers stopped harassing him.

These ten men were his brothers. They lived as he had lived; they believed as he believed. Their home was his. Differences in detail were trivia.

"Sirs." He made a lopsided bow.

They watched, but none returned his greeting.

In his elation, he barely noticed. He recognized faces: his cousin, Peter Issacs, who looked anxious and aggrieved without his captain's uniform. It was serendipity to find a relative among them, someone sure to be on his side. Three men, seated in a row together, Marcer vaguely recalled as world delegates to the Harmony's Grand Assembly. He didn't remember their names. Marcer identified two others from newsbriefs. Ahman Roger Kiku, the Ahman of Center-Sucre, an Academic position that placed him just below the six Electors, was seated at the far end of the table, near the governor. The Ahman was fidgeting like an Acolyte. The other man Marcer recognized was Evan Kolet. He wasn't a Harmony citizen, he was a general in the armed forces of the Republic of Neuland, an Altered from the world coveted by the Emirates. A Neulander medical conditioner monitor on Kolet's wrist gleamed like a medal. Marcer knew his face because ten months earlier he'd been a Supplicant, begging for aid to Neuland from the Harmony's Grand Assembly. What was a Neulander military man doing among a peace commission from the Harmony of Worlds? It didn't matter; Kolet was irrelevant to Marcer's quest.

Governor Gordan used the edge of the table for support and stood. "I apologize, gentlemen," he said in Ufazi, which few Harmony citizens understood, "but there is one other matter to which I hope you will attend." Gordan paused. After a brief hesitation, Peter translated his words, keeping his eyes averted from Marcer. The translation was merely accurate but it was music to Marcer. He hadn't heard his own language spoken without an accent since Darien. There were tears in his eyes.

When Peter finished, the governor continued. "This man claims he was deported from the Polite Harmony of Worlds by mistake; all we know is that he arrived with the Darien deportees, and that since then, there have been complaints regarding his conduct. If you want him, then we won't prosecute."

Marcer scarcely waited for Peter to finish interpreting Governor Gordan's comments before he bowed again. "Sirs," he said in the common language. He cleared his throat and tried to catch their mood, but didn't EL, inhibited by the fact they were from the Harmony. "I am Researcher Marcer Joseph Brice, a Researcher from the Academy of Darien and a legal resident of New Dawn. As Governor Gordan said, I was deported from Darien by mistake. I was entitled to a hearing, but in any event, there was no cause. I've done nothing wrong."

The Harmony delegates stared disdainfully at him, except for Peter, one other man, and the Neulander, who studied their plates. Governor Gordan seated himself and resumed eating greasy meat with his fingers. His chewing was noisy. Marcer caught a twinkle in his eyes; he was playing to Harmony prejudices.

"I apologize for my alarming appearance," Marcer said in his calmest, lecturing voice. *He* did not want to seem uncivilized. "I was beaten by a mob because I happened to see women's faces. That is the level of their religionist superstition."

In the stillness after he stopped speaking, Marcer heard the hiss of air blowing through the building's air-circulation system. One of the Harmony delegates placed a hard ceramic cup on the table; it clinked as it knocked against his plate. Marcer wished they would speak. The silence made him tense, but simply seeing them lifted a burden he hadn't known he carried. Their plain, Harmony suits covered bodies, like his own, which were leaner, taller, and healthier than those of Bralava's population, as if Jonists were a separate race of men. If humanity had begun branching into separate species, they might be based along political lines, not Alteration.

Ahman Kiku was the ranking Academician present. Marcer bowed directly to him, not generally, as he had previously. Kiku nodded with minimal politeness. "Ahman," Marcer said. "Captain Isaacs can verify what I say. I am an honors graduate of the Academy of New Dawn. I was accepted as a junior Researcher and instructor at the Academy of Darien, and this is my second term teaching there. I am in good standing, and have never been on a Flawed List. I should have been accorded the full protections due an Academic. I was not; I was deported. Please, Ahman, I want to go home."

Ahman Kiku glanced at the man on his right, one of the world delegates, then looked up at Marcer. "No one doubts that you've correctly stated your résumé, Dr. Brice. However, you assume that these matters somehow require us—commissioners to the government of the United Emirates, present on Bralava for an entirely different reason—to intervene in your case. They do not. We will not."

Marcer's stomach seemed to drop to his knees. The Ahman of Sucre, one short step below the six Electors, should have been livid at the abuse of Academic privileges. He should have felt obligated to aid a fellow Academic stranded on a barbarous world. "Ahman, I appeal to you. There's been a mistake. I'm not involved in politics. Darien deported me for no reason. Common decency . . ."

Ahman Kiku turned to the same man, and this man answered on Kiku's behalf, interrupting Marcer. "Dr. Brice, you were properly deported. You are not a citizen. You were born in the Emirates. You have no right as a former Academic to reenter our borders."

The references to him as "Dr. Brice," as though he was a private teacher and not an Academic, hadn't escaped Marcer's notice, but this was worse. "A 'former' Academic? How can I have been stripped of my Academic status? Without notice?"

"Why are you shocked?" Governor Gordan asked jovially in Ufazi, though he'd clearly understood the discussion in the Harmony common tongue. "Why did you expect them to take you back?" Maqsood seemed engrossed, as if Marcer's life was a cheap cyclone drama.

"You are an Altered man," Ahman Kiku said as though the concept pained him. "Perhaps you truly don't understand, but we can have no tolerance, none at all, for those who lead hidden lives and hold secret, un-Jonist opinions."

Peter Isaacs was not Altered. He didn't look at his cousin. Neither did Ahman Kiku or most Harmony commissioners. Those commissioners who did look at Marcer seemed to view him without empathy, as though an Altered was no longer the least human. Of those who watched him, only the Neulander, Kolet—another Altered—showed any sympathy, but it was detached, as though he was looking at a pitiable accident scene.

Marcer felt the walls closing in around him. He had to convince Ahman Kiku. "I agree," he said. "But this is all politics. I have never led a hidden life. I have never concealed that I'm Altered. My opinions are entirely Jonist."

A world delegate snorted in disbelief.

"I was born on Safi because of my parents' business trip. My father is a citizen; my mother was a noncitizen resident, a New Dawn Altered. Both were born in the Harmony. My sister was. The Harmony is my home. My future is there, and so is every place and person that I love." He felt a stab of guilt regarding Linnet, but this was not the moment for romantic confessions. "I am Jonist. I would defend our philosophy with my life. I protest the illegal removal of my Academic status. I protest my deportation. Please, sirs, accept my presence among your delegation and let me return home, if only to defend myself from these charges." Marcer looked at each of them in turn, except the Neulander. What he saw in their faces didn't encourage him.

"No." From his demeanor, the heavyset world delegate who answered was the senior member of the commission. He was able to dismiss Marcer with a glance. "This has taken enough of our time. Young man, you do not belong in the Harmony."

A sour odor clung to Marcer, something of which he had been imperfectly aware throughout the interview with the commission. He suddenly remembered the fruit he had tucked in his pocket for Linnet while at the wedding party. It had been crushed, immersed, and carried for hours. Now it was making him stink.

The soldiers took positions on either side of Marcer. They would escort him to Idryis Khan, a man who inspired fear even in his own people.

"Why?" Marcer burst out. "I can't help that I'm Altered or that I was born on Safi, but I would defend the Harmony with my last breath. Even when Purists make it uncomfortable, even when it's capricious or unfair, even if it rejects me, the Harmony is my home. What test can I take so you'll believe me? I don't deserve to be treated like this because of the politics at Center."

His outburst was met with silence. They were embarrassed, but for him, not themselves.

"The man doesn't know the charge against him." General Kolet's staccato Neulander accent made him sound boorish and blunt. Ahman Kiku protested, but Kolet spoke over Kiku's voice until Kiku stopped trying to silence him.

"Dr. Brice, your background gives them so many opportunities to expel you from your post and deport you from the Harmony, that a cynical man—I admit I am one—might speculate that you were chosen as the first Altered human in a Jonist Academy for that very reason. Your case has been discussed previously in my presence." He shot a hard look at Peter Isaacs. "To cut to the chase, Dr. Brice, you weren't deported because you are an Altered. After all, 20 percent of the Harmony is Altered, making a considerable, if nonvoting, constituency. *Officially,* you were deported because you are a secret religionist, a Jew."

"I'm not!"

Kolet shrugged and glanced at Ahman Kiku.

"Tell them!" Marcer started toward Peter, but the soldiers stopped him by grabbing his shoulder. Peter's mother was Lavi Brice's sister; though never confidants, the two boys had grown up within the same circle of family and friends. Both had pursued careers outside the family business. Peter was in an ideal position to dispel this charge.

Peter spoke to Marcer without looking at him. "I told the truth, that some of the family are Marranos. They pretend to be Jonist but secretly, privately, follow religionist superstitions. They light candles. They pray. I've admitted to these delegates that you're one of them." Peter's voice continued low and quick. "I'm sorry I had to testify against you, Marc, but it was necessary. To tell the truth." He looked at the heavyset delegate, who nodded.

"You see," Ahman Kiku said sternly. "Captain Isaacs has spoken against his own interests. You are no Jonist."

"You told them that?" The room had contracted to just Marcer and his cousin. Peter was a career military officer because, although a citizen, he had failed the entrance tests to the Academy of New Dawn a few years before Marcer applied. Because of the halo effect, Marcer had known Peter resented his Altered cousin, who had managed what he had not, but Peter Isaacs had always been an honorable man. In truth, some Brice relatives had peculiar and suspicious habits. Marcer ignored the candles and mumbled prayers since public knowledge of his relatives' failings would have reflected poorly on his own Academic career. Besides, Marcer would never have betrayed family.

"I had to, Marc," Peter whispered. He met Marcer's eyes and stared into them as though willing Marcer to understand and forgive. "I was posted to Testament . . . Some things happened. It wasn't my fault, but the governor got killed." He glanced at Ahman Kiku. "It would have meant my career."

"Instead of mine, you mean."

Peter looked at his plate, then up again. He continued in

a steadier voice. "I was recalled to Center for questioning. I was cleared—pending further investigation. While I was there, Elector Lee asked me about you. I told him that you were honest. He asked about the family; I told him the truth: your father said the Kaddish prayer when Grandpa died, and you were there. Later I heard that Lee ordered you deported. I'm sorry."

"Elector Lee?" General Kolet started to rise from the table, then thought better of it. "What did he have to do with this, Captain?"

"Kolet, you're here on sufferance," the heavyset man said curtly.

Marcer EL-ed; there was no reason not to, and the need was a crescendo of pressure and pain. He felt Peter's misery and knew it was real. So was the contempt and arrogance felt in varying degrees by the others. Governor Gordan and the Neulander general both felt some sympathy, but it was limited by a lack of personal concern.

Kolet's muscles were tense as he smiled and bowed an acknowledgment from a seated position. "We must all do our duty, Dr. Brice," Kolet said quietly to Marcer.

Marcer drew in a long breath, then regretted it. His teeth sent shooting pain through his body; it left him trembling. He turned back to Ahman Kiku. "It's simple justice to give me a chance to answer these lies."

Ahman Kiku pursed his lips in sour distaste. "You entered the Academy under false pretenses and advanced by subterfuge. You are neither a citizen nor a Jonist. We are finished with this shameful business. Captain Isaacs, tell our host that we're tired and need to rest before the treaty signing tomorrow."

Peter translated in a subdued voice as the Harmony officials rose ungracefully from the table, unaccustomed to being seated on the floor. The governor waved from his pillow like royalty ordering peasants to depart.

"Since I won't be signing anything," Kolet said more to the governor than to the Harmony commissioners, "I'll stay awhile. I'm curious about what will happen to Dr. Brice."

Marcer had failed. He wanted to throw himself at Roger Kiku's feet, to beg. He would have, if he'd held any hope that it would help. Why was Ahman Kiku even on Bralava? As Ahman of Sucre, Kiku was by tradition the next in line for an opening among the Electors. The likeliest next vacancy was for Jeroen Lee's red Elector's hat, and Lee's resignation or impeachment as an Altered could happen while Kiku was away. Why, then, was Kiku so far from Center? It was all politics, and at a level far beyond Marcer's knowledge. At a guess, if Elector Lee had been instrumental in sending Kiku out of Center at a time when he should have been marshaling his support among the other Ahman, it might explain Kiku's abundant displeasure and especially his dislike of Marcer, who, like Lee, was also Altered.

"Ahman," Marcer said. The flurry of movement wavered, and Kiku glanced back. "Ahman, I'm a victim of Elector Lee." He almost added, "like you." "I'm Altered, and my acceptance into the Academy shows the dishonor of his subterfuge, but Ahman, you have my word that I'm a Jonist and loyal to the *General Principles* of Jon Hsu."

"You have faith in Jonism, do you, Dr. Brice?"

Marcer saw the trap. "Ahman, my judgment tells me that Jonism is correct. My study of biology shows that the universe has Order, and I've never seen the slightest evidence of the supernatural. I act on reason, not faith."

Kiku studied Marcer for a moment. "You were deported on the direct order of Jeroen Lee. Without a full hearing, only he can annul that order. This mutual nonaggression treaty will, however, reopen the border. Brice, you can petition for readmittance through regular channels then. I will forward your application if it is addressed to me, and I'll add my endorsement of a request for a full hearing. At the moment, and here on a foreign world, there's nothing I can do." He bowed slightly, but courteously.

Marcer had changed Kiku's attitude, but not enough. The Ahman wouldn't extend himself for Marcer. "Sir, it's not just my career, it's my entire life. I can't stay here!"

Kiku frowned. "Good day, Brice," he said, then walked away beside the heavyset delegate. The other Harmony commission members followed briskly, except for Peter Isaacs, who lingered a moment as though his brief, continued presence was an apology. The Neulander also stayed.

Dignity was nothing against the long expanse of a wasted life, and more immediately, Idryis Khan, waiting to win. Desperate, Marcer thought that if he tried again, if he apologized and begged, Kiku might listen. Marcer started after him.

General Kolet left his place at the table and reached Marcer before the soldiers. He held Marcer back. "Don't chase them," he said. "They won't help."

The Khan's soldiers went for Kolet. He released his light grasp on Marcer's arm and assumed a wary stance. Marcer noticed a network of thin scars all over his hands and was reminded of Linnet. Neulanders.

"Leave him alone," Governor Gordan called. "He's part of their delegation." The soldiers stopped and moved into the background again.

"Though not for long, eh, Kolet?" Gordan added with rancorous respect. "You Neulanders should have known the Harmony would sell you out. They're too busy with internal squabbles. I understand there's a schism brewing among the Electors?"

Kolet didn't answer. "Governor, doesn't Researcher Brice's birth on Safi make him a citizen of the United Emirates? Wouldn't he have the right of appeal to Aleko Bei?"

Governor Gordan stood, using Maqsood as a crutch. "Birth alone doesn't make a citizen. Infidels are sojourners; they can be deported. He would need to submit to Islam."

"My mistake." Kolet glanced at Marcer. "On Neuland, we grant citizenship to everyone born there, and also to anyone who chooses to apply and has a citizen sponsor. I myself have sponsored several emigrants."

It was an invitation. The Republic of Neuland had a reputation for ruthlessness, but it was a civilized, Jonist world, a better place to make a life than anywhere in the Emirates—except for one thing. War was coming to Neuland, and sooner rather than later if the Harmony of Worlds had made a nonaggression pact with the United Emirates. Alans hated Neulanders. He remembered McCue questioning why.

Governor Gordan chuckled. "Who in their right mind would build a home in the path of a storm?"

"We like to think we live in the hurricane's eye." Kolet patted Marcer's shoulder. It hurt, and Marcer winced.

A pain-free Neulander, Kolet looked curiously at him, then leaned close as though to apologize. "Jeroen Lee always has reasons for what he does," Kolet whispered. "He wouldn't deport you without a good one. Ask yourself why he wanted you here." Kolet stepped back and studied Marcer's battered face with a medic's cool attention. "You were right that it's politics," he said more loudly, "and stupid to point it out."

"Really?" Marcer was bitter. "Exactly how did it hurt my position?"

Both the Neulander and Governor Gordan smiled. The governor started toward the door. Maqsood whispered something in his ear. "Come along, Kolet," Governor Gordan said, as though he and his antagonist were friends. "Your permission to enter the Emirates was restricted. You're not to speak with anyone except the Harmony commission and our representatives."

"Just a few words with my friend, here."

Gordan shook his head. "Dr. Brice is under arrest."

Kolet glanced at Marcer's guards, then joined Gordan and Maqsood on their way to the door. At the threshold, he turned back to Marcer. "Good luck, Researcher Brice."

Marcer was looking past him. Idryis Khan was just outside the door, regarding Marcer and Kolet with his heavy, steady stare.

"Ah," Governor Gordan said. "His warden has arrived."

III. A city of men.

Two women alone in a city of men had to move purposely. The alternative was harassment or outright molestation.

"It's almost dark," Nisa whispered to Fatima in indirect reproach. The women's curfew would begin an hour after dark, then only wicked women would walk the streets.

"Come," Fatima ordered. She ushered Nisa across the street to avoid a cluster of young men loitering on the corner ahead.

Nisa was tired. She was hungry. They'd walked the city all afternoon, and yet Nisa didn't know this woman's real name and had never seen her face. She was an authoritative voice, one too strong to belong to a woman. Who was she, anyway, this friend of a Jonist? She had a low-class, Fars-influenced, city accent.

"We need a hotel," Nisa said. "I'll be your son. Just let me find a dark corner to take this off." She had enjoyed wearing the chador, since it was by choice. The cloth was of poor quality. Its rough texture had kept her excitingly aware that it was camouflage. She had tired of it, however, and was ready to be an impostor boy.

"We're almost there." Fatima had made that claim before. Twice they'd skirted areas where police bats were out in force. Nisa suspected that Fatima's underground contacts were being rounded up. She supposed it was her fault, but the bats must have already known about them, or the arrests wouldn't have been so quick and thorough.

They passed a stand from which an unman was selling hot roasted peanuts. The fragrance made Nisa's mouth water, but a woman could not eat on the street.

"I'm hungry," she complained.

The woman stopped. "You don't know what hunger is," she said as though she were the aggrieved party, but she looked around. "Peanuts?"

"Fine, if I could eat them."

"Just slip them under your veil! It's easy." Fatima was as sharp with Nisa as her father. "Stay here while I buy them. Don't speak to anyone. You sound too rich for the neighborhood."

Fatima removed her gloves and felt in a pocket-purse for coins, then strode to the peanut vendor's stand, leaving Nisa entirely alone for the first time since she'd run away. A slovenly, middle-aged man looked her up and down as though seeing through her chador. Nisa was glad when Fatima returned. She handed Nisa the bag of warm peanuts, but Nisa gasped and dropped it on the pavement.

Fatima's hands were horridly scarred, as though she'd been in a fire and then through a war.

"I'm not getting you another bag," Fatima said gruffly.

"What happened to you?" Nisa's own hands were uncovered. She pointed, appalled.

"Oh, that. Nothing. We need to hurry; this isn't a game. If you're found, then you can't run to your father and just tell him you're sorry."

"I know," Nisa said irritably, but Fatima didn't seem to be listening.

Nisa, though troubled by Fatima's hands, followed her as she led Nisa through several narrow streets. There was no other choice. Nisa didn't even know where they were in the city.

They arrived at a wharf much larger than those they had passed earlier. Two steamships were docked. Fatima led

Nisa to a bench in a waiting area; the sign above it said
Ferry Boarding. A family group—a father and his three
sons, two of whom had the placid dispositions and hair-
lessness of unmen—was nearby, but otherwise it had the
subdued calm of a shop at closing time.

"Where are we going?" Nisa asked. A sign listed fares,
but it was angled poorly, and she couldn't read it. Fustat
Island was supposed to be pretty, but Nisa had never been
off the mainland.

"Hush. Listen." Fatima pressed close. Her voice was
muffled by the heavy cloth, but Nisa heard its tension. "We
have to pay for shelter and silence; my friends have been
arrested. I don't have enough cash for both of us. Do you
have any?"

Nisa had Ziller's purse and the money McCue had paid
her, but she didn't want to share it. "No. Nothing."

"Marcer thought you had valuable jewelry with you.
Do you?"

Nisa needed it for her future. "Not much."

"Show me."

"I don't think it's smart to go to an island; it'll be harder
to hide there and much harder to get away."

Fatima huffed, as though annoyed. Nisa couldn't be sure
through the chador. "We're not going to an island," Fatima
said. "Now, show me."

Nisa moved the chador slightly to the side, then drew
out one earring. "This is all I have." She extended it surreptitiously, to prevent the nearby men from seeing.

Fatima bent forward, the better to see the earring. "Its
mate?"

"I lost it." That was a patent lie, but she didn't think
Fatima, though skeptical, would call her on it. Nisa didn't
trust her enough to let her see the entire cache of jewelry.
In a day or two, once she got her bearings, Nisa decided
she would leave Fatima. Fatima didn't have useful contacts anymore.

"Give it to me." The woman extended her hand.

She might steal it. "I'll carry it myself."

"I need to know what it's worth. We'll have to sell it quickly.
What's the stone?" She snatched at the earring, and her
fingers closed around Nisa's hand. Her touch was smoothly
repugnant, like the glabrous flesh of Qadira's pet. Nisa
tugged the earring away from Fatima's grasp, dragging it.

The needle-sharp point of the post tore into the other woman's palm. A line of blood welled up from the cut. Nisa felt it immediately, wet, warm, and sticky on her hand. It reminded her unpleasantly of how she had killed Qadira's pet.

"Oh! I'm so sorry!" Nisa extended the earring. "Are you all right?" She was ashamed. Fatima had risked her life to help, and Nisa had met her with complaints and suspicion.

"What?" The woman looked down at her hand. "Oh. It's nothing. Never mind." She wiped the blood on the side of her black chador. "It will be fine."

"No, let me help you." Nisa reached for the injured hand. "We could wash it in a fountain." They had just passed one up the street.

"It's all right." Fatima wiped her hand against the chador again, not dabbing it gently, but pressing hard. It must have hurt. "Let's go." She started toward the ticket booth.

Nisa followed, contritely clutching the earring. The point was sharp. "I am sorry. Truly. Here, let me see how bad it is." She grabbed the woman's hand and turned it to view the palm.

Fatima's palm was scarred all over, crisscrossed by lines and a diagonal ridge which passed between her fingers and her thumb, but the only sign of the cut Nisa had just given her was a thin, pink line. Even as Nisa watched, it was disappearing.

Nisa dropped Fatima's hand and backed away from her. She had seen such healing before, in her enemy.

"You see?" Fatima said. "It's fine."

"You're one of them!" Nisa cried. "You're a houri!" She turned and ran from Fatima without direction or plan.

Chapter 10

When the Supplicant entered the hothouse garden three days later, Sanda Brauna was pacing angrily. "I called you here because *he* insisted on seeing you," Brauna said, making a broad gesture in the direction of a stranger.

The man she indicated bowed with arrogant élan. "Jeroen Lee," he introduced himself. "*Elector* Lee. And you must be the damsel in distress." He seemed delighted. "Lovely. And the human race at stake." He turned to Elector Brauna. "You've outdone yourself, Sanda."

So this was Jeroen Lee, the man who had hidden his Neulander Alteration from his fellow Jonists for decades. The Supplicant studied him as he smiled provocatively at Elector Brauna. Jeroen Lee was a handsome, aristocratic man, apparently of about forty, though she knew he was actually much older. He wore a perfectly tailored gray suit which made Brauna's crimson robe of office, though an interesting contrast with the lush green of her jungle, look crass. There was no sign that revelation of his origins concerned him unduly.

"I want to know how you learned so much." Elector Brauna slammed her dainty hand against the table, then winced. "Who told you?"

"Sanda," he said, as though she had disappointed him, "you know who writes my reports."

Sanda Brauna flushed and resumed her pacing.

The Supplicant cleared her throat. "What I've told Elector Brauna, and the data I brought—all of it is true."

"You're a liar," Lee said jovially. "Quite a good one."

"Get out!" Brauna shouted at him.

He ignored her. "Oh, not everything you've said is false, but"—he glanced at Sanda Brauna, including her in the conversation—"for an example, Revered Gangler's report says you claimed not to know Marcer Brice was Altered. You did know." He smiled kindly at her. "Didn't you?"

She wet her lips. "He never told me he was Altered."

"I haven't told you *I'm* Altered, yet you know. Who did tell you about Brice?" Jeroen Lee studied her as though he already knew the truth and wanted to see if she told it.

She hung her head. "Idryis Khan a'Husain."

"Interesting." Lee nodded, and glanced absently into Elector Brauna's lush garden, then back at the Supplicant. "And this Khan sent you here? It wasn't as you said before, that you were sent by Brice, working with the"—he turned to Elector Brauna as if for help with the name—"kitchen underground railroad?"

The Supplicant didn't dare tell another direct lie. She squirmed. Perspiration broke out on her forehead. "Marcer Brice was my friend," she said finally. "The first time I met him, I probably saved his life. He wanted the Harmony to know about Paradise. But no, he didn't send me."

Elector Brauna walked between the Supplicant and Elector Lee. "If the data is true—and I believe it is—what difference does it make how she managed to arrive in the Harmony of Worlds?"

"Sources and motivation always matter, my dear Sanda, especially when the information comes from across the border. Unfortunately the only person who knows the full truth is the man I deported. Brice."

"He's dead," the Supplicant blurted.

Lee tapped the packed-earth ground of Brauna's hothouse with the toe of his shoe. "That's unfortunate for him. Quite convenient for you, however."

"Perhaps you shouldn't have had him deported, Jeroen." Elector Brauna sounded snide.

Lee bowed in what the Supplicant suspected was an ironic manner; Harmony encounters had more skirmishing than she was used to seeing. "But then we wouldn't know anything at all, Sanda. That is, unless this Khan person found some alternate excuse to insinuate the data into the Harmony. Possible. He himself was on Darien not long ago." Lee smiled at the Supplicant. "Though I'm sure no other messenger would have been so beautiful."

"What are you implying, Jeroen?"

"I'm not implying anything," Lee said. "I am saying outright that you're being manipulated by this very pretty girl and, more importantly, by the man behind the scenes. This Khan."

"You think because you try to manipulate everyone, that others do it, too," Sanda said heatedly.

The Supplicant had assumed that because he was in disgrace, Elector Lee was irrelevant and unnecessary to her mission; she had been mistaken. Even in her own home, Lee dominated Sanda Brauna. He had intelligence, wit, boldness, and charisma; no wonder he hadn't been impeached even though having an Altered Elector violated nearly every important Harmony rule. The Supplicant needed him on her side. She needed to stop their quarrel.

"Please," she cried, "whatever you think of me, these creatures are real and dangerous. I've seen them myself. Please don't make this partisan! It might sound melodramatic, but the fate of the human race could be at stake." She went on her knees to Elector Lee. "I lied only because I thought it was vital to make you understand. You're right. I'd never have been able to leave the Emirates without the Khan's . . . influence, but I'm here because he's afraid of these things, too. He can't do anything about them. The Harmony is our only hope."

I. Pilgrimage.

Drugs are wonderful. Marcer felt his injuries yet didn't care. He knew his lying bastard of a cousin had betrayed him but was too stupefied to be distressed. He wasn't bothered that he had been discarded by the Harmony, although he vaguely wished he wasn't in the custody of Idryis Khan a'Husain. He hoped Linnet was safe. All he truly craved was water, but he wouldn't ask Idryis Khan for anything.

The young medic, who had proudly informed Marcer he was Harmony-trained, stopped tightening the cotton bindings around Marcer's ribs when Idryis Khan entered. "Finished?" the Khan asked.

"Nearly finished, Khan." As Idryis Khan looked over his shoulder, the medic grew more clumsy. He pressed stiffened fingers against Marcer's bruises until, despite the drugs, Marcer groaned.

Marcer had been placed in a large, simply furnished bedroom in Government House. Unlike most alan interiors, this one was carpeted, apparently designed for foreign visitors. When the Khan went to the window and pulled the lattice shutters aside, Marcer tried to see outdoors, but all he saw was sky. He closed his eyes.

The Khan returned to Marcer's bedside. In the face of his superior's impatience, the medic kept his head down and his attention strictly on his work. Marcer sensed the Khan's attention and looked. The Khan was staring into Marcer's face blankly, like a man in deep rapport with a utility, although Marcer hadn't seen any smart rooms in Shores, nor any house utility systems. Whatever the Khan's thoughts, his expression was unreadable.

The medic finished. He glanced at the Khan, then waited until the Khan seemed to come out of his reverie. He bowed. Strange, Marcer thought hazily. In the Harmony a bow meant respect; in the Emirates it was subservience. Or maybe he was wrong; perhaps he had never understood the Harmony.

Idryis Khan nodded rather than returning the medic's bow. Marcer felt the medic struggle not to take offense, to substitute submission for rancor. The medic revered the Khan, although the Khan was a man apart from his people. Son of the Prophet. The medic left.

"Don't do that!" Idryis Khan faced Marcer.

Marcer was too drugged for alarm. He was sheepish, however. He had EL-ed without conscious volition. "Sorry," he mumbled.

The Khan bent over Marcer, watching him. They were alone in the room. "You're mine. You are an infidel who is guilty of indecent conduct. Instead of prison, Gordan has placed you in my custody. You have no recourse. No appeal. I am your master. Do you understand?"

Marcer shuddered, remembering too much even for the drugs. He had made himself ridiculous. He had been abandoned. He had trusted his fellow Jonists. His colleagues. He had trusted Peter! His entire life had been spent believing that if he followed the rules—their rules—and did his best, he would be not just safe, but welcome. It was a lie.

"Answer me!"

Marcer's thoughts were heavy. He needed to close his eyes again. He turned his head to the wall, away from Idryis Khan, and wished for sleep.

Cold. It entered Marcer's spine like a sword, as though a spiked icicle had pierced him. It bored its way up and down his back. Frost penetrated his skull. It buried itself in his EL cavity, congealing sound into a solid. Its glacial bite made his EL-sense useless. Cold froze his eyes so that he ached to tear them out, but his fingers were brittle. The nerve endings in his hands and every other limb had petrified into thin crystal veins of ice. Frost fused his gut into a brick, then reached out for his heart.

Marcer whimpered at the bleak, frigid agony. He was dead inside. He faced a blank wall and couldn't turn or move.

"I own your life. You understand?"

Marcer's lips were stiff, as though he'd come into his grandparents' home in New Dawn's countryside after hours spent outdoors without his thermawrap. Wait, his grandmother Silvie had always cautioned. Idryis Khan was waiting. Marcer forced himself to speak. "Yes," he hissed, as though his words were steam rising from a hot pot.

The cold faded, but charred nerves, or frostbitten ones, remained. Marcer turned his head to see the Khan.

He held a slender rod pointed at Marcer. "I asked repeatedly," the Khan said. "You refused. Now you are a criminal in my custody. I require your obedience. I'll use this corrective again, whenever I need to." The Khan's matter-of-fact tone heightened the threat. "Understand?"

"Yes." Marcer's answer was quick.

"Good." The Khan dropped the corrective's control rod into a pocket of his military jacket. "The corrective was made in your beloved Harmony," he said. "It's versatile. I could make your body jump at my command, but I prefer to be more subtle. I let you choose: discomfort or obedience. In the long run, it's more effective training."

He watched Marcer, perhaps for a reaction. Marcer was grateful for the cushioning effect of the drugs. He revealed nothing because he felt so little.

"We will destroy Neuland if Aleko Bei proceeds as he plans," the Khan said. "This nonaggression treaty is an excuse for the Harmony to fail to act. Face-saving for when they do nothing." The Khan's expression didn't change, but his deep voice became louder. "Why does Aleko Bei want to kill millions of Neulander infidels? We need new lands, but space is vast; we don't need Neuland. The only answer is that the houris want it."

Idryis Khan picked up a thick, leather-bound book, which had lain on the bedside table. "A Qur'an," he said. "Actually, a translation from Arabic into your own script. You'll read it."

Ahman Kiku had accused Marcer of being a religionist. "I'm Jonist." He spoke softly, not eager to have the corrective used on him again.

"I know. And there can be no compulsion in religion." The Khan walked several steps away from the bed, turned, looked at Marcer, then said, "I'm not asking you to make the declaration of faith, the *Shahadah*, only to read. Paradise exists. It is a world men can visit. Houris originate there. Paradise has become a place where a man can get a wife without the burden of paying a bride-price and without the trouble of pleasing her family. Such men, we now say, are Blessed. Seventy-eight years ago Imam Khattab and Imam Maalouf agreed that this corporeal place was the Paradise of the Qur'an. They agreed, as others now have, that the women there are holy, that they are houris, the angels of Paradise. I want a Jonist biologist to tell me if he agrees."

Marcer's hurt pride made him reckless. "I can do that now. I don't agree."

Idryis Khan frowned. Marcer didn't need to EL to recognize its falsity. Every facial twitch expressing emotion the Khan made was calculated and counterfeit. Startled, Marcer felt the bounce-back and realized he was EL-ing. He stopped.

"I don't agree, either," the Khan said. He set the Qur'an back on the table, then kissed his fingers. "The pilgrimage commanded in the Qur'an is a pilgrimage to Makkah. The Paradise of the Qur'an is reached after death by the deserving, not a frontier world to be reached by any man with sufficient funds. If a man gets a wife on this worldly Paradise, a wife who will bear him sons, is such a man Blessed? Are his sons also Sons of the Prophet, God's blessings be upon him?"

"You're one of those Sons," Marcer said.

"Exactly. You will tell me what I am."

II. Red.

Ziller used his body to block Nisa from entering Hulweh's house. "No. It's too dangerous for the family. You can't come in, Nisa."

Filthy, famished, and exhausted, Nisa dragged feet that were raw and blistered. Her legs ached. So did her back and her arms. Her mind was alert, however, honed to a rare cunning by a night spent on the streets. "I have nowhere to go. Help me, Ziller, you're my only hope."

"I can't." He sounded regretful, but adamant.

The young unman servant who had opened the kitchen door was listening. Ziller stepped outside and closed the door behind himself, but he kept his hand on the doorknob. "We were all questioned," he said. "Hulweh is your friend; the police were hard on her. So was her father. *Your* father is frantic. The Khan says you've run, but your father won't believe it. He's waiting for a ransom demand and hoping you're not dead or dishonored."

She felt little, if any, sympathy for her father. He probably hoped she was dead. It would be simpler for him. She said nothing. The air was still. A shallow fog hung over the canal. It would be a hot, humid day.

Ziller sighed. "Nisette, go home if you can't survive the streets for a few more days. I can't do anything until the search shifts away from Shores. I won't let you involve Hulweh or the family. We're being watched."

Ziller could help; it was implicit in his attitude. He simply was unwilling. She had endangered her friends—he was right—but she didn't care. Her selfish expediency confused her, but she took a deep breath, and said, "During the night I was thinking about the kitchen express. Of course." She made a game attempt to smile. "Women live in women's quarters. Kitchens are unman territory. Why do you think it's called the 'kitchen express'?"

"I have no idea." His voice, for a moment, sounded deep as a man's. "Two men were arrested, implicated in your disappearance," Ziller said. "The ones with you in the boat."

Nisa heard the question in his statement. "I tricked them; *you* know they didn't kidnap me." She felt no guilt; she believed she never would again, not for anything she did to any man. She had helped Brice and McCue, maybe even saved Brice's life. She wondered why Brice had sent the houri Fatima to her. Should she have stayed with the houri? Some might be benevolent. She remembered Qadira's horrid creature and the ugly hands of Brice's houri friend. No, they were evil. Ziller was looking at her expectantly. "I'm sorry they're in trouble."

He shrugged. "They're infidels. They make easy scapegoats. At least it isn't one of us."

Did he mean unmen? Was he tacitly confirming her guess about the kitchen express? Or did he refer to Hulweh's family? Either excluded her. She had become an outsider, alone, exiled from her family and friends.

"Wait here," Ziller said. "I'll get money and fresh clothes." He went inside, opening the door only narrowly, as though she might try to sneak inside like a burglar if he was careless.

Nisa slumped to the ground, leaning against the polished white stone of Hulweh's father's house. The house was smaller and less grand than her—her father's—house, but its kitchen faced onto the same canal. If she stole a boat, she could return the same way she had left. The predawn sky had a pinkish glow. The canal water was smooth. No boats were out. Just yesterday she had anticipated this dawn with pleasure. She'd believed she would awaken with a gallant husband, the mistress of a beautiful house. She couldn't go back. Even if her father took her in, even if Idryis Khan divorced her, and even if Qadira suddenly became as sweet as she'd been foul, Nisa couldn't return; the sheltered, confident young woman she'd been was gone.

After running from Fatima, Nisa had ducked into an empty alley and removed her woman costume, bundling up the chador and hijab for possible later use. She had wanted to avoid being harassed, as a woman alone surely would have been. She needed rest and had Ziller's purse, so she had tried to rent a room. Twice she was turned away, once because she wanted a single and they didn't have any and once because she lacked papers proving her identity. The third place she tried was called the Inn of the Last Gate. The filthy lobby had made her hesitate, but the deskman had offered her a single room at only 78r and she had stayed. The door lock for her room had been broken, and she would have to share a common lavatory and basin but, exhausted, she'd fallen asleep on the bare, stuffed cob mattress, relieved to be invisible, behind walls again.

Only a short time later two men had intruded into her room. One had a knife. He ordered her to entertain them. "Play with" them was how they'd phrased it. She hadn't known what they meant, not exactly, and when she'd hesitated, the man with the knife had pulled her off the bed. He'd forced a kiss on her lips and his tongue into her mouth. His breath had been sour and smoky. His teeth were black at the gums, except for those that were missing. He had laughed and told the other man that she was soft as a woman. She had screamed until he punched her jaw. No help had come.

The man with the knife had tossed her bodily to the other man, then she'd been thrown back and forth between them like a rag doll. They'd joked when she cried for them to stop. They had slapped her when she tried to leave.

During their game, one man had touched her breast. He didn't send her tumbling to his friend. Instead he grabbed her breast, squeezing it so hard she shrieked. He didn't notice.

"A whore!" he shouted. "Inshallah! A woman!" He ripped off her shirt, stared, then yanked the torn cloth binding her breasts down around her waist.

They had both gawked as though they hadn't seen a woman in years, disbelief in their luck as strong and obvious as their lust. The man with the knife seized her arm, jerked her to him, bent down, and bit her nipple. "It's real!"

"I found her," the first man grumbled.

"Plenty to go around," the man with the knife had said. "And all night." He giggled. "Or maybe we'll keep her. She could be a gold mine! Not many real women around anymore."

"See if she has the rest of a woman's parts!"

The man with the knife used it to slash the waistband of her pants.

She had begged and struggled. They didn't answer, and hardly seemed to hear. They had appeared to be barely conscious of her as more than those "parts" which excited them.

Her pants fell to the ground. The one with the knife

fumbled with his and as she struggled to escape, he pitched her roughly onto the bed.

She cried as she would never cry again. They were larger, stronger, and aroused. They were two against one. Nisa couldn't stop them from doing as they pleased with her body.

Their pants were down. For the first time, Nisa saw what a man was; the organ was huge and ugly. "Please, no," she begged.

He noticed her terrified attention. "You want this? You'll have it, honey-sweet. First I want to play with you." He touched her belly and let his hand slide down. The other hand still held the knife. When Nisa squirmed, he climbed on top of her and put it to her throat. "Eager, aren't you?"

The jewelry had been released from its hiding place in her pants. It jangled as one of her rapists kicked it. The other man stooped to examine what made the noise. "Look at this!" His voice was soft, excited.

"Not now. Can't you see I'm busy?" the one on top of her said jovially.

"This is big money," the other said. "Bigger than selling her. *Look* at this stuff!"

"I'll be there, quick." The knife pricked Nisa's throat—unintentionally, she supposed—and she focused on that little pain to try to put the other, greater pain aside. He stared down at her, openmouthed, and she smelled his fetid breath as he shoved his dirty body into and against her. Eventually he stopped moving, put his head back and grunted. He stayed like that for a moment, then climbed off. "I just got a virgin!" he said.

"Yeah? Well look at this!"

He stood, gasped, then whispered a praise to Allah. "Show me all of it!" he ordered his friend.

Nisa rolled into a tight ball and listened to them exclaim over their good luck. As far as her father and husband were concerned, they would rather now that she be dead. She was polluted, but a grain of will remained to her, a desire to survive. This was her chance to escape, while they were distracted by their new wealth, though escape was too confident a word for flight that would come too late.

She had clutched her torn shirt with one hand and moved gradually to the edge of the bed. Naked, she had leapt from the bed to the door, tugged it open, and run without looking back.

If they'd chased her, she hadn't heard it. She ran without thought. Outside, the evening air cooled her bare skin. She was in an empty alley. Good fortune, if one could call it that, let her find hanging clothes. She'd stolen them, put them on, and walked.

Her new clothes had been too big and much shabbier than the servant's clothes from her father's house; she was also penniless. They had her purse as well as all her jewelry. When final curfew sounded, she had hidden from the bats, crouching just inside a neighborhood mosque. They hadn't found her, but the caretaker had walked through the mosque, awakening her from a doze. Afraid, she'd run outside. Later still, someone—she'd never seen if it had been bats or men of another kind—had chased her until finally she jumped into the canal. Never taught to swim, she'd somehow made her way to the farther side.

This wasn't the escape she'd planned. It wasn't the freedom she had wanted. She'd lost everything in a single day. Her ability to be selfish surprised her, but if Ziller didn't help, then she would die.

The door opened. Ziller held out a package. Still on the ground, too tired to get up, she took it. A clean set of servant's clothes was wrapped around a smaller bundle: a money purse.

"Five thousand rials," Ziller said. "All I had in the house. Go to a respectable part of the city; tell them you're in from the islands, looking for work. Meet me in the Frontsquare suq in Precious at noon in three days. Now go. Go, Nisa. Quickly."

"Thank you." She braced herself against the wall and stood. Even the short rest had been long enough for her muscles to stiffen. She felt the way she supposed an old woman would feel.

"Nisa," Ziller said. "You can do this. Others have."

Nisa nodded. She would get to the Harmony however she could. She straightened her shoulders self-consciously and walked away, trying not to drag her feet. It would be easier. It was normal for people to be outside in the daytime; her lack of a home was less obvious. She had all day to find a place to hide.

"Nisa!"

Nisa turned. Hulweh had run outdoors without a hijab cover. "Nisa. Wait!"

Hulweh caught up. "Come inside," she said. She put her arm around Nisa's shoulders.

Ziller had followed his mistress. "No," he said urgently. "They're searching for her. They might be watching us now." He eyed the peaceful kitchen dock as though police bats might bound, commandolike, over the top of the wall at any time.

Hulweh drew Nisa toward the open door. "Come in," she gently urged, ignoring Ziller. "I couldn't bear it if we sent you away."

Nisa let Hulweh lead her into the kitchen. Women could be strong. They could depend upon each other, maybe *only* on each other. Hulweh had overruled Ziller.

The kitchen was bustling with busy servants, none of whom looked up from their work, studiously avoiding seeing her. They knew who she was.

"Have a bath," Hulweh said. "Rest. Then we'll decide what to do."

Ziller sighed heavily. "Go out today," he ordered an undercook. "Find her a place."

The cook merely nodded.

Orders to find a place for her? Ziller was confident enough, too, to say it aloud in front of others. Hulweh was drawing Nisa away, upstairs, making a small joke as though this was just another visit. However much Ziller protested, Nisa was certain she was in the hands of professionals. She leaned against Hulweh. "I just want to sleep."

"First a bath." Hulweh grinned as she held her nose. "And look at your hair. It's so short it looks positively Jonist."

Nisa giggled to be sociable.

Upstairs, bathing seemed a luxury in a way it never had before. Hulweh put Nisa in her own bed. "You're safe," she whispered before leaving the room. "I won't let anyone hurt you."

Nisa couldn't sleep. She lay under the thin cotton cover with her eyes closed, pretending, because periodically Hulweh peered nearsightedly through the door, checking on her. Each time Nisa nearly dozed, she jerked awake with thoughts of red. Qadira's pet had red blood. She remembered it on the tile floor, being absorbed by the grout. She dreamed she ran through crimson tulips, barefoot, naked, thinking herself free, but then she was being chased. Her pursuer's face was hidden, but Nisa saw the ruby gleam in her mother's necklace, and it looked precisely as it had when she'd seen it around Qadira's neck—a drop of her mother's blood had become her stepmother's trophy. She remembered Qadira with the creature, taunting her. Nisa had washed her hands of the creature's blood in the servants' room. The bowl of the sink had been full of pink water, like the wastewater from an abattoir. Worst of all was the dream of herself, naked, spread-eagled on a table with men surrounding her, peeling away her skin, exposing the red muscle tissue and telling her it was all right, though they'd removed her skin, she wasn't really naked since she was covered by her blood.

Nisa opened her eyes. Warm sunlight blinded her. Hulweh's windows overlooked an exterior garden, not a courtyard. Nisa kicked the cover off and went to the nearest window. The street was out of sight behind a wall, but in the garden the household servants were lined up in a row of bald heads, guarded by police bats.

"No," Nisa whispered. Ziller had been right.

Next door, in Hulweh's public room, a woman screamed. Something crashed to the floor, shattered, then a man barked an order to be still. Nisa rushed to the door just as it burst open.

Two men in the maroon uniform of the Descent Assault Force entered the bedroom like they were charging an enemy position. The Khan's men.

She stopped in her tracks.

They raised their gleaming, black rifles and aimed at Nisa. "No!" she screamed, backing away.

Hulweh yelled from next door, calling for her father. There was a crack of flesh being struck, then Hulweh was silent.

"Nisa Khalil?"

Nisa clasped her borrowed sleeping gown around herself, gathering the thin material to shield her body, but there was no help for her uncovered face or her raggedly cut hair. For an instant she felt innocent and aggrieved. "Why are you here?" she demanded.

The nearest soldier grabbed her shoulder and shoved her

in front of him, into the other room. Nisa stumbled and fell, striking her chin on the threshold.

The public room had two more soldiers. They held Ziller at gunpoint. Hulweh was huddled on a low stool, her hands clenched and pressed against her mouth. She wore a thin, silk indoor chador, meager propriety in front of men. Her hair was hidden. Her face was uncovered.

Nisa rose slowly to her feet. Ziller looked alertly at the soldiers, but not at either Hulweh nor Nisa, making a show of giving them privacy despite their immodest clothes. These were private rooms. "Let them dress properly," Ziller said. "For the honor of this house."

"There's nothing honorable here." The soldier who spoke was a younger version of Idryis Khan: cold, hard, and hostile.

As though her thoughts of him were black magic, Idryis Khan a'Husain strode into the room. He surveyed them all. His eyes lingered longest on Hulweh, so long that tears formed in the corners of her eyes, but she wouldn't look down. She stared back at him as though she had the right. "This one is mine?" he asked the soldiers.

He couldn't recognize his own wife. His acre. He'd never seen her.

A soldier hit the butt of his gun against Ziller's head. "Answer the Khan."

Nisa's step forward was painful; it was toward the Khan. She was afraid Hulweh would claim to be his wife. "No. I'm Nisa Khalil."

The Khan inspected her; so did his men. Humiliated, Nisa tried to follow Hulweh's example. However immodest it appeared to the men, she stared back at the Khan. He was darkness incarnate, she decided. The houri's son. A dark angel. For simply producing these Sons, the houris were a calamity to women. "Come closer," the Khan ordered her.

"Sheik Khalil's daughter is a guest of our house. You have no right to be here." Hulweh had found her voice. She stood and faced the Khan without trembling.

"This is my wife, not the Sheik's daughter," the Khan said.

Hulweh smiled, having scored a victory by getting him to answer. She had never seemed more beautiful to Nisa than she did just then, disheveled, dishonored in her own home, displaying such vulnerable courage. "Nisa," Hulweh said, "go dress. We'll wait for my father."

"Come here," the Khan snapped at Nisa.

"I'm sorry," Nisa told Hulweh. "I'm so sorry." She had wronged her friend by entering her house; she was the architect of Hulweh's disgrace. Nisa went to Idryis Khan, head bowed, trying to think of a way to placate him. "I was afraid," she said. "My holy stepmother said you would kill me, but I was wrong to run away. Pardon me, husband."

He seemed unmoved. "You've cost me time and trouble. You've dishonored me in a way that nothing can cleanse."

"Khan . . ."

He slapped her. Despite his open hand, the blow sent Nisa spinning to the floor. Her lip was split. Blood was salty in her mouth.

"God is gentle and loves gentleness in all things." Ziller's tone was free of admonition, but the Prophet's words must have stung the Khan. He turned on Ziller.

"You are an abomination," the Khan said, "not a man. Not a woman either. How dare you quote the Prophet— God's blessings on him—to me? Me! His son."

Ziller looked calmly at Idryis Khan, but there was fire in his eyes. "How dare *you* make such a claim?"

Idryis Khan was at him in one long leap. He punched twice, both times connecting with Ziller's head. Ziller tumbled backward.

"Ziller!" Both Nisa and Hulweh rushed to him, but only Hulweh arrived. Idryis Khan grabbed Nisa by the hair, yanking her back, then put his arm around her throat, choking her.

Hulweh bent her head to Ziller's chest. She held her hand across his open mouth. She screamed at Idryis Khan, "You've killed him! Wait until my father sees what you've done! Breaking into our house! Threatening everyone. Staring at me! Forcing us to grovel because you're a Son!"

One of his soldiers raised his gun as though to bash it against her head, but the Khan gestured at him to stop. The Khan's expression didn't change. His intervention and his deceptive composure seemed to encourage Hulweh. "You're nothing but a bully," she shouted. Her hands stroked Ziller's bald head. "A murderer. He was an old man. We're unarmed women. You're certainly brave!"

Nisa was staring at Ziller. At his corpse. Dead. He was dead.

"They helped you, these two?" The Khan shook Nisa. She felt like a chew toy for a dog.

"No." Her voice quivered. "They were going to deliver me to my father. I asked if I could get clean first."

"Clean? No woman is ever clean." He shook Nisa once more, harder, then flung her aside. She staggered. "And I don't believe it anyway. You lie. I see it in your eyes."

Hulweh cradled Ziller as though he were her child.

Three of the Khan's four soldiers had the blank expressions of men who wished they weren't present; the fourth had the genuinely expressionless look of Idryis Khan. That one grabbed Hulweh and pulled her up. Ziller's head fell to the floor. The soldier dragged Hulweh upright until she was facing the Khan.

Idryis Khan spoke to her. "You helped her run away from me."

"No!" Nisa shouted. "I did it on my own." Hulweh was silent.

"You hid her. You disgraced your father's home."

"No!" Nisa saw murder in the Khan's stance. Hulweh didn't speak.

"Filthy bitch!" Idryis Khan slapped Hulweh.

"Don't you touch her!" Nisa charged him from the side. The soldier who had pulled Hulweh away from Ziller, moving as quickly as Nisa had ever seen anyone move, intercepted Nisa. He shoved her away from the Khan, and Nisa went flying toward Hulweh.

Hulweh stepped back, but although the Khan's hand had left a red outline on her face, Hulweh did nothing to indicate the blow had hurt her. When Nisa was pushed toward her, Hulweh caught Nisa in her open arms. They held each other in a tight embrace. Hulweh spat at Idryis Khan. "Bully," she said.

With easy grace, Idryis Khan reached toward his nearest soldier. The soldier placed his gun in the Khan's outstretched hand. The Khan raised it, and, without seeming to aim, he shot Hulweh through the head.

Blood, bone, and brains splattered Nisa. Hulweh died instantly. Her body sagged in Nisa's arms. Without meaning disrespect, and only because her muscles had seemed to liquefy, Nisa's arms dropped to her sides; Hulweh fell to the floor.

The Khan turned on Nisa. The gun was a long, dark tube, probing her life through its eye. Certain that he meant to kill her, she didn't flinch. The Khan kept the gun aimed at her. "Clean up the bodies," he ordered. "Apologize to the father and offer compensation." His attention traveled Hulweh's body. "Generous compensation." He lowered the gun and tossed it back to the soldier. "Bring my bride to my house, Demet. This afternoon I have other plans."

III. The women that men knew.

"Let me tell you about Paradise," Idryis Khan said. He went through a glass door into a long, open-air veranda that flanked a garden, then he held the door for Marcer. He was showing Marcer around his home, which had been built for him and his new wife. It was a mansion, if not quite a palace. Insofar as it was possible to judge his mood, Idryis Khan seemed expansive. However the Khan had spent the morning, it had pleased him.

"Paradise was found eighty-some standard years ago, not long before the Dark Exchange at the end of the Bril Wars, by a scoutship registered in Urfa, named *Hassan's Knife*. *Hassan's Knife* found the remains of a minor Bril installation, long abandoned, a crashed Bril ship, Bril bodies, and those of humans, presumably Bril captives. The human bodies had been carefully shrouded and buried. Or so it was later said."

Marcer made a noncommittal sound. The Khan had a story he wanted to tell. Let him. Marcer felt better, thanks to drugs and the medic who had prescribed them, but his right knee hurt terribly and his back ached; in a mirror, he'd scarcely recognized his face for the swelling, the cuts and the bruises. He didn't complain about the walk. He wanted to encourage this more genial aspect in the Khan.

"The crew of *Hassan's Knife* found dead men, but live women. Some said they were women captives from the crashed Bril ship." Idryis Khan walked quickly along the veranda, then waited for Marcer to catch up; it seemed he couldn't slow his gait to match Marcer's hobble. Their stroll through the mansion had been a series of starts and stops by Idryis Khan. While he waited, the Khan inspected his garden. Marcer glanced there, too. Entirely private, the newly laid garden was enclosed on three sides by different wings of the house: the main wing, with the public rooms and private suites for men; the veranda, which was in front of the housekeeping wing, containing the kitchen and servants' quarters; and the smallest wing, for women—if any. The fourth side of the garden overlooked the sea. The house was situated on a small peninsula just over an hour by ground coach from Shores.

"But these women were strange," the Khan continued as if there had been no pause. "They couldn't speak intelligibly. The mullah aboard *Hassan's Knife,* though not a learned man, recognized them and trained them to be modest—apparently at first they took wives from among the women. They were willing, and there was no bride-price."

"He recognized them as what?" Marcer was curious despite himself.

Idryis Khan looked out at the seascape. Nothing manmade was visible. "As houris. Do you know what houris are?"

They were the women from Paradise, a self-reflexive and therefore meaningless description. "No," Marcer said.

"Virgins. The eternal virgins promised to the faithful when they attain paradise. The mullah said that the world they'd found was a piece of paradise sent by the Prophet— God's blessing and peace be upon him—to guide mortals to God's will out among the stars. Another prophet is, of course, forbidden by the holy Qur'an. The Prophet, God's blessing and peace be upon him, is the last." Idryis Khan walked the three steps from the veranda down into the garden proper. As he waited again for Marcer, he picked a yellow flower, twirling its stem between his fingers in one of his rare shows of uneasiness. Or impatience. Marcer couldn't be sure.

"The mullah's interpretation was challenged. Many said it was merely another planet, and the women were survivors, as I've said. Their strangeness was explained as a result of the horrible experiments performed on humans by the Bril. The women themselves gave no answers. They could not speak any language men knew, and even now the houris don't speak well. It's claimed that they're too holy for our words, even Arabic, the language of the Qur'an." The Khan watched Marcer.

"The houris became popular brides," the Khan said, "an alternative to paying a bride-price for women, and opinion gradually agreed with the original mullah. Houris are clearly female, but just as clearly they are different from the women that men knew. And eighty years later it is impossible that they are still survivors of a crash. There are far too many of them."

"There are more women on Paradise than those the scoutship found eighty years ago?" Marcer was puzzled.

"Tens of thousands more. Plus the tens of thousands on Qandahar and other worlds of the Emirates. Bralava is backward; only a few of its most important men have made the pilgrimage to Paradise, so far. No one knows how houris are born, but they seem almost as plentiful as the men seeking them.

"Imam Nemasty wrote that the plenitude of houris is a sign, a miracle. Like manna in the desert, something sent by God to keep men holy and alive." He glanced at Marcer and began to explain. "The Jews were wandering in the desert after slavery . . ."

"I know the story." Marcer was curt. A proper Jonist would not have known. That Lavi Brice had provided his two children with a classical education as well as an Academic one had always been an embarrassment to Marcer; it had compromised him with the Academy.

The Khan nodded. "It's said that the houris carry God's design for us, so men listen to their counsel. Also, houris make good wives. They give men sons, only sons. Never daughters. They are beautiful and welcoming to their husbands. Advice of the holy ones has no force of law, and they cannot make a new Qur'an, but the holy women are eagerly obeyed. If they are messengers from Allah, then it is good and right for men to submit to them. If men do not submit, they withdraw their favor; the wife will return to Paradise. Then a man is no longer Blessed. His opinions lose all authority. And houris' Sons are important men, although they themselves are not capable of having children." He glanced at Marcer.

At the wedding, Sheik Radi had claimed it was Marcer's intended job to make the Sons capable of producing children, but the Khan did not pursue the subject of his infertility.

"So men make the pilgrimage to Paradise rather than Makkah," the Khan continued. "Old Earth is a dangerous and expensive destination, but a man who goes to Paradise is safe and comes back richer: not only a hadj but with a holy wife." As he spoke, the Khan picked the petals from the flower until it was only a coarse, hairy stem with a brown cone. He tossed it onto the path and looked directly at Marcer. "The proof that they are houris seems irrefutable. They are perpetually virgin. Every time. A man's touch doesn't soil them."

"What?"

Idryis Khan nodded gravely. "They remain intact after intercourse."

Marcer laughed. Idryis Khan didn't join in, but neither did he appear disturbed by Marcer's reaction. "Do you mean that a houri's hymen is impenetrable or that it heals?" Marcer had spoken with humor. In a different tone, he answered his own question. "It heals. Neuland."

"Exactly." The Khan placed his hands behind his back and started down the garden path. Marcer lagged behind, tired by the effort of trying to keep pace with a healthy, sound man. "Anyone could make the connection," the Khan said. "Few do, and even they claim it's coincidence. Neulander women are not houris. For one thing, they don't bear only sons; for another, they use language as well as any woman."

Excited by the connections being made in his mind, Marcer reached thoughtlessly out to touch the Khan's arm as a nonverbal signal to slow down or stop. Idryis Khan whipped around, his hand already a fist. He saw Marcer, hesitated, then opened his hand and dropped it to his side, flexing his fingers as though they were sore. "What?" he asked gruffly.

"How well do you heal?"

"Normally. Not like a Neulander."

"Do the houris have RHF? Rapid healing?"

The Khan shrugged. "Not to my knowledge. At least, not like a Neulander. I've never seen one with scars." He hesitated, then went on. "I know only my own mother and a very few others. As a son, not a husband. Sons are not permitted to marry houris."

Marcer nodded impatiently. "Just what are the houris' differences from ordinary women?"

"They use poor grammar, even when their vocabulary is complete. None of them can read. They have a different look, exotic and recognizable. Large, dark eyes. Men find them beautiful, though part of that may be their presumed holiness. They don't age. They return to Paradise once their husband dies, or earlier in some cases, but several have been married for more than fifty years with no sign of growing old. They can bear Sons throughout their lives. Most have a Son every year. Had. The houris have recently, gradually stopped becoming pregnant. They say they won't bear more Sons until Neuland is destroyed, forcing Aleko Bei to undertake a war against Neuland. A holy war. A jihad."

"No menopause?" Marcer had fixed on that difference because it was so peculiar. In the Harmony, people didn't appear to age. But like upright posture and big brains, human female menopause was a hallmark of humanity, a difference from most terrestrial animals and never found in healthy nonterrestrial species.

"No." The Khan continued listing other differences. "They're small, but not abnormally. Sons are small at birth, too." He spread his arms, displaying his size, which was large in the Emirates. "There isn't much other information, but I've provided what there is in your new lab database."

Your new lab. As though Idryis Khan was an Academy administrator assigning space.

"There it is." Idryis Khan gestured at the windows and open door of a large room which faced onto the veranda, looking out at the garden and the sea. "A pleasant location. You should have come voluntarily, but even so, there is no reason that our association must be one of compulsion, or that your visit here should be unpleasant. The work is substantive; it may even bring you fame. I don't bear you any malice."

"That's why you're carrying the control rod for the corrective."

The Khan nodded, taking Marcer's comment at face value. "I cannot afford to let this investigation become public knowledge."

They reached an arrangement of luxurious fiberfoam chairs around a sculpted stone table. Marcer used the back of a chair for support. The fiberfoam molded to the shape of his hands. He would have liked to sit and let it mold around his body, but his one physical advantage over Idryis Khan was his greater height. He didn't want to lose whatever psychological benefit it provided. "Public?" he said. "It doesn't matter what the *public* knows. The Emirates is a chrysocracy. The wealthy are powerful and the powerful openly make the rules." Marcer remembered his first dinner on Bralava with the Khan and the governor. "Does your cousin, Aleko Bei, know what you're doing? His governor gave me into your custody."

The Khan pulled out a chair and sat at the table. Rather than diminishing his authority, his position enhanced it. "A man is the ruler of his household and will be questioned on the Day of Judgment about those under his care. So said the Prophet, God's blessing and peace be upon him. You are a member of my household. *You* do not question *me*."

The Khan claimed a God-given right to command Marcer. His real control came from the governor and the corrective; his belief was the kind of idiocy that would have been amusing in the Harmony. Marcer restrained himself from a bitter reply. They weren't in the Harmony. He bowed.

Marcer glanced around the garden, inhaling the fragrance of terrestrial flowers. Nothing native to Bralava had been planted. The style was too regular and manicured for Marcer, but then, his taste was for the wild. Nevertheless, the Khan's mansion *was* pleasant. The open sea vista ahead was an invitation to EL. He didn't resist.

"Why do you do that when you can see perfectly well?"

Marcer flushed and looked at the Khan. "Why do you look when you've heard something? It's another sense. Another way to experience the world."

"I would prefer that you not do it around me anymore."

Idryis Khan reacted as though the sound was more than simple noise. Exceptional abilities by houris' Sons was within the scope of his assigned investigation. "Why not?"

The Khan stood and moved away from him. "It bothers me."

Marcer remembered the sensitivity of the demon jinn to his EL signal. Like houris, and therefore like their Sons, jinn were from Paradise. He grinned and turned aside so the Khan wouldn't see it. "Do you know much about Neuland?" Marcer asked casually.

The Khan shook his head no.

"The majority of Neuland's native animals heal normally—that is, within the average range of terrestrial and nonterrestrial animals—and they feel pain. The famous Neulander rapid healing and pain-free complex exists only in a few. The most common, excepting the Altered human population, of course, is the hummer, a hairless quadruped herbivore."

The Khan placed his hands behind his back and walked away from Marcer, down the path to a lookout point at the garden's edge. Marcer limped after him. The path consisted of loose, white stone, which crunched underfoot and rolled. Marcer watched his feet, afraid of slipping. A fall would hurt.

Marcer leaned against the rail beside Idryis Khan. "You can guess how the hummer acquired its name," he continued. "It uses sound in its social behavior. Not as language; more like terrestrial pheromones.

"I mention hummers because a friend of mine, also a New Dawn Altered, took a work contract on Neuland. They pay Harmony-trained contract labor very well, although it's a dangerous place to live, thanks to Emirates raids. Anyway, my friend had a peculiar problem on Neuland. Whenever he EL-ed where there were hummers, they flocked to him. Both sexes would try to mate with his leg."

Marcer glanced sideways at the Khan, whose expression was, as usual, imperturbable. "Apparently an EL signal is close in wavelength to the hummer signal of sexual availability." Marcer paused like a comic delaying the punch line for maximum impact. "Is there a sexual element in the sound of my EL? Is that what bothers you?"

Idryis Khan gripped the rail so tightly that his knuckles were white. He didn't face Marcer. "I am not," he said with slow, deliberate enunciation, "a hairless Neulander herbivore. I am not an animal."

"We are all animals," Marcer said in a lecturing tone. "Intelligent animals. Every one of us has antecedents and relatives. For some Altereds, those antecedents don't originate entirely on Earth. Altered Neulanders, for example. Their genetic heritage is shared not only with humans, but also with hummers. Humans with the Neulander Alteration don't seem affected by an EL signal, however. According to my friend." Marcer's knee ached. He leaned more of his weight against the rail. The apparent cliff down to the sea was only a hillock with a gentle grade, so he felt safe.

"You want a biologist to investigate the houris and their Sons. You say you want to know what you are. Apparently, however, you want most to understand why the houris are demanding that the Emirates conquer Neuland."

"Not 'conquer,' " the Khan interrupted. "They want it destroyed and all its people dead."

Marcer stared a moment, but insofar as it was possible to determine, the Khan seemed serious. "Since you've asked a biologist," Marcer went on, "you must believe there is a biological connection between Paradise and Neuland that will answer your question. We aren't sure about the rapid-healing/pain-free complex, but if your irritation regarding my EL signal is similar to what hummers seem to feel, then there is a possible link to explore." The urge to EL came again, probably caused by the Khan's hostile stance, but Marcer clenched his teeth, and it passed.

The Khan looked out to sea as he answered. His tone was cool. "When you do that thing, yes, there is a sexual feeling. Noticeable, but gentle. Pleasant. Not like anything else. I'm glad to know what it is. Thank you."

"The connection is a hypothesis, not tested and proven," Marcer said. In his heart he was certain, and also subtly pleased by the vindication of the usefulness of his Altered sense. It was another means of investigation, as well as an explanation of the Khan's personal interest in him. "I'll try not to EL."

Marcer had been holding the rail with both hands to keep weight off his injured right knee. Idryis Khan covered Marcer's left hand with his own right. "Thank you," the Khan said, "but now that I understand, it's all right." The Khan's gentleness seemed real. The Qur'an, with its super-stitious restrictions on pleasure, forbade homosexual rela-tions. Marcer had just provided an explanation for the Khan's desire which didn't shame him.

Marcer had been given a room near that of the Khan. His new understanding didn't make him dislike the arrange-ment any less. The eroticism of an EL signal was probably not enough on its own to induce lust in the Khan, an intelli-gent being, unless he was attracted in the first place.

Throughout Marcer's explanation the Khan had stared into the distance, not at Marcer. It was a change from his usual behavior. Was it a sign of strong emotion?

"There is another connection," Marcer said. "The jinn— the houris' pets—are also sensitive to my EL signal. I've seen it myself, in Shores. It's almost like calling them. They don't try to mate with my leg—fortunately for me—so I suppose there isn't a sexual feeling involved. They have tried to bite me once or twice." Marcer chuckled.

"Tell me more about these hummers," the Khan said.

It was an order. Marcer wished there was somewhere to sit; his aches had worsened during the tour. His right leg was trembling. "There is a theory that the hummers and other Neuland animals with the rapid-healing/pain-free complex were transported to Neuland from another world, since they are distinct genetically from the rest of Neuland's creatures. That theory has been discredited, however, because hummers have a significant number of genetic commonalties with other Neulander animals, too. As to a connection with the jinn because of their reaction to my echo-location, there are many differences. For example, hummers don't camouflage themselves.

"Hummers also use what would seem to us to be aggressive behaviors in apparently friendly social contexts. They scratch and bite their companions as greetings. The view of Neulander investigators is that because of RHF, the Rapid-Healing Factor, there is no reason to avoid such social rituals. Other biologists disagree. Even with rapid-healing, there is *some* risk of infection. It's especially odd that these behaviors occur during mating; theory says that all the female's energies should be spent on producing offspring, not on healing the significant wounds the pair inflict on each other during courtship." Marcer realized he had become pedantic. He stopped his lecture.

"I'm pleased," the Khan said. "I was right to want you to work on this problem. You're already full of ideas. Interesting ones."

The time seemed right. "There is someone who should be brought here," Marcer said, uncertain whether or not he was doing Linnet any favor, but he needed to know she was safe. "A woman named Linnet Wali. I was arrested at her home. She's . . ."

"A whore," the Khan interrupted. He was well informed—McCue.

"My friend."

"No. Absolutely no."

Marcer was surprised at the Khan's vehemence. "She has Neulander ancestry, which would be useful."

"No." Idryis Khan turned and set off back the way they had come. Marcer followed at his own pace, glad of the few moments alone. His inability to receive any halo effect from Idryis Khan set him on edge, and he was trying to think of a way past the Khan's objection to Linnet. Idryis Khan would not be moved by begging.

"You need a cane," Idryis Khan said irritably when Marcer was close.

A cane. Despite his Harmony training, the Khan's medic practiced old-fashioned medicine. Marcer shook his head. "What I need is an assistant. I don't know a word of Arabic; I can't read Arabic script. I assume the records are written in it." The Khan nodded. "Linnet is ideal," Marcer continued. "She can read, and her Neulander background will be useful, even with your stored data." It was sensible and true.

"No." Idryis Khan raised his voice. "I won't have a filthy creature like that in my house." He gestured at a doorway which opened onto the veranda. "That's your workroom— your laboratory. If it doesn't suit you, or you need other equipment, let me know."

"I would at least like to know that Linnet is safe," Marcer said. "You threatened her once already, and I owe her a great deal, perhaps even my life."

"You owe your life to me." The Khan gestured at the open laboratory door. "Come. I'll show your laboratory to you. Or do you need to be reminded that this is your prison?" He lifted the corrective's control rod partly from his pocket.

So much for the milder, gentler Khan. Marcer had done as much as he could for the moment. The key to making Linnet safe was to ensure that Idryis Khan wanted to please Marcer. If Marcer could discover whatever it was about the houris that caused them to want to destroy Neuland, then Marcer would have bargaining power. Beyond that, if the Khan wasn't lying about their intentions, this was something that needed to be known. Marcer heeled like a dog and walked into the laboratory, hoping he wasn't rationalizing an obedience which really came from fear.

Marcer stopped just beyond the room's threshold. He remembered the buildings crammed with instruments and techs that constituted the biology research facilities at the Academy of Darien, or even the smaller installation at New Dawn. Idryis Khan had assembled a hodgepodge of antique and antiquated equipment, scattered it randomly in a single large room, and called it a lab.

"Look." Idryis Khan pointed.

A thing was in the center of the room beneath a warming light. Marcer limped closer. The Khan remained near the door. The object's surface had the loose, sticky texture of spun spidersilk. It glowed with an opalescent gold-green light that seemed internal, though the surface wasn't translucent. Marcer couldn't see any of the structures inside. It was pear-shaped, about one and a half meters long, or perhaps a bit less, and was only about a half meter across at its widest point. "What is it?" Marcer asked, looking back at the Khan.

"You tell me. You're the nonterrestrial biologist."

Human instinct was an inaccurate judge of nonterrestrial organisms. Experience was equally flawed, if it was experience gained on a different world. Marcer didn't even know the world from which it came. Paradise? Probably. The object could have been anything: an egg, a seed, a shell, stored food, or even alien dung. The need for warmth made it likely to be living. The fact that it was here said it was important to Idryis Khan. The Khan expected an answer; this was a test. Marcer remembered what he knew of the hummer life cycle. Occasionally, if one lived long enough, it metamorphosed into—another hummer. Marcer guessed. "A cocoon."

Idryis Khan gave one of his tight, false smiles. "Yes," he said. "So you *do* know your job."

Marcer didn't return the smile. The Khan was a fool. A layman. Marcer had been lucky. Metamorphosis of a creature this size was unusual. He bent close and sniffed the cocoon. Its faint odor was of musty foliage, like earthen grass cut, then set aside in a closet. He refrained from EL-ing; it probably wouldn't penetrate inside anyway. "What is it? Is this part of the life cycle of the houris' pets, the jinn?" Marcer asked, hazarding a guess.

"No," the Khan said. "Something else went in."

He was being coy. Marcer was certain he would be told more; this was clearly part of what he was to investigate. Rather than ask, Marcer looked around the meager laboratory.

Long counters atop cabinet-style shelving lined one wall; there also was a deep sink, set low. An old-fashioned but serviceable electron and general microscope assemblage was installed on a table next to a slightly more modern DNA-scan. The equipment may have been imported from the Harmony; that would explain its age, since there were restrictions on technotrade—he knew it from his father's comments on Brice-Isaacs business. A new screen and voice/keyboard sat on another table. The single chair indicated this was meant as a desk. There were several stools, but the lab was essentially set up for one person.

Open cases of glass containers and chemicals labeled in Arabic script were stacked on open shelving. Another wall had more closed cabinets. An unused dissecting table had its own light system but no tissue analyst.

A row of windows looked out through the veranda to the garden. Beyond it, the sea and sky were visible. It was the most scenic view Marcer had ever had, much better than the flat window-screens of the Academy of Darien; it was also the worst-equipped laboratory he'd seen.

"Tell me what else you'll need, and I'll get it." The Khan was proud of the laboratory.

Marcer shook his head. "I wouldn't know where to begin."

The Khan grunted. "Don't make excuses for not working. My contacts say this is sufficient. If you need more, make a list. If it's available on Bralava, you'll have it. You can begin by studying that." He pointed at the cocoon and grimaced. His expression even seemed to be spontaneous. "My mother went inside."

IV. Buried Alive.

Shackles around Nisa's right ankle kept her from moving more than four feet from the post centered on the floor of the otherwise empty, dark, windowless room. There were no cellars in Shores, but the dampness was richer than the usual canal stench. The trip in the closed coach had been over an hour.

Though Nisa held her breath and listened, she heard nothing. The Citadel—any prison—would have been filled with noise, the cries and whimpers of the inmates and the shouted orders of the guards. These walls were very thick, or she was elsewhere.

Her homicidal husband had probably sent her to his house.

Nisa shifted position. There was nothing to look at. The cold limestone floor was polished and clean. There was no drain, as there would have been in a kitchen or a prison cell. The walls were white tile, heavily glazed since they had shone while the door was open, as the uniformed soldiers attached her to the post. The post was ironwood, set into the room later since there was a concrete mound keeping it in position. She had nothing to do except learn patience.

This was it. This was her life. Idryis Khan would never free her. Either she would be fed periodically, and therefore given a long, barren, and eventually lunatic life, or she would starve to death in a few weeks. In either case, she had been buried alive.

Chapter 11

The Supplicant described the houris' menace as an alien invasion and urged the six Electors to use their Conclave to endorse a lethal counterstrike. She emphasized the likely connection between the houris and the Bril; she called a conflict with the houris the Last War's final battle and reminded them that only a united humanity had exterminated the Bril. The six listened politely, although Elector Lee gently complained that her testimony was redundant since they had a written report and Marcer Brice's data.

If the Electors were moved by the Supplicant, they didn't show it. Their formal scarlet hats and gowns made their faces ruddy, particularly so Sanda Brauna's. She seemed to blush.

Afterward, the Electors questioned her. Jeroen Lee went first. "So you have met only one houri, your stepmother. Tell me, child, aren't stepmothers generally considered wicked?"

An Elector chuckled; another cleared his throat as if he would have, but thought better of it. The others smiled, except Sanda.

The Supplicant had also seen houri visitors to the house, but that wasn't worth explaining. "Imagine this," she said earnestly. "An alien invasion happens. The aliens come to human worlds disguised as women—and men don't even notice." She looked at each of them in turn and was surprised to see that despite his banter, Jeroen Lee looked thoughtful. He was the key to the other Electors' support. Although two Electors, including Sanda Brauna, had tried to avoid him, and the remaining three had greeted him with awkward formality, he set the meeting's tone. He was a biologist; the others were not, and they knew it.

Encouraged, she tried to use their terminology. "By the nature of alan society, women aren't seen. Unmen, the alan eunuchs, do work that was formerly women's work. All women have left is to bear children; houris can do that."

"For one generation," Elector Lee interrupted. "The data explicitly says that their children, these so-called Sons of the Prophet, are infertile." He glanced at his colleagues, seated around the austere conference table. "Based on this data I tend to discount the threat. They aren't spawning a new, hybrid race."

"If women are replaced by unmen and houris, the human race dies, with or without a replacement," the Supplicant protested. "To destroy the houris furthers Order."

The Electors frowned. The one who had cleared his throat said, "It seems to me that the problem is Emirates society, not these so-called angels. It couldn't happen here, where men and women meet face-to-face as equals. Why should we do anything? Let the alans slowly kill themselves. These alien angels just show the weakness of religionist superstitions." He looked around the table. "We might publicize this as an endorsement of Jonism's superiority."

The Supplicant didn't understand Harmony politics. Aleko Bei decided, then issued orders, without any more discussion than he himself allowed. That was how a proper ruler governed. The Harmony had no ruler; it had a system. Even if all six Electors agreed and issued their Joint Ruling, they weren't the Harmony government. The Grand Assembly of Worlds would still need to vote to send a military expedition against Paradise. The process seemed cumbersome and inefficient, but it was what she had to work with.

"It's true that Emirates society made it easy for the houris. It's true that faith"—a dirty word in the Harmony—"caused invaders to be considered houris. Angels." The Supplicant paused. She and Sanda had worked out this response together. "But there is no reason to assume that there can only be impostors who are female. There might be male impostors. They may already have entered the Harmony." Men feared other men, not women or their impersonators.

"Scare tactics," Elector Lee said when, almost involuntarily, the Electors looked to him for an opinion. "There is nothing to support that hypothesis. It seems likely from my reading of Brice's data that the creatures *must* be female. However, I can't absolutely rule it out without a great deal more information than what is available to us. Independent information." He smiled at the Supplicant. "This is tainted. It was planted in our laps by an alan nobleman—himself a houri's son with unknown motives of his own. There have been rumors about strange doings on Bralava. There is even a report, though I discount it, that this nobleman is dead."

The Electors turned on Sanda Brauna. "It's all a lie?" one asked.

"Unfortunately, no." Jeroen Lee raised his voice as he answered for her. "The houris exist. The theory connecting them with the Bril is the best rationale we have for interaction between primordial Neuland and these intelligent but nontechnological inhabitants of Paradise. Brice's conclusions are excessively alarmist—perhaps they were . . . elaborated upon by someone else—but the content of his report is sound. I have independent verification of certain points through a long-term research project I've been running."

"You have spies in the Emirates?" an Elector asked.

Lee didn't answer. He shifted position in his chair. "Despite what I've said, there remains an issue that concerns me." He hesitated. His voice dropped and he looked down at the table. "Neuland." He sighed, then met the eyes of each of them. "Hummers exist, even though all the data indicate they shouldn't. Assuming we're correct, and they are a hybrid of an indigenous Neuland and an imported Paradise species, then how do we explain them? The hybrids created by these aliens' peculiar life cycle are supposed to be infertile, yet descendants continue to exist. And let me point out that whatever native Neulander species hummers arose from is now extinct.

"Our data is suspect. I have to wonder if a human-houri hybrid species could be created, one that is fertile just as the hummers are. We need to know more. But since we can't know it anytime soon, then it's my reluctant opinion that we should consider the houris a threat to the entire human race."

I. Angels and aliens.

The manservant—a man, not an unman—bowed to Marcer to a depth which would have been obsequious in the Harmony, or else ironic. Marcer missed the affable unmen from Linnet's building; with only one exception, all the Khan's servants were unaltered men, and all were unpleasant or aloof. Several were obviously soldiers wearing a plain-clothes disguise.

Marcer set the visual display on pause, then pushed away the 3-D graphic visualization generated by the clumsy con-focal laser scanning system the Khan had supplied. "What is it?"

"The Khan wants you. He's in the sea garden." Having delivered his message, the servant left without any addi-tional courtesy.

It was unwise to delay when summoned by Idryis Khan. The sea garden was what the staff called the courtyard outside Marcer's lab. Preoccupied with his work, Marcer hadn't noticed, but now he heard voices. The Khan was not alone.

Marcer stretched. After ten days, his bruises were fading, the muscle ache was gone, but his knee still hurt. No expert, Marcer guessed permanent damage had been done.

He went outside. The weather was excellent. Marcer had arrived on Bralava during late spring; it was now early sum-mer. Rated as a Familiar, Bralava had important differ-ences from cool, dim, Extreme-rated New Dawn, but Marcer felt physically at ease and atavistically at home, as he never had on Darien. Sunlight lifted his spirits. He en-joyed being outdoors, and the Khan's mansion encouraged it. His regular reports to the Khan were often made on what Marcer thought of as garden-viewing platforms, the overlooks where benches, tables, and chairs were placed in well-maintained clearings. All the estate's gardens were manicured, unnaturally symmetrical, and emphasized water; they weren't meant to be strolled, they were to be watched. Tame though they were, Marcer was developing an appreci-ation for them. People adapt.

He limped toward the voices. They were on the sea plat-form, overlooking the water, the Khan's usual spot. Two men had joined the Khan; both wore the uniform of the Khan's staff officers. The three formed a peculiar, triangu-lar group. The Khan stood at the rail, surveying the sea. His two officers were seated. They had dragged the chairs to a maximum comfortable speaking distance from each other, and all three spoke loudly as a consequence. He heard their conversation clearly as he approached.

The alans were congratulating each other: Word had

come by special high-speed courier that the Grand Assembly of the Harmony of Worlds had ratified the nonaggression treaty.

Marcer's steps faltered. That meant the border would be opened between the Harmony and the Emirates. His family—if they hadn't all abandoned him, like Peter—would be able to contact him. He could appeal, as Ahman Kiku had suggested, if only the Khan would let him.

Idryis Khan wouldn't. He wouldn't allow anyone from Brice-Isaacs to contact Marcer, if he even let them learn where Marcer was. And then there was Linnet, about whose fate Marcer still knew nothing.

Idryis Khan noticed Marcer, but fixed his gaze on one of the officers. "Neuland is as open to us as a whore's face," Idryis Khan said. "But who wants a whore? Good morning, Marcer."

The transparent allusion to Linnet had to be a deliberate insult, intended to put Marcer in his place.

The two men turned. They stared impassively while they studied Marcer. After daily contact with the Khan, he had learned not to react as though the Khan's stares were necessarily aggressive. Their attention was of the same type. Viewed alongside the Khan, the men shared subtle commonalties with him, as though they were members of the same, close family. Their faces were broad, like Marcer's own, but also flat, with long chins. Their builds were stocky and muscular. Their eyes were alert; most importantly, their faces were without expression. They moved deliberately, without the small, unconscious physical reactions and adjustments which signaled human emotions and were the basis of his halo effect. He knew what they were. If he EL-ed, there would be nothing. "Your brothers?" To repay the Khan's insult, he asked without bowing first in acknowledgment of his superior, and he stopped close to the Khan, also at the rail.

Marcer refused to let Idryis Khan own him, consequently, he played a dangerous game, obeying without fully submitting. He could feel the spike that was the corrective's receiver; it was a cold, sharp, barely protruding needle at the top of his spine, like a tag on a released specimen. This time, the Khan didn't use the corrective.

"No," the Khan said, "but we are all Sons of Blessed men."

Sons of the houris, too—though the mothers were rarely mentioned. Sons of the Prophet, whenever a Son wanted a more copious deference.

One of the men inclined his head at Marcer. He was sun-wrinkled and apparently older than the Khan, though Marcer still had difficulty interpreting signs of age. The insignia on his cuff made him the Khan's junior in rank. "Yusef Sauri," he cordially introduced himself. "My friend is Demet Quadar." Quadar was younger than the others, rugged looking yet handsome. Unlike most alans, he was clean-shaven.

Marcer bowed. A faint breeze from the sea rustled leaftips; the petioles of a gray-green specimen plant near Sauri's bench clicked. The fragrance from a terrestrial orange tree mixed strangely with the salty, indigenous scents from the beach below. No one spoke, but the silence was unusually companionable.

Abruptly, Quadar stood. "How is your work progressing?"

Marcer had discussed it with no one but the Khan. "I'm learning," he said cautiously.

"Too slowly," the Khan added.

Demet Quadar came closer to Marcer and thus to the Khan. Quadar looked down, and the Khan turned back to the sea. Their stomachs rumbled as though both men were hungry. "Jonist," Quadar asked Marcer, "have you learned the difference yet between angels and aliens?" He sounded bitter despite his impassive face.

Angels and aliens. The Sons feared what their mothers were. Marcer glanced at the Khan. He nodded, so Marcer said, "I don't have an houri to examine, or any reading of houri DNA. I do have DNA from Sons—several samples." He hesitated, trying to decide the most advantageous way to tell the truth. All three Sons were staring at him. What did they want to hear?

"Sons are neither angels nor aliens," Marcer said. "Essentially, the Sons' genome is human. Altered from standard, of course, although not in any clearly definable pattern, the way a Neulander has a particular complex of specific changes, or I do." He didn't mention that distinctions between Altered human vs. non-human were subjective. Sons of houris had twenty-six chromosomes, but they were heterozygous hybrids. There were lost segments in the rearranged regions of their genome, and replacements

Marcer hadn't tried to interpret. It was outside his specialty. There were no obvious deleterious effects, except a certain lack of emotional affect and, perhaps, an increased aggressiveness. Based upon those segments, and what he now knew, the likeliest interpretation was, however, that houris *were* alien to the human species. And yet, how could that be? Convergent evolution on such a scale was so implausible as to be impossible.

"Then if I'm human, why don't I have sons—children?" Quadar demanded.

"Demet," the Khan said, to restrain him, but he let Marcer answer.

Marcer hadn't studied the Sons' infertility. Idryis Khan hadn't made it a significant issue for Marcer to investigate. Too personal? Too hurtful? Had he simply accepted his inability to sire children? "I'm not a medic. I do know there are a number of separate varieties of mankind, and not all can easily beget viable offspring with others." Marcer didn't note aloud that the Academy criteria for including Altered humans as members of the human species included the ability to produce viable, fertile, human offspring with a standard human mate. He was reluctant to pursue the subject when clearly the Sons would not meet that criteria. "Neulanders, for example," Marcer continued slowly, "are notorious for their difficulty reproducing with *most* other Altereds and even standard humans. And sometimes there is a basic structural incompatibility between human varieties. A woman with the Gas Alteration, for example, which entails significant cranial changes, would be unlikely to conceive with me unless we used heroic measures." He used the Emirates euphemism for genetic construction and reconstruction of the prenatal genome, the tinkering which at its simplest level allowed the Emirates to dramatically skew the ratio of male to female births. Despite the widespread use of gender selection, alans regarded genetic arts as shameful, an attitude which, together with a macho element, caused unmen to be held in low esteem.

"That's right. You're a deviant." The older man, Sauri, gazed calmly at Marcer, but his observation had a hostile edge.

Deviant. Marcer had flushed, then wished he could control his face. There were benefits to the Sons' impassivity. Deviant. His education told him he was no such thing, merely a member of one of the several recent varieties of mankind—that there was no eternal, perfect species ideal— but the word still hurt.

Quadar seemed the most self-absorbed and bitter of the three. "Haven't you heard?" he said. "It's not *our* fault; it's the women. None of them are sufficiently holy to bear children to a Son of the Prophet!"

The lack of the obligatory blessing which pious alans placed after mention of the Prophet Mohammed sounded improper to Marcer; he'd been in the Emirates too long. He smiled at Quadar because there was something danger- ous about him, more so than the others, as though he didn't check his aggression quite as well. "It's true that there *are* no females of your kind: Sons, but no Daughters. A lack of compatible partners is one possibility. If standard women aren't compatible, what about nonstandard women—the varieties of Altereds?"

"Back to the main point," Idryis Khan said. "Who are our mothers, the houris? What are they? And what do they want?"

Clearly Idryis Khan did not want to discuss the Sons' infertility. Marcer wondered why he didn't when the other two so clearly did.

Houris lived human lives as wives and mothers but their DNA seemed likely to be distinct from that of humans. What made someone human? Biogenetic history or ecologi- cal function? "I need more information."

"You have everything available," the Khan told him.

"It isn't enough. I need to meet houris and get blood and tissue samples. I need to speak with them."

"Impossible." The Khan glanced at Sauri and Quadar for support; they nodded. "Houris are wives and mothers. Secluded." He went to the chair Demet Quadar had va- cated. Quadar paced around the clearing and ended at ap- proximately the same location the Khan had first been. The three Sons were careful to give each other sufficient space; a greater social distance than in the Harmony but *much* greater than usual in the Emirates. While the Khan had shown a dislike of close physical contact previously, it was more pronounced with two others of his kind.

"You don't understand," Sauri said. "They can't know we're studying them."

"Why not?"

"They'd try to stop us." Sauri looked at the Khan.

"They're women. How could they?" None of the three answered Marcer.

Marcer was getting more information on the Sons than he had when alone with the Khan. Their body language, or near lack of it, was intriguing. *Were* they aliens? If the houris were, what was the Khan? As a fieldwork specimen, a puzzle to be solved and not a man with repellent attitudes and peculiarities, how would the Khan be classified? These Sons looked squarely into each others' faces, not glancingly and not merely as a sign of strong emotion in the manner of most humans. They kept well apart. A throaty grumbling sound, seemingly unconscious, sometimes came from them, as when Quadar approached the Khan. It wasn't loud, but given the Khan's sensitivity to Marcer's own Altered vocalization, Marcer wondered about it. What if these men's alteration wasn't a physical modification? Suppose it made them less social than standard humans? Their mothers, the houris, had difficulty with language—and speech was the social device par excellence.

"Get back to work," the Khan said, dismissing Marcer. "You've said nothing new."

Marcer had waited for this moment. He had needed something to offer Idryis Khan as a trade for Linnet. The presence of the others would be useful, too. "Before I leave, we should discuss the cocoon. I've made interesting findings."

"What findings? You claimed you didn't know what was growing inside." The Khan's flat tone was ominous. He left the chair and walked to the railing. Demet Quadar made room for him by walking several meters away along the rail.

"I said that I was unable to determine all the metabolic changes your mo . . . the chrysalis is undergoing." Marcer's slip was intentional, meant to humble the Khan without making Marcer a target. "I can't. I don't know what the imago—the mature, adult stage after metamorphosis—will be with any certainty. But I have learned something interesting." He didn't go on.

The Khan waited. His counterfeit scowl mimed great anger, but genuine or not, he was trying to show that his attention was definitely hostile. Marcer was accustomed to pleasing his superiors. To keep from saying more, he distracted himself with thoughts of rescuing Linnet.

Sauri broke first. "What is it you want?"

Marcer turned to him so quickly, he twisted his knee. He yelped at the pain, then smiled because pain reminded him so much of Linnet, and because even without the halo effect, he knew he'd won. "Where is Linnet Wali?" Marcer looked at Idryis Khan. "Her home was wrecked during my arrest. She wasn't there. Is she safe?"

Sauri turned to the Khan.

The Khan hesitated, then briefly nodded. "Yes."

It was more than he'd learned before. "Where is she?"

"Oh, tell him," Quadar grumbled.

"She's in the women's prison."

The women's prison. The infamous Woman Eater in the Citadel. Marcer recalled the terror of the deported women in the compound on Darien. He'd thought the Woman Eater was a fabrication. He knew better now. "Get her out," Marcer said. "I want her brought here."

"No. And you will tell me what you've learned from the cocoon."

Marcer wondered how alans could call the Khan's differences from standard humans *holy* when the constellation of characteristics comprising the Sons created such hard, hostile men. He crossed his arms against his chest. "No. And it's not in my notes."

The Khan seemed to relent. "No woman leaves prison unless she's released to family: a husband, father, or brothers. The whore has no one."

"Yes, she does," Marcer said. "She's my wife. I want her out."

All three Sons concentrated on Marcer. "You're lying, of course," the Khan said. "You're an Academic from a family of well-to-do shipowners. Jews, with some moral principles, unlike real Jonists. You wouldn't marry a whore."

"I did." McCue had discussed alan marriage with Marcer on their way to the Khan's wedding party. It had been a noncontroversial subject with which to pass the time. Marriage in the Emirates, like those in the Harmony, was a social contract; unlike the Harmony, Emirates marriages weren't publicly registered.

"Who were your witnesses?" Sauri asked, as if playing along with a joke.

Islam required two witnesses, but no religious official was necessary. Marcer tried to think of two people who might lie for him and Linnet, and could think of only one possibility. "I'm a Jonist. We don't require witnesses." That much was true; both parties merely registered as permanent partners. "Matthew McCue was there, however. We spoke the vows just before I left to go to your wedding. Since you had propositioned me before, I thought it was necessary."

The Khan stared. "Marriage is indissoluble in the Harmony. You wouldn't do it lightly. She brings absolutely no advantage."

Linnet's life was at stake. Stories of the Woman Eater were the stuff of nightmares. It was said to be a pit deeper than the ocean, a hole from which nothing came up alive. Marcer could almost feel the shape of Linnet inside his mind, as if he EL-ed her from across the room. He wouldn't let her die. "I married Linnet anyway," Marcer firmly stated. "For love, not advantage."

The Khan laughed. Unlike his usual tone, it had a hollow, artificial sound. He wasn't sure. "I don't believe you. None of us do." He looked in turn at Sauri and Demet Quadar.

"Ask McCue. I'm telling the truth." There were no sensors on the Khan's estate capable of saying otherwise, just crude sight/sound pickups.

"I will."

McCue was alive, then. The only one not answered for was Nisa, the Khan's wife. Marcer almost asked, then thought better of it.

Sauri made a deep, distressed, virtually inaudible rumble in his throat. "Let him have the whore," Sauri said. "What difference does it make?"

"Shut up. It's not your concern." Quadar moved a hesitant step or two closer to Idryis Khan.

"She isn't your wife," the Khan again insisted.

The Khan sounded adamant. Since the Khan had no aura, Marcer couldn't determine whether or not it was a bluff. He guessed. "I won't work unless she's safe."

"Enough." Idryis Khan removed the control rod from a pocket and rolled his thumb across its side.

Marcer had guessed wrong. There was no gradual increase in the pain. It didn't creep through his spine. He was instantly on fire.

Marcer's body was both the kiln and the burning pot. He

couldn't scream because his lungs had baked. His heart was melting. Every nerve shrieked its incandescence. His eyes were caught on those of Idryis Khan; he could not look away. It wasn't real, but Holy God the torture as his body created its own pyre was enough to believe he'd discovered hell. He tried again to scream, but could manage only a whine so high-pitched that it became an EL. As though he looked out from inside a wall of flame, his bounce-back found the Khan and his two fellow Sons. They were lumps in the outer darkness; he was their candle.

The fire was banked. The residual warmth was manageable. "Talk to me," the Khan said. "What have you discovered?"

Marcer was astonished that he was still standing. His eyes stung from the sweat running down his face.

"All right, deviant." Idryis Khan had seen him react to the word. "Pleasure is nothing in comparison with pain. Talk to me."

Marcer had EL-ed, then Idryis Khan had relented. "A moment," he mumbled, and EL-ed again.

The Khan didn't use his corrective.

"That's what you described?" Sauri asked the Khan.

Idryis Khan nodded. "An echo location signal."

"Pleasant." Sauri inspected Marcer like a specimen on a pin. "Do it again."

"A waste of time," Quadar said. "You! Deviant. Tell us what you know."

Marcer understood that the corrective-induced pain hadn't damaged his body. The mind-body dichotomy was false, however. He'd felt and reacted to pain. So, too, with Linnet. However much she denied the sensation of pain, those phantom signals scarred her body and seeped into her thoughts; she reacted to what she couldn't feel, and wherever she was being held, Marcer wanted to spare Linnet its consequences. "I need an assistant," he insisted. "The document conversion from Arabic is too slow; I need someone to scan texts and tell me what's there. A smart utility could do it, but you don't have them. Also, it might help to examine a Neulander in the flesh. Bring Linnet here. She's perfect for the job, and she's my wife."

"I have a better assistant for you," the Khan said. "One with direct and recent knowledge of the houris. *My* wife. She's a prisoner, too. So—another woman you can save, since you like them so much. I'll free her only if you make her your assistant and stop this nonsense about the whore."

II. A patch of blue.

Nisa jerked her ankle chain, rattling it like a ghoul, beating it against the floor with the force of a madwoman, and told herself she wasn't crazy. She made noise and called it music just to satisfy her craving to hear; she closed her eyes against the dark, featureless, windowless room and dreamed of color. Blue sky. Yellow sun. Red blood, Hulweh's blood. Gray matter . . . She wouldn't think of gray.

Each day an unman brought a pitcher of water, to drink and with which to wash herself in preparation for prayers. She never prayed. God had abandoned women; why submit to Him? Twice a day the unman (a guard outside the room had once called Tomo and the unman had turned) delivered flatbread or lukewarm porridge. Only when the door was briefly opened did any light enter the room, just enough to produce a washed-out dingy gray color. Tomo did not speak to her. The Khan did not visit. She waited for something to change. She waited because there was nothing else to do.

When the door opened unexpectedly, the sudden light made Nisa squint. It took her a moment to distinguish the blurred shadows as two men, Idryis Khan and a taller man. The Khan snapped on an overhead pure white ceiling bulb that Tomo had never used. Nisa closed her eyes against the bright pain.

"You Jonists don't understand women," Idryis Khan told his companion.

Nisa squinted.

The other man entered the cell and came forward ahead of the Khan. He limped. "If this is understanding them, then I hope I never do."

She recognized his voice. The man from the boat, Marcer Brice. He'd sent Fatima, the houri. Now Brice accompanied Idryis Khan, who had battered him senseless. What could it mean?

Brice knelt next to Nisa, then winced as though kneeling hurt. The limp.

Her eyes were adjusting. She looked out the door; the

Khan hadn't closed it. No landscape had ever been as fine as this one, Nisa's first use of distance vision since she'd been starved of sight in the cell. She saw natural daylight and even caught a patch of blue sky.

Light, pure and simple, was the finest form of energy in the universe, the ultimate source of life. Light filled her mind as air fills lungs; it spread throughout her body, refreshing and renewing her. With light, she could think again.

"Are you all right?" Brice asked Nisa.

"She's fine. She should be dead." Idryis Khan came fully inside Nisa's cell, but the door remained open. "She *would* be dead except I understand Jonists. Your worlds are run by women—which is why someday we'll crush you—and I was sure eventually you'd try to rescue her from justice. So she was too potentially useful to discard. Besides, her bitch houri stepmother ordered me to kill her. I don't take orders from women or houris."

Qadira had told the truth: She had ordered the Khan to kill Nisa. And he had not. Plus, the Khan had called her useful! There was hope.

"Can you read?" The Khan's tone changed. The pitch was higher. His voice mixed condescension with contempt.

Nisa had begged Tomo for help during the first few days, she had sung to herself occasionally, but she hadn't held a conversation since being placed in the cell. Words weren't easy. She choked them out. "Yes. Of course."

"You see?" the Khan told Marcer Brice. "Much better than the whore. Better educated, and she knows the houris. Since you've seen her face already, it won't matter if she works with you uncovered."

Marcer Brice patted Nisa's hand where it rested on the damp floor. His hand was clammy; there was sweat on his forehead. His eyes darted around the tiny room. "It will be all right," he whispered, then returned hurriedly to the open door, even briefly glancing outside before he faced Idryis Khan. "I still want my wife," Brice said.

"She's not your wife."

"What difference is it to you?" Brice sounded exasperated.

"I don't want that whore in my home."

With agile grace, the Khan squatted beside Nisa. He stared into her face as though she was a painting, not human. "She isn't bad-looking." He pulled a knife from his boot and placed it against her throat.

Nisa screamed. She couldn't prevent it. She couldn't stop. The worst moment of her life, the violation of her person, the incident which had led her back to Idryis Khan and this cell, was a horror replayed in her mind.

The Khan slapped her. She barely felt it. He grabbed her by the hair, shook her head, and ordered her to stop. It was impossible. The Khan seemed to understand. He disregarded her screams.

Brice hurried back into the cell.

The Khan looked at Brice. "Don't."

Brice stopped moving forward.

The Khan removed the knife from Nisa's neck, and though he still held it poised for slitting her throat, it wasn't touching her. She quieted a bit. He slapped her again. Her shoulders trembled, but her screams and sobs ended.

The Khan shifted position on the floor so that he could see Brice better. "Tell me what you wouldn't say before, or I'll kill her. She knows I will."

"You're a proud man. You wouldn't kill a helpless woman, especially one who's useful."

Sweat from the humid outdoor air and her own fear gathered along Nisa's spine and underarms. Her mouth was dry; she was afraid to move or to warn Brice about her homicidal husband, but Brice was a fool if he believed what he'd said.

The Khan moved the knife from her throat to the tip of her nose. The blade was cool against her nostrils. She dared not breathe. "You're right," the Khan said. He looked only at Marcer Brice. "But I don't care if she's disfigured and you—you seem to like it. Except *this* whore will feel the pain. Should I do it? You might find it entertaining. I would."

"Bastard." Brice wet his lips and straightened his back. "She's your wife."

"You Jonists are much too romantic. What does it matter that she's my wife? She won't give me sons. She ran away, dishonoring me, when I'd done nothing to deserve it. I'll cut off her nose, Brice, and maybe one eye, or some fingers. Unless you tell me what I want to know. Now."

"You think you've found a new 'corrective?' "

Brice was not going to agree. She had no doubt the Khan would cut her. Her nose itched. "Please," she whispered. "Help me."

"Well?"

Brice gaped at her, his mouth hanging open like a child's. He shivered and looked away. "All right," he said. "But I still want my wife." Brice moved back toward the open door. He took a deep breath. "The chrysalis inside the cocoon isn't forming properly. It was nothing that I did, since I'm fairly sure it never even started growing correctly. I'm sorry about your mother."

"What do you mean?" The pressure on Nisa's nose lessened.

"If your mother went inside that cocoon, your mother is dead. You have my sympathies."

"Not that," the Khan said as if Brice's concern was irrelevant. "The cocoon. What's gone wrong?"

"The imago—the next stage of life—is deformed. Nonviable. I am not sure what the imago was supposed to be—that is, I don't know what was supposed to come out of the cocoon at the end of metamorphosis—but I know that it's not being achieved. The metamorphosis has stopped. Inside the cocoon there is only dying, undifferentiated tissue, not an organism."

The Khan removed the knife from Nisa's face and sat back in a relaxed posture, on his heels, although still holding it. "Why?"

Brice shrugged. "My best guess is that some local condition is unsuitable. Metamorphosis is an intricate process. It will fail if everything isn't precisely right. Of course, that's only a guess. I'll know more when I open the cocoon. And I *do* need more information about houris. What's supposed to emerge from the cocoon? What triggered the metamorphosis? Just what are the houris? Human beings, no matter how Altered, don't metamorphose."

"I think the trigger was age," the Khan told Brice. "Or else the death of my father. She wanted to return to Paradise, but I wouldn't allow her to go. I needed to see what would happen."

Brice stared at the Khan as if he were a dog on the street.

Curious but terrified, Nisa didn't dare speak. In her opinion Brice was withholding information from the Khan, but either the Khan didn't see it in his face, or he didn't care because he didn't ask Brice for more.

The Khan grabbed Nisa's raggedly cut hair. "Will you take this woman as your assistant?"

Nisa glanced at herself. Tomo had allowed her to keep

relatively clean. She wore a tunic that, had she stood, would
have reached her ankles. She had been unable to determine
color, but now she saw it was pale yellow. Her cropped
hair hadn't been washed or dressed, but she was present-
able. The Khan had said so. "Please," she whispered again.
Whatever it was they wanted her to do was better than
doing nothing in the dark.

"All right. I'll take her." Brice sighed.

"Good." The Khan released his hold on her, then slipped
the knife into his boot. He stood. "Work hard, Brice. Time
is running out. The next pretext Neuland gives us, Aleko
Bei will strike at them. The Jonists in the Harmony won't
attack us no matter what we do. The treaty says, quite
clearly, that neither side will interfere with the other. The
Harmony will do no more than feebly protest an accomplished fact. So, when he thinks the time is right, the Bei
will remove Neuland from the list of inhabited worlds.
We'll sweep the planet until there is nothing left but boiling
sea and ash. Every Neulander will be dead."

"And you expect one junior biologist to stop it?" Brice
leaned a hand against the wall, bracing himself. "I don't
believe it. You would never put so much trust in me."

"You're wrong." The Khan extended his empty hands to
Marcer Brice. "We're being manipulated by the houris.
Aleko has married three of them. There are more and more
houris being brought to our worlds from Paradise. More
and more Sons are born. They whisper to him that the
Neulanders must die. The excuse that the Harmony could
crush us is gone. It seems that only Sons—and very few of
us—wonder why they want Neuland destroyed. If I know
what they are, if I can prove that they are dangerous, perhaps the Bei will cease listening to them and stop them.
Someone will."

Qadira had tried to inspire her father against Neuland.
She'd claimed that the war would be a jihad against infidels,
that it was preordained by the Prophet, God's blessing and
peace be upon him. "War or a civil war," Nisa whispered.

Marcer Brice looked at her. The Khan nodded slowly.
"She's right. Aleko Bei can be replaced by guile or assassination. If he doesn't satisfy the houris, they will find another, more easily guided man to rule the Emirates. Unless
we find a stronger one first, or justification to condemn the
houris as unholy. Go, Marcer. Work. Find out what the

houris are, and why they care about Neuland. Prove they are not angels."

Brice looked grim. He glanced down at Nisa, then studied the Khan. The Khan said nothing. "Nisa. Come with me." Brice ordered it as though Nisa had the power to obey.

She rattled the chain.

"First I want a few words alone with my wife." The Khan spoke without sarcasm.

Nisa hoped that Brice would protest, but he only nodded and limped out the open door.

III. Murder or mercy.

Fastened to a post by a chain like a dog, Nisa looked up at Idryis Khan. She hated him, so her smile was cautious. "What is it you want me to do?"

Idryis Khan turned from watching Brice's departure. He studied her intently. She didn't look away from his eyes; she didn't repeat her question. He knew what she'd asked. The cell had taught her how to wait.

"You'll do," he said eventually, and without turning away.

Nisa feared the Khan's discovery of her defiled condition, and dreaded being touched by the man who had killed her two closest friends in cold blood and then chained her alone in the dark, yet if he wanted it, she would willingly be his. Nothing would stand in the way of her chance at freedom from this room. But there was nothing sexual about his attention, except that it continued for so long.

"Was it your goal to reach the Harmony of Worlds?"

He had to know it was. "What other place is there?"

"And do you still want to go to the Harmony?"

It had to be a trick. He would be certain she was lying if she said no. "It doesn't seem likely," she said instead, though a yes was implicit.

"Women," he said like a curse.

What if she was pregnant? As a Son he would be sure it wasn't his and that she wasn't still a virgin. Would he kill her? She remembered a public stoning of an adulteress; the woman had been stripped naked first, then her husband had thrown the first rock straight at her head, knocking her unconscious. Murder or mercy? Nisa seemed to hear the woman's pleas ringing in her ears. Hulweh had died because she wouldn't grovel. "Do you want me to tell you what he discovers?" The Khan could not have enjoyed bargaining with Brice for information.

He didn't frown, though his cold response showed she had spoken out of turn. "I don't want you to spy." He pulled the knife from his boot. "Come here."

The command was a test of her temperament. He controlled her. She got to her feet and was careful not to rattle the chain, as though by failing to remind him of his coercion, Nisa's act gained an element of personal volition. She went as far as the chain allowed.

"Hold out your hand."

He had the knife. Her gut tightened but she did as he ordered, extending her right hand as though they were going to shake hands.

He reached out, holding the knife in his left hand, then sliced the blade into her palm. She had expected it, but she still flinched. The cut stung, then hurt. She stared as red blood welled up and overflowed. She clenched her teeth so as not to cry out. Blood. There had been so much of it.

"Wipe it," he said.

Then she understood. She wiped her hand against her tunic. The wound hurt more, but the blood welled up as fully as before. "I'm not a houri," she said as they both watched.

He looked into her face again. "I didn't suppose you were."

Then why the test? She couldn't afford to ask.

"Take off that smock."

She would be naked, but her face was already bare in front of a man who epitomized the word "stranger." She pulled the loose-fitting tunic over her head, which was necessary because of the ankle chain, but which also allowed her to avoid seeing him as he first perused her body. She placed the tunic on the floor and waited for him to hurt and humiliate her as the other man had.

Idryis Khan walked a circuit around her. "He likes women," the Khan said from behind her back. "Even whores," he added when he again faced her.

Nisa was uncertain who the Khan meant.

"You'll be alone with him. Often. If you touch him or let him touch you, I'll know, and I will kill you."

Marcer Brice. "I wouldn't."

"Why not? You're a whore."

Nisa stood silently looking at her husband.

"The necklace was sold. We traced it back and found the man who had you. He's dead." The Khan spat.

She nearly thanked him. Before she could, he slapped her, as hard as he had in Hulweh's room. Nisa fell. The Khan stood over her, waiting for her to get up. With the instinct of frightened prey faced with a predator which may be satisfied by submission rather than death, Nisa stayed on the floor. She whispered. "My father's houri wife told me that you would kill me, so I ran away. It was wrong. It has brought me more grief and dishonor than a man can understand." *We're being manipulated by the houris,* the Khan had told Brice. Nisa took a chance that a houri's Son disliked houris. "It's the houri's fault," she said. "I hate them." Nisa spoke fervently; everything she'd said was true.

"I think you really do," the Khan said. "If Brice won't help me, perhaps you might do."

It sounded like an offer of something better than she had. Brice was a captive, too. For now, her future was with the Khan, not the Jonist. "Brice sent a houri to meet me. I don't trust him."

"She was something else. A Neulander, not a houri."

Nisa forgot herself. "A Neulander! Ugh! An abomination. Why did he send one of those filthy Altered perverts?"

Idryis Khan studied her. "Brice himself isn't standard." The Khan waited for her to object. She didn't. "Don't let him realize you know. He becomes defensive. I want him to be comfortable around you. Keep your dislike of deviants to yourself."

"He's a Neulander?" She was confused. He had certainly appeared to be in pain on the boat when she'd fled her father's house.

"No. He has a different modification. He sees with sound. He could know your shape in a dark room. He could navigate without any light at all."

"Brice can do that?"

The Khan nodded. "The sound he uses has a pitch that disturbs me. He doesn't do it often anymore. I tell you so you'll know. Even a properly modest cover is useless around him, not that you deserve to wear one."

"He sees through cloth?"

"Yes, partly. The density of the material makes a difference—I investigated his deviance."

That was how Brice had known she was a woman! He

had touched her intimately using sound as his hands. It appalled Nisa. It was almost another rape.

She glanced down, then realized that all this time she had been naked in front of Idryis Khan. Her husband. No one would ever be truly clothed around Brice.

"You will be his friend," the Khan reiterated. "Whatever your opinions, you'll keep them to yourself. If he tells you about his abilities, you'll smile. Understand?"

A thin crust of dried blood coated her hand. She wiped it gently against her bare leg. She had a chance. "I understand," she said. "I'll be careful around him. Is there anything else you want me to do?"

"Learn as much as you can from him. Be sure you understand what he's doing. Get him to confide in you. If he won't help me, then it will be up to you. Most importantly, be sure that he is afraid of the houris, that he believes they are a threat to everyone, even to people in the Harmony. Tell him everything you can about them. Terrify him. And if you do everything I tell you, then I may let you go to the Harmony."

Chapter 12

"Tell me how Marcer Brice died," Jeroen Lee asked the Supplicant.

The Joint Unanimous Ruling being prepared by the Electors of the Jonist Academy was more cautious than the Supplicant would have preferred. It called the houris a "danger of unknown dimension" instead of alien invaders, but to argue about that would be quibbling. Further investigation inside the Emirates being impractical, and since time was of the essence, the Electors' Ruling recommended that the Grand Assembly order what they euphemistically called "a military solution." She knew she owed that consensus opinion to the influence which, even disgraced and nearly disavowed, Jeroen Lee wielded. She was also aware that this was personally embarrassing for him. He had the Neulander Alteration, which meant that alien genes and alien blood commingled with his human inheritance. In a sense, houris were his distant relatives. So she smiled at him because he'd been useful and in spite of the fact that he and his kind were an abomination. Harmony politics was teaching her to be pragmatic; despite Sanda Brauna's opinions, and his Alteration, she found it hard to dislike this quirky man.

"I didn't actually see Marcer die," she explained. "The last time I saw him he was leaving the laboratory to have dinner with Idryis Khan. The Khan intended to kill him. I warned Marcer, but he went anyway."

Lee turned to his aide, a very tall, very quiet, very handsome young man who shadowed him everywhere. "You were right, August. He might be alive."

The Supplicant shrugged slightly, to indicate her lack of agreement. She couldn't imagine that Brice had escaped the Khan, but she had the guilty sense that Jeroen Lee and his aide saw through her and knew she also didn't want him to have survived. Brice might dampen the Harmony's enthusiasm for obliterating Paradise.

"*You* were right, sir," the aide quietly said, "to grant that permission to the father."

The Supplicant cocked her head in unspoken question.

Lee said, "I issued Researcher Brice's father my imprimatur to allow his son to return to the Harmony. The man is a shipowner. I believe he's on his way to the Emirates already. If the son is alive, I imagine the father will bring him home."

I. Holy dread.

Idryis Khan was a liar. Always suspicious of him, Marcer became certain of it when the Khan asked so few questions about the cocoon. It also explained the desultory nature—one man in a home laboratory—of his attempt to obtain the houris' secrets. They were no secret to him.

Marcer felt sick. He continued investigating Paradise while wondering why Idryis Khan a'Husain wanted a Jonist Academic to duplicate what the Khan must already know. At first Marcer supposed the data was false, something the Khan wanted planted in the Harmony, so he performed his work as rigorously as he knew how in order to uncover the deceit. Within the confines of the available facility, each procedure was accurately performed. His standards were uncompromising. He kept complete records, cross-checked and repeated every test, and counted nothing as a result unless it was reproduced or he was otherwise certain of it.

Nisa's information was invaluable. It sped the work even more than her help as a technician. His EL showed no sign of deceit about her encounters with her stepmother Qadira, and even though he checked and rechecked every one of her claims that it was possible to review, her information withstood his tests. When all was said and done, it seemed irrefutable that the impossible was true. The human race was being attacked. The battlefields were weddings. And the Khan knew.

"Why are you staring at me?" Nisa asked. "Did I do something wrong?"

"No," he said, "you're doing fine." Nevertheless, after

several weeks together, Marcer distrusted Nisa. She measured her words like a liar, though she didn't actually lie. She kept an emotional distance from Marcer, a reserve that seemed to indicate dislike. She was a very serious young woman with the self-centered self-absorption of an adolescent or an artist, but it was magnified by fear. She hated houris. She feared the Khan. She mistook her judgment as truth and had decided that both the Khan and the houris were dangers not just to her, but to everyone. She told Marcer so, frequently. She spoke to him in the Harmony common tongue, and quite well, but as though practicing the language. Once she had asked what she would be wearing if their lab was in the Harmony; she often asked questions—practical questions—about the Harmony and the Academies. This was a woman trapped in a hopeless situation, the prisoner of a husband who rejected her, with whom she had no spousal relationship, yet she seemed optimistic about her future. It was more than optimism. She had confidence.

"What is it I'm doing?" Nisa often asked for explanations, though she frequently didn't remember them correctly later if his description was too technical. Her small bits of learning were too patchy for any unsupervised tech job, but at least she didn't use conversation as an excuse not to work. Her hands stayed busy.

"You're preparing cells for examination. Just like last week."

She pointed to the breached cocoon. "Is that how houris are born?"

"It's how they die."

"Huh," she said, surprised. They both scrutinized the cocoon.

It looked like a broken egg. A pale liquid had cushioned the contents, and though he had studied it and, with Nisa's help, cleaned it, a dried, white crust made a ring around the places Marcer had drilled and the larger cracks, where the exterior had been chipped, then pulled away. The viscous fluid which formed a sizable portion of the interior contents of the cocoon had been more difficult to drain. A sour odor of decay still permeated the laboratory. Worst of all to remove were the solid remains. Death hadn't come immediately to this houri. The flesh looked melted, then congealed in lumps. The bones had been absorbed, but not completely. Her shape had begun to modify. The next stage of her life would have been as a quadruped, but one so flexibly jointed that it could have stood and walked upright, on occasion. He had seen such creatures in Shores. Jinn. Demons.

Nisa had stopped work and gone to the cocoon. She placed her palm against its surface. "Then this is their coffin?"

"It was this time." Marcer didn't want to give her false information; it went against all he'd been taught. Instead he had avoided answering by either putting her off or being highly technical in his comments. However, since it seemed that all humanity might be at risk, the time had come to tell her everything he suspected or knew. That way, if something happened to him, she could tell the Harmony that, however untrustworthy the Khan, his information was true. Marcer joined her at the cocoon. "They're supposed to change, to metamorphose. Like caterpillars into butterflies."

She looked blank. Terrestrial butterflies were outside her experience.

He tried to clarify. "A season changes, hormones shift—anyway, something happens," he said. "A trigger event. It probably causes houris to become more sedentary. They want to return to Paradise. This one asked, but was prevented from making the trip. Somehow—I haven't worked out the mechanism—she extruded something which surrounded her and became this outer shell. Chemically, it's a kind of cartilage; that's why it's rubbery." He patted the side of the cocoon, feeling the spongy surface and smelling the rot which he hadn't managed to clean away. "Normally a houri stays in there and her body begins to change, drastically. I assume that for them it's like hibernation. She couldn't be awake; her brain structure changes, too. In this particular case, the change wasn't made properly or completely. She died in the middle of it. If she had lived, then like a baby, she would have eventually been ready to be born. Reborn. The cocoon would have been forced open and out would have come something different from what went in."

"A houri went in and . . ." Nisa looked to him to solve it.

"What came out?" Marcer still hesitated. He avoided EL-ing around the Khan, but Nisa was another matter. Her curiosity had an edge to it. More and more he suspected collusion between the two of them. Still, if the Khan knew the truth about the houris, why shouldn't he tell Nisa? The question of why Idryis Khan wanted Marcer to know about the houris was probably less important than the fact that what Marcer now knew was true.

"It's better if we backtrack," he said. "The existence of a cocoon tells us immediately that houris live their lives in at least two stages. One stage is the houris you have met, like Qadira. Because the Khan claims that it was a houri who spun the cocoon, and since I've been able to verify that he's telling me the truth, it seems clear enough that the houris are the earlier stage; the time spent in the cocoon is an interregnum, and then there is a postcocoon second stage. Because of the disruption of the metamorphosis of this cocoon, I can't be *absolutely* sure what the second-stage creature looks like. If I had a model-building Analyst, I could interpret the houri's DNA much better, but I've done the best I can without one; I can make an educated guess."

Nisa's eyes had a glazed look. Marcer wasn't lecturing to a class of Acolytes. She didn't need to be able to follow his reasoning, only to understand the result. "The second stage of a houri's life is spent in the form of what are called jinn on the streets, what you call the houris' pets."

"What!"

He nodded. Probably because they were the only creatures from Paradise other than the houris, the pets had been heavily commented upon in what passed for scientific literature in the Emirates. There had even been an autopsy anatomy report. "The pets aren't pets at all, they are the houris themselves in later life. Undoubtedly they are the the sexually mature phase of the houri's life cycle, in effect, the houri's—the earlier stage's—mothers. The nomenclature is bad; I say houri-stage for the juvenile form and jinn-stage for the sexually mature form; I call the species the Blessed." He was proud of his clever terminology: angels changing into demons, and a species called Blessed.

Nisa scowled. "What do you mean, that the pets are the 'sexually mature' stage? Qadira and the other houris can have children! The Sons!" She used the tone of someone exposing a fraud.

"You don't understand," he said firmly. "Children of the

houri-stage Blessed are sterile males, like the Khan. Children of the houri-stage Blessed are essentially human. They don't metamorphose. They are entirely out of the reproductive loop of either species; they don't add to the population of the Blessed species or ours. Only the jinn-stage Blessed are fertile for their own species."

"But Qadira's pet was pregnant with a talish!" Nisa made a rude sound. "Are you saying that the talish are another stage? I can't believe that! Talish are from Bralava, not Paradise."

What was unbelievable to her, fascinated Marcer. The heterogeneity of the methods life developed for solving similar problems amazed him. "You don't understand," he began.

"You're right, I don't," she interrupted him. "All I do understand is that the houris, whatever stage they are, hate real women and are replacing them. Men are stupid enough to think that houris are holy, and besides, houris dote on them. So men prefer houri wives, but the houris aren't even good mothers; their sons look human, but they're hard, cold, evil men. Houris aren't natural."

"Their behavior is natural for them," Marcer said. "And no, the talish aren't another stage of the Blessed life cycle." He walked away, toward the door to the garden. If she hadn't believed houri/pet metamorphosis—and metamorphosis was not uncommon; it was even terrestrial—how would she believe the *real* bombshell: the reproductive method of the Blessed species?

"I'm sorry." She followed him. "Researcher Brice, please. Where are you going?"

He turned around. "Spoil," he said.

Nisa shivered as if the word—which she had taught him, quoting Qadira—had special meaning to her. "Houris should all be exterminated, including their pets," Nisa said.

She was a bloodthirsty child, extremely angry and holding the anger deep inside. Judgmental. Well, she was young. To see the universe in black and white was an adolescent failing. She would grow up. "I don't believe that genocide is warranted," Marcer said gently. "We are civilized. We can find a different solution."

"We didn't with the Bril," Nisa objected. "It's self-preservation. The houris are evil."

She was right, of course. The first, and until the Blessed species was recognized, the only intelligent nonterrestrial life encountered had been rendered extinct within a century of its initial contact with mankind. "They're different, not evil," he said. "Evil is a moral judgment, Nisa. The universe isn't moral; humans are. Morality is cultural. The differences between the Harmony and here proves *that*. In my opinion the human race was, by its own standards, immoral to exterminate the Bril. We should *talk* to the houris. I wish I could meet one." These were aliens in human form, aliens with whom humanity could speak.

"It doesn't matter if they grow in cocoons or in trees. Whatever their lifestyle, there are too many houris." Nisa seemed earnest and determined to convince him. "You need to understand what a danger they are. Every year there are fewer real women. Men marry houris and have only Sons. Sons marry women and have no children. The men don't want daughters; they can't get a good bride-price because of houris, and no benefit comes from a daughter. You had better fear the houris! Between them and unmen, there's no need for women. Eventually the houris will exterminate us!"

"I'm going for a walk." He started for the sea garden.

"Do you want me to put your screen on pause?" Nisa called in a suddenly obsequious tone.

He had been reviewing DNA sequences manually, tedious work for anyone, but especially for a synecology-oriented biologist, who would rather study ecological interrelationships among communities of organisms than the sequence of nucleotides in those same organisms' DNA. The screen was stupid, so the display advanced even without his concentration on it. "Just turn it off," he said.

"Where will you be?"

It was an impertinent question from an assistant. He let it pass without answering.

"What should I tell him if he comes looking for you?" she shouted.

He. Nisa rarely spoke the Khan's name. Marcer didn't reply. He had already gone down the steps into the garden.

The humid haze of the previous day had lifted. The sea breeze was fresh, and the horizon seemed farther than it had. Marcer went to the garden's edge, to the sea overlook where he had met Sauri and Demet Quadar, and stood at the railing, gripping it with both hands. The outline of the tallest buildings in Shores were faintly visible. One may have been the Citadel, the prison holding Linnet. He felt restless and guilty at living in such comfortable confinement while she suffered in the Woman Eater. Marcer peered over the rail, looking vaguely for an escape route. He had tested other possibilities, and each had failed.

The beach wasn't far, and the path didn't look steep. Probably an animal track, the path crossed through the curly, sharp-edged native reeds. He could make it, even with his injured knee. No one had told him he shouldn't. As an escape route, it was too obvious to succeed, but Marcer lifted his right leg over the railing anyway. With his arms bearing the weight his weak leg couldn't otherwise support, he went over.

The path was more difficult than it had looked. Marcer cut his hands clutching the reeds once to brake his descent, but he finally reached the muddy beach. He looked up the path he'd just descended and wasn't ready to tackle it in reverse. He also wasn't sure why he'd bothered to descend. No one could swim the distance to Shores. There were no boats.

He EL-ed. The signal went out and out without a bounce-back. However mistakenly, he felt free. He glanced around. At the shoreline, the water was green, not blue. He removed his shoes and socks and waded into it. Wet soil was slimy between his toes, and sucked at his feet. A wave came and dampened the bottom of his pants. He rolled them above his ankles. He watched his steps, rather than looking ahead, to be sure he didn't step on anything dubious, and was surprised at the large number of animal tracks. A lumpy slug oozed through the mud. A few meters offshore a clump of the ubiquitous mangrove-form foliage was trying to establish itself.

Marcer rounded a small promontory and discovered a manicured beach tucked beneath the overhanging cliff on the far side of the house. Cleared of all natural life, well supplied with white sand the consistency of powdered sugar, it was provided not only with a small cabin but also with a trellised outdoor resting place and a half dozen loungers. Steep marble steps rose from the beach toward the Khan's mansion. He hadn't been shown this place before, probably because it was for the private use of the Khan.

"Sir?"

Marcer turned and EL-ed. A guard, or an attendant—it was a matter of perspective, but he wore household livery and carried a concealed gun—came out of the cabin. "Can I help you?" the man asked. He bowed politely.

"No, thank you. I was just walking." He smiled self-consciously. "What's over there?" He pointed ahead in the direction he had been traveling.

"The estate border." The man watched Marcer intently as he answered. "Two kilometers away. Of course, no one leaves the estate without the Khan's permission."

The edge of Idryis Khan's property was probably as well guarded as an international border. Marcer nodded casually and went to the row of loungers. His knee ached. He sat, then lay down, grateful for the fiberfoam which molded around him.

"A drink, sir?" the guard/attendant asked. "Music?"

"Nothing. Just let me rest."

The man went away, though probably not far. Marcer stared at the waves, wondering what it had cost to import so much sand and how long it would be until the tide stole it away. The Khan's wealth made Marcer's father, Lavi Brice, and all his other relatives combined, look like paupers. There was no Jonist Order in the Emirates or there would not have been such an unstable disparity between rich and poor.

He may have fallen asleep. He came back to his senses with the sun on his bare feet, as it had not been before. A creature was staring at him. A jinn, or jinn-stage Blessed—whatever. One of *them*. An alien.

Each time he had encountered them in the city, he had behaved as though the jinn was a higher order of animal. He knew better now. This jinn was pure white, having taken on the color of the sand. Her saucer eyes blinked. Brown, not the more common gray. She tilted her head the way a curious dog might, or a curious person.

"Talk to me," Marcer whispered, though he knew that the jinn-stage Blessed didn't speak aloud. How did they communicate? The Bril had used sounds, as humans did. Might the jinn use sound outside the human range, since they were sensitive to his EL?

Marcer knew better than to move suddenly, even though the jinn had the intelligence to distinguish a threat from simple motion. He sat up, slowly, in the lounger. "I would surely like to take you to my lab," he said softly. "A few simple tests . . ."

The jinn huffed: boredom. Imagine the boredom of not being able to talk! Marcer wondered how much like the jinn-stage language his EL-ing was, and if he could work out a series of trials to test its possibilities as communication.

He EL-ed. The jinn had always followed him when he did, so he had some hope of leading this one back to the lab. Would it be wrong to trap her there? He'd never confronted the ethical issues of working on a nonhuman, uncommunicative intelligence. No one had, not since the Last War.

The jinn raised herself onto two legs. Bipedalism made her look less human, like an unsuccessful imitation. She was short, compared with him, and her slightly curved backbone caused her to lean forward, but she was as stable upright as an ape, or more so. Marcer studied her paws. There was an opposable digit, on the opposite side from placement of a human thumb, but it looked clumsy. The digits had claws. "So, how do you manage?" Marcer softly asked. "Or do only your daughters work?" He smiled. "How do you tell them what to do? Talk to me."

The Neuland hummers greeted each other with a scratch or a bite. Their mating rituals involved shedding a significant amount of blood. Marcer remembered the jinn who had snapped at him in Shores. He had drawn back without noticing the opportunity. Slowly, he got up from the lounger. A minty fragrance, quite distinct from that of the surrounding sea and foliage, came to him on the breeze. The jinn.

The jinn walked closer using just two legs. Marcer extended his hand. As she reached the lounger, the jinn dropped onto her four legs, sniffed, then raised her paw to his hand. He had an odd image of them shaking hands, like a cartoon of two races meeting. The jinn brushed her paw, claws extended, across Marcer's hand. She barely scrapped his skin. There was no blood. Then she looked beyond him, high up on the cliff to the Khan's house.

"Yes, I come from there," Marcer said. "Are you watching him? Is he your grandson, perhaps?" Marcer smiled at the idea.

The jinn's attention snapped back to Marcer. She gave a low shriek. Just then, a shot rang out. It left a residual odor in the air, the sulfur smell of an old-fashioned bullet gun.

Quicker than thought, the jinn bounded away. If he hadn't EL-ed, Marcer would have lost track of her, she was so perfectly camouflaged. The guard ran up, his heavy footfalls sending sand into the air. "I almost got it," the man shouted. The jinn had reached the water and was changing color as she ran in, apparently able to swim. But all the way to Shores? She must live closer, on another estate.

"They keep coming here," the guard said. "It would have bitten you. You shouldn't have held out your hand."

"Yes, thank you for saving me," Marcer said dryly. "I'm going back to the house."

"Not yet," the guard said. "The Khan says you should wait. He's on his way down."

Marcer glanced at the stairs. Idryis Khan a'Husain was coming toward him. Marcer remembered the jinn staring upward, and her warning sound. Had she seen the Khan?

The sea breeze moved through the Khan's hair, but that and his gait were his only visible motion. His hands were still. His back was straight, regal. He was taller than anyone in his household except Marcer. Reminded of an old poem, Marcer recited it under his breath:

"Weave a circle round him thrice,
And close your eyes with holy dread,
For he on honey-dew hath fed,
And drunk the milk of Paradise."

"He is holy," the guard said reverently while looking up at the Khan. "A true Son of the Prophet, God bless and keep him."

Marcer wasn't sure whether in this instance the alan guard had blessed Mohammed or the Khan. Rather than respond, he settled back into the lounger to wait. It wasn't as comfortable as it had been. Sand had been whisked onto it by their activity. The surface was gritty.

The guard bowed in the Khan's direction, then returned to the cabin. Marcer pretended to relax, closing his eyes until the Khan's body darkened the light and the Khan's stern voice demanded, "Why aren't you working?" He was staring at Marcer, as usual.

"I miss my wife. When can I visit Linnet, since you won't bring her here?"

"She's not your wife. If you want to see that whore again, I suggest you hurry and discover the truth about Paradise."

Marcer returned the Khan's hard look with no holiness in his private dread. "Why don't we stop this charade? You already know the answers I'm looking for. Just tell me."

"I don't know what you mean."

"The Bril were masters of biological arts; we know how they experimented with human captives—it was because of the Last War that biology came into its own in the Harmony. I'd love to investigate the biology of Paradise to determine whether the houris are native or constructs of the Bril, but it doesn't really matter. The women found on Paradise were a biological trap for humans. Perhaps they were Bril allies. If they were placed on Paradise intentionally, they were deployed too slowly to save the Bril from extermination. But you already know everything I've learned."

The Khan made no comment.

"The cocoon was the giveaway." Marcer moved restlessly in the lounger and wished the Khan would sit. "You knew the chrysalis wasn't forming properly, but you waited for me to discover it myself. When I told you, that was all you needed to know—that I'd made the discovery. You had no questions. You showed no surprise."

"I had already guessed."

"You didn't grieve, although you claim the houri who went inside was your mother."

"She was." The Khan's voice matched his impassive expression.

Marcer shrugged. "Maybe grief is making you die inside. I can't tell. I get nothing, no empathy, from you. But I've been reading the Qur'an you gave me. Houris are a minor topic, but I have learned other things, such as that in Islam a proper son should see to his mother's shrouding and burial. You didn't."

"The investigation is more important."

"The investigation is bullshit!" The Khan was angering Marcer; he paused to collect himself. "You know more about the houris than I'll ever learn. You want certain information to reach the Harmony, and I was a convenient messenger. So convenient, in fact, that you worried I was a spy and waited to check on me before forcing me to do this busywork. The only thing that has ever surprised you was my ability to EL and the fact that for you it has a sexual nuance. You didn't know that, did you?"

The Khan plucked a fragile branch from a bangly-vine that grew across the trellis. He striped it of the tiny, multi-colored circlets which substituted for flowers on the world of Urfa, where the plant originated.

Marcer EL-ed. The Khan glanced at him and gave one of his false smiles. "Get back to work, Marcer. We need to know why the houris want Neuland destroyed."

"You already know," Marcer said. "And I can guess. The houris—the entire race, including the jinn-stage—want Neuland destroyed because it holds proof that they're not holy. Neuland's hummers are descended from some of the same stock as the houris. Or you."

"I am not a hummer."

Marcer shrugged. "Has anyone besides me noticed the physical similarities between the jinn—the houris' pets—and hummers?"

"What do you mean?" The Khan turned away from Marcer and gazed out over the sea.

Marcer stood. "I understand the life cycle of the houris and their mothers. The metamorphosis is interesting but the truly unique characteristic of the Blessed is how they reproduce. The jinn—that is, the mothers—don't mate in the traditional sense. Because of metamorphosis, they don't even appear to reproduce their own species. When they go into their equivalent of heat, the jinn bite a creature of another species and incorporate the DNA of the chosen victim/partner into the creation of a fetus. Just as our esophagus is used for both breathing and for digestion, so theirs would be used for digestion and reproduction, as if the jinn's mouth becomes a temporary vagina. Rather than sperm, the jinn are able to use any cells they ingest to fertilize themselves. I'd love to dissect one.

"But the child born to a jinn looks nothing like her

mother. The child is an impostor of the other parent's species, shaped like the creature that the mother jinn has bitten. To this blessed species, its offsprings' initial form is irrelevant. Their offspring are like caterpillars, temporary creatures who will eventually undergo metamorphosis into the mature—jinn—stage and become mothers themselves. In our case, the jinn must have mated with—bitten—humans who survived the crash landing on Paradise. The jinn gave birth to daughters—the holy houris that your ship found, who are functionally human. The more men visit Paradise, the more houris are born. The more houris, the more jinn mothers."

Marcer hesitated. He knew he was right because the Khan didn't contradict him, but he was thinking of Nisa's question, and the talish she said had been born from Qadira's jinn. "Sometimes the jinn, the mothers, must enter heat without wanting to reproduce," he said. There were still so many details to be worked out, and neither a jinn nor a houri to ask or to investigate. "Or those jinn off Paradise might not want to give birth to another human, since to do so would make it obvious that the houris aren't holy. Perhaps the jinn can't use any other form of birth control—I wish I could examine one myself—so when heat occurs in them, the jinn bite something innocuous. Something which could never undergo complete metamorphosis—like the talish, which are much too small. When these offspring are born, they are 'spoil.' Nisa's word, quoting Qadira."

Marcer stopped. Idryis Khan was still gazing out at the water, very unusual behavior for him. "Am I right?" Marcer asked softly. The sound of the waves was relaxing. There was even a faint EL resonance inside his head, a background signal like the white noise of normal hearing.

"They compete," the Khan said harshly. "They don't bite randomly; the mothers search for races which could harm them—their competitors, the top of the food chain—and they steal males from the females of that species by creating their own, intensified version. Gradually, steadily, deliberately they undermine their competitors. Be afraid of them, Marcer. They are much worse than the Bril. This malleable reproduction of theirs is a weapon of enormous proportion."

"It's not necessarily a weapon. The houris can be a bridge between species," Marcer objected. "Think of the value of a species which can interface with new races! Become them, temporarily. There is no reason to believe they are intentionally harming us. We need to talk to the jinn, the mothers, as well as the houris. You are exaggerating the threat. The unique circumstances in the Emirates created the problem, not the jinn. Human men went to a new planet, found aliens, and called them angels; it was exactly the same as when other misguided, superstitious men, through religion, believed their conquerors were gods."

"What are you talking about?"

Marcer had been expecting the Khan to use his corrective earlier, but the low rumble the Khan made sounded more like a purr than a growl. "My father. He insisted on giving me a classic education. I studied pre-Jonist history. Have you heard of the Spanish Conquest, for example?"

Idryis Khan spat. It fell just at Marcer's feet. The damp spittle soaked into the dry, thin sand so quickly it barely left a damp discoloration.

Marcer swallowed hard, tried to suppress the EL, and just managed it. He cleared his throat. "Remember the hummers on Neuland? I am absolutely certain, based on a comparison of the hummer genome and yours, that there is a direct genetic link; it is not convergent evolution. The link is also fairly recent. The Bril brought jinn to Neuland, or perhaps at one time jinn had their own ships.

"On Neuland, the jinn did what is natural to them, and some had offspring with an indigenous creature, the ancestral form of hummers. These offspring of the juvenile stage Blessed—like the houris—also had children, the equivalent of the Sons of the Prophet. Unlike you, however, these offspring were apparently fertile. Or perhaps the jinn bit, and reproduced with, some of their own grandchildren; in that case, I can't be sure what would happen. In any event, the hummer species was born. Its ancestors became extinct, probably because of hummer competition, and the hummers continued. They have a shape like the jinn though they're smaller; they have jinn rapid healing. If I had access to both jinn and hummers, I'm sure I could find many more common features. However, the most important difference between jinn and hummers is that hummers don't undergo metamorphosis. Interestingly, both the hummers and the Sons have a genome in which most of the genetic component is native—for the Sons, that means human—and a significant fraction is not; for both Sons and hummers, that fraction is markedly similar. There is one longish DNA segment which occurs in both hummers and Sons, but not in the genome I'm developing from the . . . material in the cocoon; I don't have the ability to be sure, but my best guess is that it turns off metamorphosis."

"So you think you know everything."

The Khan's tone sent a chill through Marcer. The flesh around the corrective implanted in his neck seemed to tense as if waiting for the pain. Nothing happened. Marcer bowed. "No, Khan," he said, less like a lecturer than a Supplicant. "I don't know everything but I know the basic outline. I know the Sons are unable to have children. You can't compete reproductively with your ancestral species, the human race and the Blessed. Humanity is safe from what happened on Neuland. There will not be a hybrid human/jinn species. We might not need to treat the houris as enemies."

"Then tell me why the houris demand that we destroy Neuland. To be rid of the hummers? You see what they are, Researcher Brice. Able to condemn millions of humans to death to protect their secret. Your interfacing houris are a threat, even if the jinn are not. This is an invasion. A conquest."

"Immigration, not invasion. Despite the power you say the houris have, they don't run anything directly. If the houris weren't holy, men from the Emirates would treat them quite differently. The houris want Neuland destroyed because it's proof that Paradise isn't unique and they're not holy. For self-preservation."

The Khan shook his head. "You are naive if you believe the houris and their mothers aren't a danger to all of humanity."

Marcer hobbled a few steps away. Alans, even including the Khan when he wasn't around other Sons, stood closer than was comfortable. Combined with his steady stare, it eventually became too intimidating. He had to break contact. As he did, Marcer wondered if this intensity was the reason Sons were so effective and respected in the Emirates. From an emotionally safer distance, Marcer asked, "Why did you keep your mother from returning to Paradise?"

"I had to be sure we could kill them. Bralava was the last world my friends and I tested. None of the worlds of the Emirates has a suitable environment for their change. The metamorphosis always fails."

"Which is why the houris always return to Paradise." Marcer nodded to himself. "But your own mother?" He studied Idryis Khan, wondering if he was typical of his kind.

"She wasn't really my mother," the Khan said. "Yes, she gave birth to me, but houris' sons are human. You said so yourself. Our DNA comes mostly from our fathers." His voice drifted into silence, and he turned to watch the waves break on the shore.

Marcer lost himself in thoughts of aggression created by doubled Y chromosomes and the bodily modifications which might be required because Sons had no human mother. He wondered at the actual mechanism. Was the paternal DNA simply incorporated into the Blessed species' pattern like a subroutine for a transient element of a larger whole? How far did the female impersonation performed by the houris go? Did they nurse their sons? How did they communicate with their mothers? How did they feel about becoming jinn someday?

"We're the same, you and I," the Khan said in a tranquil voice. "Just like me, your mother is the reason you're different from other men. You know what it is to be special. I was pleased to learn you were Altered. It explained my warmth for you." He sighed; it sounded spontaneous. "Women. Mine made me holy and yours brought you here."

"According to the Harmony, I'm here because of my father. He's the putative Marrano who made me a Jew."

"It's an excuse; you're here because you're Altered. We're both variations of humanity. I want to protect the human race from the houris' threat, but only the Harmony can do it."

Marcer was very quiet.

"No Emirates fleet commander could sweep Paradise," the Khan said. "No crew would follow those orders. A theological debate has become a menace; Paradise is protected by houri holiness. Only the Harmony has the strength to send a fleet through our territory to destroy Paradise. I'll give them the coordinates."

"Why didn't you tell the Harmony yourself, when you were there? Or just give me your data? Why this pretense that you needed me to discover the truth?" Marcer looked into Idryis Khan's eyes and EL-ed. There was a man-shape there, but without the emotional radiance of a man. The Khan was fooling himself if he thought he was entirely human.

"You would never have believed it unless you discovered the truth yourself."

There was some justice in that. Idryis Khan was betraying the Emirates, Paradise, his religion, and his own houri heritage in order to warn others of an alien threat which was real, if exaggerated by the Khan. "They just need to be confined to Paradise. They don't all have to be killed," Marcer said. He was unsettled by the idea of a second genocide.

"Of course they do." The Khan briefly touched Marcer's arm. "No one in the Emirates could ever successfully ban men from Paradise," the Khan said. "Fools would go there for wives, even through a blockade. It's demographics. No one wants daughters, and they won't need them as long as there are houris. These aliens don't need to kill every woman on every world. All they need is to control us. We make a delicious gene pool for their mothers. Eventually, this won't be a human society, it will be run for their benefit. And then they'll move on to the Harmony."

Marcer remembered something Nisa, or possibly Linnet, had told him: that the birthrate of houris' Sons was declining. He said nothing, but let Idryis Khan repeat all the reasons the human race should fear the Blessed, whom the Khan called only "houris." If the Khan was right, then why would the houris have slowed their reproduction? Nothing explained that, although it was obvious no love was lost between the houris and their Sons.

"I agree that there is danger, but the risk isn't immediate. We can take the time to talk to them," Marcer said.

"I have more information than you do. I'll give it to you now that you've understood the basic nature of the houris on your own. Review my data." The Khan gestured and escorted Marcer back to the house along the marble stairs. There was no rail, and the steps were widely spaced. Marcer's knee ached. The Khan noticed. Alans touched each other often, but the Khan's dislike of physical contact was intense. Nevertheless, he helped Marcer, standing at his side and talking all the while, and in a manner unlike his usual reserve, reiterating his reasons why the houris were a danger the Harmony should eliminate. By destroying the houris, Idryis Khan would eliminate his own kind, the Sons, yet he seemed to consider himself entirely human. The longer Marcer listened to the Khan discuss the determination of the Blessed, the more he believed that, despite the danger they did indeed represent, the supposed necessity for committing genocide wasn't chop logic of a most dangerous kind.

II. A kind man.

Nisa ran her hand along the sticky surface of the broken cocoon. A houri had died in it. Her mother-in-law.

Nisa smiled and set her work aside. She walked to the doorway and looked out at the garden. The view of the sea was lovely, though the garden showed its newness by the lack of proportion between the plantings and the garden's size. The colors were fresh; the sky was clear. The veranda would have been a perfect place to paint, but permission to paint had been refused.

This should have been her garden and her house. Had she stayed at the wedding party, had she arrived as a bride with the Khan, then he might have ignored her, but she would have been his virtuous wife. If he had slighted her, Nisa's father would have helped. Hulweh and Ziller would be alive.

She would not be impatient again.

She didn't move when she noticed Idryis Khan approaching her along the veranda. When the Khan was close enough she bowed, deeply, and said, "He's not here."

"I know."

Nisa suspected the rooms in this house had spy-eyes. She didn't care. Anything that mattered occurred in the head, not the hands. "Are the houris really the children of their pets?" she asked. Marcer Brice's statements had puzzled her.

He studied her, then answered, "Yes."

She kept her disgust to herself.

"Are you afraid of the houris?" he asked.

Truth, wherever possible. "Yes."

"And do you hate them?"

They were his mother-race. "My experiences with them have all been bad," she said.

"And Marcer Brice? Have you done as I asked? Is *he* afraid of them?" The Khan's attention on her bare face made her tremble.

"He looks at them as interesting, a biology puzzle to unravel," she said. "He's aware of the danger. Yes."

The Khan slapped her. "Liar."

To look away was to admit the lie, so she stared back into his eyes.

"No, he's not afraid," the Khan finally said. "He wants to talk to them. He says they're 'functionally human.' " The Khan made fists, then opened his hands, and glanced into the lab. "Could you integrate new data among his without the seams showing? So that it would seem to be his?"

"No, Khan. Even if I knew enough, he keeps his records in his own alphabet. I can't read or write it." She worried that if she disappointed him he would send her back to the cell, but she knew it was beyond her.

"I didn't think so. All right, I'll give *him* the data. You tell me when he has it merged with his own."

Brice was suspicious of her, but she had come to admire him in a distant, dispassionate way. However much he distrusted her, he was never cruel. He smiled when she did her work well, and told the Khan she was learning. Often he whistled while working, which reminded her of his ability to see with sound. Deviant. Altered. Ugly words, but he was a kind man. Too kind. He thought too much. He worried. He gave the benefit of the doubt to an undeserving adversary, the houris. "And when he's finished integrating the data, what happens then?" she dared ask.

"Do you care?"

"No," she said. "Not really." The Khan walked away, leaving Nisa to wonder whether or not she had lied. He intended to kill Marcer Brice.

III. An excuse.

Marcer put the finishing touches on his *Report on the*

Ecological and Competitive Aspects of a Certain Unusual Reproductive System and Its Links to Neuland RHF-type Species. After a week of diligent work, it was in excellent shape. It would convince any Academic that the Blessed species existed, metamorphosed, and (using some data supplied by the Khan) that it reproduced in a unique, economic, and flexible way, through ingestion of flesh from a "mate." Although his report avoided sounding alarmist, and he noted the possibilities of an alliance, and the potential usefulness of using jinn during nonterrestrial biologic fieldwork, he had also acknowledged the social and demographic threat and the stealthy nature of the intrusion onto human worlds. Why hadn't they announced themselves?

Marcer turned off the screen and stared at its empty plastic frame. The Khan wanted the Harmony to exterminate the houris; he expected Marcer to convince them to do it. Though he was marooned on Bralava and his Academic status denied, this report was sufficiently authoritative that the Harmony would listen, particularly because he had speculated that the Bril were involved. At the Khan's insistence, the report also included the location of Paradise and the entire panoply of its military defenses.

If Paradise was swept bare of life by the Harmony, then in a few years all houris would be dead. Could creatures so easy to destroy be a true threat to humanity? Why did the Khan want to kill off the houris? Only the Khan could answer that.

Marcer stood and looked through the open door. He went out and strolled through the garden to the rail overlooking the sea. It was a clear night. City lights from Shores were visible across the water, a pretty sight though an inefficient use of power. He EL-ed and felt the signal attenuate into the distance without a bounce-back, a peaceful sensation. He liked Bralava. Even Darien wasn't as hospitable to human beings as this pleasant world. The Emirates was a despotism ruled by a tyrant and regulated by superstition, yet Bralava itself was agreeable.

The Khan had hinted that Marcer would be sent to the Harmony with his report. He would be home, and with so much important data that overnight he would be renowned. He would be Revered before the age of forty, perhaps even made Ahman. It was what he had wanted, his ambition in life, just as Peter Isaacs's had been to command the post at Center-Sucre.

What did Bralava mean to him? Or the houris? He'd never met one. And Linnet, would he really want such a wife if he was a prominent Academic?

Yes. He wanted Linnet to be safe. He wanted her beside him more than he wanted to be an Ahman. It was the work he enjoyed; the status only allowed him to do it.

Marcer looked up at the stars. New Dawn's sun, and Darien's, and all the other worlds of the Polite Harmony were there, shedding old light on this island in the dark. So, too, did the star circled by Paradise. There was a proverb Marcer's father had liked to quote when Marcer complained about Lavi Brice's religionist family connections: *No man is an island, entire of itself.*

Marcer EL-ed, and the lack of a bounce-back, this time, felt momentous, meaningful. No world was an island, either. Each was a part of its planetary system, a part of its political group, and a piece of the universe containing all others. *Any man's death diminishes me because I am involved in mankind.* As a nonterrestrial biologist, Marcer was involved in all worlds, all life. The death of a world, the death of a species, particularly an intelligent one: how could that bring Order into the universe? How could it be right? The universe isn't moral, he had said, quoting Jon Hsu's *General Principles.* But humans were. They had to be, or human society was abhorrent.

"Finished with the report?" the Khan asked. "Usually you work later."

Marcer turned. It was possible to surprise a New Dawn Altered, but difficult. Idryis Khan must have been intentionally trying. "I was too tired to continue."

"It's a beautiful night," the Khan said.

Marcer grunted his agreement, but the night was distant from his thoughts. "You alans have always selected for males rather than females," Marcer said, continuing his ruminations aloud, "and the houris have magnified the problem, but if the truth was presented to your people, wouldn't it prevent the Blessed species from doing any more harm?"

The Khan came beside Marcer, grasping the rail only a few centimeters from Marcer's hand, conduct vastly different from that he displayed with other Sons who visited the estate. What did Idryis Khan think of other men?

"Marcer," the Khan said, "I apologize for the difficulty you and I have had. I needed your help and couldn't ask for it openly. Now you understand, although I believe you underestimate the danger." He covered Marcer's hand on the rail with his own and briefly squeezed. He pressed so tightly Marcer's hand ached, but he didn't complain.

"As to just presenting the truth to my people, it wouldn't work. You don't understand the . . . convenience of the houris. Free wives, holy wives, who make a man Blessed and bear him only Sons. You don't understand religion. Islam is not hierarchical, like your Jonism. Each Imam has his own thoughts and some—many—would continue to espouse the holiness of the houris. It is a matter of life and death. The only way to end the danger now is to destroy Paradise. Do you agree?"

To disagree with Idryis Khan was dangerous. "Of course the only way to eliminate *all* threat is to exterminate the houri race, but why are you and other houris' Sons willing to do away with yourselves to save humanity?"

"You include yourself as human while I am something else?" the Khan asked.

Marcer smiled into the dark. The Khan seemed more human when his rigid expression couldn't be seen, and as long as Marcer didn't EL. "I'm Altered," Marcer said, "but I'm entirely of human stock."

"Aren't you overlooking the fact that your ability came from animals? Porpoises and bats, isn't it? Fish and flying rodents?"

Touché. Marcer didn't say it aloud. "Small segments of foreign DNA were lifted, then modified for humans. The source was entirely terrestrial and mammalian." He changed the subject. "If the Harmony swept Paradise, then there would be a war between the Harmony and the Emirates," he said.

"No." The Khan sighed. "If the Harmony sends a fleet to destroy Paradise, I guarantee that there will be no opposition."

It was an offer, something to entice Marcer and the Harmony to act, though it was unlikely the Harmony would refuse once they—through the Academies—believed there was any possible racial threat. Jonism had its cruel streak. Marcer *had* to be present in the Harmony to mitigate the effect of the hard facts in his report. "You can't make a guarantee like that," Marcer said. "If Aleko Bei didn't avenge the houris, then he'd be toppled in a minute."

"Exactly," the Khan said. "And I intend to be the one to do it."

Marcer gaped at the Khan. "You're using the destruction of the houris as an excuse to seize power? All of this is to create the proper conditions for your coup d'état?" He hadn't removed his hand from beneath the Khan's, and the warmth was unpleasant, the sensation clammy. Aleko Bei was a tyrant who had seized power by assassination, but having held power for eight years had given a certain emotional legitimacy to his regime. Violent overthrow of any government went against Marcer's Harmony upbringing.

"It's not an excuse, it's the reason a coup is necessary. Aleko Bei has three houri wives. He lets them make policy. It's because of the Bei and his wives that we are on the verge of destroying Neuland. Which would you prefer be swept: Paradise, a world of alien impostors, or Neuland, which is settled by humans? Think of it, Marcer. Alien women control a human government, and these aliens were placed in the path of human expansion by the Bril, humanity's one certain enemy."

"That's supposition. The Blessed might be a race that had star travel of its own, and lost it. They are hardly a stable species. They may even have been placed on Paradise and Neuland by another race we haven't met. They'd make excellent biological probes. An alliance seems more possible with them than with any other intelligent alien race I can imagine. We should at least try. They *are* human for half their lives."

"They are never *human*."

Marcer, though he hadn't yet met a houri, found it difficult to believe that impostors who nonetheless had won over their misogynist husbands so completely weren't human, but how had they failed so completely to win over their Sons? "What about avenging the houris? Even if you seize power, you'll have to do that, and there will be war. The Emirates will lose."

"If we fought the Harmony, we probably would lose. So we won't fight the Harmony. We'll blame Neuland."

Stunned, it took a moment for Marcer to speak. "But sweeping Neuland is what the houris wanted! You'll have destroyed two worlds!"

"You have my word—I swear by the Prophet, God's blessing and peace be upon him—that Neuland will not be destroyed. We'll take over the administration of the world, but the people of Neuland will survive."

Neuland. The perfect scapegoat world, a pariah because of its entirely Altered population. The Khan was proposing genocide of an alien species and conquest of an innocent human world, and making both seem logical and necessary. The houris were a challenge to the human race, yet what had they actually done? An invasion required intention. Marcer wasn't certain the houris had planned anything. If they hadn't, had their mothers, the jinn?

"How much work do you have left before you finish your report?"

Marcer was finished. It wasn't safe to say so to the Khan. It made Marcer disposable. "Several days' worth, and even then I'd like to prepare what Academics call a defense of the report, where all assumptions are stated and explained."

"We don't have much time. Aleko Bei will sweep Neuland soon."

"I understand." Marcer glanced back at the laboratory. The lights were on; Nisa was still there. "I'll work as quickly as I can. I agree that the Harmony needs to know about the houris and the jinn."

"That whore you like," the Khan said suddenly. "I'll tell the governor to free her. A gesture of good faith, as soon as you complete your report."

Linnet. "And then I'll to return to the Harmony as your emissary. Can I bring her with me?"

"Yes."

Idryis Khan had overplayed his hand; he was lying. "Thank you," Marcer said. He bowed.

"Good," the Khan said warmly. "I don't think I'll ever convince you of the extent of the houri danger, but at least we agree that a danger exists. Rather than return to your work while you're tired, join me for dinner. Now that we have no more secrets, and I've agreed to give you the woman you've been begging me for, there's no reason we can't be better friends."

"Of course, Khan. I'll just close the laboratory first, then I'll join you." Marcer bowed and started to leave, but inexplicably, he felt an urge to EL, and did. For once Marcer sensed something from Idryis Khan; it was overwhelming and incomprehensible. It faded almost immediately, but whatever emotion the Khan had experienced, it was one for which Marcer had no counterpart. "I'll expect you soon," the Khan said.

IV. Kindness.

Nisa was in the laboratory. "I'm closing the lab for the night," Marcer said gruffly.

She quietly began putting her instruments away. Marcer watched. She was the Khan's wife, but also a runaway who'd been recaptured, as much a prisoner as he. His suspicion of her was probably an echo of his general distrust. "Can I trust you?" He EL-ed immediately. The halo effect was ambiguous, but there was at least a modicum of goodwill.

"Of course," she said aloud.

His hands were shaking from the feedback of the Khan's strong emotion. He sat down at his desk and hid them in his lap. "Do you know what he wants?"

Nisa frowned. She was a pretty girl, artistically talented, subdued for now, but he sensed liveliness that would return once her self-confidence did. Spunky, he had told Linnet. Nisa came around her worktable, walking closer to his desk, but hesitantly, like a child awaiting an invitation to join those she hopes will be her friends. "He wants to kill off all the houris."

"That's right," he said. "He has a plan to exterminate them."

"Good," she said.

"I understand you hate your stepmother, but condemning all houris because of her would be like wanting to kill all men because of the Khan."

"I do," she said. "All of the Sons. We have to protect ourselves first, above everything else. Kindness is a luxury. Safety comes from strength."

Marcer tried a different tack. "The Khan says he needs the Harmony to sweep Paradise so he can overthrow Aleko Bei. But why does Neuland keep entering the picture? I think there's something more he hasn't told me, that I haven't discovered on my own."

"I expect there is." She spoke calmly, her hands folded at her waist, her head submissively bent. "Don't ever trust him, but I agree with him about the houris. The universe will be better when they're all dead. Particularly it will be better for women."

Linnet wouldn't urge genocide. Marcer was certain of it, even though she'd been hurt worse than Nisa by men. "This isn't a gender issue, it's one of right and wrong."

"I thought the universe wasn't moral?" she challenged him. "Are you a Jonist or a Jew?" She gestured at him with her hands. "You think too much about intangibles. Jonists are supposed to be pragmatic. You're not really one of them. You want justice, not Order; you're a Jew."

"You underestimate Jonism." He felt his face burn with embarrassment at being lectured on Jonist fundamentals by this girl. She could be right. Many Academics studying his report would conclude that for the safety of the humanity, Jonism, and Order, the houris should be destroyed.

Nisa didn't leave. She watched him covertly and toyed with the corner of her lab coat, then brushed it down at her side. "He asked me—before he went outside to talk to you—whether or not your report was done. I told him the truth, that it was. Researcher Brice, I believe that he intends to kill you." She had spoken very quickly, in a hurry to get it all said. She looked away, twisting slightly at the hips, then looked back. More deliberately, she added, "He promised me that I'd go to the Harmony in your place."

It made sense. Nisa would make a favorable impression in the Harmony, where sympathy for alan women was widespread. In fact, she was a perfect messenger, except that the Khan had no way to control her once she was gone. But she hated the houris; perhaps that was enough. It was more than could be said of Marcer.

"You've got to get away tonight," she added.

"How?" he asked. "And why are you telling me this now?"

"I don't know," she said. He sensed truth.

Houris were said to be the essence of femininity, delightful in the eyes of any and every man, the promised angels of the Qur'an. If so, how could their Sons embody the worst of masculinity? Aggression and ambition. Cruelty. Why did aliens see that as the essence of men? Somewhere in the city of Shores, Linnet was waiting for him to rescue her. The moment Marcer ran, he was certain the Khan would order her execution. On the other hand, he had promised her to Marcer. If he could be kept to his word, if Marcer could bargain with that impostor man, then he might still save Linnet. "Thank you, but I can't escape just now," he said, smiling ironically at Nisa. "I've promised to join him for dinner."

Chapter 13

Jeroen Lee hosted a fete in celebration of his protégé's marriage; he invited the Supplicant.

"You should be proud of yourself," Lee said quietly as he greeted her after the brief registration ceremony. "You've accomplished the impossible. You've made me respectable again."

She laughed. Only one of the other Electors had excused himself from Lee's party. All significant members of the government were present, too. However, Harmony ideas of respectability shocked her; the bride was already pregnant, and she openly teased her doting husband, calling him a puppy, and generally robbed him of his dignity to the applause of the guests. From the mingling of the sexes to their dancing and the alcohol served, it was nothing like her own wedding party. It was much better. She envied the bride.

Sanda Brauna had overheard Lee's comment. "No one trusts you, Jeroen," she said. "They never will again."

Lee smiled, took Sanda's hand, and kissed it. Sanda pulled away. Though the Supplicant recognized the Jonist gallantry, Lee's unwelcome kiss was also veiled aggression.

"As long as they respect and listen to me," Lee said, "then trust is unnecessary." He turned to the Supplicant. "Do you *trust* this Khan person?"

The Supplicant cast a quick look at Sanda. She didn't want to irk her benefactor, but she answered truthfully. "No, Elector, I don't."

"And yet you're here, doing the Khan's work because you believe his message." He smiled at Sanda. "Speculate," he ordered the Supplicant. "What does he really want?"

"Marcer said the Khan wanted to depose Aleko Bei."

Lee nodded. "Of course. And we're to give him the excuse. We all understand that. But one thing troubles me."

His tone sobered. The Supplicant noticed Sanda Brauna's immediate change in attitude. She became attentive, even receptive. "Don't most despots aim to found a dynasty?" Lee asked.

"He can't," the Supplicant said. "He's as infertile as ar unman. All sons of houris are. Everyone knows that."

Lee turned and briefly nodded at a man waiting to speak to him, making him stand by while Lee studied the Supplicant. "Did Brice ever discuss the infertility of houris' sons with you?" Lee asked.

"No," she said in perfect honesty.

"What are you thinking, Jeroen?" Sanda asked. She looked to him for guidance, her dislike put entirely aside.

Lee shrugged, then he and Sanda exchanged a look which showed the Supplicant that whatever differences the two Electors had, they could work together. "We don't know everything we should about the motives of this Khan," Lee said. "He's clever. We might consider defending Neuland from him—after wiping Paradise clean."

I. Out of the closet.

Marcer blotted perspiration from his forehead with the towel-sized napkin while a servant poured him hot tea he didn't need in the excessively warm room. Dressed in his maroon uniform, but not sweating, Idryis Khan leaned comfortably against a pile of silk cushions, languidly stretched his arms and arched his back as a second servant poured tea for him. Both servants stepped back in unison, as though table service were a dance or military drill. They took positions near the door, their attention professionally absent until they might be needed.

By alan custom, dinner had passed in meaningless, courtly conversation. Marcer's back felt rigid as brick from the effort of appearing relaxed while staying vigilant. A low sound like that of a lion content with his kill came from the Khan; with the meal over, Marcer knew where the Khan's attention would turn next. The Khan exhibited no obvious intention to kill him, yet Marcer knew that Nisa had told the truth. Over the weeks he had gradually become aware that the Khan did have body language of a sort. Instead of facial expression or posture, it was a subtle dialect of unconscious sounds and barely discernible vibrations. Also, throughout the lengthy dinner, Idryis Khan had made an elaborate and perhaps unconscious pantomime of *not* touching Marcer, as though teasing himself by postponing his fulfillment. The Khan had enjoyed the grim, strained meal and was eager to be cruel.

"How is my wife's work in the laboratory?" the Khan suddenly asked, signaling a more businesslike turn in the conversational banalities.

"Considering she understands so little, Nisa is a good worker."

"Women are sly. She probably knows more than you think."

When Marcer failed to respond, they lapsed into silence. The Khan, seated beside Marcer, stared at Marcer with his usual fixed expression. Marcer wished the charade would end, but dreaded the Khan's finale. "I'll leave," he said, hoping the fragile courtesy that had until then amused and constrained the Khan would hold. "Thank you for the excellent meal, but I should get more work done tonight." Marcer started to rise from the floor cushions, but the Khan bent close, grasped Marcer's right ankle, and prevented him from going.

"Stay awhile." It was an order spoken as an invitation.

"Of course." Marcer smiled, self-consciously aware of their counterfeit courtesy. He sat back on his pillows but was unable to settle quite the distance away he had been because Idryis Khan didn't release his grip. Marcer did pull his knees against his chest; he leaned his head on them, accustomed to the dull ache from his right knee.

The Khan's fingers kneaded Marcer's ankle; his rumbling sound became a faint hum. He sighed, then reclined so that he was partly in Marcer's space, angled around Marcer's back while resting on an elbow. "Make that sound," he said. "The echo."

"I can see perfectly well." Marcer was motionless.

"Even so. I would enjoy it. Make the sound." Over the weeks, the Khan had made it clear that any overture from Marcer was welcome, but he had never pushed so hard before.

Marcer EL-ed, studying the layout of the secluded dining room for an escape route. It was all hard surfaces, with elaborate, abstractly patterned tile walls and floor; a cold, barren space, softened imperceptibly by their cushions, if at all. The bounce-back jangled against his nerves. The only furniture was the stunted dining table holding the dinner remains. The table settings consisted of a few serving spoons. Had there been a knife, Marcer doubted his boyhood hand-to-hand fighting skills could best the soldierly training of Idryis Khan.

"Good." The Khan paused in his stroking of Marcer's leg. "Your Alteration should be appreciated better. But you like women. Why?"

Marcer answered without reference to flesh. "Women—females—are the fundamental gender of sexually reproducing species. When human cultures make women less meaningful than men, they weaken humanity. Look how the houris attacked."

The Khan sat up from his sprawl. "That wasn't what I meant."

"I know."

"Are you on guard against me?" The Khan lightly swatted the part of Marcer's rump which wasn't sunk into the cushions.

"Of course." Marcer made a polite bow from his seated position. Although he had to stretch out his legs, it removed him from the Khan's easy reach. "You're a natural hunter."

The Khan nearly purred with pleasure. He gestured. "Come here, Marcer." His tone eloquently expressed his intentions. Tone. Of course, Marcer realized. Voice was sound and Sons were sensitive to sound. That was likely to be the reason Sons were capable of human vocal inflection although they lacked instinctive human facial expression. The Khan understood human body language very well, however. Marcer glanced at the two servants—shyly, he hoped.

"Do they bother you?" The Khan didn't wait for an answer. "Get out," he told the two men. "Clear the table in the morning. I won't need you until then. You're dismissed."

"But sir . . ." one began.

The Khan glared. Pronouncing every word distinctly, he said, "My order was clear. And I do not want you in the hall, peeping." He rearranged the cushions and settled into them as the servants left; afterward he tugged on Marcer's arm to draw him back, too.

"Why do you dislike unmen?" Marcer allowed himself to be pulled into the Khan's embrace. "Except for Nisa's boy, Tomo, all your servants are standard men."

"All my servants are soldiers," the Khan said. "Josip Gordan limited the soldiers I could bring off my ships, but he didn't limit my servants. This house is very well staffed. In fact, I ordered a special drill tonight, just for you. The doors are guarded, the grounds are monitored, and a scanner alarm was installed. After all, this *is* a prison."

Marcer returned the Khan's smile. "I've decided you're right. I've been studying the demographic element in the houris' assault on the Emirates. The data you gave me are conclusive. They need to be stopped. I'll convince the Harmony to destroy Paradise. That won't take much effort if houris are linked to the Bril. Linnet and I will take your information to the Harmony and do whatever you think is best."

"You're very handsome when you lie," the Khan told Marcer. He drew Marcer close and kissed him, firmly, on the lips.

Repulsed, Marcer didn't relax into the embrace. When the Khan ended the kiss, Marcer EL-ed, directing his attention outward onto a small balcony. The susurration of waves and the darkness didn't prevent Marcer from sensing the long fall from the balcony. This side of the mansion was atop a fifty-meter cliff.

"Nice," the Khan said, and shivered slightly. "Don't be afraid. I understand this isn't your favorite form of pleasure, but I doubt I'll have to hurt you in order to enjoy it."

"What?" Marcer thought he'd misheard.

Idryis Khan took Marcer's face between his two hands. He held it immobile and stared into Marcer's eyes as he spoke. "Commit yourself to me wholly. Convince me that we *do* agree about the houris, that you'll be my comfort and support. That you're not deceiving me. Bodies don't lie. Show me I can trust you. I dislike the waste of eliminating you. I would welcome you as an ally."

If the Khan could lie, then so might Marcer. He had a single, small advantage in that the Khan wanted him. He leaned his upper body against the Khan, which freed him from the Khan's grasp. "Our only quarrel has been because of your coercion," Marcer said. "And because you won't let me see Linnet. I owe her for her help."

The Khan reached around Marcer. He touched the exposed tip of the corrective in the back of Marcer's neck, wiggling it unpleasantly. "I won't remove this," he whispered in Marcer's ear, "but if you're good, then I won't use it. As to the whore, she's served her purpose."

Marcer moved away. "Men and women don't have purposes, they have lives."

"No philosophy." The Khan gave an artificial smile. "Tonight is for pleasure. You have a unique skill that could be precious to me, but only if I trust you." He touched Marcer's chest. "First, remove your clothes."

Marcer had no experience with men like Idryis Khan, who liked force, and only a limited attunement to his emotions through his involuntary, probably instinctive, sounds, but it was time to decide. What the Khan wanted from Marcer wasn't a vice to a Jonist, only a choice. Marcer had either to submit or to struggle. The Khan would enjoy a struggle. Submission was an alan virtue. It would be demeaning, but it might keep him alive. Not Linnet, however.

Marcer looked at the greasy table, then back to the Khan, and allowed his distaste to show. "Not here," he whispered. Less emotion was audible in a whisper.

The Khan's lips crinkled back in a feral smile, the first smile that had seemed natural on him. He sprang to his feet with such effortless grace that Marcer was unwillingly impressed. "My rooms."

"Outdoors." Marcer lowered his eyes. "Inside a room, I always feel confined."

"Another time." The Khan took Marcer's hand and raised him to his feet. "Tonight is *my* choice."

Marcer took what comfort he could in the reference to his future and followed the Khan out of the room. A soldier/servant guarded the door. The Khan had prepared for a struggle, and he would probably remain prepared, no matter how accommodating Marcer pretended to be.

Marcer studied the Khan's back. Broad, muscular, and strong. Marcer was taller, but the Khan had a more robust build and better training. He was more than a match for Marcer. A predator, who didn't intrinsically believe, as Marcer did, that other people were real.

The Khan's bedroom was a suite larger than Marcer's Darien apartment. It consisted of two main rooms, one for relaxing with intimates and behind it, a palatial bedroom.

Idryis Khan led Marcer directly to the bedroom. Another veranda ran its length. The wall was missing, replaced by pale draperies which fluttered in the breeze. The bed was large and low, almost a mattress on the floor. The scent of ba'na and roses had been diffused throughout, though the air flow was washing it outdoors. Marcer hesitated in the doorway between the two rooms.

"What's the matter?" The Khan had gone ahead.

It would have been imprudent to tell the Khan his bedroom was a design straight from a cyclone romance drama. Even worse to say that Marcer saw nothing with which to attack him. Rather than speak, he EL-ed, his one sure means of affecting the Khan.

"Take off your clothes."

"Not yet," Marcer said. The summer heat and humidity made him feel dirty. He walked a circuit of the room, whistling to himself, conscious of the Khan's attention and allowing the Khan to know it; he strutted; he peeked at the Khan several times. A flattopped rock had been hollowed and made into a small fountain; it was surrounded by sand-colored cushions. Among them lay the corrective's slim control rod, a translucent cylinder. Marcer glanced at the Khan.

The Khan bowed. "Only if necessary." His voice was husky.

The door to a closet dressing area was ajar. Marcer glimpsed rows of hanging uniforms and other clothing. Another door was closed. The Khan watched. Marcer stared back, then went past him, out onto the veranda. This room was also on the far side of the house from his laboratory. Steep stairs led away from the veranda, joined others from the side entrance they had used after their conversation on the beach, then continued down to the beach.

The Khan looked out onto the veranda while remaining in the bedroom. He watched Marcer.

"A beautiful night," Marcer said.

"Come back inside."

Marcer pushed the billowing draperies out of the way and returned. He stripped off his shirt immediately, much too quickly and methodically to be erotic. Marcer had no moral qualms, only an intense aversion to the Khan. He folded the shirt neatly and looked around, as if puzzled. "May I use your closet?"

The Khan leaned against the wall with his arms crossed at his chest. He nodded toward the closet door. "Go ahead."

Marcer crossed the room to the closet. He went inside. It was larger than Linnet's room had been, but the ceiling was low; he felt it coming down on him and gritted his teeth against the urge to EL, which would only worsen the sensation. He undressed hurriedly while scanning the garments and rows of closed cabinets for something useful in making an escape. He didn't know what it would be or how he would conceal it. There were belts, shirts, trousers, and shoes. Marcer grimaced at the image of hammering the Khan to death with a belt buckle.

The Khan walked into the closet. His eyes traveled Marcer's body without reaching his face. "No scars," he said. "Harmony medicine or an uneventful life?"

Marcer waited until the Khan looked up at him. "My knee."

The Khan shrugged. "It looks lumpy. Not too bad." He closed the door behind himself. "Does that trouble you?"

It was foolish to deny it. "I prefer more space."

The Khan didn't open the door. "Undress me." He raised his arms away from his sides.

Marcer hesitated, then sighed as if acting as the Khan's intimate valet was a whim he was granting. Naked himself, Marcer went to the Khan in businesslike fashion. Unaccustomed to buttons, he had difficulty with the first several on the maroon uniform jacket, which let him concentrate on it as simply a job. He tried not to feel the Khan through the fabric, but so close, the Khan's scent was overpowering. It was a mint fragrance, though Marcer hadn't noticed the Khan wearing cologne before. The thick cloth, pulled down by the heavy buttons, fell open and revealed a pure, white shirt, only a bit damp around the neck and underarms. Beneath the Khan's left arm there was also a holster. Marcer hesitated and didn't touch the stainless-steel gun.

"A Smith & Wesson double-action automatic, Model 659. Fourteen-round magazine. One of my favorites—I collect antique weapons. Death should be personal. Do you want to try it?" The Khan thrust his shoulder out as if proffering the gun.

Definitely a trick. "I've never used one."

"I'll give you a lesson." He took the gun from the hol-

ster, checked it, then laid it atop one of the cabinets.
"Later."

This reference to the future felt sinister. "Are you going
to kill me?" Marcer blurted.

"Not if you convince me that I shouldn't." The Khan's
leer was entirely in his voice, but Marcer felt it like an
unwelcome kiss. "I'm willing to be won over. You could
be useful when I'm dealing with the Harmony, and there
are many nights between now and then."

Marcer swallowed hard, controlled the urge to EL, and
continued his task. He tugged the jacket sleeves off the
Khan, whose only move to help was to turn. Marcer couldn't
resist glancing at the gun when the Khan had his back to
it, but he did nothing. "There." The Khan pointed. Marcer
deposited the jacket in an otherwise empty hamper. The
Khan removed his holster and shirt, all the while watching
Marcer. There were two thin scars across the Khan's chest,
almost lost in his damp, curly black hair, as well as one
long slash on his upper right arm.

Scars reminded Marcer of Linnet. Timidly, hoping to
please the Khan, Marcer touched one, tracing its length
across the Khan's chest. Linnet had more. He had never
traced hers with his fingers, only with his mind. Marcer
closed his eyes momentarily and EL-ed, but the bounce-
back from the Khan showed the same superficiality as an
EL of a rock.

Idryis Khan grabbed Marcer's hand. "Very good," he
said. "I don't mind that you're shy." He touched Marcer's
bare chest. "Now my trousers."

Marcer smelled the close, musty odor of his own sweat.
He could do this, if only for the chance it would save Linnet. The belt whished as Marcer slid it through the loops.
The trousers had a front closure. Marcer swallowed down
bile as his gorge rose at the thought of being intimate with
this man. Idryis Khan waited. His deep humming indicated
he was pleasantly aware of Marcer's struggle.

"A man is always better than a woman." The Khan took
Marcer's hand and kissed it, then opened the flap on his
own trousers. "A man has honor. No woman does. No
woman can. They're empty inside, or why else could the
houris impersonate them so easily?" The Khan stroked
Marcer's chest, each caress a bit lower than the one before.

Marcer tried not to brace himself against the Khan, but couldn't prevent it.

"It's all right," the Khan said, slowing his hand. "I'll be patient. This is a seduction, not a rape. So tell me, why would a decent man care about a whore? Why does someone of your elegance want an eyesore like that ugly bitch?"

He seemed to need an answer. "Because she's kind," Marcer said. "She's honest. I don't find her ugly anymore."

"I see." The Khan removed his hands from Marcer's body. "All the things I'm not, in your eyes. But there's one thing I am and she isn't. I'm alive. I'm here."

Stunned, Marcer just stood. "Linnet is dead?" he whispered.

"So, it wasn't just an act to keep a companion alive." From the Khan came a squeaking sound, aurally irritating, particularly in the close quarters of the closet, though it would have been inaudible to standard humans. "I'll forgive you, since you've submitted to me. Now remove my trousers."

Marcer looked at the Khan. If Linnet was dead, there was no reason to humor the bastard who had refused to save her.

"Come here." The Khan reached out impatiently to him.

Desperate, Marcer EL-ed. He sensed the ceiling light. He sensed the gun. As quick as the thought, he raised his arm and smashed his fist against the ceiling light, breaking the glass fixtures and the bulb. The closet went dark.

He EL-ed again. He reached for the gun. The Khan's hand was already on it. "Come get it," the Khan said. He yanked his hand away, taking the gun.

Marcer EL-ed continuously. It gave him a double advantage: audible vision and pleasure to the Khan. That pleasure might prevent the "holy rage" that would otherwise make the Khan a savage. Marcer perceived the hard metal of the gun like a bright light pulling him toward it. He ducked as the Khan took a cautious step forward. The Khan reached out his hand like the blind man he temporarily was. "You wouldn't get away even if you killed me." The Khan sounded calm. "Don't forget the corrective. It also has a homing device. The minute you left the house, you'd be hunted."

Marcer's fingers touched the belt on the floor. He picked it up. He slid his hand along its leather to the decorative buckle. Whiplike, he lashed it forward, but it caught on the clothing hanging behind him.

The Khan leapt toward the sound. Marcer plunged into the shirts, barely avoiding the Khan. Hangers jostled. Even a standard human, or a Son, could follow that noise.

"I don't want to kill you, Marcer." Idryis Khan was even with Marcer, but in the aisle. "This isn't nearly as enjoyable as I imagined. I prefer you willing and alive, but you've proven I can't trust you." He was facing Marcer, but his gun was aimed too high because Marcer was squatting on the floor. "What am I supposed to do? Give yourself up and we'll talk. My word. I swear by the Prophet, God's blessings and peace be upon him."

Marcer didn't move; he didn't breathe. The gunbarrel wavered. The Khan kicked, trying to locate Marcer, but his boot banged against a cabinet.

Marcer crept forward. He stayed low. He dropped the belt; it would only get caught again.

Marcer charged the Khan. The impact was at the Khan's waist. Marcer pushed with his arms and his shoulder, trying to topple him, but couldn't. Sharp pains in Marcer's right knee prevented him from getting a good purchase on the floor. Their sweating bodies—Marcer's naked and the Khan's nearly so—slid against each other.

The Khan floundered backward. As he moved he brought the gun down on Marcer. It connected glancingly with Marcer's neck, sending shudders of pain down his spine as it pressed against the corrective.

"Your whore," the Khan said hoarsely as he jumped back. "I killed her myself. But first I found a way to make her scream." He sprang at Marcer again.

"Linnet!" Marcer shouted. He twisted to avoid another blow. His knee snapped; he didn't feel it. The Khan's forearm, the hand holding the gun, went by the side of Marcer's head. Marcer turned and grabbed the forearm like a falling man snatching a tree branch. He sank his teeth into Idryis Khan.

The Khan screamed and dropped the gun.

Marcer jumped on top of the gun. Underfoot was the quickest method of keeping it from the Khan. Blood filled Marcer's mouth together with a lump of the Khan's torn flesh.

The Khan stumbled. He extended his injured arm blindly;

his good hand held the place Marcer had bitten. The wound was bleeding heavily; blood spurted between his fingers. "When I get you," the Khan said, "believe me, you won't enjoy the rest of your last night."

Marcer squatted. He let the Khan's blood and skin dribble silently from his mouth as he listened to the Khan's panting. The jinn passed through his thoughts: eating flesh as reproduction. Vampires. He was disgusted with them and the Sons they created. Impostor men as much as houris were impostor women.

Linnet was dead. Idryis Khan a'Husain had killed her. Marcer carefully moved his foot and took the gun. He cradled it, feeling the cool metal against his warm hand, slipping it into a comfortable position. His index finger found the trigger. He knew nothing about antique mechanical weapons, except what he'd learned from the few cyclone dramas he had seen: they shot metal projectiles which had to be loaded into them. Presumably, Idryis Khan had done that.

Marcer moved sideways. "Here I am," he taunted. "Come get me. Or do you only attack women?"

No coward, the Khan ran at him. Marcer leveled the gun, aiming for the Khan's chest. He pressed the trigger. It didn't move. Jammed? He tried again.

The Khan fell on top of Marcer, grappling in the dark for the gun. He didn't get it. Marcer tossed it away. Unhindered by the dark, he could find it again.

On his knees, the Khan swung a fist and connected with nothing. Marcer had squirmed away. Off-balance, confused about Marcer's location, the Khan retreated to the other side of the closet.

Marcer EL-ed, searching for the gun, and sensed it on the floor to his right. He edged through the clothes, trying not to disturb them and make noise. He came down on his knee. Pain lanced through his leg; he inhaled sharply.

He'd given away his position. The Khan yelled something Marcer didn't recognize and jumped at him.

Marcer just managed to reach the gun. It was hard and heavy so it wasn't useless. Marcer grasped it by the barrel. He turned. He EL-ed. With all his strength, he smashed it against the Khan's head.

The Khan grunted. He staggered sideways but didn't quite collapse, holding himself up with an arm and a knee.

Blood seeped from his forehead. He groaned. "Wait," he said. "We'll talk."

Marcer EL-ed. "Does that feel good?" he jeered, and brought the gun down again, fast and firmly, onto the same place. Idryis Khan didn't try to defend himself. His arm gave way and he went down onto the floor.

Marcer hit him once more for good measure. He waited, unsure whether the Khan was alive or dead. Idryis Khan didn't move.

Marcer was trembling. The walls were too close. The stale air smelled of blood. He EL-ed as he crouched beside the body, intending to check the Khan's breathing. He automatically avoided the shards of broken glass that glittered brightly in the bounce-back.

The taste of the Khan in his mouth nauseated Marcer. Meat. Linnet's murderer. He turned his head and vomited. A stench even worse than blood immediately filled the room.

Haltingly, Marcer moved to the other side of the Khan, then touched him. His inert body was slick and warm. Marcer felt the Khan's throat. There was a pulse. Relieved, he sat down on the floor and wiped his forehead with his equally damp arm.

In the Harmony, any basic House Utility would have rung an alarm. The Khan relied on his own prowess and standard human men. Soldiers. Marcer still had to escape the house and grounds.

Marcer sighed and reached for the belt he'd dropped, found it, and used it as a rope to bind the Khan's hands behind his back. He pulled a shirt from a hangar and stuffed the fabric into the Khan's mouth, then tied another around it, to hold it in. He checked each knot twice, then reached up, tore another garment from its hanger, and wiped his bloody mouth.

He stepped over the Khan and cracked opened the closet door. Fresh air was a blessing. Gingerly, afraid of finding a servant, he came out of the closet and into the bedroom. He EL-ed. There was no one. The draperies fluttered. Water in the fountain spilled over the rock.

The breeze began to cool him; the amply sized room cleared his head. He looked down. He was naked. Embedded in his neck was the Khan's corrective, complete with a homing device.

Marcer limped to the cushioned area around the fountain and picked up the control rod, which the Khan must have intended to use on him. A tool for violent prisoners in the Harmony, Marcer had never used one. He could only guess how the signal was controlled and sent, though he knew too well how it felt to receive one. Marcer raised his arm to smash the rod against the stone waterfall, then dropped his hand. Wrecking it might raise an alarm. He'd keep it; let them spend time searching for it. With luck, whatever homing signal the corrective sent couldn't be received by any other device in the Khan's house.

Marcer remembered that the Khan's legs were free. He hobbled to the closet. The odor made him hesitate, but finally he went in. With the door open, the closet was dimly lit from the bedroom. He EL-ed; the Khan hadn't moved. Marcer found another belt and bound the Khan's legs.

Marcer retrieved his own clothes, undisturbed from where he had set them on a cabinet. He also took the gun and holster, then returned to the bedroom.

There was the adjacent room for visitors, but in this room the bed was the only place to sit besides the floor. Marcer sat on its edge, trying to think of an escape plan. Besides human guards, he didn't know what defenses the estate had; his own weaponry was limited to the Khan's malfunctioning gun.

There was another closed door. Guessing it was a washing room, Marcer went to it. He was right. Although he longed to bathe, he merely wiped the sticky, drying blood from the gun, using one of the Khan's linen towels. Upon examining the gun more closely, he saw the safety, released it, then put it back once more. He wished he could take a practice shot but, remembering the noisy explosion of the beach guard's weapon, decided it would be too loud.

His knee hurt more than it had earlier. Marcer examined it. It was swelling, but it moved when he manipulated it. He wrapped a thin, linen towel tightly around it as a brace, then, resting his weight on his left leg, washed his face and rinsed his mouth. A large number of drug patches were neatly arranged in the Khan's cabinet, but their labels were in Arabic script. He didn't dare take anything. He dressed in his own sweat-dampened, wrinkled clothing, adding the gun and holster, then returned to the bedroom.

His shirt was too light a color for the night. Steeling

himself, Marcer entered the closet one more time and took what was surely an expensive jacket, inlaid with dark purplish blue hing-shell imported from the Harmony. Loose, but it would fit.

Marcer checked the closet cabinets for anything useful. In a small, secret drawer (revealed by his EL because of a minute gap in the surface, as when light shines beneath a closed door), Marcer found a hoard of cash, over twenty thousand rials.

The Khan groaned. Marcer kicked him, then guiltily re-checked his pulse. Fine.

Should he kill Idryis Khan? The Khan had killed Linnet; didn't he deserve death? *An eye for an eye,* Marcer's father had said to excuse certain business deals of which he was not proud. In nature, in every environment, death was a part of life. Jonists were pragmatists; he wouldn't be blamed. "Thou shalt not kill," Marcer whispered. Another bit of the classical education his father had insisted upon giving him. Besides, if he killed the Khan, the full weight of alan police and military would look for the murderer of such an important nobleman, a Son of the Prophet. If he did, he would be a murderer. Marcer stuffed the cash in a jacket pocket, then closed the Khan alone in the closet. Alive.

The beach was the most tempting escape route. He could swim or walk until he reached another house, then walk through those grounds to the road to Shores. Simple, but also obvious, and Marcer wasn't sure he could walk or swim for long. Despite that, it seemed a better chance than walking through the house, where the Khan surely had monitors watching the halls. Marcer placed the control rod in an interior pocket of the Khan's jacket and went onto the veranda. Two moons were up, reminding him of home.

He EL-ed and immediately spotted a guard. The man was alone and moving about on patrol, not at a post. Marcer watched from the verandah. The guard wore black and an infrared scatter-suit, but there was nothing to hide him from an EL. The suit indicated that the guards probably could scan in infrared, however; they would see him, too. The guard stopped, checked something small in his hand, then continued his rounds, going down the stairs to the beach. Marcer heard him exchange greetings with a man stationed on the beach, but the actual words were lost in the sound of the wind and the waves. The beach was too open; he wouldn't get past the guards.

If not the beach, where?

There could be perimeter sensor fencing around the estate. He couldn't cross it without being found. Air vehicles were seldom used, and he'd seen none near the house. The only way out would be to drive out, using a coach from the front garage. No sensor fence could cross a road—in the Harmony, at least. The driveway? He didn't know. Nor was he sure how he'd prevent being seen.

He'd do a Nisa and pretend to be a servant. The Khan used men, not unmen. Marcer felt the holster underneath his jacket, then went down the veranda stairs to the general entrance on this side of the house. The soldier/servants would recognize him if he was seen, but avoidance was one useful ability enhanced by an EL. He couldn't avoid the scanning monitors, but he could hope that they were untended. What else was there but to try? He hunched his shoulders as much as he could to diminish the appearance of his height and EL-ed continuously.

He opened the door quickly, as though he had business there. The hall was empty. He tiptoed, staggering a little when using his right leg, passed the corridor to the Khan's suite, passed the dining room and social rooms whose exact function he didn't know, and passed doors leading to servants' areas. It was relatively late; their master was occupied; perhaps that was why there were no servants around.

He reached the last corridor before the turn into the main entrance, an imposing space in every alan house, and likely to be majestic in the mansion of a Son with aspirations to be the Emirates' next leader. Majestic, and guarded.

Marcer took the gun from its holster. He unlocked the safety. His gut felt tight. He hadn't killed Idryis Khan. Could he kill blameless men whose only fault was a chance assignment by the Khan? Did self-defense stretch that far? Marcer pressed the side of the gun against his cheek and gathered his resolve. He'd probably be too far away to do anything but shoot.

A squeaky door opened behind Marcer. He turned, pointing the gun. The unman who tended Nisa, Tomo, came into the corridor with a tray in his hands. It held a teapot and two cups. He walked past Marcer as though Marcer were invisible. He didn't glance even at the gun trained on him. Marcer lowered it. Only then did Tomo nod, but he continued forward into the entrance.

The tea was clearly for the guards, but that would create only a minor distraction. Marcer appreciated the unman's attempt to help, if that was what his odd behavior was, but doubted the guards would continue to sip tea as he walked past them. Still, he knew there were two. While waiting for an opportune time, Marcer listened as the unman offered, and both guards accepted, tea. "There are cakes in the kitchen," the unman offered, but neither man wanted any. They were gruff with Tomo, who was unfailingly polite, staying with them and pouring when Marcer would have rather had him leave.

"Would you like more tea?" the unman asked. Neither guard answered. Marcer heard Tomo gathering ceramics. A moment later the unman returned. This time he smiled at Marcer. "You can leave," he said.

"Are they dead?"

"Asleep, for about fifteen minutes. They won't realize they were. They shouldn't remember me. Still, you'd better hurry. And be silent; loud noise will wake them."

"Thank you," he whispered. He peered around the corner. The two soldiers were standing, stiff as statues, at their posts. Their eyes were open. The scene was eerie. Marcer looked back at the unman. He barely knew him, except as a victim of Nisa's bitter humor, and her jailer. "Why are you helping me?"

Tomo pushed Marcer forward. As he did, he whispered, "I was his mother's servant. A lovely lady. You defend her sisters. Go."

The dead thing in the cocoon, an alien impostor, called a lovely lady. Marcer touched the unman's shoulder, then walked carefully to the doors, passing the motionless guards while holding his breath so as not to disturb them. He opened a door just enough to slide through.

Outdoors, Marcer EL-ed. No guards were nearby. One was far to the right on the perimeter of the garden inside the gate. Along with his bounce-back, Marcer heard the tinny echo of a sonic-scanner alarm. The Khan had made an error. A sonic scanner was easily avoided by anyone who could hear it. Marcer could. He dashed across the open space, zigzagging to avoid breaking the sound waves, the rush of adrenaline masking the pain in his leg. He ran toward the road. He had, at best, until morning before the Khan was found.

II. Reward.

Matthew McCue wouldn't be hurried by Marcer. He scooped sugar into his tea with a tablespoon, stirred it with a dry cinnamon cookie, then bit into the cookie and ignored the tea. "He's going to launch a coup?"

"Yes. That's what he said." Marcer rubbed his eyes; they were gritty with fatigue. He'd limped several kilometers toward Shores before being picked up by an overloaded truck taking goats into the city; he still smelled of hay and goats. "He's going to leak alarming information on the Blessed—the houris—to the Harmony, and he's depending on us to do what we did to the Bril. Exterminate them. In the turmoil, he'll depose Aleko Bei."

McCue shook his head. "It's not as though the Harmony has never heard of the houris. I myself have sold information about them. Several times." McCue adjusted his position in his air-chair so he could reach the plate of cookies more easily. As an afterthought, he added, "Although your data does cast them in a new light. Shape-shifting aliens in men's bedrooms." He chuckled as though he found the idea highly amusing. "Only an Academic could sell that. No one would believe it from me."

Marcer stood; the tiny room made him anxious. "The Harmony needs to know everything. He'll probably change my report to make the Blessed seem evil, more harmful to mankind. That's why he doesn't want me in the Harmony. I need to be there. His goal is to exterminate them by convincing the Harmony to sweep Paradise. That shouldn't happen. We should at least try to talk to them first. They know us; they spend half their lives as humans."

"Pardon me, Researcher, but this seems a very convoluted plan if the Khan's purpose is just to organize a coup." McCue sipped his tea, shuddered as though it was too hot, and set the cup back down. "There are many, many simpler ways."

"I agree. But Idryis Khan seems really to believe the

houris have to be eliminated. So does his wife, Nisa. Look, McCue, are you going to help me or not?"

McCue rubbed a mole on his forehead. "Go to the governor. He's Aleko Bei's man, not the Khan's. He may reward you for the information—if he doesn't kill you as an escaped prisoner."

"The governor won't get the truth to the Harmony!" Marcer slammed his fist onto the table, then grunted when it hurt. He had another reason to avoid Governor Gordan: Gordan had been one of Linnet's regular customers.

"What is it you want the Harmony to *do* about the houris? If they actually are a threat to the human race, why not let the Khan's plan go ahead? Then the houris are gone, and the Emirates have a new Bei. Why should the Harmony care? They ignore everyone outside their borders, except occasionally, to swat them or sell them something."

Unlike the spacious rooms in alan homes, McCue's house was a linking of tiny closed spaces. This sitting room was no more than three meters by three and it was nearly filled by McCue's chair, a hugely expensive device which used a miniature gravity generator to adjust the seat and back to any position or weight whatsoever. From the way he moved in the chair, Marcer guessed McCue was very close to weightless. The remaining furniture consisted of a comfortable standard chair and the table supporting the tray of cookies and tea. There was barely enough room to move, let alone to make a New Dawn Altered comfortable, especially since the air-chair's strange gravity played havoc with the sound waves of an EL. "What about Neuland?" Marcer said. "He'll take over the entire world."

McCue looked from side to side. "I don't see any Neulanders here."

"And you were the one to lecture me about duty! What about decency?"

"I have none." McCue dipped another cookie. "I ignore anything so fickle. Duty is something else entirely. I have none to the houris, their pets, or to you. And killing any or all of you does not injure humanity in any significant way."

"Yes it does." Marcer EL-ed. Despite the air-chair, he received a sense of McCue's aura. He was neither as cool as he pretended, nor was he so immune to Marcer's plea, but he was stubborn. "In the Last War, humans exterminated the Bril," Marcer said. "Genocide. The Blessed are only the second intelligent aliens we've met. Yes, to treat them as friends involves a risk, but they aren't the Bril. To the best of our knowledge, they haven't knowingly attacked us. They've done what is natural for them. We should meet them without these alan cultural assumptions or our own prejudices."

"We may miss an opportunity, but that's better than losing the store." McCue nestled back into his chair, scratching his head.

"What does it say about the human species if we commit genocide on every alien intelligence we find?"

"I don't know, Researcher. That we're alert? Careful? Dangerous?"

"Depraved?" Marcer locked eyes with McCue, but McCue didn't look away. It was a child's game, a game played by the Khan. Marcer turned aside. "Not everything that's different is dangerous," Marcer said. "We can gamble. After all, except that the houris replace other wives, the Blessed don't affect the human genome since the Sons are infertile. All humans have to do is not marry houris. Or the jinn-stage Blessed may agree to give their daughters a different shape."

"So you've said. I can't imagine myself conversing with a pet." McCue covered his mouth daintily as he yawned, showing his yellow teeth. "Just what is it you want me to do?"

"Get me to the Harmony."

"No."

"The border's open now. McCue, you could do it. I know you've smuggled people across the line before."

"No."

"I'll pay."

McCue hesitated. "Have you tried Viho again?"

"Who?"

"The Bralava agent for B-I Transport. Now that the border's open, he may be more cooperative. There have been a larger than usual number of B-I ships passing through Bralava system. Your family has been making inquiries on your behalf, here and in the Harmony, although nothing is officially known of your whereabouts. They haven't been successful unofficially, either. No one has come to *me*."

Marcer's father and sister seemed as remote as his last lecture seemed facile. Lavi and Miriam Brice knew nothing about the things which had become so important to him. Life was different in the Harmony. The search for Order seemed easy from within the safe confines of the Academy. Outside the Harmony, life was messier and more perplexing. He didn't want to involve his family in it. "That's too slow," he said, only partly as an excuse. "I have to get away *now,* before Idryis Khan finds me."

"Yes, and thank you for leading him here." McCue seemed unconcerned, however.

Though he had come to Matthew McCue for help, Marcer also remembered that McCue had cooperated with the Khan before. It was possible that he would play both sides: the Khan and Marcer. "If you won't help me get out, then please, get my message out."

"What message, Dr. Brice? That the houris are dangerous, but that you'd like to talk to them? That the Khan plans a coup? Or the one that the Emirates will attack Neuland—but that's old news. They've been trying to take over Neuland for fifty years."

Marcer EL-ed, despite its discomforts in that room, and sensed McCue's duplicity. For once, it encouraged him. McCue would pass the information along, probably at a profit, but to interested parties who might then question the need to destroy Paradise. Marcer wanted to see home again, but he had no other contact who could get him off Bralava. He refused to entangle his family in his troubles or bring them to the Khan's attention. "Are you going to turn me over to the Khan?" Marcer asked.

"I considered it," McCue said disdainfully, "but I have a job I want you to do. I had hoped that *you* would beg *my* help in doing it, so I wouldn't have to pay you. In fact, I'm disappointed in you, Researcher. For all your blather about decency, apparently you find Linnet Wali easy to abandon; I thought you genuinely cared for her, too. I'm not often wrong about these things."

Marcer remembered the taste of the Khan's blood in his mouth. "Linnet? I loved her." He flushed. "But she's dead."

"Did the Khan tell you that?" McCue clucked like a fat chicken and shook his head. "You must learn to evaluate your sources better, Researcher. My last report said she was alive, isolated from other prisoners by special order of the Khan, but alive. In the Citadel. Since she is a colleague of sorts, I have a *duty* to rescue her, as well as a certain self-interest. She knows more about me than I'd like the Khan or the governor to learn. I'm still under suspicion because of that damned bride. So, will you rescue Linnet from the Woman Eater?"

Dumbfounded, Marcer stared, then quickly nodded. "Of course I will."

McCue grinned. "For what fee? My best offer is a trip to the Harmony. Then we're even."

"For two?"

"Two! You drive a hard bargain, Researcher; it's in the blood, I suppose. All Jews do." Marcer didn't correct him; he no longer felt particularly Jonist. Jonists scorned passion; Academics especially were supposed to feel only cool intellectual interest in the universe.

"Don't just stand there, Researcher. You need to leave soon. Dawn is only two hours away."

With an alacrity which made Marcer suspect McCue had a House Utility, or else that they had been observed, a man opened the door. Unlike alan servants, he entered the room like an equal. "Is everything all right?" he asked.

"Researcher Brice was never here, Velkic, but you'll remove his prisoner's cuff and help him steal a respectable boat that's seaworthy enough to make passage to the Citadel. Give him a painkiller, too. We can't have him wincing each time he takes a step; it calls his disguise into question. Oh, and also forge a wedding certificate for him—do it quickly, it just needs to pass one inspection—and name Idryis Khan a'Husain as one of the witnesses."

Velkic bowed in a manner which showed appreciation of the prank. There was something reminiscent of the Harmony about the way he moved, though he was a short, squat man, physically much like McCue. If McCue was a spy, was he a spymaster, too?

"Brice," McCue said sharply. "Be at the port two hours after the *Fajr* prayer, no later than nine o'clock, or you'll be too late. Velkic, give him passes to our dock. Brice, you're on your own."

Velkic put his hand on Marcer's back, urging him forward. Marcer pushed Velkic off but started out of the tight, little room on his own, then he remembered McCue. Marcer bowed awkwardly, uncertain what to say. "Thank

you," he said in lieu of anything better. Was McCue helping him or himself?

McCue's mouth was stuffed with a soggy cookie. He
waved at the open door.

Marcer was relieved to leave the confining room. Velkic
came behind him. "Go left. To the kitchen," Velkic said.
"Our surgery. I'll remove the cuff, but since you've worn
it so long, you'll be sore for several days. The painkiller
will help for a while."

"Who is he? Really?" Marcer knew he sounded ungrateful, but he didn't understand McCue.

"I couldn't say, sir." Velkic had a smooth, discreet manner, like a private secretary to an ambassador. He slipped
past Marcer and opened a door, turning on the electric
lights with a manual switch like those in Linnet's home.

Suddenly nostalgic for sun-stones, imagining himself back
in the Harmony, Marcer hung back, watching Velkic gather
medical instruments from kitchen cabinets.

Velkic turned to Marcer, waiting.

"Who does McCue work for?" Marcer asked.

Velkic shrugged. "Does it matter, sir?"

III. Your responsibility.

Only the youngest infants cried, the Citadel guard told
Marcer as they passed rows of cells containing silent, hopeless children, the unwanted daughters whose mothers had
died in the prison. Many lacked the strength to raise their
heads from their filthy cots. The possibility of adoption was
a cruel joke; boys, perhaps, but never girls. Horribly, the
prison smelled of warm, yeasty bread. The Citadel kitchen
was just above the children's level, according to the garru-
lous guard, and the cooks were baking bread for the garrison and the city beggars, who placed themselves under the
Bei's direct protection. The fragrance taunted the prisoners,
including the children, who received only gruel. The guard
thought it a joke and looked askance when Marcer failed
to smile.

"Clever of the Khan to send you instead of coming here
himself," the guard said.

Marcer grunted. His request for Linnet, his marriage certificate, and the other documents with which Velkic had

supplied him had first been met with bewilderment by prison officials. "I thought the Khan wanted his special prisoner kept here," the recently awakened warden had said. "Anonymous and secure until he came for her, he told me. Why this?" He held up the forged marriage certificate.

Marcer immediately understood. Idryis Khan had safeguarded Linnet in the Citadel, and probably bought off the warden, in case he needed to coerce or bribe Marcer. Events hadn't worked out that way. Marcer smiled at the warden and claimed he was Idryis Khan's messenger, sent to keep the matter private. After a half hour of questioning, during which Marcer hinted at a special relationship between the Khan and him, and after verifying the Khan's signature against a written record, the warden had finally instructed the guards to release Linnet to Marcer. It was already seven-thirty.

"Where are the women kept?" Marcer asked. The sight of dying children was oppressive. One could at least pretend that adults had done something to deserve their situation.

"I'll show you where most of them are." The man licked his lips and led Marcer to the end of the corridor. There, he opened a sealed, pressurized door and let the two of them into an enormous empty space, cool and damp as a cavern.

Back in Shores, Marcer had thought the Citadel was a fortress built on an island, but he'd discovered instead it was a hulk which floated in the bay. The prison levels formed its ballast, a deep stabilizer for the tower, administered separately from the garrison. They were on the lowest level, and there was a huge depression in the open space ahead. The guard grinned. "The Pit," he said. "Look down."

Marcer went a few careful steps forward and looked down into the darkness. He EL-ed and finally sensed the women. A roiling mass of female shapes were at the bottom of the stabilizer fin that kept the Citadel upright in storms: a straight-sided pit, entirely dark, which extended two hundred meters deep. The Woman Eater. "Holy God," he said.

"Me, I'd rather go to Paradise than the Pit for a wife," the guard said, "but there's some as come and claim a wife or a daughter out of there. They always come up filthy, and sometimes they come up crazy. Naked, of course." He shook his head as if this reflected on the women, instead of the men who put them there.

Marcer took a deep breath to collect himself, then got a whiff of the stench of blood and excrement mixed with female pheromones which rose up even from the deep cavity. He gasped.

"Yeah, wash-out day is tomorrow, so they're ripe."

"Is the Khan's prisoner down there?"

"Nah. She's a special. Has a room to herself." The guard led the way back through the pressurized door and into a corridor with closed doors rather than open cells. It was dim. A small amount of light came from underwater portholes at either end of the corridor, and from wave-generated electricity, but the walls seemed to absorb most of it. Marcer EL-ed and even the EL signal was unpleasant. The painted metal walls sent a harsh bounce-back that reverberated along the corridor. He wanted to get out. He wanted to get Linnet out.

The guard slapped a query tap-on against a function screen on the wall, then a Tell spoke aloud; it was the most advanced technology Marcer had seen on Bralava, reduced to prison record keeping. Oddly, the Tell used a female voice. "Room three," it said.

"Good. Let's go." The guard ushered Marcer to the proper door, then held his palm against a smudged reader. The lock mechanism made a loud, mechanical click. "Stay back," the guard warned. "Sometimes the bitches are vicious; I don't know about this one." He put his hand on his weapon, an entirely modern stick gun.

"I do." Marcer shouldered the guard aside and pushed through the door.

There was no light at all in the cell. Marcer EL-ed but almost missed her. Linnet was huddled on the floor, pressed against the bed which, with a metal basin and a drain, were the sole other features of the room. "Linnet?" Marcer said.

"Come on, bitch," the guard called with benign crudeness. "You're free."

He backed out and slapped the door panel again. A bluish white light flickered, then stayed on inside the room. Her facial scars cast strange shadows that made Linnet seem alien. Not human.

Linnet's eyes darted wildly from the guard to Marcer. She didn't move.

"Your *wife* is very ugly." The guard winked. "Wonder why the Khan wants such a nasty thing."

Marcer extended his hand to Linnet who, though skeletally thin, was no more blemished than she had been. Her belly was a bit distended, however, like those of starving children. "It's all right," he said. "I'm your husband, come to take you home."

The guard chuckled. "If she don't get up pretty quick, we can flush her out."

"No!"

Linnet merely watched as Marcer squatted in front of her. "It's all right," he whispered. "I've come to free you, but we do need to hurry." They would have to clear the Citadel, take the boat to Shores, and then find a way to reach the inland hoist station to the interstellar port in an hour and a half.

She started to reach out to him, then seemed to think better of it and jerked her hand back.

"Please. Linnet, we have to leave." He touched the hand with which she had almost touched him. He EL-ed and felt her misery wash through his mind.

She turned her hand so that she could grip him, and grip him she did, hard as a drowning woman clinging to her rescuer. "Marcer?"

He helped her up, trying to shield her naked body from the curious guard. She had no bruises; her body was probably incapable of them. There were no open wounds or sores. She wouldn't have felt physical pain, but she had known terror.

"So, this is the one?" the guard asked.

"Yes. My wife. Get something to cover her." Marcer remembered the alan horror of uncovered women and understood the prurient interest of the guard. They needed to hurry. Besides McCue's deadline, there was no telling when the Khan would be found.

"Wife." Linnet trembled as she said the word.

Marcer put his arms around her and was drawing her out of the cell as the guard unfolded a huge black cloth. Marcer grabbed it from him. "Here. Hurry."

"There's a full outfit for her at the depot," the guard said.

Marcer nodded and draped the cloth over Linnet. She relaxed a bit.

"She needs a medical exam before she goes," the guard added. "Else we're not responsible for any complications."

"I'll waive it. I just want to leave." Marcer started back the way they'd come and kept his arm around Linnet.

"If that's the Khan's choice," the guard called dubiously after them. "Then the baby is your responsibility. We thought it was the baby that he cared about."

Marcer hesitated, but kept going. He EL-ed as he walked alongside Linnet, examining her swollen belly with new attention. The guard was telling the truth. Linnet was pregnant.

Chapter 14

"Peace be upon you." Elector Jeroen Lee made a trifling bow in the direction of the Supplicant.

Startled, she drew back. She hadn't noticed him in the crush of people in the Great Hall's lobby. He wasn't wearing his red Elector's gown, though he should have been. In only a few minutes the Electors were scheduled to read the final, official version of their Joint Ruling to the Grand Assembly of the Polite Harmony of Worlds. Then the Grand Assembly would begin its debate on the destruction of Paradise.

"Isn't that the proper greeting in the Emirates?" Lee asked.

Flustered, she blushed and bowed to him. "It's not used much anymore. I've never heard it spoken in your language."

"It does have an ironic sound, in light of our reason for addressing this meeting of the Grand Assembly." He seemed grave, not smiling. "To incite genocide."

That was what Marcer Brice had called it. "Unfortunately, it's necessary. The houris and their mothers threaten all of humanity."

"'Humanity,'" he said thoughtfully. "An interesting word. A species *and* a virtue. Both are often too narrowly defined." He looked around the lobby of the Great Hall. The Supplicant followed his gaze, her aesthetic sense unimpressed by what she saw. The lobby was dim and poorly designed; it made everyone appear insignificant. The artwork was tediously grandiose.

Lee sighed. "Well," he said, watching her as if he wanted to say more, "I need to change." With that, he walked away.

Sanda Brauna immediately came to the Supplicant. "What did Jeroen want?" she asked.

The Supplicant shook her head. "I have no idea."

The carillon rang to announce the start of the Assembly session. At Sanda's suggestion, the Supplicant attached herself to a group of Ahmen; she filed into the Great Hall among them and was ushered to an aisle seat at the front of the Near Gallery. In short order, Sanda came onto the dais with the other Electors, the Grand Marshal and the Speaker of the Assembly. Jeroen Lee, properly gowned, entered with the Electors, but stayed separate from them. The Supplicant fidgeted in her seat and kept her attention on him. She told herself that the destruction of the houris was inevitable, even if the wait was nerve-wracking. She had learned patience.

The session began. The world delegates and guests sat, stood, then sat again in an unpatterned paean to their god Order and its messenger, Jon Hsu. The Supplicant smiled; it seemed to be a rudimentary *rak'ah* prayer. She supposed every culture needed rituals, no matter how they rationalized them.

The Speaker read a carefully crafted Fact Statement about Paradise, the houris and their mothers. It acknowledged the Supplicant as the messenger sent by Researcher Marcer Brice, who was described as a deceased junior staff member of the Academy of Darien. His deportation from the Harmony went unmentioned, though the statement did assert that he had been murdered by a houri's son.

Next, Elector Kurioso asked permission to use the Great Hall to read a new and pertinent Joint Unanimous Electors' Ruling. Just as the Grand Marshal began to answer that formality, Elector Lee walked to Kurioso at the speaker's center of the dais. The Supplicant held her breath. With everyone's focus on him, Jeroen Lee said, "I withdraw my imprimatur from this Ruling." Lee looked out at the world delegates, then his eyes seemed to meet those of the Supplicant. "Here is my reason," he said, and pointed at the rear doors.

I. To free the pigeon.

Nisa watched from the laboratory window as armed men dashed around the garden inspecting bushes and flowers for clues. First they had searched the laboratory; their hunt continued to widen as they found nothing. It now encompassed the seashore and the scrub forest inland. Nisa smiled. Marcer Brice had escaped the Khan.

"Where is he?" Idryis Khan himself strode into the laboratory and glanced about as though his men might have missed seeing Brice. "Why did you help him?"

"I didn't." She spoke softly, to placate him, and kept her eyes modestly downcast. "I haven't seen him since he left the lab last night."

The Khan raised his arm. She was sure he was going to hit her. Maybe he intended to, then changed his mind. Instead he smashed his arm across a nearby counter, scattering a case of slides and a specimen jar onto the floor. "Then how do you explain the fact that the scanners in the house were sabotaged last night?"

His spy-eyes had been turned off. Nisa wished she had known; she might have run away, too, if she had found a way to prevent that dratted unman from locking her in. "He must have done it himself," she said in a near whisper. She had seen the Khan enraged before. She did not want to be nearby when it happened again.

"How?" He kicked a cabinet. Its locked door popped open and the lamp on the counter toppled over. "He was with me."

She wet her lips. "He must have learned how in the Harmony."

The Khan snorted. "You warned him I would kill him. Why?"

She wished the sabotage had happened earlier in the evening. "He's a good person; he was kind to me." She shrugged. "I thought maybe he could persuade you to let him live."

" *'He was kind to me,' "* the Khan mocked. "Kindness is a lie; everyone acts from convenience or self-interest. Haven't you learned that yet? Wife?" He grabbed her shoulders and shook her. Her head flapped; her neck hurt. So close, she felt actual physical heat emanate from him, as though his body was a fire that had just been stoked. His arms trembled when he stopped. His face was calm. He looked into her eyes. "My men were here and your face is bare!" He slapped her. She fell back across a cabinet, tumbling her tray of prepared tissue samples onto the floor.

The Khan was an animal, a creature born of the houris, an

alien without empathy. That was the difference between him
and Marcer Brice—between him and any human. Human
men were *capable* of understanding others, although they
rarely had much sympathy; the Khan's understanding was
distorted. She had listened to Marcer Brice speak his notes
into his records. She had absorbed more information than
she had let him realize, and had reasoned out the rest.
Idryis Khan looked like a man in the same way that Qadira
looked like a woman. He was as much an impostor as a
houri. His mind had a deviant logic. Those around him
must submit or fight. Or escape.

She watched. He moved methodically around the laboratory smashing equipment, mangling it not like a child in a
tantrum, but with the self-control to avoid the two data
screens and equipment not easily replaced. Uncertain
whether she fell into that category, Nisa stood stock-still,
expressionless except for uncontrollable wincing at each
sudden explosion of glass. She wished she was invisible. A
holy rage. If there was one thing she'd learned from Marcer
Brice, it was that there was nothing holy about Idryis
Khan a'Husain.

His destructive frenzy apparently satisfied, the Khan
stared at Nisa across the length of the room, then through
the window at the search going on outside. A slight but
telltale skin color variation showed that a skinsack dressing
covered part of the Khan's forehead. Marcer Brice hadn't
just escaped; he'd hurt Idryis Khan.

"Why are you smiling?" The Khan stalked toward Nisa.
Just then an older man, a uniformed officer, ran through
the lab door, saw the Khan, nodded, and backed out.

"Yusef!" The Khan stopped as he shouted, and slammed
his fist down on an empty table.

Yusef returned but stayed a respectable distance from
the Khan. "Control yourself," Yusef said. He waited. The
Khan nodded. "He's got her," Yusef said.

The Khan's face reddened, but that was his only
reaction.

"An hour after dawn. A forged marriage certificate. I
have a copy." Yusef extended a paper toward the Khan
though he was too far away to take or read it. "You wit-
nessed their marriage."

"McCue!"

Yusef nodded. "We've been there. No trace of him anywhere. No tracking signal. McCue is gone, too. An unexpected business opportunity, his man says. He left surface a few minutes ago. Brice wasn't with him. Neither was the whore. We're sure."

"Good work." The Khan's voice was shaky.

"Intercept McCue? Any of our ships are faster than a private carrier."

The Khan stared at his subordinate for a long time. Yusef didn't seem uncomfortable. He looked back with just as little expression as the Khan. As she studied their tableau Nisa realized that Yusef was a Son of the Prophet, too. "No," the Khan said finally. "Not worthwhile, since he left without Brice or the bitch. And McCue may have uses, later."

Without warning, first the Khan, then Yusef, turned to Nisa.

"Time to free the pigeon," Yusef said.

"Yes." The Khan went to Nisa. She bit her lip but didn't flinch. He grabbed her hand, holding it in an uncomfortably tight grip that seemed unconscious. Yusef had meanwhile moved away from the Khan and now stood in the doorframe. "They're somewhere in the city," the Khan told Yusef. "You and Demet find them. Don't let them get to Gordan. I'll kill you if you let them get offworld." He made the threat matter-of-factly.

Yusef nodded without a show of surprise or concern. "Kill them both?"

The Khan hesitated, then said, "Not the whore, if you can avoid it. Not yet."

Yusef saluted and backed out of the room. Nisa had felt safer with him present. Unreasonably so, since he was a Son. The Khan's pressure on her hand increased. She imagined her bones breaking. She shivered.

"You'll go to the Harmony," the Khan said.

"As you wish." She bowed to a servant's depth, anxious to leave.

"No insolence."

Nisa hadn't intended any. "I apologize. I'm eager to go to the Harmony, for myself and because I understand the houris' threat. I've watched Brice; I've listened. I can present his material and add to it. I hate the houris and their mother-pets. A houri killed my mother and ruined my life. Bad as they are for everyone, they are a disaster for women. I'll tell the Jonists. I'll do everything I can to see the houris annihilated, every one of them."

He dropped her hand. "You're telling the truth."

"Of course." Nisa wondered if he had a truth-sense, like Marcer Brice, then decided that he lacked the insight. He was simply a good observer. Let Idryis Khan rule the Emirates. It wouldn't be for long. With no more houris, there would also be no more Sons. She wanted an end to both. She meant to get it.

"A tech has been regularly copying Brice's data and adding a bit of fire to it, on my instructions. The information will be brought to you. There's a Harmony mixed transport leaving for Darien at local noon. You'll be on it. Remember, you are a refugee running away from your husband. You carry a message from Marcer Brice to his Academy, a matter of life and death. The future of humanity is at stake."

Nisa took a breath. "I want one thing in return," she said and quickly added, "Divorce me. Now. I'll be a cast-off wife whose family wouldn't take her back. I'm doing what you want; I want a new life."

He stared. She had no idea what thoughts were behind his dark eyes. "I divorce you," he said. "I divorce you. I divorce you." His face showed no anger, no satisfaction, nothing. He grabbed her shoulders. "If you don't succeed, if the Harmony doesn't destroy Paradise, then remember: the border to the Harmony is open. I'll find you, and I'll kill you." He shoved her away and walked out of the lab.

II. I do.

It wasn't his. It couldn't be. Despite her occupation, when they were far from the Citadel, Marcer had to ask.

Linnet shivered beneath her coarse, black, prison chador. "I didn't bother taking a pill after visits to Government House," she said, extending her hand to him like a Supplicant. "Everyone knows the Sons are sterile."

The stolen boat rocked in the water. "I thought your customer was Governor Gordan." Marcer didn't take her hand.

Linnet hunched forward as though hiding her stomach, which was inconspicuous anyway because of its still modest

size and her voluminous chador. "I know you did. It was
easier not to tell you. It seemed to me that if I did what
you had refused . . ." She held up her empty hands, then
brought them to her covered face as if trying to hide it
even more. "I was ashamed, but too afraid of him to stop.
He said, the very first time, that he'd kill me if I did."

Only Linnet's eyes were visible. Trapped in the Khan's
mansion, Marcer had yearned for her. The fabric of her
flesh—not silky smooth, that trite cliché, but rather the ex-
traordinarily elaborate cicatrix, her sweet striations—had
been among what he had missed. Scars could be erased
with a healing skinsack, but that had nothing to do with
her true beauty, which went deep. It was in her halo, in
her heart, not in something evil done to her which, unac-
countably, he found fascinating. "You don't have to explain," he said. "And you shouldn't be ashamed. Idryis
Khan was your customer at Government House. It makes
no difference." That Idryis Khan had hurt her only made
Marcer more protective. He gently tugged her hands away
from her face.

She looked up at him. Tears glistened on her eyelashes.

"You're my wife," he said.

"I'm not." She turned away.

"A marriage is when two people believe it," Marcer said
firmly. "I do. I've told everyone, even Idryis Khan. Linnet,
will you let me be your husband?"

She stared with the intensity of a houri's Son. "Forever,"
she said, then, as if correcting herself, she added, "For as
long as you want me. Husband."

Marcer had a sudden, terrible thought. "Did *he* send you
to find me—that first night? Is that why you took me to
your home? To keep an eye on me for him?" Marcer EL-ed.
It showed him everything he needed to know, and left him
contrite for having asked.

"Of course not," Linnet said. "I told you, we don't talk,
and anyway, he was having one of his fits. The old man,
the governor, was generous; he told a servant to send me
away. He said the Khan was too dangerous that night."

"And every night," Marcer said under his breath. He
glanced at the sky. Bralava's sun was higher. The canal
stink was worsening as passing boats stirred up garbage and
dead fish. "We have to hurry. We need to meet McCue.
He's taking us to the Harmony!" Marcer started the engine

and moved the boat away from the canal edge, where it had drifted, and out among the traffic. He dodged a barge loaded with fish and trailed by flies. "No more wema!" Marcer shouted, and revved the engine. The prow lifted into the air, and the boat surged forward.

Linnet grabbed the edge of her seat; her face was covered, but she suddenly ripped the veil off and bent over the side of the open boat, vomiting. Marcer immediately pulled back on the power. That was why she was so thin. Of course. They'd fed her, but she was pregnant. As he waited, he EL-ed for the simple pleasure of feeling her shape inside his mind. She turned, probably to tell him to continue on. He saw her face and seemed able to read her thoughts. After the Khan's impassivity, after Nisa's mannered defenses, to see and feel Linnet's honesty was breathtaking. He stared. He turned off the engine. "Holy God," he said.

"Marcer? What is it?"

"You're carrying the Khan's child!"

It was her turn to stare. "I . . . uh . . . thought you understood . . ." Her words trailed off without conclusion.

"This changes everything," Marcer said. There was a barely perceptible vibration, not enough to ripple the water. Marcer looked up. White, fluffy clouds—a kind never seen on New Dawn—dotted the pastel blue sky. A hoist ship had taken a curving path to the port, lifting people and cargo to an interstellar ship, perhaps even one from the Brice-Isaacs line. There was still time to reach McCue. He looked back at Linnet. "*That's* why he wants Neuland! The Sons are fertile with Neulander Altered women! And the houris must know it. That's why *they* want Neuland destroyed." Marcer wished he had access to a proper utility, or at least a field recorder. His thoughts were coming so quickly he was afraid he wouldn't remember them all. He had to work out exactly what was going on. Hummers.

"Marcer? What's the matter?"

He ignored Linnet, too rapt in his thoughts to answer.

The hummers on Neuland were the hybrid descendants of the alien Blessed species and a native species. They had been so successful that their ancestral native species had become extinct. If, as the hummers had done, the Sons of houris could reproduce themselves, then they had the capability of competing, perhaps successfully, against their ancestral species, mankind. The real threat would come not from the jinn-stage or the houri-stage Blessed, but from their spoil, their waste: their Sons.

It all involved Neuland. Of course. Its people had most of their genome in common with the Sons: the human portions and some of the same alien ones. The Sons needed Neulanders—Neulander women, anyway—to bear their children. The Khan's plan wasn't just to replace Aleko Bei, it was to create an alien dynasty to rule the Emirates.

If the Harmony destroyed Paradise and the Emirates took Neuland, the Sons would have won a foothold on the future; mankind would have a dangerous adversary of its own making.

Linnet touched Marcer's arm. She had scrambled close. "What is it?" she asked again.

Marcer stared at her. Many in the Harmony claimed Neulanders were beyond the pale of humanity, despite their fulfillment of the biologic demarcation, the capacity to have children with other humans. It was said that their inability to feel pain gave them a different psyche from the rest of mankind, that it made them cold, heartless killers. It wasn't true. His own Altered senses could distinguish the enormous difference, the chasm, between Linnet and Idryis Khan. The Khan lacked the healing factor; he felt pain; but unlike Linnet, the Khan had the strong desire to inflict pain, an aggression so deep it had to be innate. "I love you," Marcer said.

Linnet smiled, looked down, then up and back at him. She whispered, "I love you."

Embarrassed, Marcer looked around. The sun had just cleared the horizon; the light had a gossamer quality, as though the view was through a fine film of sheer, delicate cloth. The towers and palaces of Shores looked like a fairy-tale land. Bralava was a magnificent world, but it was real. There was also poverty and abused women. It was Linnet's home.

"Hey!" a man shouted across the water from a freight-laden barge bearing down on them. "Out of the way!"

Marcer restarted the engine and moved them out of the canal entrance into which they'd drifted. He headed for the central district rather than inland toward the port. Alans, men and women, were human; he had a duty to them. Neulanders didn't deserve the fate in store for them if Sons ruled that world. Kolet had offered him a place; besides, Linnet was one of them. Marcer had a duty to warn Neuland. There was the Harmony, too, which had expelled and abandoned him, but it was his home anyway, the place he most wanted to defend. He had a duty there as well. Marcer smiled ruefully, reminded of McCue.

And what about the Blessed? Did his duty extend to them? Aliens, who clearly wanted to destroy Neuland, a human world—but to protect themselves, and humanity, from their own Sons. That was the explanation for the conflict between the houris and the Sons. Whether from distaste, unwillingness to be discovered themselves, or fear of vying with the Sons for a niche within the human race, the houris did not want the Sons creating a hybrid species. They had even stopped bearing Sons. Yes. He had a duty to them.

Hummers. Marcer's thoughts returned to where they had begun. *I am not a hummer,* the Khan had said. Hummers were a hybrid between the Blessed and a native animal. *Animal.* Hummers were quadruped vertebrates with minds not much more complex than those of dogs. What if the Blessed had never impersonated an intelligent creature before? If prior to the discovery of Paradise, the houri-stage were unable to think or plan, and their offspring, the spoil, were no more than dogs—then the current situation would be a unique conflict within the Blessed species.

"We can't leave Bralava yet," Marcer told Linnet. "We have to warn and defend our . . . people." Marcer looked and EL-ed in all directions, using his Altered ability to its fullest, trying to locate the place from which McCue had driven, with Marcer half-conscious in the boat. Nisa had been there, too. Nisa. She would be sent to the Harmony by the Khan. How would she do? Spunky. Quite well, he guessed. She had to be stopped. She didn't know the truth.

"Why can't we leave? Marcer, talk to me. Please! You're frightening me."

He explained, as briefly and persuasively as he could. He told her about the Blessed—the houris and their pets, the jinn—and about the Sons and Idryis Khan's plans to rule the Emirates and to have many, many children. As he spoke, he drove.

It seemed a long time before he located Sheik Radi's mansion. Once he found it, it was obvious. Built of a very white stone, it shone under Bralava's rising sun like a beacon. He pointed. "There, up ahead. That's where I was beaten and dumped in the canal."

"How auspicious."

Marcer grinned. The Linnet he knew was being reborn from the Khan's special prisoner. "Ready for an interview with an alien?"

She had replaced her veil, but Marcer heard uncertainty in her voice. "Are you sure they're really aliens? If houris *look* human, if they *feel* human, if they *live* as humans do, then maybe they are human."

"Functional humanity. I've wondered about that myself. But I am certain that yes, biologically, they are nonterrestrial. Alien. Their appearance means next to nothing. It isn't convergent evolution, it's imitation that creates the houris. Camouflage, just like the jinn change the color of their skin." He slowed the boat and glanced at Linnet. She was a Neulander. All this talk of their alien inheritance must have made her insecure. "Neulanders are different," he said. "They are human, with only a very few specifically introduced modifications. They can have children with standard humans." He wished he could explain the halo effect, and that Neulanders had auras, but there wasn't time; she didn't even know he was also Altered. Would she mind when she found out? He stopped the boat, having suddenly realized his greatest duty was to her. They were at a busy cross-canal. "I'll let you off," he said. "There's no reason for us both to be in danger; he'll search Nisa's home eventually."

"Wherever you go, I go," she said. She patted her belly. "And I can help convince them."

Marcer didn't insist. They were both silent as he docked on Sheik Radi's wharf. He helped her off the boat in a dignified, deferential fashion for the benefit of watchers.

The enemy of my enemy is my friend. It was an alan saying. Marcer hoped Idryis Khan would not expect him to seek help from a woman.

III. Sanitized.

One of the Khan's officers, Demet Quadar, escorted Nisa to the hoist ship, then rode it with her to the quickship, a

Harmony-registered vessel named the *Miriam* which smelled of disinfectant. Quadar wouldn't let her board. They stood on the ship's transient skirt as a dozen traders and several students bade farewell to the most tenacious of their friends and family, those few who had paid to accompany them off-surface. Finally, a tech arrived. He delivered a black case to Quadar, who handed it to her.

She wasn't wearing a veil, though her hair was properly covered. Quadar gazed stonily into her face. "Remember," he said, "if they don't kill the houris, then you die." He turned his back on Nisa and went to the down-run waiting area. She sent her ticket and other papers through a reader, which quickly produced her permission to board. Nisa crossed the threshold and entered the sovereign space of the Polite Harmony of Worlds.

She opened the case as she waited to be sanitized to Harmony specifications. Inside was the material taken from Marcer Brice's screen, part journal, part draft scientific report and part hard data. There was a bit of alien tissue in a miniature refrigeration unit. Atop it all was a note written in Ufazi using Arabic script. The calligraphy was elementary and obvious, an attempt to show off a skill the writer actually lacked.

"Nisa," it read, "It is up to you. Tell them I will ensure that there is no war against the Harmony. If they act against Paradise, I will be indebted to them." The note was unsigned, but she had no doubt from whom it came.

She destroyed the note before she stowed the case. She tossed aside her chador, vowing never to wear one again. The Khan had provided the cheapest possible passage to Darien. Two women tucked Nisa into the semiadhesive webbing and explained shipboard routine. She cursed the Khan as she watched the better class of passengers led away to cabins. She would arrive in the Harmony as an impoverished refugee, for the Khan had not provided any money.

Marcer Brice had been a good man. Idryis Khan was not, but Idryis Khan was right about the houris.

IV. Maybe baby.

"What are you doing here? Do I need to throw you out again?" Sheik Raul advanced on Marcer through the grand

entrance room of his mansion. He ignored Linnet. When
covered properly by alan standards, a woman was only eyes
and a vaguely human shape, socially invisible. Marcer
hoped it would be enough to keep her safe.

"Sister visit," Linnet said. It had been her idea to pretend to be a houri.

Sheik Radi hesitated. He turned to the unman who had
allowed Marcer and Linnet into the house, despite his obvious recognition of Marcer. From Nisa's description, Marcer
guessed this was Gidie, the head housekeeper. Gidie had
been overawed by Linnet; he feared houris. "You shouldn't
have let *him* in!" Sheik Radi exclaimed. "He's the Khan's
prisoner!"

Linnet stepped forward. "Get she. Your wife." She was
haughty as a princess.

"My wife is a houri," Marcer said with dignity. "She
insists that we meet with your wife. You can stay, if you
like, but this is urgent."

"Wife!" Sheik Radi snorted. "Don't be ridiculous. You
haven't been to Paradise; you're an infidel. Either this
woman isn't houri, or she isn't your wife. Lady," he said
to Linnet in a more restrained tone, "who are you?"

Linnet made a huffing sound and went close to the Sheik,
causing him to retreat a step. "Wife to him," Linnet said,
without indicating Marcer. "Sister to wife to you. Get she."

Sheik Radi stroked his beard while looking searchingly
into Linnet's eyes, all that he could see of her. He glanced
indecisively at Gidie.

Sadness echoed inside the walls of Sheik Radi's house,
relayed to Marcer in the tones in which the Sheik and his
unman servant spoke, and by diffuse, mournful music, perhaps imaginary, the aural equivalent of a dark cloud ob-
scuring the sun. Marcer EL-ed. He hoped the houri,
Qadira, would hear and investigate.

"Get she," Linnet repeated.

The Sheik looked at Linnet, stroked his beard, then
looked resentfully at Marcer. "Bring them to the south sitting room. Get refreshments," he ordered Gidie. "I'll ask
my wife if she'll see you," the Sheik told Linnet. He
walked away.

Gidie bowed to the Sheik's back, then curtly to Marcer,
and led them past the large social rooms in which the wedding party had been held, along a corridor and to a more

standard-size room. It was furnished with built-in benches along two walls, an oversize lounger, and several chairs around a low table. There were pillows, of course, on the benches and a long, narrow window at ceiling height, too high even for Marcer to see out. The room was large enough that Marcer wasn't disturbed at being enclosed, but it was oppressive simply to be in this house again. The knowledge that it was past the time for them to have met McCue weighed on him, too.

"You convinced him," Marcer said quietly after Gidie closed the door and left. Even if this wasn't the Harmony, with its ever-present monitors and sensors, someone could be listening.

Linnet was trembling. He brought a chair to her and helped her sit. He stood behind her, like an accompanying servant, pressed her shoulder comfortingly, and whispered in her ear, "When have you met houris?"

Nisa had described Qadira's speech as that of a foreigner who, though she knew words, didn't know the language. Her comments and the Khan's data pointed to a grammar deficiency in houris, something reminiscent of the ungrammatical speech of patients with untreated Broca's aphasia. A defect in the alien impostors was reasonable. Human grammar was a particularly species-specific ability. Marcer had forgotten to mention it to Linnet.

"Other women told me," Linnet whispered.

A servant arrived with tea and sweet cakes. He looked curiously at Marcer while setting them on the table, but avoided glancing at Linnet's shrouded form. Almost as he left, a covered woman arrived with Sheik Radi. Her chador was silkik. A hint of green sleeves showed. However fine the fabric, a chador remained a cloak of invisibility.

"My wife." Sheik Radi's introduction sounded as if it had been cut from his flesh. The alans had encountered a nonhuman intelligence and hadn't recognized it. They'd brought aliens home and made the imposters their wives.

Marcer bowed to Qadira, an unheard-of courtesy—or perhaps discourtesy—in the Emirates, where politeness meant a man should ignore any females present. Qadira's face was veiled, and there was a gauzy black material over the slit for her eyes, but Marcer saw them: dark, lovely and hard. Her hands were bare, not gloved, like someone in an imperfect quarantine. She had long, narrow fingers; her nails were painted a pale yellow-green. Green was the color of the alan Paradise. He EL-ed, to know her better.

"Beautiful man," Qadira said warmly, in a voice as individual and as mellifluous as the strings of a harp being played.

The question of whether houris were susceptible to his Altered ability to EL was answered. Like the Khan and like the jinn, she was a blank to his empathic perceptions, but he scarcely noticed. She radiated an uncomfortably intense sensuality, enhanced by the mystery of a chador. There were probably pheromones at work, too.

She was near the door, though she had come farther into the room than Sheik Radi. Her movements were a delight to the eye. Marcer thought he recognized something familiar about her, too, and remembered the woman who had waited in the courtyard garden to speak with Idryis Khan at Nisa's wedding. "Talks, you," Qadira commanded Marcer.

Simple sentences, he reminded himself. Houris probably had difficulty understanding grammatically complex speech. "Lady," he said, glancing behind her momentarily to where Sheik Radi glowered, "my deepest sympathy for the recent death of your mother." The pet Nisa had killed.

"Her mother!" Sheik Radi exclaimed as if the concept had not occurred to him. Did angels have mothers? Qadira said nothing.

"I came to warn you that Nisa is probably on her way to the Harmony," Marcer continued. "Sent there by Idryis Khan."

"Nisa," the houri hissed. She had been gazing steadily at Marcer, but she glanced at Linnet, perhaps suspecting Nisa was behind the veil. Her attention lingered on Linnet's hands. Linnet had tried to hide them in the cloth of her coarse chador, but where they showed, so did scars.

"What? Where is my daughter?" Sheik Radi advanced on Marcer until Qadira stopped him by placing her hand on the Sheik's arm. "Husband," she said, making the word music. Nisa and the Khan had never mentioned the siren song of a houri's voice. With her hand on Sheik Radi, ostensibly for support, she used it like a rein to guide him toward the door. He must have supposed she meant to leave with him, because he didn't object until she spoke.

"Go." Qadira's single syllable felt like a sentence. It was both a command and reassurance to the Sheik.

"I can't leave you alone with *him*. And I want to hear what he has to say." He glared at Marcer.

Marcer had no objection to Sheik Radi's presence. Qadira clearly did. "Go," she told her husband.

Marcer EL-ed again, seeking contact. Qadira turned to him, then back to Sheik Radi. "Good man he," she said.

Linnet got up from her chair. "Sister talk," she added to the argument.

Qadira froze. An instant later, using the same lightning speed as Marcer had seen from the Khan, she pushed Sheik Radi back, slammed the door on him, and turned the knob to lock him out. The three of them were alone. "You!" Qadira screeched at Linnet. "Spoil?"

Spoil was what Qadira had called the talish Nisa had cut from the mother/jinn's body. Spoil was trash of the Blessed. Linnet was spoil? Was that how the Blessed saw Neulanders? Not as humans?

Linnet stood motionless. Qadira stalked toward her. Marcer came around from behind Linnet and stood protectively at her side.

Sheik Radi banged on the door, shouting for Marcer to open it, though his wife had been the one to push him outside. The sound was muffled. That door was solid.

Qadira reached out and yanked off Linnet's veil. She stared into Linnet's scarred face. "Spoil," she said definitively.

Linnet looked at Marcer.

"Do you know my wife?" It didn't seem possible.

"Spoil, she. Of us. Stupids bited us Son." Had her voice been less beautiful or her tone less expressive, the houri's garbled grammar would have rendered her speech into nonsense. As it was, Marcer was uncertain he grasped its gist. He pulled the chair around and sat down. "Linnet," he asked, "are you a houri?"

"No!" Linnet grabbed the houri's veil and pulled it off, then did the same to Qadira's chador. "Do we look at all alike?"

Nisa had drawn a portrait of her stepmother; it hadn't done justice to the . . . woman. By any standards, Qadira was beautiful, the very essence of womanhood as judged by an alien race. And how right they had gotten it!

"Do we?"

Marcer had nearly forgotten Linnet. The houri's beauty

and sensuality had momentarily driven all other thoughts
from his mind. Of course alans called them angels. Of
course men wanted them.

Marcer forced himself to turn away from Qadira. Linnet's face had never seemed more ghastly than it did in
close comparison with the houri's. It was Linnet he loved.
Marcer EL-ed and felt viscerally Linnet's pain and her
unique beauty. Qadira was a vacancy, a siren waiting to
ensnare men with her false song and impostor beauty, able
to lead men to their deaths. "No. You don't look alike,"
he said. "You look much better to me."

"Liar," Linnet said, but he felt her flash of joy.

"Difference man." Qadira's tone was that of a compliment spoken in the midst of a seduction, but it ended on
a questioning note. She knew he was Altered; she'd heard
his EL. She walked closer to Marcer.

"None of that." Linnet sounded truculent.

Qadira stopped.

There was so much to say and too little time for questions. The pounding on the door had stopped. A bad sign.
Sheik Radi had gone for a key or a means to force it open.

"We came to warn you about your Sons," Marcer said.
"Idryis Khan is sending Nisa to the Harmony to tell them
that you are alien, not holy. She will claim that you're dangerous to humanity. She'll ask them to destroy Paradise, to
sweep it with weapons that will leave no life and nowhere
to go to make your change."

Qadira watched. In that she was like a Son, but where
the Khan's expression seemed permanently callous, Qadira
smiled. She even smiled as he told her more.

"I think the Harmony will do it. Genocide. They have
before. The Bril." Marcer stopped. He was concerned that
she understand him. He could determine nothing from her
face, so he went on. "The Sons want all of you dead. Without Paradise—no more houris. Without houris—no more
mothers."

"Harmony man." Qadira stamped her foot. "Nisa must
is stop. You go at Harmony, Harmony man. Tells them
Nisa lies."

McCue was gone. Marcer couldn't get home to the Harmony without her help, but he didn't tell her that. "The
Khan will blame Neuland."

"Spoil there." Qadira still smiled.

"The Sons won't *destroy* Neuland," he said, speaking slowly. "The Sons will *conquer* it. They will take Neuland's women." He held out his arm to Linnet and she came to him. "Now I know why. My wife is a Neulander. She is pregnant with the Khan's child. The Sons are fertile with Neulander women. They will start a new race--not houris, not human. Because you want Neuland destroyed, I believe you understand and don't want that to happen. It did happen once already on Neuland. The hummers. But Sons are smart; Sons could kill everyone: houris, mothers, humans. We can work together to stop the Sons."

Qadira had stopped smiling. She had stared at Linnet throughout the latter part of Marcer's explanation. She turned back to him, and enunciated with care, speaking slowly. "Her is spoil. Neuland is other. Not safe other. Not safe spoil. Neuland is babies of Sons. Harmony man and me, you stop Nisa, stop Sons."

There was nothing wrong with houri intelligence, but without clear speech, communication was frustrating. Marcer gave up on the issue of "spoil" for the moment. The banging had resumed, and someone other than Sheik Radi had shouted at them to open the door, but there was also a scratching sound. Something was being done. Time was running out.

"You *are* infiltrating human worlds," he said. "You *are* a danger to humanity. I'm not a traitor. You must stop this imposture and leave human worlds."

It was difficult to resist seeing Qadira as a woman. She swayed with what seemed to be indecision though Marcer felt nothing as he EL-ed. "We tell," she said. "We go."

She'd agreed to everything.

"Don't trust her," Linnet said, moving threateningly closer.

Qadira sniffed at Linnet. "Smells baby of her," Qadira said. Linnet grimaced. Qadira touched her own belly, displaying through the heavy cloth that her waist was flat. "Not baby of my. No plus baby. Too much spoil is, we decides. Neuland must is dead. Maybe baby then. Harmony man says not."

"Neuland must not die," Marcer said earnestly. "Neuland is human. To kill Neuland is wrong. No more Sons." Unintentionally, he had raised his voice.

The door burst open. In walked Idryis Khan.

V. What he had to do.

"Cover yourself," the Khan snapped at the houri. "You, too, whore."

Neither woman moved. Linnet was defiant; Qadira looked to Marcer to defend her.

The room quickly filled with local police. Demet Quadar stood out among them because of his maroon soldier's uniform. Instead of a police handgun, he carried a soldier's deadly stick gun, which could melt a hole through a body instantly.

Sheik Radi pushed through to the front of the men. He gasped, either because his wife's face was uncovered, or else at Linnet's disfigurement.

"We are guests in your house," Marcer told Sheik Radi. "What is this about?" He motioned at the police.

The Sheik seemed not to hear him. "Cover your face!" he shouted at Qadira. He passed the Khan, stooped to grab his wife's veil and chador from the floor, then draped them loosely over Qadira's head, blinding her.

She tossed the fabric off. "You!" Qadira pointed at Idryis Khan. "Disgrateful Son!"

Marcer's warning had been understood, but now he doubted that, among alans, a woman could help him, even a holy houri—especially a houri, with their difficulty using human speech. Qadira was trapped in a dependent female role by her impersonation. Marcer felt surreptitiously for the gun he'd taken from the Khan. Badly outnumbered, he didn't bring it out. He'd have to find another way to protect himself and Linnet.

Linnet. Marcer looked at her and felt a glimmer of what Sheik Radi must feel. He wished her face was covered. It was repellent that these men could see her, jeer at her, hurt her with their eyes. "Move out of our way," he demanded as though he had the right. "The holy one has ordered that the three of us go to the Harmony."

Sheik Radi and the policemen gaped, but the Khan laughed, and glanced at Demet Quadar. "The houris do not give orders to men, infidel," he said smoothly. "They are *gifts* to men from Allah. Paradise is a reward, and so are they. Not our commanders." He looked at the slowly nodding listeners and smiled one of his false smiles, which were so much more convincing in public than in intimate surroundings.

"Sheik Radi," Marcer called without looking at the older man. He raised his voice so those in the hallway could hear, and hoped there were no more Sons. "Idryis Khan a'Husain plans to destroy Paradise. He sent your daughter to the Harmony to persuade them to do it. He wants to kill all houris and become emir in place of Aleko Bei. That's why I came here, to warn your wife. Idryis Khan is a traitor to Aleko Bei and an apostate from Islam! The governor should be called!"

"Not a word he says is true." Idryis Khan turned around to face the police jamming the door and hallway. "This man is a Jonist infidel and a liar. He has disgraced this household twice." While everyone watched, Idryis Khan bent and took a thin-bladed knife from his boot.

"Ask the houri! Let her tell you what is true!" Marcer tried to convince the men, but when they heard the word infidel, their minds seemed to close.

"The holy one has been shamed enough," the Khan shouted over Marcer's voice. "Sheik Radi. Cover your wife's face! Take her away from the scene of her defilement by men's eyes while I, your son-in-law, avenge the disgrace."

Sheik Radi frowned. He grabbed Qadira. She jerked sideways, away from him.

"You shame yourself!" Sheik Radi said harshly.

Idryis Khan bounded forward, grabbed Marcer, then held him with his arm across Marcer's neck. "What is the proper punishment for a man who rips the veil from a holy houri's face? A man who encourages misbehavior in women? A man who accuses me—me, a Son of Paradise—of wanting to harm that sacred place? Should I take out his eyes?" The Khan raised the knife above his head.

They clamored for Marcer to be blinded. Marcer EL-ed automatically. The human police were furious at the dishonor to a houri. Impossible that they would believe anything Marcer said.

The Khan subvocalized. Marcer, but no one else, could hear. "I'll build a box *exactly* your size. You'll spend your life there, in your coffin, until you beg to die. I'll own you."

Marcer struggled against the Khan. The knife pricked his throat. The Khan chuckled. "I own you," he said.

Qadira, still uncovered, walked calmly between Idryis Khan and the gaping police bats; she planted her feet wide. "Sons is bad!" she said. "Neuland and him Sons!" She pointed at Idryis Khan. "All spoil him. Her!" She pointed at Linnet. "Die Sons!"

The men quieted as the holy alien spoke. They listened without looking at her, but they did look at Linnet. Her scar-tissue face couldn't blush, but she trembled and gazed at the floor.

Sheik Radi studied first Idryis Khan, then Marcer. "Let him talk," Sheik Radi told the Khan. "He came here of his own accord. As my guest. My wife seems to . . . prefer him to you."

"And look what he did!" The Khan used the crowd. "Now a dozen men have seen your wife's face. Is she still holy?"

Marcer swallowed, and tried once more to pull away. He failed, but gained a bit of breathing space. He used it to shout. "The houris aren't holy! They're aliens. So are their Sons!"

Idryis Khan shoved Marcer away. He staggered at the unexpected release. The Khan reached out, seemingly casually, and punched him.

The blow to his head disoriented Marcer; it sent phantom EL signals and, temporarily, he lost his sense of balance. He stumbled across the chair, then fell sideways with it. He went down. As he started to get up, the Khan kicked him in the groin. The Khan laughed as Marcer doubled over; so did others.

The Khan set his foot on Marcer's neck. The pressure was slight, just enough to keep Marcer aware that the Khan would not let him get to his feet. The Khan placed the knife just below Marcer's eyes. The blade was all Marcer could see. "Should I do it?" the Khan jovially asked the men.

Marcer tried to roll away. Men laughed as the Khan pressed his booted foot hard against Marcer's throat.

"No!" Linnet screamed. She ran forward and pushed the Khan away from Marcer. The Khan staggered, then slapped her. It had no effect. "Cut *me,* Khan," Linnet taunted, dancing away from him, sideways, away from Marcer. "You've done it before. Do it to me instead. You like to hurt women, but you've never hurt me!"

They faced each other. The Khan shifted position, balanced for an attack on Linnet. Temporarily overlooked, Marcer rolled away.

"Neulander whore!" The Khan slashed the knife across Linnet's face.

She hadn't tried to prevent it. She didn't move. A red stripe appeared on her forehead, crossed her cheek, and went down her chin, dripping blood. She grinned at the Khan. "Is that the best you can do?" Her wound was already closing.

The Khan watched it, and her. He had an erection.

Marcer lurched up from the floor and lunged at Idryis Khan, EL-ing as he moved. Excited by the blood, two police bats rushed to the Khan's aid. They seized Marcer and held his arms before Marcer connected with Idryis Khan.

The Khan turned to Marcer, holding the knife like a boxer readying a crude thrust. An EL had no calming effect on him. "You won't defile another woman with your Jonist eyes if you're blind." He jabbed at Marcer's face.

Marcer ducked, his ability giving him an edge in anticipating the Khan. He avoided the knife, this time.

Linnet ran at the Khan. He tried to knock her away, but the impact only stopped Linnet briefly. She grabbed his knife by the blade, a move so unexpected that it succeeded. The edge cut into her hand. Blood gushed between her fingers. Oblivious, she gripped the knife harder and yanked it away from Idryis Khan.

Blood streaming from her newest cut, Linnet faced the Khan. "Let him go," she said. She turned the knife, making it a weapon she could use.

The police bats aimed their guns at Linnet. The knife was a toy, a David to their Goliath. Several of the bats smirked, as though Linnet's bravery was funny.

The Khan grinned like a dog barring its teeth. "Once it's born, you're dead, whore."

Ignored for the moment, Marcer got silently up. He felt inside the jacket for the Khan's antique gun. His hand closed around the handgrip.

With the speed of the fearless, Linnet stabbed Idryis Khan. She aimed for his chest, but he twisted and raised his arm to block her. The knife entered his upper arm. He grabbed the hilt before she could pull it out. He grasped her arm, used his outlandish speed to wrench her around, and held the knife against her throat. "If I cut the artery, will you die before you heal?" The police were motionless, an audience eager for blood, not justice.

Marcer would not let Linnet be hurt. None of the guns were trained on him. He pulled out the Khan's antique handgun and aimed at Idryis Khan's chest. "Cut her, and you'll die before you're done." Marcer felt calm. For the first time since he'd been deported from the Harmony, he knew absolutely what he had to do.

The Khan looked at Marcer. "I don't think so. You didn't kill me last night, when you had a chance. You won't now."

"It's like you to imagine I'd do more for myself than for my wife. And last night I made a mistake." They were so close and so intent upon each other that it seemed as if everyone else had left in the room. None of the police intervened, but Marcer's EL showed Demet Quadar inching toward him, his weapon in his two hands. "Don't move, Quadar, or I'll kill him now."

"Standoffs are unstable," the Khan said in a tone of brotherly advice. "If you have a demand, you'd better make it before I order them to shoot the whore if you shoot me."

Marcer saw the smug, malicious grins of the police behind the Khan. "My wife is pregnant by Idryis Khan," Marcer said loudly.

The knife stayed at Linnet's neck. "Liar."

The Khan didn't want to admit it because "everyone knew" that Sons were infertile. Marcer smiled. "Ask her. You tortured her and raped her."

"Yes." Linnet tried again to get away, but the Khan's grip only tightened.

"Yes," Qadira said suddenly, startling everyone. "You spoil, you dirty Son, you father on spoil." She spat at Idryis Khan. It hit his arm.

Demet Quadar started toward Qadira, glanced at Sheik Radi, and stopped. "Immodest bitch," he said.

"Apologize!" Sheik Radi's angry demand was joined by murmured agreement from the police.

"Sorry." Quadar made his insincerity obvious.

Idryis Khan shrugged, then winced as the bleeding from his arm increased. The knife edge slid against Linnet's neck. "What difference does it make? She's a whore."

"Do you want to kill your own son?" Marcer glimpsed the Sheik, frowning.

"I can have more."

"But only with Neulanders. That's what he's after. That's what this is all about." Marcer felt possible victory in the changed atmosphere of the room. The Khan had admitted he could have children and that he was threatening a woman now pregnant with his child. That revelation required a rethinking of his character by all these men.

The room was silent but for the shifting of the men's feet. "This is *my* home," Sheik Radi said finally. "They are my guests. I want to hear what the Jonist has to say."

Marcer lost a bit of his tension. "I'm not a Jonist anymore," he said mildly as he met Linnet's eyes and smiled.

Linnet returned his smile as she relaxed in the Khan's grip, trusting Marcer to free her.

"Put down your weapon, Brice," Sheik Radi said, "and then we'll all listen."

"When he releases my wife."

Sheik Radi walked away from the crowd of men, toward Idryis Khan. "Do it," he ordered.

"No." The Khan didn't take orders well. He pulled Linnet closer against himself and changed position. Marcer would have to shoot Linnet in order to kill the Khan.

"Did you hear him?" Marcer addressed Sheik Radi. "He'll have more sons. But not with your daughter. Sons are infertile with *human* women. They're aliens and can only sire children on Neulanders."

"Shut him up, Demet," Idryis Khan said.

"Officers," Sheik Radi immediately said to the police, "don't let anyone harm my guests."

For the first time, Marcer was pleased that police were present. There were six inside the room, and four of them threatened Demet Quadar, albeit vaguely, without looking at him quite directly.

Marcer couldn't explain everything to them, but he had to turn the Sheik and the police decisively against Idryis Khan and Quadar. "Listen to me. The Sons want to use Neuland as their private harem and are willing to kill all the houris—their own mothers!—because the houris want to stop them. That's what this call for a jihad is about. The houris hope destroying Neuland will stop the Sons from subjugating all of humanity. Ask your wife, Sheik Radi."

Qadira held her arms tightly against herself. "Yesss," she said and swayed side to side, just slightly, then puffed air from her mouth as if blowing out a candle. She stopped. She seemed to decide something. Qadira, who had resisted doing so before, picked up her chador from the floor and put it on, though she left the veil. Her husband and the police watched, nonplussed. She walked out of the room like a queen making a stately exit. The police made way for her

Sheik Radi began to follow his wife, then he hesitated and looked back at Marcer. "I'll call Governor Gordan. Brice, you and your wife come with me. Khan, release the woman." He spoke without looking at Idryis Khan.

"She'll call them." Demet Quadar spoke without urgency or anger, but his bearing seemed alight with an urge for action.

Idryis Khan eased his grip on Linnet.

Qadira was already out of sight down the corridor. Marcer EL-ed. None of the police wholly trusted the Khan anymore, but they were unsure of Marcer and the Sheik, too.

An unearthly screech began. It was like the sound of cats fighting and dying. The sound seemed to build. Marcer wasn't sure where it originated except that it was outside the room. The police exchanged grim looks and terse, shouted commands, then all but three left to investigate. The three who stayed were those most strongly converted by Marcer. Oddly, the Khan and Quadar seemed to relax.

Marcer caught the incipient motion as he EL-ed. Before he could shout or shoot, Idryis Khan had slit Linnet's throat. Blood fountained from her neck, bathing her face red. Her eyes met Marcer's for one last look, then the awareness in them disappeared.

Marcer pulled the trigger. This time there was no safety on. The explosive noise crashed through even the shrill, expanding screech. Marcer's hand had jerked with the recoil. The Khan flinched, dropped Linnet, but wasn't hit.

Unencumbered by Linnet, the Khan pulled a weapon from his jacket. Marcer expected to die, but he threw himself to the floor, EL-ing continuously despite the increasing interference from the screeching sound, which pounded into his head like an auditory missile. It had to be Qadira;

what else but an alien song could interfere so well with his EL?

Sheik Radi began to protest. Demet Quadar shot him. Instantly, the room was warmer. The awful scent of charred flesh filled it. Sheik Radi's headless corpse tumbled across Marcer. Marcer jerked away from it, clutching his gun.

The Khan turned on Marcer.

A policeman shouted for everyone to put their weapons down. He had pointed his own gun at Quadar. The Khan wheeled around and shot the policeman through the left eye.

Marcer aimed at the Khan, though his hands were shaking and his head was filled with false, random bounce-back signals. He pulled the trigger. The bullet missed. He wondered how many he had.

The remaining two police bats backed away from the two Sons, moving toward the door. Demet grimaced—perhaps he tried to smile—and fired at them. Set on a wider angle, the heat wave caught them both. They had time to scream as their bodies melted. The wooden molding of the door-frame caught fire.

Marcer saw Linnet's motionless body. He aimed at the Khan and shot again. The Khan's side spurted blood, but the Khan didn't go down. Instead he jumped forward, then kicked the gun from Marcer's hand.

"I'll kill her before they get here," Quadar said, capturing the Khan's attention. Marcer used the interruption to crawl in the direction his gun had gone.

"Get the strays, too." The Khan shouted to be heard.

Quadar turned his weapon on Marcer.

The Khan rumbled angrily. "He's mine!" He knocked the stick gun down, ruining Quadar's aim.

Quadar shrugged. "And the servants?"

"If they interfere."

Quadar nodded. He jumped gracefully over Linnet's fallen body, then across the melted, fused, and steaming bodies of the policemen and through the dying flames around the doorway to look for Qadira and strays to kill.

The houri's shrill scream must be both a protective mechanism and a weapon Marcer thought as he tried to find humanity in the noise and couldn't. The sound seemed to raise the air pressure in the room. Marcer's balance was deteriorating. He wasn't sure he could stand. His hand closed around his gun. Phantom figures danced in his head and he couldn't EL. He clenched his teeth. It didn't stop the waves of pain inside his head or stabilize his equilibrium. He forced himself to turn, ignored the dizziness, and raised the gun again. He fired just as the Khan moved. He heard the discharge but there was no impact on the Khan.

"You're a poor shot," the Khan shouted. He glanced down at the wound Marcer had made earlier. "I'm not." He shot Marcer's right hand, shattering it and the gun it had held. "Never aim a weapon at me."

The new pain was a distant dullness. Linnet's body lay near the man-shaped creature who had murdered her. Marcer thought he saw her fingers twitch, then knew it for an illusion created by his pounding head. Idryis Khan had killed her. He was watching Marcer, anticipating the sight of suffering. Pain was the only bridge between them, the only human sensation Idryis Khan perceived.

"You hate me," the Khan said. "Good. So did she." He grabbed Marcer's shoulder and hauled him upright. Marcer thought he would vomit.

Qadira's screeching suddenly ended.

"Even better," the Khan said.

VI. Impostor.

"I didn't want to kill the whore," Idryis Khan told Marcer. "Really, I thought she would heal."

Marcer stopped walking. "Please let me check her," he begged.

The Khan pushed Marcer forward with the gun barrel. "No, she's dead."

Marcer guessed the Khan's verbosity meant he was nervous. Sheik Radi's house had the frightening feel of a cemetery, not merely sad, but dead.

The Khan muttered, "Where's Demet?"

While heading toward the mansion's main entrance, they had encountered telltale signs of Demet Quadar's passage in the form of burned, half-melted corpses, but they hadn't found Quadar himself. Qadira was absent, too.

The Khan stopped in the middle of the immense foyer. The oversize bronze double doors opened onto the streets of the city of Shores, not the canal. Marcer had come through those doors to attend the wedding of Idryis Khan and Nisa Khalil. Then the sounds of happy guests had suffused the entire mansion. Now, except for the talkative Khan, the only sound was silence.

The Khan kept well back. No windows faced outdoors, and the security system, if one existed, wasn't obvious, and would have been keyed exclusively to residents. Any guards the Sheik usually posted were gone, though there was an unidentifiable lump of melted flesh near a wall.

"You should have left the whore in prison, Brice. At least she was safe." The Khan chuckled. His humor was patently false. "I suppose I have a claim against you for killing my son. Was she really your wife? A Neulander whore? You should thank me for getting rid of her. I'm rid of mine. The little bitch is on her way to the Harmony, but first I divorced her."

How had Linnet ever endured Idryis Khan?

"Do you think you're bothering me when you don't answer? I don't care. You're a walking dead man." He prodded Marcer. "Demet is probably outside with the police. Open the door. Go out. Tell me what you see." The Khan moved to where he could not be seen from an open door.

Marcer's right hand was useless. Blood still oozed from it; only his thumb was recognizable. He used his left hand awkwardly; the door was heavy. The Khan did not hurry him. If Idryis Khan was capable of human emotion, Marcer would have said that the Khan dreaded what might be beyond the door.

Marcer tugged one ponderous door open. An odor like wet Rockland stinkweed, or manure spread with vinegar, struck him.

The Khan inhaled, then instantly retreated. "Close it! Come back inside!"

Marcer hurried outside. With Qadira's horrible noise gone, he could EL. He did.

The raised terrace separating the house from the street also afforded an excellent view. Twenty-four mothers—jinn-stage Blessed—watched the front of Sheik Radi's house from the street. More were arriving. They were all colors, like pebbles gathered randomly on a shore. None tried to camouflage themselves. Strewn among the rainbow-hued creatures were taller, black-clad, woman-shaped impostors. Houris. Qadira was at the forefront of them. Like the call of a crying infant, her screeching had drawn mothers to her defense. Aliens. Real ones, but also their impostor daughters.

"What's out there?" Idryis Khan whispered from behind the door.

Demet Quadar was dead, lying at Qadira's feet. He'd been picked clean to the bone. The remnants of his maroon uniform and the chewed remains of his stick gun were all that identified him.

Qadira turned. She wore her chador, but was still unveiled. Hers was the only face he could see. She stepped blithely over Quadar's bones and smiled at Marcer. "Beautiful man," she said. "Hurted?"

"I'm fine," he said. The pain of his ruined hand, the throbbing of his knee, the ache of fatigue throughout his body were nothing. He was alive, talking to aliens, but Linnet was dead.

The door into Sheik Radi's house began to close. A rustle passed through the Blessed, both the jinn and the houris. Nearly faster than his EL bounce-back could resolve, two moving figures streaked past, followed by most of the other jinn. A shot from a bullet gun stopped one, but her fallen body blocked the narrowing doorway from closing fully. The rest charged through.

Marcer listened to the jinn hiss and growl. He heard Idryis Khan's screams. They sounded very human. When they stopped, Marcer walked away from the half-open door. He met Qadira at the bottom of the stairs. Her attention, and that of the other houris, was fixed on the door. They stared like fans at a rangeball game, though there was nothing to see and the only sounds were the scrambling of crowded bodies and the tearing of flesh.

The jinn were eating the Khan. Marcer had seen predators in the field bring down their prey and been less indifferent. With the detached satisfaction of solving a puzzle, he guessed that those jinn not partaking of the Khan's flesh were those in heat. None would want a daughter of Idryis Khan.

That reminded him of Qadira's comment about Linnet. He thought back. *"Spoil, she. Of us. Stupids bited us Son."* Spoil was the houri word for unwanted things, specifically— *perhaps* specifically, he corrected himself—the unwanted offspring of their mothers, the jinn. Is that what Linnet had been? No, she was a Neulander; she had every aspect of one. How could jinn, the houris' mothers, be *"Stupids"*?

Silence returned. The jinn came out with bloody mouths, their bodies now patchily crimson. A few walked on two rather than the faster four legs, and wiped their mouths with their hands. No, paws. Those appendages weren't capable of significant object manipulation. They had a panda's thumb, not a man's.

"Dead," Qadira said unnecessarily.

The jinn who had killed Idryis Khan passed Marcer cautiously, their saucer eyes those of bloodthirsty wolves. He EL-ed. They continued on but they watched him. How had he failed to find deep intelligence in those eyes? Yet even now he saw only the cunning look of satiated beasts, not reasoning killers. Stupids.

Marcer met the gaze of one of the closer mothers. "Talk to me," he said. The jinn licked her mouth. Her body odor was sweetening, but the aroma was still closer to the butcher shop than to the perfumery. Marcer extended his good hand.

Qadira touched Marcer's hand and pushed it gently down. "Harmony man, my husband?" Her tonal inflections sounded truly worried.

"Dead." He pointed to Quadar's skeleton. "He did it."

More jinn and more houris were entering the street. The jinn milled about, apparently at random, but the houris clustered, coming to Qadira and Marcer.

"Spoil wife of you?" Qadira sounded less concerned.

"Dead." He swallowed and EL-ed. A police cruiser was gently nosing into the area. Marcer guessed the men inside had pulled back earlier, intimidated by the arrival of the houris and jinn. No one else was on the street. Until he felt tears on his face, Marcer hadn't realized he had cried. Linnet was a Neulander; she had to be. Anything else was impossible. *Stupids bited us Son.* Qadira's words echoed in his head like an intangible EL. He had to know. "Why is Linnet spoil? Was Linnet born from a jinn? A mother?"

"Yes." Qadira looked at another houri behind herself, and the woman—the impostor woman—came forward.

"One of mother. One of Son," the covered houris said. "Spoil is. And gives to canal." Her voice was firmer than that of Qadira, more fluent, but she corrected herself. "*Deaded,* and given to canal."

Linnet had been the daughter of a jinn. In that sense, she might even be called a houri. Instead of a human father, Linnet's father had been a Son, an accidental choice by a Bralava jinn. Such offspring were dumped in the canals. Somehow, Linnet had survived and been picked up by a sympathetic person who had eventually abandoned her again, probably when her differences became apparent. Had Linnet known?

He'd been up too long. He couldn't assimilate the implications of Linnet's heritage. He had to do one thing, then whatever happened didn't matter. Marcer EL-ed. Qadira, the other houris and the jinn all turned to him. "Nisa is on her way to the Harmony. All of you must go back to Paradise. I want to tell them myself. How do I talk to them, your mothers?"

"Not talking." The covered houri sighed. "Stupid. Stupid." She crooned the word like an endearment. Qadira nodded and repeated it herself.

Down the street the police cruiser opened. Two uniformed bats came out. They took hesitant steps toward Marcer, then jinn intervened to block them.

Another cloaked and covered form came forward. She made a low, unhappy snapping sound in the back of her throat. "All good?" she asked in the beautiful tones of a houri.

"Yes," Qadira said. "Bad spoil dead is. Good husband dead." Her tone was somber. "Houris us go home."

They used human language to communicate among themselves, however poorly. Nisa had said as much. Logical, since they had human form, but Marcer wondered. It was unthinkable, too horrible to be true. "Are your mothers stupid?" he asked anyway. "Do mothers talk, think, plan?" He took a breath. "Do mothers talk to you?"

All the closer houris made a sound like sizzling fat. The nearest jinn came protectively toward them. Their smell worsened.

"Stupids, yes," said the covered houri, the one who seemed more fluent than the rest. "Pets." Her sadness made the word long and difficult. One jinn brushed against her. Others went to other houris—their daughters—and faced Marcer with their bloody teeth bared. Qadira motioned them to calm using a very human gesture. She and

the other houris made another, subtler sound in the back
of their throats, and the jinn became more acquiescent.

The houris' lack of complete grammar made them sound
simpleminded or mystical, but Marcer repeated the first
rule of nonterrestrial fieldwork to himself: Don't judge the
alien by familiar standards. The houris were intelligent.
They spoke, they thought, they planned. Did that mean
their mothers were also intelligent? The *houris* didn't seem
to believe their mothers could comprehend more than attack or protect. *My mother, the pet.*

It was worse, much worse. Houris were the juvenile, the
larval stage. They would eventually metamorphose into
adults, into jinn—into animals. Every bestial mother in the
street, watching him with feral eyes and shallow mind, had
once been an intelligent woman, or woman-thing, capable
of speech and thought. "Holy God," Marcer whispered. An
intelligence born to be lost. Metamorphosis would be the
death of their minds.

"I'm sorry," he said as gently as he could. "I'm so sorry."

Qadira, the only houri whose face he knew, was smiling
beatifically. She looked directly at him with that smile and
he saw grief behind her heavenly, only temporarily
human eyes.

Qadira touched Marcer's good, left arm. "Harmony man,
tell Harmony we stops spoil. No houris. Not talking more
again."

She and the other houris walked among their mothers.
They dispersed in twos and threes, mothers and daughters,
animals and aliens, beasts and their impostor human daughters. Marcer sat down hard on the bottom step of Sheik
Radi's house and watched them go.

When the departure was well established, as if it had
been waiting, a lifting hull settled slowly into the street.
The pilot took care not to crush anyone. Marcer's broken
hand brushed against the ground. Pain shot through his
arm; his entire body was in pain that he was too exhausted
to contemplate. He blinked and looked away as dust blew
in his eyes. Someone had come, some human authority to
sort out the mess. He supposed he would be a prisoner
again.

The lifter had a mirrored surface, a cheap version of a
Harmony scatter-field. Marcer couldn't see inside. The ve-

hicle doors didn't open until all the houris and their jinn mothers were out of sight.

Marcer's mouth was dry. His head ached. He was tired. His hand was an oozing mess. He stared straight ahead, waiting for someone to take charge of him.

The doors opened. Governor Gordan was the first man to leave the lifter. Marcer was too tired to be surprised.

The governor surveyed Marcer. Perhaps he waited for Marcer to speak or bow. "Researcher Brice," he said finally, "you'll receive the medical aid you clearly need. I want to understand what has happened here." He hesitated, but Marcer didn't respond, though he noted with petty curiosity that the governor had used his Harmony title. "First, then I have a pleasant surprise." Governor Gordan gestured at someone inside the lifter.

Marcer roused himself. "Please, check my wife. Linnet Wali. She's inside the house. Dead. Please. I'm not certain."

Gordan frowned. "Idryis Khan?"

The answer was the same whether Gordan had asked if the Khan had killed Linnet, or if the Khan was dead. "Yes." He closed his eyes.

"Marc?"

Marcer looked. Speechless with disbelief, he only stared. Lavi Brice, his father, had come out of the lifter.

"Marc?" Lavi spoke as though he barely recognized his son. "I'm here to take you home."

Epilogue

I. Qadira.

Along with everyone else in the Great Hall of the Grand Assembly of the Polite Harmony of Worlds, the Supplicant looked where Elector Jeroen Lee pointed. With expert showmanship, the rear doors sprang open. Marcer Brice walked into the room.

The Supplicant jumped from her seat, gaping. He wasn't dead.

"Delegates and colleagues," Elector Lee said, "let me present our greatest living expert on the houris, their mothers, and their sons. Researcher Marcer Joseph Brice, lately of the Academy of Darien."

Marcer Brice wore a white Academic robe. At first he hesitated, his mouth slightly agape, then he advanced toward the dais. Several steps behind, Elector Lee's aide escorted a beautiful woman into the Great Hall. From her fixed smile, the Supplicant guessed the woman was a houri.

Brice had brought one of *them*, uncovered and lovely, to plead their case to the Harmony.

On the dais, Elector Kurioso left Lee alone at the speaker's center in order to confer with the remaining electors and the Grand Marshal. Below, the world delegates argued about unauthorized entrances; some accused Elector Lee of playing tricks. One even stood on his chair to be heard. "Brice is dead!" he bellowed. "It says so in your Fact Statement. This is an impostor!"

Another shouted, "That's Brice! I saw him on Bralava!"

Marcer Brice tensed, but continued forward. He would pass directly beside the Supplicant.

"This is no trick." Lee's sonorous voice rolled over the

others and filled the room. "The only trick is the one played on all of us, including me." It might have been her imagination, but the Supplicant thought Lee looked directly at her. "Researcher Brice was delayed by injuries, but he is here just in time with important information. Listen to him."

The Supplicant was on her feet facing Brice as he approached. His steps faltered, then stopped as he noticed her. He smiled. "Nisa!" He extended his hand. "I'm glad you're here."

Brice must have come to dispute the Joint Electors' Ruling. Elector Lee's withdrawal from the Ruling proved it. They would listen to Brice because he was an Academic; she wasn't. In his own way, Brice was one of them. They would be swayed by Brice's Altered empathy. All her work would be undone.

Brice was wrong. As loudly as possible, Nisa called, "Were you sent to stop us from destroying these impostors? How did the houris corrupt you? With a houri wife and a chance to breed more aliens? Ones with your Alteration?"

The Jonists listened to her accusations and were silent.

"No," he said quietly. "Idryis Khan is dead, Nisa. So are most of the Sons on Bralava, guilty or not. The houris have incited a jihad against them." Nisa was disconcerted by his failure to defend himself against her impromptu slander. He glanced at the roomful of people straining to hear with the expression of someone unhappy at being called away by business. He came closer. "I have bad news: Your father is dead. I'm sorry." He touched her shoulder.

Surprised by her unexpected sadness, she pulled away from him.

"Come to the dais, Researcher," Elector Lee commanded.

Brice glanced at the houri, who had stopped a few rows back from Nisa. The houri smiled, as they always did, nodded, and Brice continued ahead while Elector Lee's aide ushered the houri to vacant seats at the front of the hall held for them by a bailiff.

Brice went to the speaker's position with conviction in his stride, but no enjoyment. He bowed to the Electors—it seemed a bit perfunctory—then bowed specifically to Elector Lee. Lee moved aside. Brice took the speaker's center, cleared his throat, and assumed an orator's relaxed stance. There was no lectern. He looked out at his audience. "Jon Hsu wrote in his *General Principles* that the human form is the one best suited to searching the universe for Order." Brice paused, smiled slightly, then added, "An alien race agreed."

There was muted laughter. The delegates eased back in their seats. After all, none had ever met a houri.

"No!" She shouted it. "They didn't *agree*. They *attacked*!"

"There was no attack," Brice said over Nisa's voice. He had the advantage of the speaker's sound system, but many in the room heard her. "At worst, there was an infestation. It is the natural reproductive strategy of this species to imitate other species during one stage of their life cycle. A competitive camouflage. Anyway, it's over. The houris are on their way back to their world, Paradise. There will be no more houris unless we agree."

"Liar!" Nisa ran toward the dais, the better to be heard. She saw Sanda Brauna whisper to another Elector. Sanda was frowning, probably worried that Nisa would embarrass her. Sanda didn't really care about stopping the houris; she had only wanted to win points against Jeroen Lee—then he had taken over her crusade anyway. "The houris are dangerous!" Nisa shouted. "They replace women. You said it yourself, Marcer Brice! They're a threat to the human race." She reached the stairs and started up to the dais. The confused bailiffs didn't stop her.

"I was wrong," Brice said. He looked out at his audience with his hands open, an honest man admitting an honest mistake. "There is information I didn't have when I wrote my report," Brice said. "It changes everything."

Nisa was atop the dais with him, but Brice continued speaking.

"First of all, we are not dealing with an intelligent species." Brice glanced at the Electors to his side, then Nisa. "Pity them," he said directly to her before facing the delegates again. She hesitated and listened.

"When houris lose the human shape in metamorphosis," he said, "they also lose their memories and their minds. They become animals; they become their pets, the jinn, without self-awareness, language, or abstract thought. And the houris know it will happen. They have years to dread it." He frowned, looked down, then back up. "Imagine it," he said as though he had. "Imagine *them*—not as impostors but as a fragile race of *temporary humans.* They are no threat to us."

Nisa almost, but not quite, was moved, then she remembered her mother's death. "Don't trust them," she said. Her voice carried. "They're evil. Don't underestimate them. *All* life is temporary, not only the houris'."

Brice continued before Nisa could say more. "The second, and most important point is that the houris' Sons are fertile with certain human women, although not standard humans." He glanced at Jeroen Lee. Lee nodded. "Specifically," Brice continued, "the Sons can have children with Neulander-type Altered women." He hesitated again. As though it hurt, he added, "Like my wife. She's pregnant with the child of a houri's Son, Idryis Khan a'Husain. Because the Sons are fertile, they have the potential to create a hybrid species: part human and part Blessed—houris, that is."

Brice gestured, and the beautiful woman stood. Her pregnancy was clear enough if one knew to look. His wife. The woman the Khan had called a whore. The Khan's whore. Not a houri? Was this Fatima? Nisa looked, but couldn't see her hands to be sure.

Nisa didn't stand beside Marcer Brice; his height would have made her look childish. She stayed where she was, watching as the beautiful whore turned to the delegates, letting them see her and her pregnancy, dazzling this Jonist audience. Pregnant by Idryis Khan? Impossible, yet Brice wouldn't dare fabricate this. She was a Neulander. Like Jeroen Lee. Inspired, Nisa said, "Then she must be an alien! All Neulanders must be. Like him!" She pointed theatrically at Elector Lee, taking back the respectability she had given him. "The houris and the Neulanders are both aliens!"

Lee was motionless.

"My wife has the Neulander Alteration," Brice said into the silence. He fell into a lecturing style which, Nisa hoped, was unlikely to gain him the support of people who made policy. "I'm Altered, too. Not like a Neulander, but Altered. Yes, the Neulander Alteration incorporates some nonterrestrial genome segments, but Neulanders are human."

His whore wife was still standing. She probably didn't know the Harmony common language because she continued smiling, though she flushed and visibly forced herself to stand still under their inspection. She kept her attention on her husband, Brice.

Nisa smiled too, grimly. The argument could become about Jeroen Lee, not whether to destroy the houris. That one she could win, despite not being a Jonist, an Academic, or a citizen of the Harmony. She, at least, was human. "Who are the houris' champions?" she asked rhetorically. "Two Altered men, and one not even Jonist!"

"Compared with the cyclic changes of this species from Paradise, all human Alterations are trivial," Brice quickly said. "But I'm not here to tell you my opinion, only facts. Neulanders can have children with standard humans; Sons cannot. Therefore, by definition, Neulanders are Altereds and Sons are aliens. And if Neulanders are not human, then I'm a dolphin and all of you are still apes." Some delegates giggled nervously.

Nisa let him continue; he'd offended some delegates.

"The differences between Neulanders and Sons of the houris are real and significant. As for the houris, they are leaving human-occupied space. Most are already gone. They are returning to Paradise where, in a few decades, when they're all metamorphosed, only animals will be left."

"How can we believe they'll stay away?" Nisa demanded. "The alans would come instantly if they were invited back."

Brice answered without turning to Nisa. "It isn't in the interests of either race to let a stable, fertile hybrid replace them. Houris are intelligent until their metamorphosis; they understood the threat of letting their Sons conquer Neuland. Their first plan, to destroy Neuland, is unworkable. Instead, there will be no more houris. Therefore, there will be no more Sons. That is the only way to prevent a hybrid from becoming established—other than genocide."

Nisa shouted, "Self-defense, not genocide!" She had the attention of fewer delegates.

He ignored her. "The houris and their mothers are on their way to Paradise; they are leaving in order to save us."

Finally, the other Electors took action. Elector Kurioso went around Elector Lee toward Brice. "You claim these imitations are human, but your own data show that they're not."

Brice bowed to Kurioso, who didn't return the courtesy.

"My data show the history and the present state of the Blessed species, which includes houris. It doesn't show their future. It can't. This species is multiform and adaptable. They have *learned* to be human while imitating us. They have achieved a modicum of ethical understanding. They hope that if they surrender, we won't commit genocide. They know we can."

"And you say we shouldn't?" Kurioso chuckled as if in disbelief.

"There's no reason. They are sacrificing their minds for us. They are giving up their lives as reasoning beings in order to prevent their spoil—their offspring—from overwhelming us. Or them." He looked around the Great Hall as if just realizing where he was. "The definition of human used to be simple," Brice said, "but that simplicity is gone. There are different forms of humanity, Alterations. The houris are another form. They have an essentially standard human genome, which is used to create a type of human during a portion of their lives. Temporary, but human. No one form of humanity is higher or better. There is no evolutionary progress. There is no ideal. No matter what Jon Hsu's *General Principles* say."

Brice had just disputed with the Jonist substitute for God; with the one phrase, he should have lost his support. He sighed and looked around the room. "If the houris don't fit within your definition of humanity, if I don't, if my wife doesn't—then shame on you," he said. "Perhaps the houris have surpassed us in humanity."

Nisa was surprised they didn't remove him bodily from the dais. Elector Lee had winced, and shaken his head, disassociating himself from the sentiment, but Brice continued uninterrupted.

"Meanwhile," he said, "until the Sons are all dead, I suggest you defend the Republic of Neuland at all costs." He took a step back. No one asked questions. Even Kurioso seemed to wait for Brice to finish, so Nisa stayed silent, too.

"I've left a more detailed report with Elector Lee," Brice said quietly. He nodded at Nisa, bowed to the Electors and the Grand Marshal, then walked off the dais, collected his wife, and left the Great Hall.

Nisa watched the door close on Brice and his wife. "Shall

we continue with the Joint Ruling?" she asked in a stage whisper to Sanda Brauna.

"Sit down," Sanda Brauna said. "There is no Joint Ruling."

Jeroen Lee smiled at Nisa but spoke to the room. "I believe we all need to review our opinions after examining this new information. Perhaps a quarantine would be more appropriate than extermination. I'll make the report available to everyone. It contains interesting ideas on the possible usefulness of this species." He turned and began to lead the Electors off the dais.

"What about the whore's child?" Nisa shouted. "Isn't it a hybrid? Shouldn't it be destroyed?" Nisa was talking to backs turned on her. The Electors filed off the dais, departing through a side exit. The world delegates also were leaving. They all were quiet, and though she wasn't certain Brice had convinced them, yet he had created doubt. Nisa watched them go. How could she win them back? They didn't understand. Human or not, houris were evil. Despite all she'd done, they were abandoning the crusade against Paradise.

Idryis Khan was dead; so was her father. Hulweh. Ziller. There was no one left alive from her past life except, possibly, Qadira. She thought she heard Qadira's laughter in her mind.

II. Linnet.

Marcer missed the rough texture of Linnet's scars. Her medically polished perfection pleased her, however, and the gain from her happiness more than made up for any loss of individuality or interest.

Jeroen Lee had invited the two of them to stay in his apartment. Months earlier, Marcer would have been uncomfortable. The offer would have seemed an honor. He no longer cared about such things and had accepted because it was more convenient than seeking private rooms.

"So Neulanders are aliens, artificially produced hybrids." Lee grimaced. "And I'm one of them." Lee offered Marcer a drink.

Marcer shook his head; he'd lost the taste for alcohol. He EL-ed and felt a bit uneasy at the revelation of an

Elector's insecurities. It seemed a bit ridiculous to reassure Jeroen Lee, but he did it anyway. "No, Elector. I believe otherwise, just as I said. Neulanders are human. We've known about recombinational speciation since before Jonism. The consistent result of recombinational hybridization between mankind and the houris—I mean larval-stage Blessed who are human impostors—is a Neulander-type Altered human. Certain gene segments from one of the two ancestor species are prone to combine with certain ones of the other. That same combination happens whether the hybridization is artificial, such as on Neuland, or not. In nature—starting with the mother or jinn-stage Blessed and a human man—several generations are necessary before reaching the stable form." He inclined his head at Linnet. He had kept her strange inheritance out of his report, though he had privately told Jeroen Lee. "My wife isn't the child of any Neulander, but she is a Neulander-type Altered. Some combinations of foreign genes with those of *Homo sapiens sapiens* are favorable. Our children together will be Neulanders, since it's dominant. I believe that the Khan's child will be a human Neulander, too."

Linnet nudged him gently from the side. She stayed close. His ELs showed that she felt vulnerable and exposed, unsure of herself without the dual covers of her clothing and her scars.

"You hope so," Elector Lee said, smiling. "The prudent course would be to abort it. I don't understand her refusal."

Marcer glanced at Linnet. He didn't quite understand it, either, but he respected her ability to choose. "Who knows?" he said, putting his arm around her shoulders. "Maybe the people in the Republic of Neuland are humanity's future. Maybe Neulanders are tougher, more adaptable, and generally better able to survive."

Elector Lee, one of them, frowned and began to protest. Marcer overrode him. "I doubt it, too," Marcer said. "The worlds we live on now have too much variety. I think the human race is alive and well, and because of its vitality, we're separating into new lineages, sibling branches of the human species." He stopped abruptly. An Elector didn't want his opinions, and he already had given too many.

Lee smiled indulgently, then looked for his aide. August was subvocalizing a message through the House Utility, but he nodded when Lee gestured for him to come.

"Why not stay awhile in Center?" Lee asked. "Your position on Darien is secure, but if you wait a bit, I'm sure that something will turn up here. Such a bold young man deserves a reward."

Marcer was unsure whether or not Lee was being ironic, so he took the comment at face value. "Elector, I don't want a reward."

"Call it a penance, then." Lee smiled at Linnet. "I am the one who changed your life by ordering you deported."

"Changed it for the better," Marcer said, and pulled Linnet close against his side. She was constantly uneasy; she didn't know the language. She would have wanted to return home, if either of them had one.

August arrived from across the room. He bowed. His hearing was even better than Marcer's, though over a narrower spectrum. He spoke as though he had been present and listening all the while. "I believe a significant position in the Academy of Center-Sucre will be offered to you very soon," he said. "I overheard a pertinent discussion in which Elector Lee was *not* involved."

Marcer smiled and shook his head. "Thank you, but no. We have other plans." He EL-ed merely to sense Linnet's presence, alive and with him, and sent a small, silent, embarrassed message of thanks to whatever Power or Fate inhered in the universe that Linnet was a Neulander and that she had healed. Any monitors that reported his EL didn't matter. He had no one to impress.

"Are you returning to New Dawn?" Lee asked with polite, but genuine, interest.

Marcer glanced down at Linnet. "No. We've decided to go to Paradise. Houris have sacrificed themselves for us and for their animal mothers. I want to know them better. I still think the Blessed species is an opportunity. I'd like to find a way to help them out of the trap of the danger they present to humans, to find a way to give them back their minds." Though open affection was considered rude in the Academy, he lightly kissed Linnet's forehead before continuing. "And here is the best argument in favor of helping their race that I can imagine."

Valerie J. Freireich is the author of three critically acclaimed prior novels, *Becoming Human, Testament,* and *The Beacon,* all published by Roc. Ms. Freireich is a practicing lawyer in the Chicago area, where she lives with her husband, Jordan, and son, Jared, and where, every winter, she dreams of moving to Tucson. She invites you to e-mail her at JKaplan@concentric.net.

CUTTING EDGE SCI-FI NOVELS

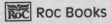